NYWENING

Hidden Grace Trilogy - Book Two

THE
CHARADE

A Novel

MW01598896

THE CHARADE

Copyright © 2011 by Cassandra Nywening

All rights reserved. Neither this publication nor any part of this publication may be reproduced or transmitted in any form or by any means, electronic or mechanical, including photocopying, recording or any information storage and retrieval system, without permission in writing from the author.

This is a work of fiction. Names, characters, places and incidents either are the product of the author's imagination or are used fictitiously, and any resemblance to actual persons, living or dead, businesses, companies, events, or locales is entirely coincidental.

All Scripture quotations are taken from the Holy Bible, New International Version. Copyright © 1973, 1978, 1984 by International Bible Society. Used by permission of Zondervan Publishing House.

ISBN: 978-1-77069-222-0

Word Alive Press
131 Cordite Road, Winnipeg, MB R3W 1S1
www.wordalivepress.ca

WORD ALIVE PRESS
Just Write!

Library and Archives Canada Cataloguing in Publication

Nywening, Cassandra
      The charade / Cassandra Nywening.

(Hidden grace trilogy ; bk. 2)
ISBN 978-1-77069-222-0

      I. Title. II. Series: Nywening, Cassandra. Hidden grace trilogy ; bk. 2.

PS8627.Y93C43 2010   C813'.6   C2010-908135-8

To Uncle Jake

The Lord your God is with you,
he is mighty to save.
He will take great delight in you,
he will quiet you with his love,
he will rejoice over you with singing.
Zephaniah 3:17, NIV

ACKNOWLEDGEMENTS

Nothing as big as a novel is truly possible to complete without the help of so many different people. Though the author gets most of the credit, it only seems fair to acknowledge those who have helped me along the way. So, to Jake Hogeterp, an awesome editor who sees the worst and best of it all. You have helped shape *The Charade* into the novel it is now. To all those at Word Alive Press who have patiently worked through the process of publishing a book, and have given up much time and effort to make this book the best that it can be. And to all the friends, family, and other supporters who have encouraged me with enthusiasm, helped me with so many different things and stuck by me to the very end. All of you have been a blessing that has made this book possible.

PROLOGUE

BLOOD DRIPPED GENTLY FROM HER lip and traced a path down her chin. Its red stain stood bright against her pale face. She shuddered. Her breath was shallow; her hair matted. The dress she wore was torn from top to bottom. It clung to her only by a few tattered threads.

Seth stroked her brow gently with a single finger. He bit his lip trying to prevent the quiver. It was done. There was nothing else to do. He had done all his father had said. There were no other directions. No other thoughts in his head.

Her eyes opened and horror filled them. She jerked away from him and gasped at the pain. She pushed herself from his grasp and fell onto the forest floor.

She screamed.

Seth covered his ears and began to rock. Tears streamed down his face and he shook. The scream tortured him, taunted him. *Liar, liar*, it said. He moaned and tried to stop the scream, but it only grew louder and more hysterical.

He hit her.

She stopped crying and more blood dribbled from her lip. Seth's eyes widened when he realized what he had done. He pulled her back in his arms and began to rock her. "It's all right. It's all right," he whispered.

She didn't respond.

He needed to get moving. He picked her up in his arms and walked toward the town. There were no other options—he would have to kill her or bring her to town.

He wasn't a murderer.

Liar, liar, the trees whispered. Seth shook his head and ignored them. They didn't know what they were talking about. He wouldn't kill her. She would be okay. He would bring her home. She would heal. She would forget. She wouldn't remember him. He would make it right.

He *would* make it right.

The town was dark. It was late and everyone was asleep; everyone but one family. A candle glowed in the window. A shadow paced back and forth behind the curtains. Step, step; look out the window. Step, step; look out the window. Seth watched from the shadows. The pattern repeated over and over again.

Her breaths became shallower. He didn't have much time. He stepped out of the trees and walked toward the door. It loomed closer, closer, and there it was. He laid her there and knocked.

The steps inside stopped. There was a heartbeat stutter as the pacer made a choice. Step, step, step. Seth could hear them coming closer, closer, closer.

He should run.

He waited. There was a pause at the door. The latch clicked, and the hinges creaked as the door opened.

He needed to run.

Shock was the man's first reaction. He hadn't been expecting Seth. Shock turned to horror when he saw his little girl on the doorstep. A twisted grimace pulled his face into anguished lines. He reached for his daughter but thought better of it. He grabbed at Seth. He shook him with all his might.

Seth went limp with horror. What had he done? What in the world had he done? He broke free from the man's grasp and fell to the ground. He scrambled to get up. The ground slipped from beneath him. "I'll kill you, Seth Hepton. You hear me? I'll kill you!" the man shouted hoarsely.

Seth ran.

He ran for his life. He ran from his life. The night's events bit at his heels, goading him, compelling him to move faster. He screamed out all his pains as he ran. He stumbled, he fell, he picked himself back up. The night surrounded him. The night consumed him. He was overwhelmed.

He kept running.

ONE

SMILE. SMILE. BOW SLIGHTLY. SHAKE hands. *Good morning how are you?* Smile. Nod head. Bow. *Thank you, Miss May, I'm glad you enjoyed the service.* Bow. *I hope you enjoyed your visit.* Smile. Smile. Keep smiling.

Miss Monks stepped forward and curtsied. "Oh Curate Taylor!" she gushed. "Your message was just lovely. I would have never thought of it from that perspective. You truly are a talented man."

Keep smiling. "Thank you, Miss Monks. I always try to bring a fresh perspective to all my sermons. I wouldn't want to bore all the pretty young ladies in the crowd."

Miss Monks blushed, and Caleb hoped she would move on. Such was not his luck. "Oh, you don't have to impress any of us. What should you care about a few silly girls?" She batted her eyelashes like the best of the good-mannered girls. Caleb tried not to roll his eyes.

He forced the smile on his face. "I care what all members of my congregation think, even if they are silly girls." There was an awkward pause as Miss Monks stared up at him, and he tried to think of a way to send her on her way. He stepped uncomfortably from one foot to another.

"Good morning, Curate."

Caleb let out a sigh of relief. Josh was always the answer when it came to Miss Monks, and there he was, come to the rescue just in time. Caleb stepped around Miss Monks and shook Josh's hand. The exchange was brief as Josh had other things on his mind. He looked past the curate to the person of his true interest and then excused himself. Caleb watched as he left.

At the age of nineteen, Josh was a fine-looking young man. He was handsome, talented, and one of the gentlest souls alive. It was a pity he had fallen for one of the silliest girls in Emriville.

Miss Katy Monks was a force to be reckoned with—young, vivacious, and beautiful. Any girl had the right to be jealous of her, and any young man should have the sense to be wary of her. Unfortunately, Josh seemed to lack that sense.

He loved the girl, or so it seemed, and nothing could persuade him to leave her side; not even the blatant rejection of Katy herself. Most people just shook their heads and let the two be. Some pitied Josh and tried to deter him. One person had even gone to the extent of restraining him. With kind persuasion, Josh soon convinced his mother that he was old enough to look after himself, and she was forced to let him leave the house.

Caleb shook his head and laughed at the odd pair. They were bound to get married some day; at least, it was likely they would marry some day if Josh was able to persuade Katy to turn her affection away from the curate. The only question was how long that would take.

Caleb sighed as he thought of the past six years. They had been six wonderful years spent as the pastor of the small church of Emriville. The work had been tough but worthwhile and peaceful. The only downfall to the position thus far had been Miss Monks. Caleb shuddered as he recalled all her eyelash-batting, girlish swooning, and, most dreadful of all, the enormous teardrops rolling off her quivering chin as she pouted.

How was any man supposed to reason with a girl when she pouted? If it were up to him, Caleb would ignore them altogether, but decorum required a gentleman to comfort a crying female no matter how silly she was being, and if a gentleman went so far as to scold a girl for her pettish ways, he would suffer the severest consequences. How could the male gender understand the whims and vices of the fairer sex? It would be better for them to comfort the female than to try to help her overcome such vices that cannot always be explained.

Caleb groaned inwardly. Such decorum had made women weak—much too weak. But, they were the fairer sex, and they must be catered to despite what he thought. Perhaps they could not be stronger. Perhaps it was true that women were much too delicate to handle the stresses men took on every day. If that were so, it would be better for him if he put up with pouting.

Caleb's rambling thoughts came to a standstill as the line of churchgoers dissipated. The building was very nearly empty, and there was no other service for the day. It was time for him to relax.

Caleb made his way up the aisle to the front of the church. He stepped up to the pulpit and looked at where his notes lay.

The sermon had gone over very well. The congregants had responded well, and many had gone home pleased. In his head Caleb could picture a scale with one side weighted down, and the other lifted high in the air with only a slight mass on it. With a small smile, Caleb pictured the sermon adding a little extra weight to the lighter side. The scale shuddered, and Caleb grinned. It had been a good day.

He picked up his notes and folded them neatly. It was time to go home to dinner. Perhaps he would have a good meal, a celebratory meal, because today had surely been a day to celebrate.

The parsonage was not far from the church, but the winter weather made it a cold walk. January was the coldest month in Samaya, but Caleb didn't mind. He loved the snow. Snow was pure and white and clean. He inhaled deeply and felt the crisp cold clean out his system.

Caleb stomped his boots on the parsonage stoop and removed them. Bending down, he placed them neatly against the inside doorpost. He hung his coat and scarf next to them on the coat tree and made his way into the warmth of the house. A hymn played in his head, and he began to hum.

A stack of letters sat on the table. Caleb looked at them as his stomach growled. Food first, he thought, then he would get down to the tasks required of the minister. His meal was simple. He had been given some sausage from the farm family down the road. The sausages cooked quickly enough, and beans and potatoes did not take long to prepare either. It wasn't twenty minutes later that Caleb stuck his fork into his meal and began his celebration.

The letters stared at him as he ate. They spoke of his procrastination, and the negligence toward important ministerial duties. The meal began to sour in Caleb's mouth, but he forced himself to finish eating. He justified his tardiness by claiming he had been busy. He assured himself that it was not a big deal, but no matter how hard he tried, he still felt the weight added to the heavy side of the scale.

Caleb scowled and pushed his empty plate away and grabbed his letters. He took a deep breath to settle himself, and broke the first seal. He scanned the contents and found it to be inconsequential, so he moved on to the next one. He grimaced. There was another funeral to be held in the next town, and they needed a pastor. He would have to leave tomorrow if he was to be of any service at all.

The third letter was to announce a wedding, the fourth was like the first, and the rest of the letters followed in much the same way. Because of the lack of content in the letters, it did not take Caleb long to diminish the pile to the last remaining letter.

He looked at the return address on the letter. It was unfamiliar to him and the handwriting was very messy. He looked to make sure it was addressed to the right location. He had to laugh at the spelling when he read it: *Cureate Caleb Tayler.* It was probably a letter from one of the travelers that sometimes stopped by the church. Perhaps they needed a pastor for a wedding. Without hesitation, Caleb ripped off the seal.

His heart leapt into his throat and stayed lodged there, making it impossible to breathe. He read farther down the letter and began to gasp for breath. There had to be a mistake, a dreadful mistake. He stumbled from his chair and made his way toward the stove. He opened up the hatch and went to throw the letter in, but he stopped himself. Perhaps it would be better to keep it. A reminder of sorts, perhaps. He would hide it in a box somewhere, but he would keep it.

Caleb pulled himself up off his knees and began to breathe. He took in deep, shuddering breaths until he was calm. He went up to his room and found a small, wooden box that had been given to him years ago. He placed the letter in the box and shut the lid tight. Taking some candle wax, he sealed the lid. Once the wax was dry, he went to his chest of drawers and buried the box under his clothes. He wouldn't think about it anymore. It was done. The box would serve as a reminder, but he would not think of the letter that resided in it. Not ever again.

Smiling to himself again, Caleb picked up the book he had been reading and flipped to where the page marker was. He began to read, and with a sigh, paged back to remind himself of what had been occurring in the story. It had been so long since he had last been reading for pleasure. The thought of reading reminded him of the letter in the box. Dropping the book down on the table, he stared around the room.

This was silly. A single letter should not keep him from celebrating. Once more he picked up his book, and with determination, he made it through the first few paragraphs. As he continued to read, his mind drifted into the land of the story where there were no nagging letters and weighted scales. Where the past wasn't remembered because it had never been written.

Darkness set upon the house, and Caleb began to have trouble reading. With a sigh he put away his book and began to prepare for bed. He said his prayers slowly and with care, slipped under the covers, closed his eyes, and waited for sleep. It avoided him. He squeezed his eyes tighter, but consciousness demanded more of him before he passed into the land of dreams.

Growling under his breath, Caleb got out of the warmth of his bed and made his way to his chest of drawers. He rummaged through his clothes until he found the box. He broke the wax seal and pulled out the letter. His hands shook as he opened it, and began to read yet again.

Deer Seth,

Yup, I figured it out. It was reel reel swift of ya to cum up with the hole minister idea, but it sure made it dificult to find ya. Well the truth is thet I found ya a couple'a yeers ago or I thought I had but Mark went to check tha out and when he didnt tell me what happened with tha I figured I had been wrong but I wasn't.

But I gess I should tell ya why Im righting now. Well you see a couple'a yeers ago I got to wonderin what happened to my brothers you no. Well I figured I could just check up on them kinda idea. I found Mark reel easly. He was in the army you know I gess. He looked good then but I dont no bout now. I wondered if hed stay with me and we could make ourselves reel comfertable like you no with double the money. But he'd gone all reelijus on me.

Any ways. By thet time Id herd rumer that you was up in a small town Emriville or somin pretendin to be a preecher. I had to pay gud money for thet there information so's I'm hopin that itll do me sum good.

11

At first I was reel scared cause I dint no how you would take to yer little bruther butin in on yer hole sceem so's I sent Mark instead. He was willin to go so's I thought it would be ok. But he musta run scared cause I haven't herd one wit out of him since a couple'a yeers past.

Well I gess to get right down to it. I was hopin you would be willin to take on yer little bruther fer a while. I no I'll probably be a bit of a newsance. But I'll be reel good if ye'll allow me to stay and I wont bring up the hole Sarah thing if ya dont want me to. I wont menchen a word of it to a single sole.

Sinseerly,

Bill

Yes, Bill would have to mention Sarah. Even if it wasn't intended to be mean spirited, Bill would be the only one cruel enough to mention Sarah. Caleb closed his eyes, and he was back at that night with Sarah. He shuddered, and the image broke.

There was no way he would allow Bill to enter his house. No possible way he could allow the person responsible for all the misery in the world to sleep one night underneath his rafters. He worked too hard to keep the place spotless to allow that piece of scum to step in and dirty up everything. No. Bill would just have to go without knowing the truth. For all he cared, Bill could live as if he didn't have any brothers. Mark was dead, and so was Seth. Seth Hepton no longer existed. He had died the night Sarah had, and there was no way to revive him.

Caleb placed the letter on the nightstand and closed his eyes. This time, deep sleep came quickly. A sleep so dark and terrible, it sapped all energy and left Caleb unconscious as he screamed.

Terror wracked his body all night, pulling at his sanity. It ate away at the core of his being, taunting him. In his mind he saw her eyes: lifeless, dead. He saw the blood drip from her lip. He saw her father. He heard him scream. *I'll kill you, Seth.* But most of all, he ran.

All night long Seth ran. What he was running toward, he didn't know, but whatever it was, it was just out of his grasp. One second he thought he had it, but then it slipped from his fingers. Another time it played around his face, but when he reached for it, he only ended up clawing his cheek. He tried to coax it, but it wouldn't listen. His honeyed persuasion sounded coarse and evil. He screamed in frustration, but it just laughed at him.

He began to run again. His feet were weighted down. They became heavier, heavier, heavier. He was sinking. Farther, farther he sank. He began to drown. He couldn't breathe. His life was fading. As he grasped at the last vestiges of life, it came. Closer and closer it sauntered. He could almost reach it, but his fingers refused to clasp. He dropped his arms in defeat. He was going to die, and it was teasing him. It caressed his cheek. It kissed him lightly. Everything went black.

Caleb took in a gasp of air as he woke from the nightmare. His entire body was covered in sweat, and his sheets were soaked. The sopping mass was twisted around his body, and he had bitten a hole in his pillow. He felt the hoarseness of his throat as he let out a hysterical laugh. He took gasps of air trying to calm himself.

His body shuddered and collapsed as he began to weep. He had been so close. It had been there. He had felt it touch him. It was going to fill him. He was so, so close to it, but it had left him. The complete emptiness of this thought left Caleb wailing. It just wasn't fair. He had searched for it his entire life, all thirty years, yet it evaded him. What did he have to do to grasp it? What was *it*?

With shuddering sighs his weeping ended, and he was able to rise. He made his way to his wash basin and splashed water on his face. It didn't help much to clean him, but the normalcy of the action was comforting. He rinsed his hands over and over. They were clean and wet when he finally quit. They trembled as he dabbed them dry.

The sun peeked over the horizon. There was no time left to sleep. Caleb stripped his bed. He would have to have the sheets washed again. Perhaps he would wait awhile. He had a fresh set in the closet that he could use for the time being. He inhaled deeply and quickly changed his mind. The mass of sheets in his hands stank. If he waited to wash them, the entire house would smell putrid. It was better to have them washed and deal with the rumours than to leave them sitting.

Sighing, Caleb began to get ready for the rest of the day. His eyes drooped as he cleaned the rest of himself and got dressed. The night had left him wanting. He slapped his cheeks to try to give them some colour. He cleared his throat, then he was ready to face the world.

His brother's letter waited for him on the nightstand.

TWO

KATY PUSHED HER WAY THROUGH the crowded market-place. It was busy for a winter day, and she had many things to do. She needed to stop by the butchers to buy a portion of meat for dinner, she needed to look in the mercantile to see if they had any new gloves, and she needed to stop by the post office to see if there were any letters from Rose. It was not bad to be busy in town, and she did not mind having to go about her tasks, but she did hate it quite passionately when Josh was there, as he was now.

He was a nice boy and all, but he was just that: a boy. Of course he was older than she was, but only by a single year. What novelty was there in marrying a boy only a year older than she? It was much too mundane for her taste. Besides, he was terribly obnoxious when he wanted to be, and today he seemed to want that very much.

He followed her from store to store, keeping up a constant dia-logue about the weather, the store owners, or the ever-present useless facts that seemed to pop into his head on the spur of the moment. His very presence was enough to cause a headache. Why he had to pester her all the time, Katy had no idea.

She sighed softly to herself and picked up her pace. Perhaps he would get lost in the crowd. Fat chance! Josh's long legs easily kept up with her smaller strides, putting her petty attempt at losing him to shame. She would have to think of something much cleverer if she wanted to get rid of him.

She could pretend he wasn't there, and hopefully he would get the hint that she wanted him to leave. An unlikely solution. She hadn't so much as acknowledged him in the past hour, and he hadn't even come close to understanding why. Lacking all necessary skills for recognizing when he was not wanted was a very prominent flaw of his.

She could have a fit in the middle of the streets and hope to scare him off. Katy considered this option for a while. It was possible that it would scare him, but it was unlikely that he would run off. It was much more likely that he would end up coddling her while trying to decipher what the problem had been. Nothing good could ever come of such an attempt.

Perhaps she could suggest he leave. She had tried that once before, and it had worked for about five minutes. He had left to go about a task she had sent him on, hoping it would be nearly impossible, but apparently it was much easier than she thought to procure a bouquet of flowers in the middle of winter. This time she would have to come up with something a little more challenging, or perhaps she could bluntly tell him the truth.

She stopped in her tracks and turned on him. He faltered in what he was saying, but finished with only a few more blunders. Then he fell silent. The silence stretched as the two of them stood facing each other. Katy couldn't decide what to do. She could tell him to leave her alone, and he would, or she could get him to do something for her, and he would.

"Why do you keep following me?" she asked.

Josh pondered the question for a while before a grin broke out on his face. "You decided you are going to talk to me now, have you?" He laughed and shook his head.

Katy scowled at him and turned to keep walking. "Wait!" he shouted. He grasped her arm. "Come on, don't leave. I was just surprised that you actually talked to me, and I guess a little startled and..."

Katy turned back to see what could have kept him from finishing his sentence. He stood there with his mouth gaping. "Well?" she demanded. "What do you want?"

Josh let out a relieved sigh. He gave a nervous chuckle as he began again. "I was hoping that you would let me walk with you, and that you would actually talk to me, maybe." A blush bloomed across his cheeks at the revelation of what he wanted.

Katy made a face at him. "Why in the world would you want to walk with me? Don't you have anything better to do with your time? Honestly, the way you carry on, one would think you are possessed!"

Josh chuckled nervously again. It grated on Katy's patience. "Well, some have accused me of worse. I guess I can stand to be called possessed."

Katy glared at him. "You still haven't answered my question."

"Right!" he stuttered. "Your question. Why am I following you?" He took a moment to think it through. "I guess," he began, "I'm following you because I enjoy your company. Is that a good enough reason?"

"It is the silliest reason I have ever heard of. Someone your age should be about your job, or perhaps doing something useful with your time instead of bothering respectable young ladies. Now, I would appreciate it if you would leave me to go about my own business. Unlike you, some of us actually have set tasks for the day." She glared at him, and he smirked at her.

"I suppose I should have seen that one coming. But, I don't think that I am going to listen to you today."

Katy stopped dead in her tracks. He wasn't going to listen to her today? Since when had this become a possibility? Had Josh suddenly grown a mind of his own? Was he now free to follow her whenever he wanted to, even if she didn't want him to? She groaned at the possibilities.

Josh laughed outright. "Come on, Katy." Another one of his flaws; he lacked all sense of social propriety. "I've been bugging you for over a year and a half, and for the first time in this entire time you speak to me, and now you are so quick to dismiss me? Surely it is your turn to speak for once."

"You have been bugging me on purpose! You mean to say that I have been trying to be polite and send your annoying presence away without being rude, and you have been intentionally bugging me? You, you..." Katy glared at Josh as she tried to think of a word strong enough to convey her utter dislike for him. No words came to mind. Everything she could think of was much too kind. For once in her life she wished she had not been so sheltered.

In frustration, she stomped her foot on the spot and stuck out her tongue at him. This only brought on a fit of laughter. She let out an angry growl, and he tried to hold back his laughter. She turned and began to tramp away.

Josh paced after her and grabbed her hand. She yanked it away, but he grabbed it again. "Mr. Deplin, this is highly inappropriate. Can you imagine what all these people will think if they see your hand holding mine? The scandal that would ensue is far less than my retaliation once you let go of my person." She resorted to formalities hoping Josh would listen to her, but he didn't seem to want to pay attention.

He took her hand and slipped it into the crook of his arm where it bent at the elbow. "Pretend I'm the curate, and then you shan't mind this one bit."

Katy bit back her retort. She had been ready to respond to anything but that.

Josh gave her a stiff smile when she didn't respond. "You see, I'm not completely dense. It's not like I don't see the way you practically drool over him. Now, all I ask of you, is that you give me this one afternoon as a friend, nothing more. I will say something, and you will respond, and we will be content just to be friends. Then, when the day is over, we can continue as friends and you can keep ogling at the curate when you don't think he is looking, or you can totally ignore me while I keep following you around whenever I get the chance." He stopped briefly to gauge her reaction. She didn't let anything show on her face. "It's up to you." He shrugged his shoulders as if he didn't care either way.

Katy's mouth gaped as she stared at him. What in the world could he be talking about? Could he seriously be asking just to be friends and nothing more? Could she trust him? "What do you mean by *ogling* over the curate? I don't do that, and you know that's the truth."

Josh let out the breath he had been holding. "Oh, please! Anyone with eyes can see how you adore him. I bet if you had your way, you would christen him a saint."

Katy let out a snort. "Well, he's more of a saint than you will ever be. At least he has a job. That's more than can be said about you. And, he is well respected throughout the entire community. If I were married to him that would mean that I would be held in the same high esteem."

"You wound me, mademoiselle!" teased Josh. "Is that what you think of me? I'll have you know that I hold a steady job despite what you think. It just so happens that I have this particular day off. Do you have a problem with that, Miss Snooty Monks?"

Katy couldn't hold back the giggle that built up in her throat. She tried, but when Josh looked down at her with a mock high-and-mighty look, she couldn't. Her laughter burst out. "Okay, okay. You win. I'll be your friend, but for today only, and don't you dare try to weasel out any more from me."

Josh's grin split his face, but he didn't say anything. The silence grew and Katy began to get uncomfortable. "Well, you could at least say something. You only have the rest of the afternoon, and then I am back to ignoring you. You'd best use your time wisely."

Katy didn't think it was possible, but the smile on Josh's face grew even larger. "Sorry about that. I figured if I opened my mouth, I might shout for joy, and then some people might think we had gotten engaged or something, and I figured you wouldn't want that to happen, so I decided it was better not to say anything at all."

Katy groaned. "This is going to turn out very bad. I can see it now. You are going to get the wrong idea in your head, and I am going to be stuck for the rest of my single life trying to shoo you away. Oh, woe is me!" Katy followed her little spiel with an overdramatic slap of the hand to the head.

Josh chortled and Katy joined in. It would be nice to be friends for the afternoon. Perhaps after that, Josh would leave her alone. Perhaps. Or, perhaps after the day was done, she wouldn't dislike Josh so much. It was a possibility, but it was unlikely. He was already chattering about swords and other such weapons that only men could find interesting. Katy rolled her eyes and settled in for the day. She had promised him that much at least.

Josh took her to the butchers and helped her get the best deal on a piece of pork, then he took her to the mercantile, and he didn't even complain when she took over half an hour picking out a pair of gloves. In the end he was the one who made the final decision between two pairs that were very nearly identical.

The entire time, he kept the conversation going. If Katy tired of a topic all she had to do was suggest something more interesting, and Josh was sure to take to the new topic and supply her with insights that she had not originally had. He knew something about everything. He even knew the names of all the lately born children in the town; something that most men would not admit their knowledge of.

Katy was so enthralled by their conversation that she almost forgot to stop by the post office as Josh escorted her home. She halted suddenly as they passed the building. Josh stopped talking and looked at her questioningly. "Sorry," she shrugged. "I forgot that I need to check if there are any letters for me or my family. It's been so long since any of us has checked."

Josh nodded that he understood, and he waited outside while Katy stepped into the tiny building. Miss Mede stood at the counter sorting through mail and sliding it into the appropriate slots. She smiled sweetly at Katy, and Katy shied away from her. It wasn't that Katy was naturally timid, but she had heard stories about Miss Mede that made her shudder. Of course, she didn't know if those stories were true, but it was better not to get too close.

"Are there any letters for me or my family?" she asked a bit brusquely. Miss Mede nodded her head and rummaged around until she found the pile she was looking for. She handed them over the counter, and Katy snatched them out of her hands. "Thank you," she said sharply, and walked out the door. As she passed through to the outdoors, she took a deep breath of clean air and let it out through pursed lips.

Josh looked at her questioningly. "Did you get your letters?"

Katy held the stack up for him to see, and shrugged off his look. He held out his arm for her to place her hand on, but she ignored it and began to rummage through the letters to keep him from inquiring about the look on her face. She read the names on the addresses and nearly dropped the entire stack when she came to one in particular.

She pulled the fancy paper out from the rest of the less important scraps and looked again at the address. "Well, who would have thought?" she murmured to herself. Josh let out a slight whistle as he read the name over her shoulder.

They stopped in the middle of the road looking at each other. Katy turned her face away first and gaped at the letter in her hand. It wasn't everyday that a commoner got a letter from the queen, but there it was, a letter from Queen Rose Arden. And, it was addressed to her alone. Not to her father, not to her family, but to her, Miss Katy Monks.

Josh let out a slight chuckle. "So, Rose finally decided to contact you? I thought you would have gotten a letter from her sooner, but apparently not, by the look on your face."

"What do you mean by Rose finally deciding to contact me? This is a letter from the Queen of Samaya, not just your everyday average Rose. Of course it hasn't been my habit to be in contact with *Rose*. Honestly Josh, do you lack all sense of propriety? The only Rose that I would dare send a letter to is Rose Wooden, or Rose Hyden as I suppose she is now called, but that is a far cry from the queen. Besides, I have only sent a letter to Rose just recently because I was particularly missing her company."

Josh fought to keep back another laugh, but failed miserably. When he had better control of himself, he encouraged Katy to open the letter in front of her. Slowly, with shaking hands, she listened to his advice.

My Dearest Katy,

I know this letter may come as a bit of a shock to you, for which I am greatly sorry. When I left Emriville, I thought you and your family had understood all, but judging by your past letter, I suppose I assumed much too much.

Forgive me, I have not fully explained, and I fear that I have lost you completely. Perhaps I should have written this letter on different stationary, but it is far too late for that now. Now, without hesitation, I shall explain to you fully the already far too confusing contents of this letter. But, where to begin?

Perhaps I should begin by giving you my name. I am in fact Queen Rose Arden of Samaya, but you better know me by my former name of Rose Wooden. Perhaps this then already explains all to you, but perhaps not, so I shall go on in explaining.

When I lived with your family in Emriville, there was a certain traveler claiming the name of James Hyden. This man, though appearing to be common, was in fact the Prince Henry Arden. You of course know the goings on of the year I spent in your company, but you most likely do not know what occurred when Henry left.

On the night that I was injured, Henry and I had a slight falling out, and he left. When he heard of my injury, he thought I had died, but his father, King James Arden, thought it was best to check and be sure. King James brought me back to the palace in Silidon (your family was given a modified address I presume) where I fully recuperated and made peace with Henry. Soon after this, we were wed.

Forgive me, Katy, for not explaining this to you earlier. I thought you had understood completely, but I was much mistaken. Silidon is so busy that I tend to forget that word travels a lot slower to the country towns and villages. Besides that, I forget how so little has been said about Henry's and my stay in

Emriville that it is unlikely any news has travelled to your town except perhaps the fact that there is a new queen by the name of Rose. Forgive me, it is my mistake for not informing you, and I can only hope that you will not be too put out with me.

Now, on to other matters. I was very glad to receive a letter from you and to hear about all that is going on in Emriville. I have not received a single letter since the time I left, except from Mrs. Jennings. But I suppose that is my own fault for making myself so difficult to contact. I am sorry to hear about your troubles with Josh. He is a good boy, but I suppose he could possibly become obnoxious. Please give him my greetings, and tell him that I hope he is keeping up with his lessons.

Henry would also appreciate it, and I would to, if you would send our regards to Caleb. It is odd that we have not heard one word from him. He has always been slightly strange about some matters, though, and I guess we cannot expect anything more from him.

I miss you terribly, Katy. I always did regard you as a younger sister. Henry and I will have to come and visit sometime soon. Until then, I hope you are in the best of health.

Your friend,

Rose

Katy's jaw dropped when she looked at Josh. "You knew?! You knew that Rose married the prince and became a queen, and you didn't tell me?!"

Josh shrugged. "I thought you would have known. Besides, it really wasn't my place to say. I didn't even know until the king came and Colonel Jasper made it so easily obvious. I thought the entire town would have known by now, but apparently not. What I wonder is how so many people in Emriville failed to notice the connection. Prince Henry Arden marries Rose of an obscure background and nobody asks questions. It is all very strange to me."

"We were told that the queen-to-be was from Golan! Rose is not from Golan, why did they lie?"

"It was really quite well worded. They didn't want to emphasize the fact that she was a commoner. It was really the problem of the aristocrats. They were worried about what the masses would think about a commoner queen so they tried to hide it. I think it was a pride thing really. But they never lied. Rose was from Golan before she lived with her relatives. And they never did specify a last name. No one ever really asked."

Katy glared at Josh. "You never told me, and you knew she was the queen. How did you even know she was the queen, and why didn't you tell me?"

Josh shifted from foot to foot uncomfortably. "Sorry?" he murmured in an attempt to get Katy's glare off of him. It didn't work. "Look, it's not that big of a deal. I only found out because I walked in on a conversation between Rose and the king when the king came to Emriville in disguise as Henry Hyden. Besides, this should be a good surprise, not something to get angry about."

Katy began to walk away from him, but he kept up the pace. "Don't you think this is a good surprise? I mean, think about it. The person you shared your room with for a year is now the queen of the country. Surprise! You now have a friend in a very high place."

Katy spun on the spot and poked a finger into Josh's chest. "You should have told me! How long were you planning on keeping me in the dark? You know, I could have gone my entire life not knowing that I knew the queen. How absurd is that? And you, you would have been laughing the entire time because you knew, but you couldn't tell me."

Josh's face darkened. "It's not like that, and you know it. I wasn't keeping this from you purposely and I wasn't laughing at you. I just didn't think of it, okay?"

Katy let out a groan. "Boys."

"What was that?"

"Oh, I was just saying that Rose sends her greetings. She hopes that you are keeping up with your studies, whatever that is supposed to mean. How do you know Rose anyway? You really didn't start bothering me until after she left."

Josh laughed. "I had the chance to meet her on the rare occasion in town. We formed a general acquaintance before she left. She is probably referring to a study of justice that she got me interested in."

"Hmm," Katy muttered and kept walking.

"So, do you forgive me? Because you're supposed to be my friend for the rest of the day, remember?"

Katy let out a dramatic sigh. "I suppose so. But, if there are any other important little tidbits of information that you forgot to share with me, now would be the time to speak about them."

Josh laughed. "I assure you, about everything else I am completely and utterly in the dark. Wait, I might want to mention that Rose's cousin John is also serving in the palace as a lawyer or something like that, but I am sure that is not very important to you. But, I suppose he is your cousin as well."

"How did I miss out on all of this?" Katy wailed. "It is like I am living inside of a very dark box, and you have just lifted the lid briefly to give me a peek at the world I have been missing out on for all of my years. It is slightly depressing, you know."

"Perhaps you should open your eyes a few more times, and you will notice that your world is not nearly as sheltered as you claim it to be."

Katy opened her eyes wide and looked at Josh. He laughed at her newly opened eyes and she smiled back. Then, shrugging her shoulders, she kept walking. She had a lot of news to share with her parents. It wasn't everyday that she got to tell them about a letter she received from the queen.

THREE

ELIZABETH WOKE WITH A START. The dream had been the same as always. The same repetitiveness. The same awfulness. She took a deep breath and let it out slowly. The images faded, and she was ready to face the day. She dressed in a simple frock and went out to milk the cow. The sun was just rising as she made her way back into the house.

Silence sang as she prepared breakfast. It was a small meal, since she would be the only one eating. She did set aside a small portion of porridge to carry down the hall to the sick room. She sat down to eat. The emptiness made the meal lonely. Her spoon tapped against her clay bowl. It was the only sound in the entire house. Tick, tick, tick the spoon drummed. A cough sounded down the hall, and Elizabeth jumped.

In a flurry of motion, she cleaned up her dishes and took the porridge to her father. He lay pale and weak on a hard straw tick in the corner of the room. She would have gladly given him her bed, but he would not hear of it. They could not afford another bed, and seeing as she did all the work, he often declared that she deserved to have the bed. No form of persuasion could convince him otherwise.

His eyes were empty today as he looked at her. They didn't recognize who she was. That was alright, though. She brought him his porridge and fed him with the same patience that a mother uses to feed her infant. He didn't eat much of it before he collapsed onto the tick, exhausted. Elizabeth kissed his cheek and went to prepare for work.

She brushed down her dress to make sure it was clean. She brushed out her long, dark hair. It was horrid hair—raven black and dirty. Nothing could change that. She pulled it up into a tight bun and pinned it into place. It stayed without making much of a fuss. She looked at herself in the mirror. A crack cut her image in half, but it did not hide the pale bleakness of her cheeks. She pinched them to gain some colour. It didn't help much.

She needed to leave. She was late for opening the post office which was abnormal for her. People already detested the little Miss Mede who ran the post office. It was best that she didn't give them any other excuse to hate her. She stopped by her father's room once more and looked in. He was sleeping fitfully, but at least he was sleeping. She left him to his slumber.

She used to worry about leaving him. She would fret about him while she went about her work, but each day she would come home and find things much the same. Eventually she had given up on worrying. Perhaps it would be better if her father died while she was away. At least he would be out of his misery.

The day was cold. It bit at her as she trekked toward the post office. She tried to ignore it, but it nosed in, refusing to be put off. Perhaps she should be thankful for it. It would bring some colour into her face.

When she reached the post office, the morning had broken into its full, sunny glory. The snow-topped roofs sparkled and dazzled, and the frost-covered windows decorated each store front. The mail carrier was waiting, stamping his feet next to his horse. Elizabeth apologized, but he still glared at her as he handed over the bag of mail for Emriville and the surrounding area.

She sighed as she heaved the heavy sack into the building. She let it drop with a thud onto the floor. Dragging it behind the counter, she began to sort it. There was a lot of mail today. It would take her a while to get through it all, but she did have all day.

She hummed to herself as she looked at addresses and filed each letter into the appropriate mail slot. The door opened and she jumped to her feet. Mr. Walters, one of the church elders, stepped into the warmth of the post office and glared at her. She shied away from his glance and went directly to his mail slot. There were three letters for him and he would want them directly. She slid them across the counter toward him, and he snatched them up, tossing down a generous coin offering for her work. She thanked him quietly, but his glare intensified. He left in a hurry.

He was the usual morning welcome. Often he was the first to arrive, and it was always the same. He never wanted to talk to her. He never wanted to touch her. He just wanted his mail and nothing else, but seeing as he was an elder, he was expected to do his good Christian duty for the poor. So, he always left a generous tip for the poor Miss Mede. When she said thank you, he would not respond, he would walk out the way he came and let God handle the wellbeing of the poor beyond that.

What else was she to expect from an elder? He would not want to soil himself by touching the likes of her. What would the congregation think of him then? He was a good man, Elizabeth was sure of that, and she could not expect him to get involved in something that was not his problem. It would only harm his family and cause all sorts of hurt. Elizabeth did not wish to feel guilt over that.

She went back to sorting the mail. She smiled when she recognized the handwriting of a friend sending a regular letter, then she would slip it into its slot. She tsked when she realized that John Read had another letter from his admirer a couple of towns over. What a scandal that would be when his mother found out that her boy would be moving a ways away. Each address had a story behind it, and Elizabeth knew nearly all of them.

It wasn't that she was nosey, but it was nearly impossible to work in the post office, sorting the mail and sending the mail out, without noting particular trends. It was probably wrong of her to live vicariously through the letters, but she had no other connections, so she felt no guilt over it. When looking through addresses, she became a part of the town, a part of the life that took place there. Without the addresses, she would be hopelessly alone.

The door banged open and Elizabeth looked to see who could have arrived. Mrs. Atkins strolled coolly into the office. She was tall and lean. She looked down her nose at the young girl and sneered. "I'll have my mail now, please." Elizabeth turned and, as slowly as possible, retrieved the lady's mail. It was probably terribly wrong of her, but she couldn't stand the woman, and as far as she was concerned, Mrs. Atkins deserved to be knocked down a peg or two. Unfortunately, she would not be the one to do that.

She procrastinated as much as she could in finding Mrs. Atkins' mail slot and then crept around and handed the mail across the counter. The woman snatched it up and left the building in a hurry. Elizabeth let out a breath as she disappeared. That woman was enough to vex any sane person. It was a wonder she had ever married.

Elizabeth sighed. It was time she got back to work. The day dragged on as she went about her tasks. She tidied up the office and sorted the rest of the mail. She marked the mail appropriately for the night shipping and made sure everything was ready for the next day.

People came in and out while she worked. Many of their reactions to her were predictable and much the same. The younger people avoided her eyes, the older generation scowled at her, and the rare naïve soul smiled at her. Oh to be so blissfully ignorant, but that was never to be. She was always polite, she always smiled, and she rarely spoke. The job was perfect for that; she hardly ever had to speak.

She was just about to close up for the day when the door opened once more. The curate walked through and glared at her. That was a change. The curate was usually one of the blissfully ignorant who smiled at her. It must have been a bad day for him. He held a letter in his hands which shook, and his entire being looked stressed.

"How may I help you?" Elizabeth asked in a near whisper. She normally didn't speak first, but the curate looked unable to form a coherent sentence without some prodding.

He shook his head. "I... I was hoping that you would be able to keep some letters from coming to me." Elizabeth gave him a confused look, and he shook his head again. "I mean to say, I have been getting letters from a particular address, and their contents are slightly disturbing. I was hoping there was some way that you could just not give me the letters. Perhaps you could burn them or something so that they don't have to disturb anyone else." The curate stuttered to a halt, and with a look, Elizabeth prodded him to continue.

"I would have to know what the address is from which the letters are coming," she stated when he did not oblige.

"Yes, yes of course." He held the letter in his hands out to her. She looked at the address and began to write it down. Checking it over twice, she finished, and placed it where she would be sure to remember it. The curate glanced at where she placed the slip of paper and looked at it anxiously. "You'll remember to burn the letters? I mean, I wouldn't want you to have to fill a drawer up with useless letters."

Elizabeth smiled politely up at him. "Sir, I am sorry, but I think you misunderstand. I have the address and then I will speak to Mr. Walters. If he says that the letters should be destroyed, then I will do as you say. Of course, Mr. Walters may ask to see the letter for himself..."

"No!" the curate cut in. He cleared his throat. "What I mean to say is you can get rid of the letters. I will talk to Mr. Walters, and it will all work out. Just make sure I don't have to see another one of those letters."

"Yes sir," Elizabeth murmured. She waited to see if he would say something else, but the curate just stood there.

Elizabeth started to go about odds and ends. She really didn't have anything to do, but she couldn't close up the post office until the cur-ate left. He didn't seem in a hurry to leave the spot where he stood holding the opened letter. She bit her lip trying to come up with a solution to the predicament. She walked around the counter toward the solitary figure. She tapped him on the shoulder and he flinched.

"Oh, Miss Mede! You startled me." He shook his head again, but he continued to stand on the same spot.

Elizabeth cleared her throat. "Is there anything more that I can help you with, Mr. Taylor? Or, do you just need this time to think?" Her voice was quiet, but it still seemed to startle the curate with each new syllable.

He looked at her curiously when she finished speaking. "Why in the world would I need time to think while standing in a post office? The very idea is preposterous. No, I'll be on my way now, I think. I was just enjoying the warmth. It is a cold one out there tonight. Goodnight, Miss Mede. Make sure you make it home safely." He gave her a large smile and then he was gone. Elizabeth shook her head in wonder.

The curate was a different character, but he was kind, and that was more than she could say for most other people in Emriville. There was no need to complain about a person who had a ready smile on most days. Besides, he was almost always a gentleman in her presence, which was a refreshing contrast to the other crude persons who tend-ed to enter the post office.

Elizabeth put on her wraps and locked the door as she left the office. It was dark outside, and the wind had begun to blow. Snow whipped against her cheeks and stung her nose. It was on nights like this that she sometimes wished she were rich. If she were rich, she would sit in front of a large fireplace and let the warmth seep into her bones. She would close her eyes and hum softly. Then she would lull off to sleep without concerning herself with finding her bed because the chair she sat in would be as comfortable as any bed found in the entire kingdom of Samaya.

The picture she formed in her head was old and well used. It comforted her on the cold nights when the wind whistled and made the entire house shake. She used it when sleep evaded her because of the nightmares that tormented her. But, she used it most often when her heart wrenched with the misery of being so utterly and miserably alone.

When she got home she went immediately to the barn to feed the cow and milk her. The warm milk frothed in the pail and sent up a delicious scent. It tickled at Elizabeth's nose, and she was thankful for it. Not many families had the luxury of fresh milk, but fortunately she and her father had this one blessing.

She carried the bucket carefully toward the house, attempting not to spill a single drop as the wind whipped about her ankles and tried to knock her off balance. It was a struggle with every step, but she eventually made it to the kitchen door and into the house. She set the bucket down and began to take off her wraps.

It was cold in the house, which meant that her father had been unable to get up and tend to the fire. She raced down the hall to make sure he was still breathing. The gentle rise and fall of his chest under the layers of quilts spoke of his continuing existence, and Elizabeth was able to breathe more easily. She tended to his needs before she thought about any of her own.

When her father was content, she went to the kitchen to prepare her supper. There weren't many options. She sliced off a piece of bread from a loaf on the table and fried a couple of eggs. She topped this off with a glass of milk. She was just finishing her meal when a noise from the other room startled her. She raced to see what had happened.

Her father lay on the floor, wheezing. His cheeks puffed in and out, but no air seemed to make it down his throat. With a frightened cry, Elizabeth raced to his side and began to pound on his back. He still couldn't breathe well. She pounded his back harder until he began to cough. He took in a great gasp and began to pant.

Elizabeth let out a sigh of relief. Her pounding turned to a gentle massage as she quietly reassured the old man. He began to breathe easier, and he was soon fast asleep. Elizabeth let the tears fall as she lifted her frail father back onto his tick.

He was light and feeble, and it didn't take much effort on her part to get his entire body back onto the tick and under the covers. She stroked his tired faced and wished him a good night's sleep, then, bending over him, she kissed his cheek and walked quietly back to the kitchen.

She cleaned up the kitchen and washed the dishes. She cleared cobwebs and dusted down any surface she could find. It was getting late, and she had an early morning the next day. It was best that she got herself to bed. She checked the stove to make sure it was well stocked for the night, she checked on her father once more, then she slipped under the thin covers on her bed.

The wind howled and groaned. Its noisy bawling made it nearly impossible to sleep. It ranted and raved about its winter power. It snickered at the way the town folk cowered in their houses. It taunted, it teased, and it tormented. Elizabeth tried to ignore it, but it wouldn't consent to such treatment. She closed her eyes and tried to drown it out with her cozy image from before, but the wind would not be pushed from her thoughts.

As sleep stole over her, the wind snuck into her dreams in the form of soul-twisting shrieks of agony. The dream, of course, was the same as always. It was the same scene as before, the same face, the same person, but the wind brought the person to life.

It started out in a small kitchen. She was four years old and very sad. The wind whispered her name gently and persuaded her to look around the room. She didn't want to listen to the wind. She knew what she would see if she looked up from the floor, and she didn't want to see it. But the wind became more insistent and demanding. It yelled at her to look.

She lifted her head, but she didn't look in the corner. Instead, she looked at the stove where dinner was cooking. She looked everywhere but the corner. The wind started to whine. She wasn't cooperating with what the wind wanted, and it was going to have to be angry with her unless she actually looked at the rest of the room.

She ignored the wind and tried to think of something else. She thought of her father and his face. She tried to see his smiling face one more time. It appeared, but the wind screamed at her, making her lose the image. She yelled back at the wind, but it ignored her screams. It demanded that she look in the corner. She refused, but the wind was insistent.

The Charade

The wind tried another method. It coated its voice with honey and began to croon. It was all right if she didn't look in the corner, but she would be missing out. It wasn't a bad thing in the corner. It was actually a lovely picture that she would enjoy looking at. She should trust the wind and look in the corner.

She knew the wind was lying, but she wanted to look. She wanted to see, to make sure it was the truth. She started to turn toward the corner, but she stopped herself short. She knew better than to listen to the wind. She would not look into the corner.

The wind growled at her stubborn nature, but did not give up. The wind never gave up. It started to call her names. First she was a coward, then a weakling. She was incapable, unworthy of looking in the corner. It was probably best that she didn't look anyway. She would be unable to handle the beauty of what lay in the corner.

She yelled back at the wind, but her four-year-old mind was hurt by the taunts that had been thrown at her. She began to pout. The wind laughed at her—deep, hysterical laughter. She tried to ignore it. She plugged her ears and shouted at the top of her lungs. The wind laughed even louder.

She begged the wind to stop, but it wouldn't, not unless she looked in the corner. The wind waited to speak as she came to a point of indecision. Her bottom lip quivered as she tried to fight the urge to cry. Slowly, uncertainly, she turned toward the corner.

Horror filled her entire being as the image she saw scalded her eyes. She tried to close her mind, to stop thinking. She covered her eyes, but the image still hung there. She screamed in terror, and the wind laughed at her. The wind had won yet again.

She sat in terror as the image hung before her. Her screaming stopped, and she was left to study the corner as the wind continued to laugh.

It was a person, of that she was sure. It hung from a bed sheet tied around a hook in the wall. Its face was blue and bloated. The tongue stuck out from swollen purple lips and the eyes bulged out from deformed sockets. The hair was a mass of matted blond locks that stuck to the face. Bugs could be seen crawling in and out of various areas in that mass.

The corpse wore a dress. It was yellow and dirty. It had a tear in the hem, and the fabric swept soundlessly across the dirt floor. A stench came from the body that resided in the fabric. It was putrid and rotten, and it filled the room so much that Elizabeth was shocked she had not noticed it before she had looked in the corner.

A broken chair was next to the body. It rested on its side, as if it had been kicked away in haste. It was the only witness to what had occurred. It was the only one who could tell what had happened to the woman. Elizabeth asked the chair what had happened to see if it would answer, but it was the wind who responded.

Don't you see? It mocked. *Can't you understand?* It teased. It laughed and forced its way into the corner. It climbed into the corpse and brushed past the ruined vocal cords. A shriek wracked the body and tormented Elizabeth's ears. She covered them, but nothing would help. The terrible shriek continued on and on.

She woke with a start. She was screaming, but she couldn't stop herself. She took in deep breaths to try calm her shattered composure but the terror persisted. She began to gasp and then sob, but the image would not leave her. She could still see the face. She could still hear the scream.

Slowly but surely, her sobs subsided. Her gasps turned into small hiccups and she was able to calm herself. She shuddered and tried to ease the tension in her shoulders. It remained. She picked herself up from her bed and began to prepare for the day.

They would be expecting her at the post office soon. She needed to tend to her father as well as the cow, and it would be necessary to find some food before she left. Her stomach recoiled at the thought. But, she knew it was necessary.

She walked to her father's room. He was sleeping peacefully. Her tortured screams had not woken him. That was a good thing. He often slept fitfully as it was.

She went out to the small barn and began to milk the cow. The gentle rhythm soothed the last frayed ends of her nerves, and she was even able to smile. She patted the cow on its haunches and then left with her pail of milk. Dawn had not broken as she made her breakfast, but the wind had stopped, for which she was thankful.

She prepared a small portion of porridge for her father and carried it to him. He ate it all, which was a good sign. She stoked the fire and set some bread and cheese on the nightstand close by her father's head. Perhaps he would get hungry in the middle of the day. That had not occurred in a long time, but there was always a first time for everything.

The sun was rising. It was time for her to leave for the post office.

FOUR

KATY LOOKED IN THE MIRROR and patted at her hair. It sat perfectly in place, yet still she stared. She looked blankly at her eyes and tried to see what the curate would see. She tried to understand what it was about herself that he didn't seem to like. Surely, there must be something. Perhaps her eyes were too pale, or her cheeks too plump. Perhaps she was too white and sickly. She could try wearing some rouge. She shuddered at the idea. Colourful cheeks would be nice, but not at the expense of being mistaken for a woman of unseemly sorts.

She sighed and turned away from the mirror. There had to be a reason why the curate didn't like her, and she was determined to figure out what it was. She could change to be what he wanted. It couldn't be anything too terribly difficult. The only problem was she didn't know what he wanted from her.

She picked up the letter she had received from Rose and walked out the door. It was time for her to pass the message on to the curate. He would be pleased to hear from Rose again, and it would most likely be a surprise to him as well that she was the queen. Maybe Katy could convince him to stop and talk for a while on the topic.

She dreamed of this as she walked down the road. She pictured his eyes lighting up and dancing like they did when he was passionate about the topic of a sermon. His hands would start moving with expression, and any person who heard him would be drawn in by his charisma. She smiled to herself as she imagined herself being part of that conversation. It would make her day perfect and wonderful—one of her most treasured memories.

As she approached the curate's door, the dream dissipated and reality set in. Katy's stomach twisted into a knot that pulled itself tighter and tighter with each step. She tried to form an introductory sentence but couldn't think of any. She tried to think of ways to get inside to the parlour, but nothing seemed reasonable. She took a deep breath as she knocked on his door.

It opened and the curate stepped out onto the front stoop. Katy looked up, until she found his eyes. She took a deep breath before she began. "I have a message for you, from Rose." She blinked quickly, trying to hide her nervousness.

Caleb fought the urge to scowl at her. Her eyelashes batted up and down at him, and she looked absolutely silly. He would have sent her away politely, but she had a message from Rose. It was best that he allow her in and listen to her politely until she gave him that message.

"Please come in and have a seat," Caleb said as he opened the door further. "I'll bring you a cup of tea if you would like."

Her eyelashes began to bat even faster. Caleb could have sworn she was about to swoon as well, but she must have thought better of it, for she collected herself and thanked him for the small offer. He grumbled under his breath as he went to the kitchen for the drink.

When he came back to the parlour, Katy sat politely at the edge of her seat. Her back was straight and stiff with perfect posture. He placed the cup in front of her and she accepted it politely. He sat across from her, and she tilted her head down and blushed. Caleb turned his head away and pretended not to notice. "You said you had a letter from Rose."

Katy blushed again. "Yes, I do. It was probably silly of me to come all this way just to tell you that she and, and... Oh, how do I say this?" Katy faltered. "I guess I would have to say that his highness sends his greetings." She started batting her eyelashes as she looked up at him.

Caleb took the news in for a few seconds. So, Rose and Henry had finally let the cat out of the bag. They had made their position known to the poor, lowly commoners had they? "So *King* Henry and his wife have been in contact with you then?"

Katy looked up at Caleb. "You knew as well, and you didn't tell anyone?"

He looked angry, and her nerves did a little jump. There was no way of telling what he was feeling. He was so hard to read in that way, yet he was so terribly handsome. She felt her face heat up, and she quickly took a sip of tea to clear her throat.

"I was told to keep that particular information to myself when I learned of it. But yes, I knew. When I heard the wedding announcement, I decided it was still a big secret and I had better not let it out. But now I see that it is information that everyone is to know."

"Oh," Katy squeaked. "Rose said they were hoping to stop by sometime soon. Wouldn't that be lovely?"

Caleb didn't respond at first. "Yes, that would be wonderful," he sighed. All conversation ended as Katy finished her tea. She sat watching him, not sure what to say, not sure if she should say anything at all. Caleb avoided looking at her. He looked out the window; he glanced at the clock; he looked at the ceiling. Finally, the fifteen minutes passed, and Katy made her escape.

She politely said her goodbyes and very nearly ran out of the house. Caleb watched as she left and let out a sigh of relief. How was he supposed to talk with such a silly girl? It was a good thing she knew when she was not wanted, because he did not know how he would have asked her to leave politely.

He picked himself up off the chair and made his way toward his office. He had a lot on his mind. Henry and Rose would be coming again. He hadn't been expecting that. They were royalty now. They had enough things to occupy their time now that they didn't have to waste any of it visiting those less than them. But, if they wanted to come, he wouldn't begrudge them that.

He honestly didn't mind that they were coming. It would be good to see Henry again. He had been a very good friend when he had been just Henry, but now it was different. Henry was no longer just Henry. He was King Henry, and he had a wife. Rose.

Caleb cringed when he thought of her. Beautiful Rose. He had loved her, or so he thought. She was kind, compassionate and loving.

Being in her presence was enough to make anyone a better person. But, he didn't deserve her, and she had made that perfectly clear to him. She was a queen now, and did very well at it. From what he heard, those in Silidon were quite pleased with their young queen.

If Rose was to come for a visit, he would have to guard himself from all sorts of evils. He could picture the bars going up on his heart, shutting out the scum. He tested their strength. He watched as jealousy took a shot at the barrier. It held strong. Pride and boasts tried next, but both were useless against the strength of his barrier. Finally came lust. It snuck up to the barrier and tried to deke around his defences. With a nod of satisfaction, Caleb stopped it in its tracks. He would be well prepared if the royal family decided to pay a visit.

He walked over to his writing desk and began to work on his sermon. The words flowed through him and he felt the strength of his arguments come alive and take root. It would be another good sermon. He could feel the scale shudder in anticipation of the added weight. A smile cracked the corner of his mouth.

Perhaps the week hadn't been all bad. He hadn't received any other letters from Bill, or if he had, he hadn't heard about them because Miss Mede had taken care of them. His sermon was falling into place, and he could be expecting a visit from the king and queen sometime soon. Yes, this week could turn out to be a very good week after all.

Katy let out a sigh of relief as she walked out the curate's door. She closed her eyes and counted to ten before she could keep moving. She was about to open them again when she heard a soft chuckle coming from the street. She knew that laugh and she glared in its direction. "What do you want, Mr. Deplin?" she demanded.

He laughed at her again. "Nothing at all, Katy girl. I was just wondering if you had a nice little visit with the curate." His voice dripped with sarcasm, and Katy wished she could inflict some sort of physical damage to his being, but he was much too big for her to even attempt to hurt.

"I'll have you know, that I had a very lovely visit with Mr. Taylor. I was telling him that Rose sends her greetings. He was very grateful for the news and then we had a nice conversation over a cup of tea." So it was a bit of an exaggeration, but she would never let Josh know that.

"Was that what you were dreaming about when you came out, or were you dreaming the entire time you were visiting, and the illusions were just breaking as you left the house?" He tried not to laugh as Katy glared at him, but he couldn't help himself when she stuck her tongue out at him.

Josh grabbed his stomach and tried to stay upright as Katy stomped her foot on the spot and began to walk away. "Wait!" he shouted between fits. "Wait!" he called a little more desperately. "I was only joking, Katy, dear. You were perfectly respectable when you left the curate's house, I just couldn't help myself."

Katy turned on him. "If I were you, Mr. Deplin, I would refrain from using endearments in my presence, or I may have to resort to some form of corporal punishment. It is not polite or proper for a young man to call a young lady by such familiar names unless there is an engagement of sorts between the two. Seeing as such an engagement does not as of now, or ever will exist, please restrain yourself from speaking to me in such a manner."

She tried to emphasize her point by staring him down, but his height put him at an advantage, and she had to tilt her head back to find his eyes. When their eyes did finally meet, his were filled with such merriment that she was forced to turn away with a blush. She turned to leave. He took her hand and placed it in the crook of his arm.

"Please, allow me to escort you home."

"I don't think I would like that very much." But Josh didn't listen. The two walked in silence for some time. There was nothing to talk about, and neither of them deemed it necessary to break the silence. Their footsteps sounded on the snow-covered road in slow, steady thuds; each one creating a beat in a familiar rhythm.

Finally Josh broke the silence with a sigh. "It is a lovely day out, don't you think? Perhaps it is a bit cold, but nothing that is too much of a bother."

"Yes," Katy agreed and silence again fell.

"It seems a shame to waste such a beautiful day indoors. It would be better for one to spend the time out of doors when the sun is shining as it is today. Would you not agree?"

"I suppose," she replied.

Josh inhaled deeply. "Can you smell the pine? Scent always travels better on days like today. It makes the outdoors so much more enjoyable—"

"Is there a point to what you are saying? Because if there isn't, I would very much appreciate it if you would keep your comments to yourself."

Silence fell and the two continued to walk. They were drawing closer to the Monks' house, and Josh's pace had noticeably slowed. Before they reached the lane, Josh stopped altogether and turned to Katy. He opened his mouth as if to speak, but paused for a moment. When he had gained his thoughts, he began again.

"I was wondering, Miss Monks, if you would join me on a walk throughout the rest of the afternoon." He paused and looked at her shocked reaction. "I don't mean anything by this, of course, just as friends, I mean. I wouldn't want to impose on your time at all, and if you don't want to, that is all right, but I would greatly appreciate your company," he finished lamely.

Katy considered him for a moment. He seemed sincere, and it was a nice day. "What will people say when they see the two of us walking together? There will be many assumptions that will lead to rumours."

"Oh. But, if we go into town, and if there is no chaperone, people will think I am just nagging at you again, which I probably will end up doing. I might even start rambling if you don't get too annoyed with that. People will be able to see we are just friends, and if you are really worried about it, I won't hold your arm at all. There shouldn't be any rumours then."

Hesitantly, Katy agreed. It would be a good way to get rid of the extra stress that was currently weighing on her shoulders. She was still feeling flustered after her visit with the curate. It would be nice to visit with a *friend* for while. It wasn't like any assumptions could be made if they were walking through the middle of the town and they weren't even touching. And, if there were any rumours, they could easily be quashed.

A grin split Josh's face at her consent, and he began to ramble as he placed her hand back on his elbow and steered her toward town. She let out an overdramatic sigh, and he hooted with pleasure. She couldn't keep herself from giggling at that. Josh was so easy to please that it was pleasant to be in his company. She tried to think of a time when he had been angry but couldn't find any memory of such an event. He was always so happy. She was jealous of this.

Josh looked down at her and smiled again. He was infatuated by her. She was pretty and somewhat intelligent. No one would argue that she was the most intelligent being, but she was quite charming in her own way. He tried to think of a fact that would interest her. "Did you know, that a lamb is usually walking a half hour after it is born?"

Katy rolled her eyes. "And why is that important?"

Josh shrugged his shoulders. "Don't you find it interesting that we humans take months to learn to take our first steps and then to start to run, but after an hour of life, a lamb can be running around on sturdy legs?"

"I suppose it is interesting in its own way." Katy turned to look at the scenery that they passed by, and Josh tried to think of something more interesting to amuse her.

"Did you know that if the lamb takes too long to start walking, the ewe will start pawing and nudging at it? It is a type of instinct, and it can almost appear to be violent at some points."

"Do you have an avid fascination with sheep, Mr. Deplin?"

Josh blushed. "Not in particular. I just thought that you might find some things about sheep interesting. I mean, they are interesting creatures to a certain extent."

Katy gave him a look and then turned back to the road and waited for him to keep talking about whatever it was that he would come up with next. Josh took a deep breath and continued to ramble about nothing in particular. Katy took the time to close her eyes and relax. She breathed in the crisp, clean scent of winter and let the gentle hum of Josh's voice ease the tension out of her muscles.

It didn't take them long to get to town. The streets were empty except for a few women and children going about their business. No one took much notice of the couple, and the couple didn't take much notice of them. As the last of the tension eased from Katy's shoulders, she decided she should probably relieve Josh of some of the conversation.

"How have you been, Mr. Deplin?"

Josh grinned. "Well enough, I suppose. How have you been, Miss Monks?"

Katy smiled politely. "I have been quite well, thank you. I have just recently received a letter from the queen of Samaya. Would you like to hear the contents of the letter?"

Josh laughed. "I believe you have already passed the message on to me. If you don't remember, I was with you when you received that particular letter."

"I suppose. But, I do love relaying that bit of news. People are always so excited to hear more about my correspondence with the queen. I mean, who would have thought that a commoner would or could ever become queen. Such a thing is so... so unthinkable, unreasonable."

"What is so unreasonable about it? Rose and Henry are perfectly suited for each other. It would have been peculiar of Henry if he had chosen to marry anyone besides Rose. I can understand if he was forced to marry, but when given a choice why wouldn't you marry who you are compatible with no matter their social status?"

Katy rolled her eyes. "I wasn't thinking that deep into it. I was just thinking about how uncommon it is for someone who has no connections to be placed into a position of such power. It is astounding."

"Sure," Josh grumbled jokingly, "you find this interesting, but you think that sheep are absolutely boring." He let out a longsuffering sigh. "I will just have to figure out what pleases you."

Katy laughed. "Why would I be interested in sheep? They don't apply to my life in any way. This, this applies to my life in many ways, so it is interesting. Surely, you can see the huge contrast between the two."

"I suppose."

"I sent a letter back to Rose. Do you think she will be glad to hear from me?"

"Of course she will be! What would make you think otherwise?"

"Oh, I don't know. It's just that it's different now that she is royalty. Now she has a reason to look down on me. She will be rich and have servants, and I won't have any of that. And, it's not like I can give her anything that will make her like me. Perhaps she will think worse of me for that."

Josh looked at her incredulously. "Do you actually believe that, Katy? I mean, it's not like we are talking about a complete stranger here. This is Rose we are talking about. I am sure she will love you just as much as ever when she comes to see you again. Why else would she reply to your letter?"

Katy hesitated. How was she supposed to respond to that logic? What Josh said made sense, but she still felt nervous about the whole coming of the king and queen, if they ever did come. "She could just want to rub it in my face," Katy said shyly.

Josh snorted at her response. He stopped and looked her in the face. "My dear, I am sure you are imagining things now. Rose would never rub something like that in a person's face. You have to remember that she herself was once in your position, actually she was in a worse position than you."

Katy stiffened at the familiar way the endearment rolled off of Josh's lips. "I told you not to use endearments, Mr. Deplin. If you allow such slip of a tongue again, I will not be responsible for my actions."

A smirk crossed Josh's face. He turned back to the road and pulled her hand back to his arm. They continued their walk. "I am sure Rose will be the exact same lady she was the last time she was here—only with a bit more money."

"A *bit* more money? That is the most severe understatement I have ever heard. A bit more money would be a few extra coins to throw about, or an extra penny in the offering at church. When Rose comes, she will have trunks of gold coins to dispose of as she wishes."

Josh laughed. "Then, my dear, you should hope you get on her good side so she can dispose of some of those gold coins on you."

Katy yanked her hand from Josh's arm and turned on him. Without thinking, she slapped him across the face as hard as her unpractised hand would allow her. She felt the shock of the force in the stinging of her flesh, but it was worth it. She jabbed her finger into Josh's chest and began to rant.

"I told you, it is improper for you to call me by endearments, but did you listen? No, you pigheaded fool, you would not listen, and now look what you have made me do. I will not have it. You will apologize for your actions, and you will refrain from ever calling me 'my dear' ever again."

Josh blinked as he looked at the vixen before him. He tried to stop himself too late. A hoot of laughter escaped his lips. He tried to pull it back in, but he couldn't catch his breath. He grabbed his stomach to try to hold it in place, but his knees gave out. Before he could control himself, he was on the ground howling with laughter.

Through tear-streaked eyes, he watched as Katy stomped her foot. If he had been listening more closely, he might have heard her mutter "Boys!" under her breath as she left him rolling in the streets.

FIVE

ELIZABETH WOKE WITH A GASP. It was the dream again. The same old dream, but it still left her shivering. It would seem that one should get used to the images seen only in the head, but there was no way to protect the vulnerable mind of a slumbering person. As soon as that person closed his eyes, his defences dropped and he was left unprotected. This knowledge did not in any way comfort Elizabeth.

She looked about the room as the last remnants of the bloated, swaying body left her mind, and she was able to once again take control of her sanity. It was early—earlier than normal. Elizabeth groped around the cold room until her hands landed on her work dress stiff and frozen on the hook she had placed it on that evening. She pulled the rigid fabric over her head and waited for it to warm.

It was too early for her breakfast, but the cow would not mind an early appearance. She trudged through the snow to the barn. The wind nipped at her hair, yanking it out of its pins and tossing it in her face.

She tried to pull it back, but it wouldn't cooperate. It was determined to obey the wind, to slap against her cheeks, to blind her, and make her life difficult. In frustration, she let it have its way.

The barn door creaked and groaned as she pulled it open. The wind pushed against it, keeping it in place, but Elizabeth pushed through into the warmth of the room. Once she was inside, her hair fell limp, shuddering only slightly with faint breezes that found their way through cracks. She moved herself farther into the warmth of the building. It was hard to see, but experience told her where to find all that she needed. Taking the stool and pail, she sat by the cow and began to milk.

The steady rhythm of the *splick splick* splatters of milk in the bucket was comforting. The cow was warm and gentle, and at that moment, the barn felt like the safest place in the world. "You know," murmured Elizabeth to the cow, "I don't know why I still dream. It would seem wiser just to ignore the dreams, or perhaps to never sleep unless absolutely necessary. Then, when I did sleep, I would be too tired to dream." Big cow eyes turned and looked at her. They rolled, and Elizabeth sighed.

"You are probably right. If I slept deeply, I might still dream, and because I was so tired, I would not be able to wake up and then I'd be stuck in the corner with, with... well with you know what." The barn fell silent again except for the *splick splick* of the milk. Elizabeth sighed and finished her task.

The sun had not made an appearance when she left the barn, and the moon greeted her cheerily from the wind-whipped ceiling. The clouds scowled at the shining one, and went quickly about their tasks in the sky. They hurried from here to there in such a rush that sometimes they collided, but this did not slow them in any way.

Elizabeth prepared her breakfast slowly, but no matter how long she took, there was only a certain amount of time one could take with morning preparations. So, when she accomplished all she could at home, she decided to head to work early. It was still dark when she reached the post office, and it would not be wise to burn candles or lamps in such a building if it could be avoided, so she decided to walk a little longer while she waited for the sun to make its presence known.

Elizabeth tried to ignore the cold, but she pulled her wraps closer anyway. There were not many places to walk at such an hour. The streets were off-limits because of the possible nuisance to the neighbours and townsfolk, and it was better to avoid any place with even a slight population. By this deduction she ended up in the pasture.

It was a quiet place that emitted an overwhelming sense of peace. The snow rested unmarred and unsoiled by foot prints. The only thing that protruded from the smooth surface was a large boulder and something or other in the back corner. Hesitantly, Elizabeth took a step onto the untouched surface to discover what the other protrusion could possibly be.

The snow crunched under her shoes. It was a nice crisp sound that could brighten anyone's day. For a moment she was satisfied with just the sound of it. She kicked the dusty flakes and watched as the wind carried them swirling away. She smiled, but regretted it when she saw the deep rut she had made in the once perfect blanket. She cringed and hurried about her task.

The object of her curiosity was nothing spectacular, but it was rather peculiar. It was a wooden cross, slightly dilapidated, but still erect. It was a strange place for a cross, considering most crosses such as this one marked graves, and most graves resided in the cemetery outside the church building. Perhaps there was a reason why the cross was in this particular place. Perhaps someone did not wish to bury their loved one in the church graveyard. But, why in a pasture where no one would see it?

Elizabeth could only think of one reason why someone would want to bury a person away from the church, and she was repulsed by the thought of it. It was unlikely and uncommon. It would not and could not be the reason for this cross. The soul under that cross must have had a different story than the one that had come to her mind. She bent and touched it lightly, tracing its wooden structure. There had to be an explanation.

Elizabeth sighed as the first rays of light broke over the horizon. It was time for her to open the post office. She would not want to be late. Sadly, she left the pasture behind, hoping to return to it soon. It would be a nice relief from the stresses of every day.

No one was waiting at the post office when she arrived. She was still early, but that gave her enough time to at least open the doors. She pulled the key out of her pocket and unlocked the door. Pushing against it, she discovered that it wouldn't move. She pushed harder and hoped that it would swing open, but the door refused to budge.

In frustration she began to batter it with her hip and then pummel it with her fists. Nothing seemed to work. Elizabeth took a step back to contemplate the situation. This had never happened to her before, and she wasn't entirely sure what to do. She thought about kicking at the door, but that was more likely to cause her physical damage. It was best she continue as she was.

She pressed her shoulder against the stubborn structure. It didn't move. She applied more pressure. Still the door did not budge. She was about to again add more pressure when a throat cleared behind her. With a start she jumped and sagged against the building. Suddenly the door gave, and she found herself tumbling into the building with a frightened squeal.

There was a slight commotion as the throat clearer bustled to her assistance. She tried to pick herself up, but he got in her way, and with a frustrated grunt she was knocked back to the ground. Before she could respond, she felt herself being picked up off the floor and placed lightly on her feet. She wobbled trying to regain her balance. The stranger held her tighter, mashing her head against his chest.

"Are you okay?" he asked politely.

Elizabeth tried to respond but it was difficult because of the way he held her. "I'd be much better, sir," she gasped, "if you would unhand me. You are making it rather difficult to breathe." She felt herself suddenly released, but couldn't prevent the stumbling that followed. His hand reached out and steadied her.

When she had regained her balance, he quickly pulled his hand away and cleared his throat. "You should make sure there is no ice in the door. That is probably why it wouldn't open. It was probably frozen," the stranger explained to his feet.

Elizabeth looked up at the stranger. He was tall, incredibly tall for any man. His head would have brushed the top of the door when he entered—he might even have had to duck. Elizabeth couldn't help but stare at him. He blushed under her scrutiny, and she quickly turned away.

"I will do that later. But, as of now, how may I help you, sir? I believe you came to the post office for a very express purpose, but I am afraid that I do not recognize you, so you will have to tell me your name if I am to be of any service to you." She looked at him pointedly and he blushed again. What an odd man he was that he would blush.

He cleared his throat. "Yes," he murmured. "My name is Sir John Borden. I am a member of the king's court, and I was hoping that you would be able to give a letter to a particular person in your community. Would you perhaps be able to deliver this letter to Miss Katy Monks?" He held out an envelope to Elizabeth and she took it confidently.

"So, the queen has decided to continue her correspondence with Miss Monks? That is very kind of Rose indeed," she murmured to herself as she looked at the letter. She flipped it back and forth then responded to the gentleman. "I believe I am capable of that. Miss Monks is sure to stop by the post office today. After all, it is Thursday. I will make sure she gets this today."

The gentleman nodded his thanks. He turned to leave but then hesitated. "I would like to apologize for my behaviour earlier this morning. It was boorish and ungentlemanly. I hope that you will forgive me." He finished his apology off with a curt bow.

Elizabeth smiled. "It is quite alright, sir. There was no harm done. You only startled me, which I am sure to easily get over. All is forgiven."

Sir John grinned from ear to ear and then left the building. It wasn't common for a member of the king's court to stop by the post office. In fact, it was unheard of. But, seeing as the queen had once been a resident of their small town, it was sure to be expected a little more often. At least the man had been polite. It was more than she could have expected from a member of the court.

Elizabeth shook her head, and went to file away the letter where she would remember it. The mail bag came soon after, and she was forced to go about her normal task of sorting and dividing the mail. The bag was small, so it would not take her long. The week had started out busy, but it was uncommon for that to last an entire week. It would be even slower tomorrow. The regulars came into the post office and went about their business in the same ordinary fashion. It was as if the morning events had not happened, and in many ways that was alright.

Though it was slow, by the time lunch hour came, there were still letters in the bag to be sorted. Elizabeth ignored her groaning stomach and sat down to them. She smiled as she looked at the story told by the addresses, and she was soon lost in her task. An hour of sorting and dividing passed, and it wasn't till the end of the bag that she took note of reality around her.

She had been so engrossed in the stories of the addresses that when she came across the unfamiliar one, it startled her. She looked at it again and blanched. The address was not as unfamiliar as she had first thought. It was dirty and marred in the same way as the last time. The spelling was a bit off, and the handwriting an uneducated scrawl.

Elizabeth fidgeted with the letter, deciding what to do. The curate had told her to burn these letters, but what if he had not spoken with Mr. Walters? She couldn't give the letters to the curate if he had spoken with Mr. Walters, but if he hadn't, she certainly couldn't destroy them.

Pocketing the letter, she continued her work. It could not be considered wrong for her to do such a thing. After all, if the curate decided that he would like to have the letter, she would hand it over immediately.

She returned to her work with a little less passion. The stories in the addresses did not speak in the same tongue. They were boring and dull compared to the one that now resided in her pocket. It burned there, reminding her of its presence. She would not forget it there. She would read it sometime if the curate never claimed it, or perhaps she could read it now. He had turned it over to her care.

The door creaked open and one of the townsfolk stumbled in. He glared at her, and Elizabeth tried not to sigh. There was no use sighing. Sighing would not change the glares. If anything, it would only intensify them. She found the necessary mail and handed it over. The customer snatched it up and walked out again.

The day returned to normal. One day could only hold so much excitement, and excitement could only last for so long. It was best not to dwell on what could not last. It was getting dark again. Soon it would be time to close up. Elizabeth felt her heart pound as she thought of home. She would be able to read the letter at home.

She began to clean up the office. Reaching into her pocket she grabbed the key and was about to lock up when she remembered the gentleman from the morning. She had promised him that she would get the letter to Miss Monks that day. Miss Monks had not come into the post office. She would have to deliver it to her. With a slight grumble she went back into the office to fetch the letter.

Closing the door and locking it behind her, Elizabeth headed off in the opposite direction of her home toward the Monks' house. The wind was blowing again. It whipped snow around and played with it, making the walk more difficult. It blurred the path and wrapped Elizabeth's skirts about her legs, tripping her. She tried to walk straight, but the wind refused to let her.

When the Monks' house finally came into view, she was chilled to the bone and very tired. She knocked on the door, but no one answered. She knocked again, harder. The door opened suddenly and Mrs. Monks stared down at her. Elizabeth shrank away from the hardened gaze. It was one thing to get glared at in the post office, and quite another while she stood on a front stoop in the cold wind.

"Well, what would you like?" demanded Mrs. Monks.

"I, I... I was asked to deliver a letter directly to Miss Monks if that is at all possible." She felt herself blushing for no good reason besides the fact that she was nervous. She tried to hide it, but she could feel it burn deeper onto her cold cheeks.

"Well, where is this letter then? I will have it, and then you are relieved of your duties. Now, be quick with it. You are letting all the cold air into the house standing there like that." She held out her hand and waited.

Elizabeth fumbled, pulling out the letter. She handed over the exquisite envelope and was about to explain when the door was slammed in her face. She took a deep breath and tried to ignore the sting caused by the blatant rejection, but it didn't help. Tears began to run down her face and freeze to her skin. She wiped at them, but they flowed freely.

She wrapped her arms about her stomach and headed back toward her house. It was a long walk. She felt numb inside and out. She felt nothing as she made it to the barn and to the cow's side. The milking rhythm did nothing to calm her. The cold house did not register as she removed her wraps. Nor did the lonely silence.

She checked on her father. He inhaled and exhaled, the only evidence of life. She made supper and ate. She attended to her father. She cleaned in the dark. She checked on her father once more. He was fine, just fine. His condition hadn't changed for so long. Perhaps the doctor was wrong. Maybe her father would go on living in this state forever, hardly eating and hardly living. He would be her burden for eternity. Or, perhaps her father would leave that night, and she would be completely and utterly alone.

She dressed for bed and crawled under the covers. She closed her eyes, welcoming sleep, begging the dreams to come, anything to replace the numbness that smothered her. Tears squeezed past her closed eyelids and slid down her cheeks. A wail escaped her throat and filled the silence. She tried to stifle it, but her heart still groaned. It ached for someone to listen.

How long she wept, she did not know. It was hard to determine when night was only greeted by more night, but somehow, as time passed, she was able to slip past the numbness into sleep. At first it was a luxury, empty and peaceful, but the dream would not let her win that easily. As her defences dropped, it slipped in.

It brought with it the familiar images, the taunting, and the dead, swaying body, but that was not all it brought. This night was different. This night the cross was in her dreams. It was not in the corner with the corpse. It was on the floor next to her. It sat there silently, and she was able to study it, but it was only a minor distraction. It was not enough to hold her attention when the wind started taunting.

She tried to use the cross. She said she was more interested in the cross than in the corner, but the wind reminded her that the cross and the corner had much in common. The wind crooned to her, reminding her of another cross just like the one she was then interested in. This other cross was also in the corner. She didn't want to believe the wind, but the wind was, of course, right.

In the end, she looked to the corner. It was the same image, the same body, the same death, and there the other cross also hung, but it was different than the one on the ground. This cross was much smaller and it hung from a string that choked the corpse. It... Elizabeth woke with a start and the image disappeared. The dream still remained, but the image was uncertain. All she knew was that she had to find the cross in the meadow again. It was the only way to know for sure.

Mrs. Monks looked at the letter in her hand. It was fancy and thick. The envelope itself spoke of wealth and elegance. She knew immediately who it was from, but that didn't make reading the address any less thrilling. The queen! The queen of Samaya had once lived under her roof, and was now corresponding with her daughter. She could almost imagine that the queen was sending the letters directly to herself.

A chair scraped across the floor in the next room, and Katy came into the parlour where she stood. "Who was that?" she asked. "It's an awful dreadful night to be walking about. Didn't you invite them in, Mother?"

Mrs. Monks jerked out of her reverie and looked at her daughter. "It was that insufferable Miss Mede. Of course I didn't invite her in. If she was fool enough to come out here on a night like this, then she will have the tenacity to be able to make it back to her home." Katy eyed her mother with shock. She had never heard her mother speak so ill of another soul.

"Was there a reason why she came?"

Mrs. Monks looked at her and then sighed. "That girl does have some use. She brought a letter for you. It's from the queen," she said, giddy from the joy of it. "You must read it immediately. We must know what Rose has to say to us. It has been so long since we have heard from her."

Katy took the letter gingerly, and broke the seal. Before she looked at the contents, she took a deep breath and sat. She lifted the upper fold and began to read.

> My Dearest Katy,
>
> I was much relieved to get your letter of response, and I am glad that you wish to keep up correspondence. It is busy here at the palace, and I look forward to a time in the day when I can sit down to a letter that seems normal and familiar. Don't get me wrong. I love my life at the palace. It is wonderful beyond compare, and I will never regret it, but it is something to get used to, even after two years of it.
>
> I hope you are faring well. I have been very well. It seems that I have had an abundance of energy lately, and Henry has been dragging me around to party after party. We eat so much food, I feel as if I shall explode, and the food is so rich! There

are dances and formal events. At every dance we are to be the first on the floor. It is odd to dance while everyone watches, but Henry tries to make the most of it, claiming that we put everyone to shame anyway. He is much too generous though. I have never seen such good dancers as the ladies of the court. They practically float across the floor.

Of course, I am in charge of the order of the palace. I never thought I would have the charge of servants, but here I am in charge of hundreds of souls, and such sweet souls they are at that. I am sure that I love every one of their dear sweet faces. They take pleasure in so many little things and take great pains to please everyone around them above themselves. I think I better understand what our good Lord means by becoming first by becoming a servant to all.

Though I do a lot with Henry, it is often that I will spend a day going about meetings of my own. It is important for the queen to keep up appearances. I am required to meet with certain associations, and I am affiliated with certain boards that I never knew existed. It is amazing what the women of Samaya have accomplished even without the education that men have received. It is quite startling, actually.

Here I am rambling, when I should be getting to the point. I have sent our cousin John with this letter because I am hoping that you will receive it as soon as possible. Henry and I have been planning a small tour of the country and we are hoping to stop in at Emriville for an extended period of time. If it suits *you, we should arrive within a few weeks for an unspecified amount of time.*

Henry's father is not appreciating retirement, and he is hoping that we will give him a few months to be the king he misses being. We know the kingdom will be in his secure hands, and I am determined that the palace will be content in the hands of the Queen Mother. We shall have some time to be away and study the country with these arrangements.

John is on his way to Thespane and will return to Silidon by way of Emriville. When he returns, he will prepare for our coming. If this is not a good time for you, we will better arrange, though I do not know if that would be in the immediate future.

Send greetings to Josh and to Caleb from both Henry and me. I pray that you remain in good health, and that all will come together so that we can meet again soon.

With love,

Rose

"So, what does it say?" Mrs. Monks asked impatiently. She started tapping her foot when Katy looked up at her blankly. "Are you going to answer me?"

Katy shook her head to clear her thoughts. "The queen is going to come for a visit very, very soon."

Mrs. Monks let out a squeal of delight. She bounced on the spot trying to contain her glee. The queen was coming to their town. The queen would be under their roof. With one more squeal she ran off to find Mr. Monks.

THE CHARADE

Katy remained sitting in the same spot. She looked at the letter blankly. The queen was coming. Rose was coming. Would the queen still like her, or would things be different? The queen was coming with her king, and they were sure to be different. That thought scared Katy more than anything else in the world.

SIX

I T WAS THE SAME DREAM. Caleb was still searching, always searching. He was looking for something, but it evaded him. When he woke, the haunting feeling did not leave him. He was still looking for it in his mind's eye though he no longer slept. He felt the urge to run and search and find it, though he had no idea what it was.

He groaned and tried to get out of his bed. It was early, or very late. It was hard to tell because the sun had not yet made an appearance. He groped around on the nightstand trying to find his pocket watch. He knocked something to the floor and let out a soft curse when he bent to pick it up and cracked his head on the corner of the stand.

He couldn't find the watch, but the restlessness wouldn't leave him. He decided to dress and get out of his room. He snatched up his shirt and trousers from the chair in the corner. He pulled them on and left the room, slamming the door behind him. What did it matter if he made lots of noise? There was no one to hear him except the heavenly hosts that never slept.

The kitchen was no better than his room, or the parlour, or his office. Caleb paced restlessly back and forth, but the *it* from his dreams called to him, begging him to catch it, to take it in. Whatever it was, it haunted him. He tried to ignore it, but it would have none of that. It screamed in the wind, rattled the windows, and shook the entire house.

Caleb muttered under his breath, then, grabbing his cloak and boots, headed out the door. How long he walked, he did not know. All he knew was that as long as he walked, it left him alone. So he kept walking, and just as the sun cracked the horizon, he came to a meadow and stopped.

It was a familiar meadow. In the centre was a boulder, a stone weathered by time, but still a permanent fixture in the pasture, though not its most memorable feature. Caleb already knew what lay on the other side, and what it meant. He didn't want to be here, but it wouldn't let him leave. He walked toward the distant object.

He would have laughed disgustedly. He would have sworn, cursed, and done all sorts of unseemly things. In some ways he wished he had, wished he had let all the emotion out. But, it would not have him do that. It would not let him say anything profane because he was not the only one in the pasture. At the far end, next to the object of his intent, was a solitary figure, just standing.

Caleb froze in his tracks.

71

The morning was like any other morning after a nightmare, but this morning Elizabeth worked with a purpose. She did not let the dream haunt her; she pushed it aside. She did not want it to take her concentration as she rushed through her chores and breakfast. When they were all done and out of the way, she blew a kiss to her father and raced out of the house.

The wind howled its usual gusts and hisses, but none of that mattered. Elizabeth pushed on. She did not stop at the post office, but rather, she searched for something else. She had time. It was still very dark, darker than the last time. That didn't matter. She was sure she would be able to find her way.

The meadow wasn't really all that far off. She found it without much difficulty, and without hesitation, she crossed to where the cross stood. When she got there, she halted, unsure of what to do next. She considered talking, but the idea seemed silly and somewhat childish, so she just stood there and studied it.

It wasn't anything spectacular. It was really rather plain. There were no adornments or carved letters. There were no suggestions as to its meaning or purpose. It was just a cross, a plain wooden cross. It didn't stand out, and it was not strategically placed. There were no other symbols around it, but it had to have meaning. Why else would it have appeared in her dream?

Elizabeth let out a sigh and thought back to her dream. She shuddered when she remembered the corner and the image there, but she ignored that part and thought of the cross. She was sure that the cross had been the one that she was now looking at, but it wasn't really the same. Yes, both crosses had been plain and wooden, but the cross in her dream had been almost reverent and holy. This cross in the meadow was just that, a cross in the meadow.

She was about to leave when she heard a noise behind her. She stiffened but did not turn. She was not in a very safe place for this time of day. There could be any number of horrible people about who would do her harm if she were not careful. She took in deep breaths and waited to hear the noise again. It didn't come.

Hesitantly, she turned around. She almost let out a shriek of terror when she saw the man standing not far behind just staring, but realization came soon enough to stifle her fear, and she was able to contain herself. She was staring at the curate, and he was staring back. Neither moved.

Elizabeth took the time to study the man before her. He was tall and handsome, but his eyes were blank and lifeless. They weren't always like that. On Sundays, as he stood before the congregation, his eyes would have an inner glow that built and radiated as his sermon came to life. But, today his eyes were dead.

He didn't look the part of a curate either. His shirt tail was untucked, and his buttons were mismatched. A fresh and tender-looking bruise was forming on his forehead. His whole being spoke of sleepless nights and stressful mornings. There was none of the peace or security that one would expect from a curate, just undeniable vulnerability.

Elizabeth cleared her throat with a small cough. "Good morning," she whispered.

He nodded his head in acknowledgement, and moved forward, toward the cross. He walked slowly, decrepitly, as if his entire life had passed by him in a single night. He looked down at the cross and just stared. "It's not here," he muttered to himself. Elizabeth decided it would be best not to comment. She stood quietly beside him and waited. Neither of them spoke for quite some time.

"Did you know this man?" Caleb asked. He did not look up from the grave. He just stood there, staring at the cross. He was searching it, contemplating it. It was hard to say if he even had asked her a question.

"No. I did not even know this was a grave. I came here only for the cross." She waited and wondered if he would respond. The silence lasted for a while.

"Private Mark Hepton was a soldier in the King's army. He died of gangrene in the end. He had no family around to bury him, so Miss Rose Wooden had him buried in the meadow. It was the most she could do for him. But, then she left to become the queen, and his grave has been left unattended. There is no one to care about him. There is no one to pluck the weeds from around the grave marking, no one to place fresh flowers over by his grave, no one to cry for him..." his voice trailed off.

Elizabeth waited for him to continue. His voice was eerie, yet somehow, knowing the story of the cross comforted her. It was as if the story in itself was enough to give the cross a supernatural power of sorts.

"In the end, the meadow was the best place for his resting place. In the spring the flowers bloom, and rain weeps fat tears on the grave. When winter comes, the weeds are built high around the cross, but then the snow crushes them. The natural elements of weather seem to take the time to care about the *poor, dead private.*" These last words he issued with a sneer.

Elizabeth stood silently. The sun was rising, and the birds were singing in the trees. She needed to open the post office, but she was intrigued by the conversation with the curate. She didn't want to leave. "Why did you come here, sir?" She didn't know how else to address him.

He looked at her sadly. His eyes were worse than dead—they were hollow, somehow emptier than the eyes of death. She wanted to look away from them, but she couldn't; she needed to keep searching them, and find out what it was about them that made them dead one moment and so alive the next.

"I knew Mark, probably better than anyone in the town. He had something that I wanted, but I'm not sure that he still has it." Caleb let out a short laugh. "That probably doesn't make any sense to you. How could a dead man have something that I would want? After all, he is dead. But he did have it. In those last days he had it, and how it nagged at me."

Elizabeth didn't respond. How could she respond? It was possible that the curate had gone mad, but she didn't think so. There was something more he wasn't saying, but he did not seem about to elaborate. He had clammed up as if he had said too much already. She waited, hoping that if she were patient, he would slip back into an easy dialogue.

Her patience paid off.

"You know," he began again, "I used to think that I could be content in all situations. I mean, the Bible demands it. We are to be content and not covet what our neighbours have. But, no matter how hard I try, I still long for what he had. He is dead, but I wish I were him because even in death he has what has haunted me for my entire life. The sad thing is that I don't even know what it is."

He stopped again. There was nothing more to say. How could he explain what he wanted more than anything else in the world when he didn't even know for himself? He would have to discover it for himself before he tried to share it with another.

Caleb turned to leave when sudden fear stole over him. He had said too much. He had let too much go. He looked frantically at Elizabeth. He tried to form a plea on his lips. He wanted to make her promise she wouldn't say anything to anyone, that she wouldn't pass what had been said on to anyone else.

She looked back at him. She didn't say anything, she just looked at him. Then, briefly, she nodded her head, and he knew it would be alright. She wouldn't tell anyone. She would keep it to herself. Perhaps it hadn't been such a bad thing spilling this to her. It wasn't haunting him as much as it had been, and he felt a little more rested.

Caleb turned once more to leave. People would be missing him if he did not return home soon, and there could be some very negative repercussions if he was caught in the middle of a meadow with a young lady from the church. He picked up his pace and nearly started to run for home.

Elizabeth watched him as he left. He seemed happier, more content. Something about his countenance had changed when she had nodded. There was no logical reason except that he had gotten something off his chest that had been bothering him for quite some time. She tried to think of what he could have meant about being content, but it made no sense to her. She shrugged her shoulders and walked off toward the post office. She was exceptionally late. There would be angry customers if she did not get there soon, and she did not want to lose her job over a silly little excursion.

The post office unlocked easily today. The door did not stick or jam, but Elizabeth couldn't help but blush as she remembered the other day's encounter. What had that man been thinking sneaking up on her like that?

She shook her head, causing the memory to dissipate, and walked into the building. She hadn't made it very far when there was a thud outside. She looked out to see the mail deliverer disappear, and the letters sprawled out on the ground, spilling from the bag. Apparently his frustration with her tardiness had caused him to carry out his duty without waiting for her to receive the mail bag.

She glared after the sleigh and driver, but he had already disappeared. A silent wind crept up, and began to blow about. She let out a screech of horror as the letters began to blow away. She raced after them and tried to catch all of them. She had almost caught every last one when her feet came out from under her, and she fell with her legs sprawled and her arms flailing, sending the letters once more out into the wind.

She let out a frustrated growl, and rose sorely from her haunches and went about once again gathering the scattered papers. A throat cleared behind her, and an angry Mr. Walters glared at her as she lifted her head to look up at the noise.

"What do you think you are doing, Miss Mede?" His face was a deep red, tinged with purple, and a vein popped on his forehead. It began to pulsate as his blood pressure rose. Elizabeth shuddered at the sight of it. "Are you going to answer me?"

"I, I..." she started. Blood rushed to her face, and she could feel the heat of it. "The mail bag collapsed and some mail fell out and I was collecting it when I fell, and I had to collect the mail again." She stuttered to a halt, and Mr. Walters just glared.

"You should be more careful!" he growled at her. "You could lose your job over a foolish mistake like this, and there are not many people who will hire you after that. What would you do then, Miss Mede? We gave you this job in good Christian charity, but if you cannot work at it responsibly, we will have to replace you."

"Yes sir," Elizabeth replied as she looked at her feet. Taking hold of the mail bag, she dragged the heavy sack with one hand while trying to hold all the letters in the other. Mr. Walters did not offer any assistance. Once inside, Elizabeth set the letters down on the counter and retrieved Mr. Walters' mail. He did not leave his usual tip. He just snatched up his mail and left. Elizabeth looked dismally at the empty counter.

The day did not continue in any better fashion. The letters that had fallen out of the sack were wet and crumpled. Many people complained when they saw the condition of the ink on the sheets of paper, and many of them blamed Elizabeth for that condition. She had never had to talk so much in one day, but each person wanted an explanation.

By the time lunch had come and gone, and the sun had begun to set in the west, Elizabeth was exhausted. She dragged her feet about as she tidied up the post office, then she haphazardly threw her wraps around her shoulders and trudged home. It was difficult to make it through dinner awake, but she persevered, and when her father was tended to, she slipped into bed and slept.

The night was mercifully peaceful. No dreams taunted her. She saw no corpses. She was not forced to look into any corners. She just slept, long and peacefully. It was the first time in years that her night had not been broken by dreams, and her throat was not scratched by the terror released in a scream.

Morning came much too soon. Elizabeth opened her eyes and smiled to herself. She felt rested and ready to face the day. Perhaps someone would smile back at her today. Perhaps her father would eat an entire bowl of porridge. Perhaps she would be able to sleep a full night again tonight without waking up screaming.

She walked excitedly to the post office. The sun was just rising, and it promised to be a warm day. They could be expecting a thaw soon. No wind blew, and there was a hint of spring in the air. Elizabeth smiled to herself and tried not to get too excited about a day that could still go so sour. But the day was too nice, too wonderfully blessed to turn out awful.

This conviction disappeared rapidly as she turned the corner. Mr. Walters stood by the post office tapping his foot impatiently. He glowered at her from a distance, and she tried to hide the terror his look invoked. Hesitantly she made her way to his side and looked up at him. "Is there a problem, Mr. Walters?" she asked politely. Her smile wavered when he scowled at her.

"As you know, Miss Mede, I am in charge of your salary, and your job. Does that not mean anything to you?" Elizabeth looked up at him, not sure what to think of this. He rolled his eyes at her slow wittedness.

"It is common for an employer to do a surprise visit of sorts on his employees to make sure everything is on the up and up. In light of what occurred yesterday, I decided it might be best to check on the everyday activities of the post office. I arrived early, and immediately went into the office. Do you not see anything wrong with this story, Miss Mede?" he growled.

Elizabeth shrank away from the anger in the man's voice. "I'm sorry, sir, I don't understand what your point is. Forgive me if I have missed something, but I surely don't understand what you are leading to."

"The door, Miss Mede!" Mr. Walters snarled, and Elizabeth had a hard time holding onto her wits. What was the man's problem? What could she have possibly done to invoke such anger? "The blasted door! You didn't lock up when you left the office last night. Can you imagine all the dreadful things that could have occurred? Did you not once consider that such a mistake could cost the entire town dearly? What if someone had gone into the post office late at night and decided to play a prank? What if we woke up in the morning and all the mail lay strewn across the town? Worse yet, what if someone decided to read the personal mail of the occupants of the town? Did you not think, Miss Mede? You were responsible, and you did not take that responsibility seriously!"

Elizabeth fought back tears as the man continued to rant at her. She felt for the key in her pocket and produced it. She raced to the door and tested the handle. It flew open without the assistance of the key. She let out a gasp of shock. She was sure she had locked it. She was almost positive. There was no way she could have left without locking up. It was one of the things Mr. Walters had stressed when she had first gotten the job.

The post office was in perfect order, but that did not matter. Something horrible could have happened, and she would have been responsible. She turned to Mr. Walters and considered pleading, but thought better of it. He was already calming down, and pleading would only make the situation worse.

She watched as Mr. Walters took in deep calming breaths. He looked at her sourly and took another deep breath. Letting go of it slowly, he began to speak. "Miss Mede, I have decided to be gracious. This appears to have been a onetime mistake. Judging by your reaction, this has never occurred before, and never will it occur again. Despite that, action must be taken. I will not take your job from you today, but I will observe you as you work, and if there are any discrepancies, they will be fixed today, or you will be fired. Do we have an understanding?"

"Yes sir," Elizabeth replied, trying to hold back the tears. Taking the chair she normally used, she offered it to Mr. Walters and then set about the normal tasks of her day. Mr. Walters watched as she sorted the mail proficiently, then as she went about cleaning the office. It was immaculately clean, but she didn't dare sit still while Mr. Walters was watching. When people came in, she smiled politely and got their mail quickly and quietly.

The entire time she worked, she fought to hold back tears. She didn't want Mr. Walters to see her cry. He might very well accuse her of smearing ink and ruining the letters.

When the day finally came to a close, Mr. Walters gave her an unusual smile. "I can see you know your way about the office, Miss Mede. You shall go about your tasks as usual." Elizabeth let out a slight sigh of relief a little too early. "But, if I hear of any more inadequacies, or if I ever catch this door unlocked, you will be fired on the spot. I will not have any of my employees slacking. Money is too valuable to be wasted on nonsense like that." He turned and left the building to Elizabeth.

The tears finally flowed as she left the building. Carefully she locked the door and walked out onto the street. It was dark out, and most people were inside eating meals with their families. There was no one there to notice the young girl as she cried the entire way home.

SEVEN

KATY RUMMAGED THROUGH HER CLOSET. Dress after dress, she pulled from their confines and tossed them onto her bed. The room was covered with lace and fabric. There was hardly any room to walk, but this did not stop her. Surely, she could find one suitable dress in her entire closet. She continued her search until her closet was completely emptied into the room.

Katy stood sighing with frustration. Nothing, absolutely nothing would do. Some were too old. Others were far too simple. Another was torn and needed mending. And still another was much too ugly. Of all the dresses Katy had, not one was suitable for greeting the queen.

Katy glowered at the piles all over her room. She couldn't recall the last time she had felt so poorly dressed. She had always considered herself adequately suited, but she had never thought she would have to dress to impress the queen. Such formalities left her quite at a loss.

She looked hopelessly at the piles of clothes and whimpered feebly. Then she flounced onto the floor.

What was she supposed to do? Rose was coming. Rose was beautiful, smart, and perfect at everything she applied herself to. To add to this perfection, she had married the prince of the country. Now, she was the queen—the beautiful, smart, perfect queen. Some people had all the luck in the world.

Rose had liked Katy well enough while she had stayed with them, but that was sure to change. No married woman would tolerate a young, foolish girl. Even if Rose as a married woman tolerated her, as the queen, Rose certainly wouldn't be able to spend her time in the company of such youth as herself. She would have to be much more mature if she was to stay in the good graces of the queen.

Then it came down to a matter of clothing. Would it be appropriate to meet the queen in her Sunday best, or would it be better to be modest and wear a simple frock? Was there a specific way she was to curtsy? If so, was it difficult? Would she be expected to address her as *Your Highness*, or would Queen Rose do just fine? Such questions as these buzzed through Katy's mind as she sat staring at the dresses.

There seemed to be no answers to her questions. Who could she ask? In such a small town, it was unlikely anyone had entertained anyone higher than a wealthy merchant. Perhaps one of the richer members had entertained a Lord or Lady, but even that was unlikely. It wasn't common for the noble classes to mingle with the lesser citizens. It just wasn't natural.

With a final sigh of frustration, Katy picked herself up off the floor and left the room in disarray. She didn't know what she would do, but she had a while to think about it. It would be best that she get some fresh air and clear her head from all these worries for a time. They would last, and they would be sure to make their presence known in a few hours when she let her guard down. She would think about them then.

The sun was warm on her back, and it was evident that an early spring had made its arrival. The road was slick and muddy from the thawing snow. Patches of brown grass peeked out in soggy marshes. Snowbirds sang cheerfully from the barren tree branches, and the whole earth seemed to heave a sigh of contentment.

Katy tried to let the weather relax her nerves, but she still felt tense. She rolled her shoulders to try to loosen them, but they were non-responsive. She determined to ignore the stiffness, hoping it would leave voluntarily, but as she walked it only seemed to intensify, demanding to be attended to. She gritted her teeth and walked on.

She made her way into town. The streets were crowded. The weather was the warmest it had been in a long time, and many people were out enjoying the day. Katy said her polite hellos, but she did not stop to chat. There were too many things on her mind, and if she stopped, they might all spill out and embarrass her beyond all imagining.

When she came to the bridge at the edge of town, Katy continued to walk over it, not knowing where it would lead her. Leaving the town seemed to contain a certain tonic. As soon as the sound of the hustle and bustle of swarming bodies disappeared, Katy could feel herself relax.

Her shoulders drooped, her back sagged as her spinal cord released the tension, and her lips parted in a gentle sigh. This was much better than anything had been in many days. She closed her eyes and allowed herself to completely relax. Opening her eyes once more, she kept walking. She paid no heed to time or direction. She cared little that the sun was setting or that it was starting to get colder. All she cared about was the lack of tension, the absolute relaxation, the release from all stress. All else would work itself out.

Josh stood in the door of the blacksmith's shop and watched as Katy disappeared over the bridge and out of sight. He wondered if she knew where she was going. It wasn't common for a young lady to leave the town without a chaperone, but propriety meant little to Katy. It would have been easy for any other person to let the girl be, but Josh didn't feel comfortable with that. There were too many things that could meet a girl on the road away from town.

"Jimmy!" Josh shouted. "There's business I need to be about. Don't expect me back till tomorrow." A low rumbling grunt was the only response from the back. Josh checked his workplace, rinsed his hands, grabbed his coat, and left the shop. He would be lucky if he hadn't already lost Katy. But perhaps there was a chance he could catch up.

Surprisingly, it did not take him long to find her. She wasn't travelling quickly or with purpose, but rather she moseyed along swaying her hips gently back and forth as if dancing to an unheard song. Every now and then she would let out a contented sigh as if there were nothing better in the world than an empty forest road.

Josh watched from a distance. He didn't know why, but he didn't want to be seen. It seemed rude to interrupt her when she appeared to be so at peace. So, he kept off the path and followed quietly behind her.

They travelled farther and farther from the town. The sun began to set, but Katy continued on, oblivious to the changes in her surroundings. Josh began to worry as the weather got colder and the wind picked up. Darkness began to descend. Josh hoped Katy would soon turn around, but she continued in her mindless meandering.

So, they continued on. Josh's nerves began to fray as they travelled into the ragged, less-travelled paths of the woods. Out of habit, his hand went to his sword hilt. It rested snugly against his side. The cold metal brought reassurance, and he was able to press on despite his better judgment.

Josh bit his lip. They should turn back, but that would require alerting Katy of his presence. He would most likely startle her, and she would be angry with him for following her. But, if he didn't stop her, she would wander all night in the woods and most likely catch her death of cold, or worse. There were many dangerous people who roamed the forest at night.

As if she had heard Josh's thoughts, Katy suddenly stopped. Josh held back a sigh of relief, but his victory was short-lived. Katy did not turn around. Instead, she looked into the distance, contemplating it. She seemed rooted to the spot, tense and scared. She let out a squeal of terror and began to back up quickly.

Josh tried to see what was scaring her, but he could see nothing. Terror flamed in his throat when Katy started to whimper. She backed up farther and farther. In one fear-filled shriek, she tumbled to the ground. Logic lost all grounds as Josh burst out of the woods to protect his dearest. He placed himself between his lady love and the enemy and drew his sword. Looking in front of him, he tried to size up his foe, but all enemies had disappeared.

That was when it hit him. The smell satiated the air, and nearly knocked him off his feet. A fetid scent like that of rotting straw mingled with animal waste filled his nose and caused bile to rise in his throat. Josh looked down at his feet. The black and white tail was still pointing straight up, and the noxious fumes seemed to intensify with the motion of his head.

Letting out a groan of disgust, Josh swung his sword in a gentle arc and watched as the severed skunk head rolled off into the woods. It did nothing for the smell. It was probably a useless waste of energy. But it did make Josh feel better.

He stared at the dead skunk body, not wanting to turn around. He didn't want to see her. He was angry, and he didn't want to have to see the cause of his anger. He tried to push it off, but the sound of retching brought forth the inevitable.

Katy sat at the side of the road spewing her lunch into a thorn bush. Josh raced to her side and tried to assist her. Katy shoved him away, but could do nothing to stop him as a fresh wave of nausea hit. She was crying by the time she was done, and Josh was kicking himself for not bringing anything to drink. It was a long walk back to town, and the taste that Katy would carry the entire way would not be a comfortable companion.

He tugged her into his arms and let her weep. She didn't smell very pleasant, but then, neither did he. Everything around them reeked of skunk. Its rancid scent had penetrated every little speck of dust, and had ingrained itself into their very skin. They would have to live with the smell until they returned home.

Katy's sobs subsided and she began to push him away. "What in the world did you have to do that for!" she screamed at him. "You didn't have to kill the darned animal!"

Josh looked at her, shocked. What was he supposed to say to that? Anger replaced shock. "Well, what in the world were you doing walking around in the woods so late at night! Now we both stink like rot!"

Katy glared at him and turned around and began to walk away. Josh grabbed her arm to stop her. "Let go of me!" she screamed. "I want to go home! Let go!"

She stomped on his foot, and Josh had to bite his lip to keep back the cuss words that wanted the right to flow freely. "Fine, go home! But, if you go that way, you'll be walking for hours on end and won't arrive there!"

Katy stopped in her tracks and turned. "What did you say?" she sneered. "Are you saying that I am going the wrong way?" Josh nodded his head cockily. "I'll have you know, Mr. Deplin, that I know exactly where I am, and that the town is in the opposite direction to what I have been walking. If I have been walking that way," she pointed, "then I shall now walk this way," she pointed again, "to get home."

"I'll have you know, Miss Monks," that when you were busy disposing of your lunch, you changed directions, so if you would like to go home, you must travel west," he pointed to the correct direction, "in order to get home." He smirked at her, and she scowled.

"I won't have you mention my feeble stomach again," she said as she grasped the mentioned body part. "It was your fault anyway. But, seeing as you seem to be so intelligent, why don't you direct the way, *all-knowing supreme one.*"

Josh wished he could respond in kind, but that would only get him into trouble. He turned his back on her and began to walk. He didn't care if she could keep up. He wanted to get home. The sun was long gone, and if they did not return soon, there would be talk, and talk was never a good thing. He stopped briefly to clean his sword, but otherwise he kept up a steady pace.

Time dragged by. It didn't feel like they were getting anywhere. Josh's anger began to fade, and he slowed his pace. He could hear Katy behind him panting as she tried to keep him in sight. He scowled at the thought of her. His anger may have been fading, but what sensible girl went into the woods without a chaperone? His pace picked up again as he thought of a warm bath and supper.

Suddenly, the panting behind him stopped.

Josh spun around and searched the darkness for Katy. She was nowhere in sight. She didn't call to him, or he couldn't hear her. Fear was building inside him, and he tried to push it down. It was nothing, she was alright. He let out a slight groan and backtracked to find her.

When he found her, she was sitting on a log, panting. She looked up when she smelt him. She tried to scowl, but her teeth chattered. It was cold, and she didn't have many wraps. She stood slowly and stiffly, but nearly slipped on the icy ground. Josh grabbed her and helped her steady herself. "S-s-sorry," she muttered. "I'll keep up better. I was just t-t-tired."

Josh sat her back down onto her log. Shrugging out of his coat, he held it out to her, but she hesitated. "Oh come on!" he exclaimed.

"You smell just as bad as it does, and you're obviously freezing. Just take the darn coat and don't talk about it, okay?" Katy took the coat and shrugged into it. She let out a slight sigh of content as it began to warm her almost immediately.

She closed her eyes to rest a little, and Josh took this as his opportunity. Stepping up beside her, he picked her up in his arms and began to walk. Her eyes flew open in shock, but she didn't struggle. "What are you doing?" she asked him.

"You're tired, and I am going to be cold unless I do something to exert myself," he stated bluntly. He avoided looking in her eyes. He just kept walking. Katy didn't know how to respond, and she was just too tired to care. She closed her eyes and fell fast asleep.

Josh tried to remain angry with her. He reviewed in his mind all the woe she had caused him. He had lost half a day's work over this, and Jimmy would have his head for it. He smelled like skunk. He was cold. He was tired. And, his feet hadn't seen so many miles in years. No matter how often he pounded Katy's shortcomings into his mind, he couldn't help but justify them.

She was most likely stressed and needed the distraction. She didn't realize how far she had been walking. She had every right to be afraid of a skunk. He had been the idiot who had jumped out in front of the animal. It was his choice to follow her. Every fault on her part seemed to be justifiable. He grumbled under his breath at his own stupidity and kept walking.

The bridge came into view. Leaning over, he whispered into her ear, "Katy girl, you need to wake up." Her eyes fluttered open and widened when she realized she had slept in his arms, but she soon recovered and was able to stand on her own two feet. Josh offered her his arm, and she leaned on it heavily. They crossed the bridge into the town that was oddly bustling about even at the late hour.

The smell must have alerted the throng, because as soon as Josh and Katy came into view, every citizen still out on the street turned and looked. There was silence as the two of them walked down the main street. Josh realized that there were no women about, just men. Realization dawned in his mind, and he felt like an idiot for not thinking of it before.

"It's alright!" he shouted. "You all may return to your families now, she has been found, and she is quite alright. There is no need for you to worry any longer." Some men glowered at him, some sneered and others just shook their heads as they walked off.

Josh just kept leading Katy through the crowd. There was no need for her to deal with this mess tonight.

"Joshua!" The call came from behind him. Josh turned to see the curate standing in the gentle glow of a single candle. His face was hardened into severe lines, and his entire countenance told of unspoken rage. Josh tried to ignore this as he greeted the man.

"I'll have a word with you, Joshua, after you return *Miss Monks* to her family."

"Yes sir," Josh replied politely, but he groaned inwardly. He had been looking forward to a nice hot bath, but apparently that would have to wait.

The streets emptied out as Josh and Katy drew near the Monks' house. The entire place was ablaze with candlelight. Mrs. Monks sat near a window peering anxiously out, and she burst through the door as soon as she saw the two shadowy figures trudging down the lane. She stopped short when she smelled them.

Katy ran to her mother and hugged her. Mrs. Monks scrunched up her face trying to hold back her repulsion. She coughed prettily and pretended she needed a drink. Katy quickly let go of her, and the two of them walked into the house. Josh watched as they disappeared. He sighed and walked back into town.

The curate was waiting in the entrance to his house. Josh would have knocked, but the door was opened before he could get that far. The curate stared down at him in disgust. "We'll have our discussion here, seeing as you are not fit to enter any building in your—present— condition." Josh just sighed, hoping the conversation would not take long.

The curate looked down at him as if waiting for him to confess something. Josh just waited. "I hope you are happy with yourself, young sir. Your actions were highly inappropriate and they deserve strict punishment. Now, I cannot delve into that matter without the consent of the elders, but I do think it is necessary that I get your side of the story before I discuss the matter with them. So, boy, speak!"

Josh stared at him, mouth agape. "My side of the story? What story?"

The curate just stared at him, and Josh felt himself squirm. "What were you doing out in the woods with Miss Monks, Mr. Deplin?" the curate asked in quick staccato notes.

Josh let out a hoarse laugh. "Is that what this is about?" Another chuckle escaped his lips. "Curate, do you think that if Miss Monks and I were about... mischief, that we would come back smelling like skunk?" Josh couldn't keep from laughing. He was exhausted, and sense had no control over his mind. "Shoot!" he laughed. "I would take that any day over a skunk." He snickered to himself. "I'm not saying, curate, that I would ever—outside the wedding vows I would never even consider. But, that is far from what happened tonight. That's for spitting sure." Josh shook his head and chuckled to himself. "Nah," he muttered. "Miss Monks is really the cause of all the trouble. I was just minding my own business when I saw her wandering off into the woods out yonder. Of course I thought it was odd that she didn't bring a chaperone, so I followed.

"That silly female was walking around senseless until the sun near set. I just followed her until she started getting all jittery. I thought a band of gypsies was going to attack her when I jumped out to save her. It's a real pity that it wasn't gypsies. I might have won some favour with the lady if it had been. Turns out it was a blasted skunk.

"The rest of the story isn't too hard to figure out. I slew the skunk and then Lady Fairest took her time preparing herself to head the wrong way home. I pointed her in the right direction and then I made sure that she made it all the way." Josh cut his explanation short. There was no need to add in the little details.

The curate stared down at him. His face was so severe that Josh wondered if he ever laughed. The thought of the curate genuinely smiling brought another chuckle to Josh's lips, and the curate's scowl deepened.

"S-s-sorry, sir," Josh laughed. "I think I'm a little tired. Do you mind if I leave now?" The curate didn't seem to like it much, but the skunk smell must have been getting to him. So, Josh was dismissed.

Caleb watched as the lad laughed himself near to hysterics as he made his way home. It was late, and he had probably been walking most of the time. He had every right to be exhausted, and Caleb wished him a long and blessed sleep. He deserved it if his entire account was true, which it probably was.

Caleb shook his head and walked into the house. The night was beginning to smell like skunk, and it was not a pleasant way to end the evening. He heard a bird chirp in the distance, and he wondered if it really was still the night, or if the morning had come to greet them already. He pulled out his pocket watch and let out a low, slow whistle. The morning had greeted them some time ago. It was best that he spend what time he could in sleep. He turned toward his room and bed, but sleep never did come. Every time he closed his eyes, *it* took over. Going without sleep was easier, so Caleb picked himself up off the mattress and began to walk.

EIGHT

CALEB WALKED THE SAME PATH as the last time. He ended up in the same place, but why he went, he did not know. It was like an unknown sense pulling him toward the one place he hated the most. It was like a longing to understand, yet not knowing what he sought to understand. He fought the feeling. He hated the feeling, but it was as prevalent in his life as the dream. There was no escaping either of them.

He stumbled as he entered the clearing. Miss Mede was already there. She turned when she heard him and smiled. Turning back to the grave, she became lost in a world of thought. She did not speak. She just stared at the grave. Caleb joined her.

When he had reached her side, she broke the silence. "Tell me more about Private Hepton. I would like to know his story."

Caleb let out a hoarse laugh. "It is not as easy as just telling a story. His story hurts. Anyone who touches it is sure to be burnt from just the telling of it. I would not want to tarnish your innocence by telling you any more than that."

Miss Mede turned and looked him full on. He tried to hold back a gasp as he saw her blank, dead eyes for the first time glimmering like cold onyx stones in the pale shimmers of the remaining moonlight. Her eyes spoke of horrors unknown, and he knew that innocent was not the word to describe her person. "I don't know if I can tell his story," he muttered and turned away from her.

She turned her gaze back to the grave and did not respond. Caleb did not know how long they stood there, but slowly the cold crept in. It started with nose tips and ears, turning them pink. Then, it moved along their toes, up their legs, and down their spines. Caleb started to shiver, but he didn't want to leave.

Suddenly, Miss Mede looked up at the horizon where the sun was just beginning to show pink. She let out a deep sigh. "Will you be back here any time soon?" she asked.

Caleb looked at her, wondering what she wanted to hear. "I think that I have no choice. If I cannot sleep, I will be back before dawn breaks. At least, I will be here until I can sleep again." Miss Mede nodded her head and then disappeared across the meadow and through the thicket.

Caleb watched her as she went. There was more to her than met the eye. What was her story? What had stolen the innocence from her eyes? What brought her to the grave before the sun rose? Perhaps he would have to get to know her better. Perhaps she would have some of the answers that he so steadfastly searched for.

Caleb sighed and turned to leave. It would be a long day. He hadn't gotten any sleep, and he would be required to speak with the elders as well as with Miss Monks. He groaned inwardly as he pictured the meeting they would have. He cursed Josh for putting him in such a situation. It just wasn't fair. Couldn't it have been anyone other than Miss Monks?

Caleb pushed the thoughts aside as he thought of food and clean clothes. It would be nice to freshen up and have some breakfast in his stomach before he went about the day's duties. It would be easier to think if his stomach wasn't constantly nagging at him. Hopefully there would be something moderately easy on hand when he got home.

Katy stared at the curate who sat across from her, straight and regal. There was nothing shameful about his appearance. He was clean-shaven and his hair was neatly tied back. His eyes were a soft grey, and his nose was perfectly straight. He was entirely too handsome for his own good.

Katy tried to concentrate on what he was saying, but it was no use. She was too distracted by the fact that she still smelled like skunk, and he had noticed. She had tried not to be embarrassed when she had answered the door, and he had scrunched his nose, but it was far too humiliating to not be embarrassed.

Now, she sat across from the curate, as he droned on about something or other, and she tried to hide the smell in any way possible. She had thought that perhaps lemon would work, but they had not owned enough lemon to clean her entire self. Soap had helped a little bit, but there was nothing to be done about her hair, which still reeked of the blasted animal. Katy hoped Josh smelled just as terrible.

"Have you listened to a single word I have said, Miss Monks?" Katy jolted out of her reverie at the pastor's words, and tried to hide her blush. It was no use. It covered her entire face—ears and all. She took out her fan to try to cover the heat in her face, but when she swished it back and forth, the skunk scent wafted over and up into the curate's perfect nose. Katy quickly snapped her fan back when Caleb scrunched up his nose.

"Forgive me, Mr. Taylor," Katy tried to state calmly, "but I have been completely distracted today. Could you possibly repeat your question?"

Caleb scowled. "Could you just give me an account as to what occurred yesterday? It is important that no rumours are spread and it would help if we know what happened."

It was Katy's turn to scowl. "Why don't you ask Mr. Deplin what occurred?" She turned away from the conversation.

"As I explained already," Caleb said in an exasperated voice, "Mr. Deplin has already been spoken to about what happened, but it is important that we get the story from your perspective as well. Do you think you can do that, Miss Monks?" Caleb gentled his voice, hoping it would help. Katy looked at him with expectation, and he immediately regretted his choice. How much had she assumed by the changing of his timbre?

"Alright," she sighed. "I'll tell you my half of the story." She readjusted her position on the chair and made sure her cup of tea was in close proximity before she began. "It was really all Mr. Deplin's fault. I was frustrated, so I went for a walk. While I was walking, I lost track of time, and it began to get dark." She stopped to take a sip of her tea.

"Anyway, I was just deciding to turn around, when I came across a skunk in my path. It would have left me alone if Josh hadn't jumped out in front of me and scared the critter. You should know the rest of the story. The skunk retaliated, and Mr. Deplin and I left the woods smelling like the horrid creature."

"Is that all that happened?"

Katy hesitated. Was she supposed to give every detail, or was her account enough? She decided to leave it as it was. "That is all."Caleb studied her quizzically, and she began to squirm under his gaze.

"It was really stupid of you to enter the woods without a chaperone. What would have happened if you had gotten lost? What if Mr. Deplin had not followed you? You could have met with any sort of wild animal, or a band of highwaymen, or something far worse than that! Promise me that you will not enter the woods again unescorted." Caleb hoped that the fatherly tone would work with the young girl, and she did seem properly repentant, but she obviously had other things on her mind.

"I promise, sir, that I will not enter the woods without a chaperone again. Now, I have news that I must give you before it has spread all the way around town." Caleb didn't know how to respond. There were so many things she could say, but what would she say? All he could do was wait and see.

"I received another letter from Rose." She turned her eyes from his gaze and seemed to become a little shy. Caleb became instantly interested in the topic. "She and King Henry send their greetings. And, I will tell you first, though I think that others already know. She has told me that she and her husband will be visiting soon. It seems that they have some time to be about the country, and they have chosen to spend much of that time in Emriville."

Katy looked up at him as he felt himself fall back against his seat. It was as if the air had been taken from his lungs. Horror crossed Katy's face as she stared at him. "You aren't feeling well, are you? I'll get you some water." She raced out of the room, and Caleb took deep breaths to calm himself. He was reacting badly and he knew it, but he couldn't seem to shake the numb feeling.

Rose was coming with Henry. The two of them, married and happy. The world was a cruel place. He could picture the scale in his mind. He remembered all the lustful thoughts he had had for Rose, and the one side became more and more weighted. She was a married woman now. He could not be thinking about her in that way for any reason at all. He did not deserve her.

What would she say to him when they saw each other? Would she be angry with him? Would she even care about him at all? Would she ignore him? What horrors would her presence bestow on him? He tried to picture the iron bars holding back all lustful thoughts, but the reality of Rose's upcoming arrival burst through them. He shuddered at the thought of it.

Katy returned with the water, and she knelt at his side as she gave him the glass. He took it gratefully and gulped down a large swallow. Closing his eyes, he breathed in and out once, then looked down at Katy's worried face. "Forgive me. I don't know what came over me. Perhaps the smell. I should go now." He clattered to his feet. Katy had no choice but to stand as well. "I'll be going now." Taking his hat and his coat, he left without another word.

Katy watched as he disappeared and couldn't help but wonder if he had told her the entire truth.

Caleb walked stiffly and silently out of the Monks' house. He did not look back once as he walked down the road. He just kept walking until he reached the parsonage. He had work to do, but what did it matter? No matter how hard he worked, it was all useless now. Rose was coming, and with her—temptation. He wouldn't be able to resist, and the scale would just get heavier and heavier and heavier. He could see it now. He could feel it deep in his gut.

He let out a slight moan as he sat on the edge of his bed. He was so tired. Why couldn't he just sleep? If he could just sleep, and sleep, and sleep for eternity without ever waking up and without dreaming, what a heaven that would be. But, that would never happen. He would never lay claim to that. It would be fire and brimstone when he slept for eternity. That was all that he could look forward to.

Perhaps God would be merciful, but then again, his sins went beyond mercy. He laughed hoarsely. The overflow of emotion caused the mirthful sound. It wasn't a real laugh. It was more just the air passing through his voice box.

He brought his hands to his face and scrubbed roughly up and down. His eyes watered as he peered through his fingers. The room was dark. The curtains were closed, and there were no candles lit. He looked at the matches on the nightstand and considered them for a while.

Why shouldn't he end it? It would come no matter what, why not help it along? At least then he would get a taste for the place before he actually walked through the gates. No one would miss him. He wouldn't have to pretend anymore. He wouldn't have to force a smile, and he wouldn't have to consider the scale because it would already be decided for him: fire and brimstone.

He walked over and picked up the matches. He lit one and watched as it burned slowly down. The flame touched his fingers, but he didn't care. He ignored the pain and let it sear into his skin. The flame went out. He lit another and went through the same process. He considered dropping this one on the floor, but decided to wait.

The third match was much like the first and the second, but the game had lost its lustre. There was no wonder in the little spark. It was petty and useless. It did not fulfill any task or purpose. It was worthless. Caleb blew it out and placed it in an ash tray. Fire and brimstone would have to wait. He had more things to do before he joined the demons with their sulphur breath. It was best that he went about it.

Josh spent the day working at the shop, all the while grumbling about his life. He stank. Skunk permeated every breath he took, and eventually left his nose tainted with the scent. The lack of sleep didn't help any. When he had gotten home, he had fallen straight to sleep in his smelly clothes, and now his entire house reeked of the rotten animal. He had tried to wash the smell out, but nothing seemed to work.

Work, ha! He had been late for work. He had overslept, apparently. He never overslept, but today was the first for that too. Now, his boss was running him over for that as well. The drunken louse of a man accused him of all sorts of evil, including stealing and charging for time he hadn't worked. He would have to work overtime to appease him.

Josh didn't mind the work. In fact, he loved the work. He spent most of his time in the shop working with metal and swords and all sorts of other things. He could make whatever he wanted to with metal, and his pieces had lasting quality. He couldn't picture himself doing anything else, and he hoped some day he would be able to own his own shop, but chances of that were very slim. In no way could he afford it with his current rate of pay.

Josh dropped the hammer he was working with, and felt like cussing. He never felt like cussing, but today, he had felt like it on more than one occasion. He tried to calm himself, but he was feeling bitter. He was angry, and there was no one to shout at. He decided to take it out on the iron. He beat on the metal, swinging his hammer in wide arcs. The iron was submissive.

The physical labour felt good, so Josh pushed himself. He piled the work on and continued to work until the smell of melting iron outdid the smell of skunk, and the pain in his joints surpassed that of the fatigue from the night before. Night came. He knew he should quit, but he didn't want to. He worked longer and harder, pushing his body past its limits.

He ran out of work.

With a frustrated grunt he threw the hammer aside and, grabbing his coat, headed out the door. He didn't want to go home. It smelt like skunk at home. He walked toward the meadow where he had practiced so often. He didn't care if the ground was slick and there was a great danger of falling. He hadn't expended enough energy yet, and he needed to push his body farther.

It was early morning. The sun hadn't risen yet, but hints of it played on the horizon. He shoved his way through the brush and the trees. Then he stopped cold. Normally, the meadow was unoccupied. No one came to it because it was out of the way and sometimes difficult to get to. No one owned the land. It was just there in the middle of nowhere. But, today someone stood at the far end.

She was small and poorly dressed for the weather. She only had on one wrap, though the early morning temperature had to be somewhere close to the negatives. She turned expectantly when he came stumbling through the brush, but her face fell when their eyes met. She looked at him curiously for a while, but then turned away again.

Josh watched her as she peered down at the ground. If he was right, she was standing by Private Hepton's grave. He wondered what the man was to her, but he didn't ask. Instead, he went about his own business. Unsheathing his sword, he started to go through some practice routines. The girl seemed to get bored with the grave and began to watch him.

It was odd practicing in front of an audience. Josh had never had a need to show off his skills, and the only girl who had seen him handle a sword had been Rose, but this girl watched him with open curiosity until he stopped. He looked at her and she blushed.

"I'm sorry," she murmured to the ground.

"It's alright." Josh resumed practicing, and the girl went back to watching him.

It was not long before he stopped again. "Is there a reason why you came here?" the girl asked.

Josh turned to reply, but the girl was not looking at him. There was no need for her to look at him because there was no other person she could be speaking to. Josh didn't look at her when he replied. "I needed somewhere to get rid of some anger, and this was the first place that came to mind."

"Do you come here often?" she whispered.

"Mostly during the summer, just to practice." Josh turned and looked at her, and she stared back. "Do you mind that I am here now?"

She shook her head. "This is a good place. I have not been in the summer yet. Is it pretty then?"

"Yeah, I suppose it is." Pretty was one way to describe the meadow in full bloom and blowing about in a gentle summer breeze.

"I thought so," she whispered. "I better get going." She left him then.

Josh stood there for some time, not quite knowing what to do. Exhaustion crept over him, and he knew he needed to go home, but still he did not want to go. There was nothing there waiting for him except the skunk smell. He shrugged his shoulders and walked that way anyway. There wouldn't be anything for him to do at work for a while. He could sleep at least till the afternoon.

Caleb didn't go to the meadow that morning. *It* had not visited him that night. Instead, fire and brimstone had filled his nightly slumber. It touched his fingertips and toes. It seared his brow and left its mark all over his body. He could feel the violent abuse of it tear and burn at his insides.

He felt himself call out for a breeze just to cool the burns, just a slight breeze of mercy. The only response was the stench of hot, sulphurous breath in his nose. He screamed to be heard, but the heavenly hosts laughed at him as the demons crawled onto his back, pinning his arms behind him and gagging his mouth.

He fought against them. He struggled. He couldn't catch his breath. Pain wrenched at his arms and legs. He bit down on the gargoyle arm in his mouth and spit out the copper venom. The demon hissed at him. The copper taste did not leave his mouth, and he continued to spit.

He felt pain all over. It jarred his being and made him vomit. He pulled his legs to his chest and whimpered, but the demon still haunted him. It spit acid on him, and the saliva burned his cheek. He tried to wipe it away, but the burning continued.

The demon came in closer. It was going to kill him. Caleb knew that's what he was going to do. Its eyes bulged bright red. He hissed *Seth, Seth.* The sky above cracked with a flash and a rumble of thunder. The demon cowered and disappeared.

Seth looked up and was blinded by the dazzling brightness. *Seth,* the voice whispered as soft as a feather, as firm as iron. *Rest now, my son.* And then it began to rain. Seth slept peacefully. He did not wake. He did not dream. All he was sure of was the rain that healed and cleansed and felt so marvellously good.

When Caleb woke in the morning, he did not know what to think. He did not remember the demon, but he remembered the horror. He did not remember the fire, but he remembered the pain. He would have thought it all false except for the blood on his pillow and the cut on his tongue where he had bitten it. He did not remember the light, but he remembered the calm. He did not remember the rain, but he remembered the peace. His emotions were a mix-match of reality and impossibilities. He tried to sort them out, but none of it made sense. He tried to understand, but he found it all so incomprehensible.

How could he understand something he did not remember? How could he comprehend something so much larger than himself? With a sigh, he forgot about the dream and went about his day.

NINE

AYS FLEW BY AND NIGHTS passed slowly. For Caleb, time was only a matter of nightmares and daydreams, and the occasional morning in the meadow. On Sundays he gave his sermons, and on Thursdays he got his mail. Other than that, there was nothing to break the routine, nothing to tell him that anything was different.

For Elizabeth it was much the same. She spent her nights in dreams; the same dream, over and over again. She lived quietly through the days, keeping herself busy. The only time she rested was the time she spent in the meadow. It was her time. Sometimes she shared it with Caleb, but more often than not, she spent it alone.

It was after another of those long days that Elizabeth sat at home working on her laundry. Often she procrastinated. It could be strenuous work and not one of her favourite tasks after working all day at the post office.

She pulled out the large tub and filled it with boiling water. She gathered all the soiled garments and dipped them in one at a time after checking their pockets to make sure they were empty. The routine was simple. She would scrub out the stains, rinse out the soap, then hang the garments to dry. If there were any holes that needed mending, the garment would be set aside after it was dry.

It took some time, but Elizabeth was able to content herself with the fact that it was a necessary task. Her pile was small, and she was soon down to a simple frock and an undergarment. She picked up the dress and stuck her hand into the pocket. Her fingers closed around an envelope. Releasing the object, she yanked her hand out unsure of what to do with the envelope. Once more, she reached into her frock and this time she pulled out the envelope. She stared at the letter.

It was addressed to the curate—the one he had told her to dispose of. It was a curious-looking thing. Dirty and smudged. She had been wanting to read it. Now, she wasn't so sure. Perhaps it contained something about the curate that she didn't want to know, but perhaps it would explain more about Private Hepton. It was also possible, and likely, that it would not say anything good at all.

Elizabeth took the letter and set it on her nightstand. She had to finish the laundry. She would decide if she wanted to read the letter later. It would be better not to think about it at the moment. She finished with her task and then went to bed. She needed to go to work tomorrow, and she wanted to be able to go to the meadow.

She closed her eyes, knowing that with sleep came the dream, but with sleep also came some bits of rest. Her lids fell shut, and the terrors began their haunting. She tried to ignore them, tried to change the dream, but it had more power than she did. It held sway over her mind and controlled it.

It did not last long. It seemed as if the nights were becoming shorter and shorter. Probably the changing of the season: it was spring now, and the days were getting longer. She would not have to spend as much time with the dream when the night was no longer so dark.

She made her way toward the meadow. The ground was soggy because the frost had forgotten to come the past few days. Water was everywhere, and it slopped up over the hem of her dress. She ignored the soggy mess and continued toward the grave. Caleb was standing there already. He greeted her politely.

The two fell into their normal quiet states. Neither of them needed to speak. Neither of them knew why the other was there. They only shared the companionship of the need to be there. It was an incomprehensible need, but a need none the less, and it provided an acquaintanceship of sorts.

The birds hummed softly in the background. Every single living creature was ready to greet the dawn, but it held back on them. It waited for its cue to enter the morning stage. Elizabeth stated her usual morning demand: "Tell me more about Private Hepton." She never expected a reply, but she always hoped that maybe someday...

"His was a horrible life," replied Caleb softly that day. Elizabeth was surprised at his words, but she looked at him expectantly. He continued to gaze at the grave. There was a pause as he seemed to think it over, then he looked up at her. "If I tell you this story, you must promise to keep it to yourself, and you must not be horrified by what you hear. I warn you now, it is a dreadful tale."

Elizabeth nodded, and Caleb sighed. "I do not know where to begin except at the very beginning. But, I remind you, it is not a good beginning. Perhaps no beginning is good. It is the end that must justify the beginning, or is it the other way around?" Caleb looked at her, but she didn't respond. She did not understand what he had said.

"Mark was born on August thirteen, twenty-six years ago. I can remember the date because it was a Friday, and his mother was told that it was bad luck. She didn't think so; she thought her boy was the most wonderful, beautiful creature in the entire world. Of course, she thought that of all her sons, but she named him Mark because she said he would be the fighter; he would be the one to fight and find the truth.

"You see, Mark's father was not as good as his mother. His father was evil to the very core. He beat his boys to keep them in line, and when he was not satisfied with beating the boys, he beat his wife until she was bloody and bruised. So, the boys grew. The oldest was Seth. He was like his father. He looked like his father. He acted like his father. He, too, was evil.

"The next in line was Bill. He was not evil like his father, but neither was he good like his mother. He wasn't the most intelligent one either. His full name was William, but that never suited him. It was far too regal for the likes of him. He was a fool in every manner.

"Then there was Mark. Mark was the good one for the most part, but like the rest of them, he had his faults. His biggest one was that he didn't fight. He was the only one with sense enough to stand against his father, but he never did. He just stood in the background and watched. He could have changed things. The people in the town would have supported him, but he never did anything.

"So, the days went by, and they lived in a house in the middle of the woods. The townsfolk called them cursed. They would spend time in their churches praying up a storm for the cursed family in the woods, but not one of them ventured out. They all stayed inside their pews protecting their innocence and quite possibly their lives." Caleb's voice was filled with bitter contempt as he cut the story off. He could not continue.

"Did Mark ever stand up and fight?" Elizabeth whispered.

Caleb turned to her and smiled. "That is a story for another day. Look," he pointed, "the sun is rising. It is time that we are about our normal lives." He turned and left her standing there.

Elizabeth sighed as he disappeared through the brush, then she turned and went on her own way. Curate Taylor was an enigma to her, and she wasn't sure she would ever figure him out. She wasn't entirely sure she wanted to figure him out. Something about knowing what lay under all his layers terrified her, yet fascinated her as well.

She looked down the road as she drew near the post office and stopped abruptly. Horror filled her, and she began to run. It was impossible—she was sure she had locked the building. She wasn't late either. The sun was just rising. He couldn't be there already. It had to be some mistake. She couldn't lose her job, she just couldn't, but if that was Mr. Walters down there waiting impatiently, she was sure to be replaced with great haste.

She flew down the hill. She made it to the door of the post office and came up short, panting. She looked at the man waiting at the door and very nearly swooned with relief. It wasn't Mr. Walters. With this realization, anger took charge of her emotions.

She shoved her hand into her pocket to take out her key. She jammed it into the lock and, with great effort, opened the door. Storming into the back, she took up her post behind the counter and glared at the man who entered behind her. She recognized him. He was the one who had delivered the letter from the queen. He was Sir John, the one who had nearly trampled her the last time he had come.

"How may I help you?" she asked angrily. He blushed when he looked at her, but she ignored this, and glowered at him.

"I was wondering," he began, "if you had any letters posted to the palace. If not, I will have to wait around somewhere until a more appropriate hour."

"Appropriate hour!" Elizabeth grumbled under her breath. "You wouldn't know an appropriate hour if it hit you in the centre of your forehead."

"What was that you said?" Sir John asked politely.

"Nothing at all, sir, I was just commenting on how early in the morning it is now. It is uncommon for someone to arrive at the post office so early."

Sir John blushed. "Forgive me, Mademoiselle, I probably should not have come so early; I did not think of the stress that you would feel from having someone waiting at the post office. I should have considered that."

For once in her life, Elizabeth felt like rolling her eyes. She refrained from doing so. "There are no letters here marked to go to the palace. If you are waiting for a reply from Miss Monks, you will have to wait until later on in the morning. I usually do not see her about until at least after ten in the morning."

"Thank you," Sir John said and went to stand at the side of the room.

Elizabeth didn't know what to do with him standing there. She started clearing up any messes she saw, and he stared at her while she worked. She tried to ignore it, but it was an odd sensation. She soon ran out of work to do. The mail carrier was late, so she was unable to sort the letters. She resorted to polishing the already spotless desk.

When she heard the jingle of the mailman's coach, she bolted around the counter to the front door. The bag was tossed to the ground, and she raced to pick it up. Sir John was right behind her. He grabbed the bag from her hands and carried it inside for her. She felt herself blushing. Perhaps he thought her incapable.

He placed the bag behind the counter beside her chair, and she began to sort the letters. He just stood there watching. Mr. Walters came in, and Sir John greeted him kindly. Mr. Walters took the time to converse with him briefly, and then he was about his usual habits. He took his mail from the counter with his slight sneer; he dropped his coin, and he was gone.

Sir John gave her an amused look, but kept to his post by the wall. The usual people poured in with their usual attitudes. Elizabeth did her best to smile and be polite, but their scowls and John's steady stare made her nervous. It was impossible to ignore someone staring, and it became rather obnoxious after a couple of hours had passed.

"It is a more appropriate hour now, sir. Perhaps you could call on Miss Monks and get your reply. Then, you can be on your way." Elizabeth had tried to put it politely, but her voice had come out sharp and a little bit cross. Sir John nodded his head.

"Yes, you are correct. I should be about my business. Rose will be quite disappointed if she doesn't receive a response soon. Please, excuse me. I will be back briefly with the note." He turned and left the building. Elizabeth let out a sigh of relief, and turned back to her work. It was so much easier to concentrate without someone constantly staring. She wouldn't have to pretend so much with him gone.

Her victory was short-lived. Sir John had been gone but an hour when he again came bursting through the door. He had to duck in order to get through the frame, but that didn't seem to bother him. It must have been a normal occurrence for him. He carried a letter with him, and he brought it right to the counter and placed it down in front of her.

"Mademoiselle, I am hoping that it is possible that this letter could be sent out tonight to make it to Silidon as soon as humanly possible. Could you see to that for me?"

Elizabeth smiled at him like she smiled at all her other customers. "It can be sent out with the evening mail. I'll make sure of it."

"Thank you," he murmured, and then reached into his pocket for the proper payment for the mailing service. He pulled out a handful of coins and placed them down on the counter. Elizabeth counted them and then laughed. Taking two of the smallest ones, she pushed the other eight back at him.

"These two will be sufficient to pay for your mail, sir. The rest is unnecessary."

Sir John pulled at his cravat then turned his face down to look at her. She squirmed under his gaze.

"The extra is for you. You have so kindly put up with my presence all morning, and I am greatly in your debt. A few extra coins are the least I can do to pay you back."

Elizabeth shook her head. "Sir, those coins are a bit more than a thank-you. I cannot accept them. It is too much. It would be inappropriate." Elizabeth pushed the coins back at him with greater force. He picked them up from the counter, then, taking her hand gently in his, he opened it palm up and forced her to take the coins in them.

"These are a gift," he whispered, "and I fear, I cannot take no as an answer. If you will not take them, neither will I. I have no use for them, and they will just go to waste. You must take them and use them for something that will be beneficial." He let go of her hand, and hesitantly she pulled it back to her side and placed the coins in her pocket. It was a lot of money, and she was not used to the feel of it weighing her pocket down.

She turned to go back about her work. She took his letter and marked it properly for the evening post, and then she went about sorting the rest of the mail. Sir John took up a position at the counter, staring at her once again. Elizabeth let out a sigh of defeat and waited for him to speak or to leave.

"Mademoiselle," he started, "I would ask one thing of you."

Elizabeth waited to see what it was he would ask.

"I beg your pardon, but, could you please tell me your name?"

Elizabeth looked at him. Of course he wouldn't know her name, but that didn't explain why he would care what it was. "My name, sir, is Miss Elizabeth Mede." Sir John nodded, and then bowing courteously, he left the post office and her to her peace.

Elizabeth shook her head as he left. He was an odd one, that was for sure, but who was she to judge. He had acted perfectly respectably; he just wasn't like the rest of the town. Perhaps the men of the court acted a lot differently than the average male citizen. She was sure to find out, if rumour was correct. She would get to see many men of the court because surely the royal couple would not travel without an entourage from the court, but perhaps not. She would have to wait and see.

The evening post came, and she sent her letters on their way. Darkness came, and it was time for her to lock up the post office. She stepped out into the cold and pulled out her key. She locked the door and turned to leave. Standing not a foot away was Sir John with a horse and buggy. He smiled shyly and made his way toward her.

"I do not want to impose on you, but it is a cold night out, and I was wondering if you would like a ride home. I have a carriage, you see, and there is no where I need to be."

What was with this man? Elizabeth wondered. He seemed to coddle like a mother hen, and she hardly knew him.

"I'm sorry sir, but it would be highly inappropriate for me to accept a carriage ride from you, when I hardly know who you are, and there is no chaperone. It would never do." Elizabeth began to walk toward home. She heard Sir John mumble something as she left, but she couldn't be quite sure what he said.

She soon disappeared out of his sight and let out a sigh of relief. It was a good thing that the man would be leaving soon. Elizabeth was not sure she could handle much more of his presence. It was too close, too trying. There were too many things that could go horribly wrong with him so near.

118

It was late when she got home. She went about her chores. She tended to her father. She had her supper. She slept. It was a normal day, and a normal night. When she woke in the morning, she was able to go about her normal morning and make it to the meadow for a brief visit with Private Hepton.

She went to the post office and opened the door. Mr. Walters came at his usual time. And the day followed its normal course. Sir John was not about, and Elizabeth was quite alright with that. It was better that way. There was a routine, and his presence only disturbed that routine. It was better if he just stayed out of her life. It was just better.

The time had come. John had arrived the other day, and Katy had to tell him that it was alright if Rose came, and it was alright if Henry came. It was alright if the entire palace came for all Katy cared. She was sure to be mortally terrified no matter who came. She would be entertaining royalty, and she had no way of knowing if they would still like her.

She had written the letter quickly hoping that John would leave with it and carry it himself directly to Silidon, but such was not to be her luck. John was staying in Emriville to prepare the way. He said he had to make sure the inn would be able to take care of all the queen and king's needs. He had to make sure the town would be able to handle the presence of royalty, and most of all, he had to make sure the town was safe.

It wasn't that they expected trouble in their own country, but one never knew what an angry peasant would do, given the chance. So,

John was sent to prepare, and prepare he did. He went immediately to send the letter, then he went to the inn and set the rooms aside. He checked at the livery to make sure there was enough feed for the horses and enough room for the carriages. This was all done on the first day of his arrival.

In truth, there was not much for him to do. There were not many people in the king and queen's party. It was what many people would call a vacation party. There were a couple of men-at-arms to attend to the demands of the king, and a few ladies-in-waiting to care for the queen and whatever she needed. All else would be provided by the town itself.

John would have two weeks to go about his business, and much of that time he would be visiting a select number of people, and getting to know the rest of the locals to make sure there were no trouble spots. It really was a simple job, and Rose had only given it to him after she found out he was going to Thespane.

She claimed it was on his way back, and he was the only one she trusted with such arrangements. John knew the truth was that she was hoping he would take the time to relax. She always claimed he was working too hard. He needed to unwind, she would tell him. Work was not the only thing a person need do. When he told her the same thing applied to her as well, she had scrunched up her face at him and challenged him to a duel.

She had defeated him soundly.

John slept long his first night. It was a singular joy to sleep past normal hours. He had breakfast in the inn's dining room where he was treated with the highest respect. The serving girl was still in awe of his position, and had a difficult time speaking to him coherently. It took her two attempts to get out an audible good morning.

With a full belly and a smile on his face, John was able to set his schedule for the day. He needed to speak with Curate Caleb Taylor. Henry had requested that be done as soon as possible. Then, he was to locate Josh Deplin. This was of course a request of Rose's. These were the two main people of interest. The rest of his day John would spend mulling about the town. He would go to the market and check what types of sales went on there, and he might ride into the countryside.

That would be the majority of his day. There was only one thing he did not dare to consciously think of putting on his list. He would stop by the post office. He did not know yet why he would go. He had already spent an unruly amount of time there after only being in town for a single day, but he would think of an excuse to go. He was intrigued by Miss Mede, and he wanted to find out more about her; he only feared he had scared her a little the other day by moping around the office. He would have to apologize for his behaviour. With a smile on his face, John left the inn to go about his day.

TEN

CALEB SAT SILENTLY ACROSS FROM Sir John. He didn't speak; he didn't move. He sipped tea from his mug and listened, or at least pretended to listen. John droned on and on about the upcoming visit of the queen and king. He didn't say anything of much interest; he just kept talking. He seemed to understand Caleb's need to think.

Caleb set his mug down and looked at John. John stared back. The silence stretched before Caleb finally spoke. "Will the royal couple be staying long in Emriville?" His question was polite and stiff. He didn't want to show emotion. Emotion would give him away.

"It is uncertain how long their stay will be. Quite literally, it all depends on the welfare of the country. As long as no wars break out or revolts take place or any other such matters, they may be able to stay for several months, but then again, they could be called away after a couple of weeks."

"Very well," Caleb soughed and picked up his mug again. John took the time to study him. There was nothing more to talk about. The two men did not know each other, and neither of them was prone to small talk. Caleb could feel his heart beat with every tick of the clock. The rhythm was steady and even and constant: *tick, tick, tick.*

The chair groaned as John switched positions, and Caleb looked up at him. It would be best if they found something to talk about. "This may be a bit of vanity speaking, but I wonder," began Caleb, "does the queen often speak of her time in Emriville? Or the king, for that matter?"

John chuckled. "More often than not. The two of them often share stories about the town and their cherished memories here. Of course, there are only a few select people they can actually tell the stories to. I mean, there are people who do not want to hear that the queen was once a commoner. But, Rose and Henry find ways around offending anyone too seriously."

Caleb raised an eyebrow. "Why would people be offended that the queen was once a commoner? That seems like such a silly notion."

John sighed. "Silly? Yes, but also very true. It is already known that Rose grew up in Thespane without parents, and that is enough to send shivers down some Lordships' backs. They are a prissy bunch, some of them, but then there are the few you wouldn't trade for the world. Anyway, Rose doesn't let that bother her one whit. She has friends, and that is all that matters to her."

Caleb leaned back in his chair and ran a hand through his hair. "The queen has many good friends left here. I ran across Mrs. Jennings the other day, and she was quite excited to know that she would be visited soon. She is quite lonely now that there are so few children in the orphanage. She gets by, though."

"Ahh, Mrs. Jennings," John muttered. "I had forgotten about her. I will have to speak with her as well." He looked up at Caleb. "I believe I have overstayed my visit. Rose will be in Emriville within two weeks. She and Henry would like to visit you immediately. When the date becomes more exact, I will speak with you again."

"Pardon me!" gasped Caleb. "What were you just saying?"

John looked at him in confusion. "I was saying that Rose and Henry would be visiting you soon. Within the next two weeks, in fact. I will contact you with more information when I can. Is there a problem with that?"

"No, no," Caleb hurriedly replied. "I just didn't understand that the king and queen would be coming directly to see me. I thought they would remain at the inn where they would be quite comfortable."

John looked at the curate quizzically. "Forgive me, sir, I thought I had made it perfectly clear from the beginning of my visit that Rose and Henry would be visiting you directly. They are quite fond of you, and they wish to spend some time with you."

"I see," whispered Caleb. "Very well, I shall see you about town then, Sir John?"

John nodded, and began to walk toward the door.

"You know, Mr. Taylor, you really don't have to be nervous about their visit. They're still Henry and Rose. They are the same people as before. Just think of them in that manner, and it will all go perfectly fine."

"I am sure you are right," Caleb replied and opened the door for the man. John stepped out, and with a farewell salute, disappeared.

Caleb closed the door and let out a haggard sigh. Rose would be coming to his house. She would sit with her husband across from him. They would sip tea, and she would smile and laugh. She would move about in her delicate ways, and he would watch.

He felt his heart pounding in his chest. It was wrong. It was lustful. He should condemn himself; punish himself before he could get to that point. He could make himself sick, and then the queen would not come to visit. He could move away, he could pretend to be too nervous to meet the royal couple; he could pretend he had chosen to live a solitary life.

None of these options fit. They all required lying, and lying would tip the scale just as much as the lust. He would have to go through with the visit, and he would have to guard his eyes. He would not look at her. He would avoid her. He would only address himself to Henry. That way, he would not see her face; he would not think about her, he would not lust after her.

Caleb lifted his hands to scrub his face. He was tired, and the visit had only taxed him. He needed to sleep more, but every time he closed his eyes, the dreams took over. He walked toward his office and yawned as he went. He needed to prepare his sermon, and it would have to be a good one. If he could gain some weight for the lighter side of the scale, perhaps he would make it through the next few months.

John made his way to the livery after his visit with the curate. He needed to find Josh, and he had no intention of going about that task on foot. Two men sitting by the counter eyed John as he walked past and continued their conversation in animated whispers when he was out of earshot. After saddling his horse, John decided it would be just as time-consuming to wander about on a horse looking for a man as it would be on foot.

So, clearing his throat, he turned to the two men and inquired of them. "Excuse me gentlemen, but by chance could you tell me the whereabouts of a Mr. Josh Deplin? I have certain business with him, and I would like to be about it as hastily as possible."

The two men looked at each other and smirked. "I told you he didn't recognize me," the younger one shouted victoriously, and he held out his hand for payment. The older man grumbled, and pulling a coin from his pocket dropped it into the lad's hand.

"It's not fair to him. You were just a wee bit of a boy back then. Matter fact, you've hardly changed any. Ye're just a big brat of a boy now." The boy laughed and tucked the coin into his pocket. "And," continued the older man, "you smell like skunk." The lad's face fell, and the livery owner hooted with laughter, slapping him on the back.

John watched the two, amused by their antics. It had been too long since he had been among the members of a small town. It was much more relaxing than Silidon. He was cheered almost instantly by it, but he still needed an answer to his question before he left. He cleared his throat once more to gain their attention.

"You had better answer his question," the older man stated. "He may end up leaving on you, and then where would you be?" The man's laughter burst forth as the younger man pushed him away with a mockingly severe face, leaving himself and John alone to stare at each other.

There was silence.

The younger lad began to fidget. He didn't seem to know what to say. He cleared his throat. "Do you really not recognize me, Sir John?"

John looked at him closely, but no name came to mind. He tried to think clearly, but there was nothing.

The boy grabbed the back of his neck. "Wow," he murmured, "I must have grown more than I thought." He looked up at Sir John with slight bewilderment. "Well, Sir John, today must be your lucky day because I am Josh Deplin. Just didn't think that I had changed that much."

John took a step closer to look at the young man in front of him. "Well, I'll be darned," he whispered. Then, slapping the boy on the shoulder, he gave him a friendlier greeting. "It's been a long time, Josh. What have you been doing besides growing?"

Josh chuckled. "Nothing too difficult. I got a job down at the blacksmith, and now I own my own place. Mom's a bit worried about that, but I told her I'd be alright. She has all the girls living with her, and they don't need me around bothering them none. They get along just fine. They sell those little doily things to the mercantile, and they make enough to satisfy themselves. How about you? What's it like working for the king and queen?"

The two began walking around the horses. "Well, it's not that bad at all. You know, there are some perks to being close with royalty. It seems once the prince is off the market, all the fair ladies go for second best. Right before I left, there was a ball, and I think I danced with every single lady present and I was asked to about just as many dinners."

Josh smirked. "I don't know if I could handle that. One lady is enough for me. The rest can all go find some other man."

John turned a long face toward the young man. "There are also many downfalls to having the ladies cling to you. I am positive that Miss Kayla Beton was ready to sink her claws into me and hold on for the rest of the night. I would have been a lost soul then." The two men laughed at the light banter. There was nothing important that needed to be discussed at the moment, and it was nice to catch up on old times.

"Listen, Josh, do you have some time to talk? There are some things that I need to discuss with you before the queen and king come, and it would be better if we talked about it in a more private area."

Josh took a deep breath. "Well, I need to get back to the shop before my boss gets after me, but if you don't mind burnt dinner, you can stop by my place tonight, and we can talk then. How does that sound?"

"That would be great, Josh. I'll see you at closing then?"

"Yeah. I live in the small house behind the butcher's shop. Come by when you're ready. I'll get dinner ready, or at least attempt to. You might wish that you were eating with Kayla Beton once you've tried my cooking."

John laughed. "Don't count on it. I think I would rather spend supper with one of the great cats than with that particular lady. It will be a relief to all men when she chooses a husband. Except for the poor soul she catches."

The two men said their farewells and John was on his way. He had all afternoon to do with as he pleased. He would have to think of something to fill that time. His first stop would be at Mrs. Jennings' place. The older lady deserved a visit.

THE CHARADE

The old orphanage was just three doors down from the curate's house. It was in much better shape than two years before, but there were still some minor repairs that needed to be done. There was no sound coming from inside. The place stood hauntingly quiet. No toys littered the front yard, and the walkway was freshly gravelled.

John knocked on the front door and waited for someone to answer. There were silent thuds and a quiet flurry of motion before the door opened and a young girl peeked her head around the corner. John smiled down at her, and stooped to greet her. "Hello lass," he said cheerily. "Would Mrs. Jennings be around?"

The little girl's eyes went wide with surprise, and she nearly shut the door in his face, but she quickly corrected herself and held the door wide for him to step in. As soon as he stepped over the threshold, she slammed the door and began to walk away. John picked up his feet to follow.

The halls were quiet except for a whisper every now and then. John looked around to see if he could find the owners of the whispers, but they seemed to be well hidden. The girl stopped in the middle of the hall and pulled open a closet door. John thought she wanted him to hang up his coat, but that didn't seem to be her intention. Shyly she took his hand and pulled him into the closet and shut the door.

The two stood in silence in the dark for a moment before John could no longer contain himself. "Lass," he whispered, "is there a reason why we are standing in the closet?" He heard a childish shush come from beside him, and he shut his mouth. Soon he heard the gentle calling of an older lady.

"Where are you, Lisa? You are the last one, you little rascal, and I will not be searching for you all afternoon again. Now, where would you hide your little self?" John recognized the voice of Mrs. Jennings and he stepped forward to greet her. Lisa grabbed his hand and yanked him back, but that didn't prevent the noise.

Mrs. Jennings stopped in the hall and walked up to the closet door. "Would this in fact be the spot where you hide, Miss Little Lisa?" The closet doors burst open, and Mrs. Jennings looked up at John then down at Lisa. She let out a shriek of terror and nearly fainted to the floor. John jumped to her side and caught her before she could knock her head on anything. Lisa giggled at their side.

"Mrs. Jennings? Mrs. Jennings!" John exclaimed. She looked up at him with large, terror-filled eyes. He picked her up and carried her to a chair where he set her down. He bit his lip trying to think of what to say. "Er, I am sorry that I startled you, Mrs. Jennings, but Lisa answered the door, and then she pulled me into the closet, and I didn't know what was going on... I guess I was a bit of a fool." He smirked and tried to cover it, but knew the evidence was all over his face.

"You sir, have to be the biggest idiot I have ever met! What type of fool follows a four-year-old into a closet and just stands there? You about made my heart stop. Could you imagine what that would have done to the children?"

Lisa walked over and climbed into Mrs. Jennings' lap. She snuggled her head into her shoulder and peeked out shyly at John. He couldn't help but smile back. Mrs. Jennings shuddered and pulled the girl closer. John reached out, and taking the girl's hand in his, he bowed over it. "Good afternoon, Miss Lisa, my name is Mr. John. It is very nice to meet you."

Lisa smiled up at him, and gave his hand a quick shake, then, pulling her hand away, she jumped from Mrs. Jennings' lap and disappeared around the corner. John laughed as he watched her go. He took a seat across from Mrs. Jennings and waited for her to catch her nerve again.

She inhaled deeply once or twice more, then turned on him. "Now, Mr. John, what may I ask is your business here? Are you looking to adopt a child, or is there another reason for you to hide in a closet and scare the living daylights out of a poor unsuspecting woman?"

John felt himself blushing again. "Forgive me, Madame. My name is Sir John Borden. I am Queen Rose's cousin, and I was..."

"Rose's cousin? Well, why didn't you say so in the first place!? How is Rose? I hear she is planning on coming for a visit soon. At least, that is what she says in her letters. I do hope it is true, because I have missed her so terribly much. A letter is not the same as seeing the person face to face."

John smiled politely. "Rose will in fact be coming with King Henry very soon. They should be here within a few weeks, I believe. They will be leaving as soon as they receive my letter. That is why I thought it might be wise to stop by here and make sure that you would be willing to visit with them soon after they arrive."

Mrs. Jennings let out a snort. "Would I be willing to allow the king and queen to visit? What type of question is that? Rose and Henry are welcome here any time they see fit. If they didn't come and visit me, I would be tempted to rush over to the inn and demand a visit with them."

John looked at the feisty little woman in front of him, and he didn't doubt it for a minute. She would probably take on the entire guard that went with Rose and Henry if she thought they were keeping her from the royal couple. "Very well, they will most likely visit you on the second or third day after they arrive. I know Rose would like to stop by immediately, but I believe they think it is necessary to visit the curate first."

"As it should be. The curate needs someone to put him first in their life. He is much too serious, that fellow. You would think that he was living with the weight of all damnation on his shoulders, but you wouldn't want to tell him that. I think that man has a temper on him if you ask me."

John couldn't help but agree. Caleb had not been the most welcoming person he had ever met. In fact, John had thought the curate was rather cold. He did not see what Rose and Henry saw in the fellow. If he had the choice, he would leave Caleb all to himself to live in whatever cold misery he inflicted upon himself.

The room fell silent as the two contemplated their opinions of the curate. Neither spoke for quite some time, and John began to get uncomfortable. Decorum said he should remain for another few minutes, but he really did not know the lady, and he felt like there were many other things he could be doing. His thoughts turned to the young lady who was working at the post office. Yes, Miss Mede was definitely enough to distract the thoughts of any young man. It was amazing she wasn't already married.

John felt a smile spread across his face, and he tried to prevent it. The resulting face must have been quite humorous because Mrs. Jennings started laughing at him, and John felt a blush creeping up his neck.

"If my intuition is right," laughed Mrs. Jennings, "I would say that you have something else on your mind besides this conversation we are having here. Am I right, Mr. Borden?" John tried to pretend it wasn't true, but nothing got past Mrs. Jennings. He nodded in agreement.

Mrs. Jennings let out another hoot of laughter. "Let me guess, that particular something is a little lass that has caught your eye." There was no denying that one, for the blush had probably turned John's face a scarlet red. Mrs. Jennings clutched her side with laughter.

"Sorry, lad! It's just been far too long since I have had anything interesting in my life. I think I might have to start living vicariously through others. It is much more interesting than living the life of an old widow woman. I fear I only lack the knack for couth."

John bit his cheek to prevent an angry retort. There was nothing wrong with what Mrs. Jennings had said, it was just embarrassing to be caught thinking about such a topic. He tried to take control of the conversation. He cleared his throat. "Mrs. Jennings, how many children do you have in the orphanage at the moment?"

"Eight, but never mind any of that. Is your lady friend close by?"

"Mrs. Jennings, I hardly think this an appropriate conversation. Besides, the girl hardly knows my name."

"Nothing is inappropriate conversation when you are a widow and you are old; every other person thinks my lack of couth is cute and something to be ignored. They blame everything on age once you get past fifty. It really is quite a relief. Now, what were you saying about the girl hardly knowing your name? I am quite sure most women would remember you after meeting you once. You are hardly a figure to forget."

John fought the blush. There was nothing to blush about at all, the old woman was just teasing. "This particular girl is probably quite good at ignoring anyone or anything that she wants to. I'm afraid I must go, Mrs. Jennings, there are still things I have to do today." He rose from his chair and walked toward the door.

Mrs. Jennings followed him. She had a grin on her face and a sparkle in her eyes, but John ignored them. There was no point in inviting her to tease him more. "Come again, Mr. Borden. Perhaps when Rose and Henry come. I should have a more civil tongue in my head when they are around."

"Perhaps," replied John as he disappeared down the path and onto the road.

ELEVEN

E LIZABETH LOOKED DOWN AT THE letter. It was addressed to the curate, but he wouldn't want to see it. It was from the same place as the last one. It was in the same messy scrawl, with the same dirty smudges. She should probably burn it, but she couldn't bring herself to do such a thing. She still had the other one sitting at home in a cupboard. Perhaps she could place this one with it.

The door creaked open, and Elizabeth quickly shoved the letter into her pocket. She placed a smile on her face and looked out at the new customer. She had to fight back the groan. Mr. Borden was not an unwelcome man, but he made her nervous, and she did not want him standing in the post office the entire time like he had done the other day. It really was quite obnoxious, and she didn't think she had the patience to deal with it today.

Elizabeth turned her face from him and pretended to be working.

"Excuse me, Miss Mede, but I was wondering if I could have a word with you."

Elizabeth looked up and smiled politely. She had to fight back a laugh. The man was blushing, for Pete's sake. What type of man blushed so often?

"How may I help you, Mr. Borden?"

"I was, um, I was wondering if you would forgive me for my behaviour yesterday. I was obnoxious and rude, and I shouldn't have intruded upon your space so much, and I was hoping that you would forgive me."

Bother, thought Elizabeth as she felt a blush come up to her cheeks. Why did she have to blush just because he was blushing? It wasn't as if the conversation was all that embarrassing. "There is nothing to forgive, Mr. Borden. This is a public building, and you should feel welcome to stand in it whenever you please."

Bother, that came out all wrong. "What I mean to say, Mr. Borden," Elizabeth was trying to prevent the blush from covering her entire face and neck, "is that there are no rules about you standing in the post office, and if you want to stand there, then feel free to do so at any time." *As if that had come out so much better!*

They stood uncomfortably in the room, each scarlet red. Of course, there was no reason to be embarrassed, but that didn't matter any. John tried to think of something to say, and Elizabeth tried to ignore him. Both of them let out a sigh of relief when the door creaked open.

"Good afternoon, Mr. Taylor!" Elizabeth exclaimed in relief. Caleb looked at the two beet red adults and pretended not to notice. He walked up to the counter to retrieve his mail.

"Good afternoon, Miss Mede. How are you today?" Elizabeth turned her face down and did not respond.

"I have your mail in the back. I will only be a moment." She turned and disappeared into the back mail room. When she returned, Mr. Borden was gone, and the curate stood waiting at the counter. She handed him his mail, and after a brief farewell she was once again alone in her small office. She let out a small sigh of relief and wondered what in the world was the matter with her.

John made his way toward the butcher's shop. It wasn't quite time for his visit with Josh, but he did not think it would matter if he was early. Besides, he planned to take as long as possible with his walk. He needed some time to mull over what had happened at the post office.

What had gotten into his head back there? Why did he have to blush every single time he entered that place? It wasn't like he had never apologized to a girl before. He had apologized often; in fact, he should be used to it. Yet, he had never blushed as often as he did now, and it was getting to be embarrassing.

It didn't take long to find Josh's house, and it turned out he was far too early, and Josh wouldn't be home for quite some time. He walked around the market centre and visited the mercantile. He saw the doilies Josh's mother and sisters made and sold, and he was tempted to buy one for no good reason except to support Josh's family. He could give it to Rose, perhaps.

There wasn't much to do, and the time dragged by slowly. He really needed work of some sort to occupy his mind. He walked down a path in the woods, but it didn't lead anywhere interesting, so he walked back, but Josh still wasn't home. Finally he decided to just sit on a log and wait.

He watched as people walked by. There were the rich couples who couldn't be bothered with a stranger. There were the poorer fellows going about their tasks, and every now and then there was a child who would come by and look him over before their mother came along and dragged them away. As time passed, the crowd waned, and night began to take hold.

Josh did not appear until the last legs of light disappeared over the horizon. He seemed tired and did not look like he could make it all the way to his house. John greeted him, and the boy began to walk a little straighter. "Sorry I took so long. There was a lot to do at the shop. We had a couple of farmers come in with emergency orders today, and that took up most of our time. Anyway, I'm here now."

They walked in silence until they reached the house. John couldn't help but scrunch his nose at the smell as he entered the building. He tried to keep Josh from seeing his reaction, but it was no use. Josh just laughed. "You thought that Miss Beton was bad; at least she didn't sick a skunk on you. Don't worry, you get used to the smell. I'm hoping it will wear off soon enough." He shrugged his shoulders and made his way toward the kitchen area.

The building was quite small. There were only two rooms. The one large room was split into an eating area and a kitchen, and the smaller room was a bedroom. Josh began to pull out some supplies from different cupboards. There wasn't much in them, but he didn't look like he was starving. John wouldn't complain.

Josh shoved around some items on the counter and cleaned up a spot to make the meal. He tossed some things in a pot, put them on the stove and watched as it began to boil. He looked around for a spoon, found one and began to stir. Soon the entire room was filled with a smell that wasn't quite skunk, but wasn't necessarily pleasant either. John began to wonder what he had gotten himself into.

Josh pulled the pot off the heat and dumped the contents onto two plates. He placed one in front of John and sat down with the other. "Sorry if you don't like it. It's the only half-decent thing I know how to make." John looked down at his plate. He wasn't sure he recognized anything in front of him. With a quick prayer before the meal, the two dug in.

John held his breath as the first scoop went in. It was a little slimy, but if he could look past the texture, it wasn't half bad, whatever it was. He swallowed. It slid down his throat and hit the bottom of his stomach. It would have to do.

"So, what is the visit for? You said you had something to talk to me about?"

John nodded around another bite. "Have you heard that Rose and Henry are coming for a visit?"

"Yes, I've heard the rumours."

"Good, because Rose wants to meet with you again, and I have to make sure that it is alright with you."

Josh laughed. "Alright with me? Why in the world would the queen have to ask if it is alright with me to visit with her? What sane person would reject such a chance?"

John shrugged his shoulders. "You know Rose. She doesn't want to impose herself on anyone, and so she will be ever polite and make sure it is alright that she visits. She was also thinking of having a bit of an informal meeting, too, if that would be alright." John looked at Josh to see if he caught the drift.

"An informal meeting? What does she mean by that? Am I supposed to dress up for when I meet her formally?"

John shook his head. "You really don't get it, do you?"

"I am completely beyond understanding." "She taught you how to fight. Don't you think she wants to see how her pupil is doing? If it is alright with you, she would like to have an informal meeting with you out in the pasture while she is visiting. Of course Henry will be with her, but she wants to know if you are still open to meeting to practice some time."

"Well, I'll be! The Queen of Samaya didn't give up fighting with the sword. Well, won't that be something. I would love to have an 'informal' meeting with the queen then. Perhaps I will be able to beat her this time."

"Hah, you wish! She still beats Henry half the time, and I swear she lets him win the other half, because she doesn't want to wound his pride. Besides, even if you disarm her, she's as quick as a whip, and she's learned a few more punches and kicks. I wouldn't get on her bad side if I were you."

"That'd be something to see," murmured Josh.

"I'll set up the informal meeting for a Tuesday night, most likely. Other than that, the formal meeting is up in the air, and don't feel pressured to dress up for it. Rose will probably throw a fit if she sees you in your Sunday best around her. She's still trying to get used to all the frills, and she won't force them on anyone else."

"Sounds like what I remember of her." Josh turned back to his meal. The two spent the rest of the evening playing checkers and enjoying each other's company, and it wasn't until very late that John returned to the inn. It had been a nice evening. He looked forward to more time with Josh. Though, maybe next time he would bring the food.

The morning wind was chill but not bitter. Elizabeth walked toward the pasture. It was part of her morning routine now. She would wake from the nightmare, she would take care of her chores at home, and then she would walk to the pasture to stand by the cross.

There was no purpose in standing by the cross. She didn't gain anything from it; it did not calm her or give her peace. But, ever since she had stood there the first time, it had been a part of her dream, and she was determined to figure out why.

Caleb joined her on most mornings. He was always tired and didn't like to talk much, but that didn't matter. He would stand with her, and the two would wait until the sun touched the horizon. Then, Elizabeth would say that she had to go, Caleb would sigh, and both of them would walk toward the town. Today started like any other day.

Caleb was at the cross before Elizabeth. He looked up at her and smiled when she approached. She smiled back feebly. Both of them turned to look at the cross. It was dark outside. It was always dark when they were there, but the days were getting longer, and that would soon change. It would be warm then, and maybe not quite so wet.

Elizabeth looked at the grave and wondered if she would ever know the full story behind it. Sometimes she wanted to ask Caleb to tell more of the story, but she was afraid he would stop coming if she pried. So, each morning that Caleb was there, Elizabeth would stand patiently waiting, waiting for him to speak first.

"Where did I leave off in Mark's story?"

The question startled Elizabeth. She didn't think Caleb was ever going to speak again, but now he did, and she would take whatever she could get. "You were saying that Mark could change something, he could fight, but he never did. I asked you if he ever did fight."

Caleb nodded, and Elizabeth waited for him to go on.

"The three boys grew into young adults. Seth became more contemptible as he grew. He would go into town sometimes, and he would visit the bars and the women of ill repute. He was only seventeen, but he already had a reputation for being mean. Bill wasn't far behind him. He was sixteen, and just starting in the ways of his brother, but he never was quite as evil. People thought that he was too stupid to be so formidable, and they were probably right.

"Mark was fifteen, and he was different again. He had no intentions of doing as his brothers did. He never went to the bars or those other places. He did go to town though. He stuck by his brothers' side for the most part, just to make sure they didn't get into so much trouble, or at least so they wouldn't hurt anyone. He wasn't strong, but he knew the power of words.

"Sometimes Seth would get in a temper, and he would want to beat whoever was in sight, and Mark would step in his way. He would say to Seth, 'What you doing? Do you think that makes you a man?'

Sometimes it would work, sometimes it wouldn't. If it didn't work, Mark would take the beating, and all three of them would slouch their way home."

Caleb ran his hand through his hair. "I remember one time Seth gave Mark such a bad beating, he had to carry him all the way home. Of course, he might have just left him in the streets, but he knew his dad would be furious, so he carried him all the way back and dumped him outside the shack they lived in. The next day, Mark was up again and ready to step in Seth's way once more if necessary."

Caleb paused, and Elizabeth took the time to think over what he was saying. Mark wasn't a fighter. He probably never fought, but he had to have done something, because something had put him in the grave in Emriville, and it wasn't his brother.

"You know," continued Caleb, "I never understood Mark. I always wondered why he didn't just go to the authorities. His father could have been jailed along with his brother. Bill would have gotten by as a stupid drunk, and Mark would have lived a happy life, but he didn't do it. He refused to do it, and because of that, someone got hurt.

"He could have prevented a lot of pain, Mark could have, but he didn't, and I don't think there is a soul in this universe who can forgive him for that." Caleb looked at the cross and spit on it. Elizabeth tried to ignore the action, but it was too awful, too degrading.

She turned on Caleb in anger. "Why did you do that? Why don't you give him respect? He's dead. He can't change anything now, and for all you know, he could have saved countless lives. Were you with him his entire life? Did you see all the good he might have done? Do you even know how the story ends?"

Clenching his fists, Caleb turned on her, his eyes ablaze. "I know the rest of the story, and I can't forgive him because of the rest of the story. You shouldn't make a hero out of him until you know the entire story. For all you know, he could have been a tyrant, a murderer. You don't even care about the other characters. All you care about is Mark. I'll have you know, he's dead. He can't change anything. He's dead and he left too much baggage behind!"

Elizabeth stepped away from the curate. She didn't want to be near him. He frightened her, and she didn't know why. She turned to leave him, but he called to her. She looked into his face and saw the need that was there. She hesitated, but then turned back to him. What harm could he really do her? He was the curate after all.

"I'm sorry, Miss Mede. I will behave myself from now on. It's just that the rest of the story is painful and it hurts me to tell it, to say the words, to form the thoughts in my mind. He could have done so much to prevent it, and that is what hurts the most.

"Seth wasn't always bad. Yes, he was evil, but evil can be tamed, and the best tamer of an evil man is woman. There was one girl that could tame Seth. Her name was Sarah. She was sweet and blonde. She had a heart-shaped face, and she wasn't afraid of anything. It was the horrible truth, but Seth Hepton didn't scare her one whit.

"One day, he made a lewd comment as she walked by, and she turned on him, and she railed at him. 'Mr. Hepton, if I hear one more such comment come out of your mouth, I will take a bar of soap and clean it right out. Such filth shouldn't reside in a man.' Of course Seth got a good laugh out of that, and he wanted to put her to the test. So, the next time Sarah walked by, Seth was ready.

"He came up with the lewdest thing he could think of, and he said it right out for Sarah to hear. Now, Sarah was a lady, and she had the sense to take the time to blush, but after that, she turned on the spot, pulled a bar of soap out of her reticule, and marched right over to Seth. If he hadn't been in shock, she never would have gotten that far. She shoved that soap into his mouth and began to scrub.

"That was the talk of the county for quite some time, only topped when Sarah started having regular conversations with Seth. The entire county was in an uproar over that, but it didn't matter what others thought. Sarah did what she wanted, and there was nothing anyone could do about it."

Elizabeth looked at Caleb. He was getting off track, she thought. He was supposed to be talking about Mark, but apparently he had gotten Mark and Seth mixed up. She would have to bring his attention to this. "Sir," she whispered, "what does this all have to do with Mark? I'm sure Seth has an interesting story, but you were telling me about Mark, his younger brother."

Caleb turned to her and smiled sadly. "I know," he whispered. "It all fits in. You will see." He turned and looked at the horizon. The sun was starting to show. People would be missing them soon. They should be on their way.

"Mr. Taylor?" whispered Elizabeth again. "How do you know so much about Mark? I thought no one ever bothered with the Heptons. How then do you know so much of their story?"

Caleb turned away. "I was close to the story. I am, in a way, part of the story, but that won't make any sense to you. It is no matter though. I know the story, and that is all that matters." There was silence again.

Neither of them wanted to be the first to leave. There was still a lot to be said, but the sun demanded that they go about their day.

Elizabeth sighed. Mr. Walters would have her job if she didn't open the post office on time. She turned to go. Caleb stopped her one more time before she could get very far. "Elizabeth. Do I scare you?"

She looked at him. How was she supposed to respond to that? He wasn't a terrifying man, but there was something about him, a mystery of sorts, that didn't make sense. Did that scare her? Perhaps it did, but then again maybe it didn't.

"I don't know." Caleb studied her briefly. "If I am to tell you the rest of Mark's story, you must not be afraid of me. What I have to tell you is terrifying enough. You must *trust* me. I know that is an odd request, but I think you will understand when you hear the story. Do you think that you could trust me with this?"

It was Elizabeth's turn to study the curate. She wanted to know Mark's story so badly, and it seemed that the curate was the only one who knew it. She would *have* to trust him. She *would* trust him. She would make herself trust him. "Okay," she whispered. Caleb nodded back; then, turning on the spot, he left.

Elizabeth stared after him. There was so much about the curate that she didn't understand. He was an enigma in every sense. One day he was hollow, dead, mournful. The next day he would be changed, almost revitalized, but his eyes were always dead as if life could no longer live in them, at least not around the grave.

Elizabeth wondered what he saw when he looked at her. Would he see the stain that everyone else seemed to see? Would he see the hurt, the pain, the unending nightmare? Sometimes she thought he could see it all, and that he understood it all, but other times she wasn't so sure. All she knew was that he was in the same place as she was, and it was nice to know she didn't have to be alone in it.

TWELVE

KATY LOOKED OUT OVER THE marketplace and froze. The curate wasn't far off. He was standing alone in front of a booth of knickknacks. She stared at him and watched as he looked at one item and then another. Taking a deep breath, she began to move toward him. Slowly, slowly, each step brought her closer to his side. She reached the booth and looked down.

"Good afternoon, Mr. Taylor," she said cheerily. He looked down at her with evident frustration, but she didn't look up to see his expression. Her fingers moved from a wooden doll to pen nibs and to whatever else was displayed.

"Good afternoon, Miss Monks," replied the curate. He turned as if to go. Katy looked up at him, at a loss of what to say.

"How have you been faring?" She blushed when he turned to her, but she refused to turn her face down. She would look at him. He was handsome, and she would have the pleasure of looking at him.

"I have been quite well, Miss Monks. I hope you have been faring as well. I am sure you are quite excited about the forthcoming arrival of the queen." Katy ignored the clipped and practiced tone of his voice. They were having a conversation, and there was something to be said for that.

"I must admit that I am actually quite nervous. I do not know how it will be when Rose comes, and the entire prospect of it has my stomach in knots." She felt herself starting to blink as nervousness took hold. She tried to stop herself, but it couldn't be helped.

"There is nothing to be worried about; the queen is a respectable woman, and will not discredit you because of your position in life. She also came from such a dire background."

Katy stiffened at the curate's words. *Dire background?* She did not consider her position in life so dreadfully terrible. What did the curate have against them? "I do not understand what you mean by dire, Mr. Taylor. I find my position in life to be perfectly respectable. There is nothing in my situation to be ashamed of."

The curate pasted a grin to his face with a look meant to appease. "I meant no offense, Miss Monks. I was just stating that the queen will not look down upon another with less than herself. She is a lady after all."

"That may be so, sir, but that is not what has me worried. It is the fact that Rose is now in a position of power that is making nervous. It has been my experience that when people are given a higher position in life, they tend to change. This possible change is what makes my stomach churn."

"Very well."

The conversation died, and silence hovered between them. Katy looked up at him every now and then, but the curate did not look back. She tried to think of a conversation starter. There was nothing she could think of. The curate came up with one for her. "Do you know when the queen is coming?"

Katy looked up at him with shock. He had never started a conversation with her before. She smiled to herself. "I believe Rose will be here within a week. At least, that is what John has been planning for. Has John not talked with you?"

The curate nodded. "He set up a meeting with me. I am to meet with the king and queen as soon as they arrive. Can you imagine that? The king and queen want to visit me."

Katy sighed with his last words and looked off into the distance. "I understand how you feel. Can you believe that the king and queen want to see me as well? It is just so unfathomable. Who would have thought that such a thing could have happened in Emriville?"

The curate laughed bitterly. "Yes, in Emriville of all places. It was supposed to be a safe place from all things wonderful and splendid. What being deemed it necessary to bestow such bliss upon such a small little speck?"

"Bliss for one, but absolute misery for another. I know for myself this waiting is absolute misery. I shall be much better once Rose and Henry are here. There will be no more questions then."

Mr. Taylor smiled down at her. "You may be right, Miss Monks. You just might be right. But, I must go now. I have much to do. Saturdays, unfortunately, are very busy days for me, and if I am to have a sermon for tomorrow, I must return immediately."

The Charade

Katy smiled politely and curtsied as the curate bowed and walked away. She bit her lip to keep back the giggle, but it came anyway. She had just had an entire conversation with the curate, and it hadn't been all that bad. Perhaps she would have an even easier time of it when next it chanced.

"Now, what is that giggle for? Why would a young lass such as yourself be so happy?" Katy jumped because of the voice coming from behind her and nearly fell to the ground. She grabbed at her pounding heart and exhaled when she noted Josh grinning at her from the blacksmith shop. She walked toward him.

"And, why would a young lad such as yourself be about scaring young ladies? If you ask me, it is quite atrocious."

Josh laughed at her and straightened his posture. "Most young ladies are not so easily scared, but seeing as it is the young Miss Monks, it is probably best that I offer my most sincere apologies for fear she'll set a skunk on me."

"Why you, you..." Katy was at a loss for words. "It was your own blessed fault. There was no need for you to follow me into the woods, and it was you who startled the creature. He would have been quite content to leave me alone if you hadn't jumped out with such bravado. I smelt like skunk for three days after that incident."

Josh smirked and sniffed the air. "I'm not sure if you are accurate in saying it took three days to get rid of the smell. I'm pretty sure that I can still smell something faintly over this way, and it's not me."

"Quit teasing, Josh. I know very well that I don't smell like skunk. You're just being unpleasant."

"Honestly, Katy girl, I smell something over here. Come see for yourself if you smell it. Perhaps you will know what it is." Josh shrugged his shoulders in a look of complete innocence. Katy squinted at him, then she took a step forward.

There was a smell. It wasn't a bad smell. It was an interesting smell. She stepped closer. It was a good smell, in fact, a very good smell. She closed her eyes and tried to concentrate on what it was. She took another step and slipped on the muddy ground. She felt herself falling and tried to catch something, anything. Josh reached out and grabbed her. She looked up at him with round, startled eyes. She righted herself and turned away.

"Dewberries," she muttered under her breath.

"What did you say?" asked Josh politely.

"The smell. It smells like Dewberries. If that's what they are, they are extremely early this year, which is odd because the winter has been colder than normal."

Josh nodded his head and stared at her. "Is there a reason why you are staring at me, Mr. Deplin?"

Josh shook his head. "Did you have a nice conversation with the curate?"

"Very pleasant," replied Katy as she began to walk away.

Josh raced after her. "Aw, come on now Katy girl. I did not mean to offend you. I was just trying to be polite. How are things going for you?"

Katy continued to walk. "Things are going quite well for me, Mr. Deplin. Like I said, I just had a wonderful conversation with Mr. Taylor. I think he is becoming friendlier toward me." Josh stopped walking.

"You can't mean to say that you still like the fellow?" he asked.

"Whatever can you mean by that? Of course I still like the curate. He is a perfectly respectable man, and if I were to ever become his wife, it would be an honour."

Josh laughed. "What an honour that would be. I honestly don't know if the man ever smiles anymore. He is so severe, I doubt he will ever marry, and if he does, what a pity it would be to be his wife."

"Stop it Josh. The curate is simply misunderstood. He has a lot on his shoulders as minister to such a large congregation, but even with all that stress, he is kind and considerate to all people."

"As kind and considerate as a stiff, old man can be. Sure, he smiles when he is supposed to. He says the right things and bows at the right time. He is polite, honest, and dead as a mouse in a trap. Anyone who really sees him knows that. Haven't you wondered why all the other girls have stopped chasing after him? Is he any less handsome or available? No. He is just dead, that's all."

"Don't say that, Josh. He is a good man, and I can't bear to hear you speak of him in this way. I will not be deterred. I will give my utmost respect to the curate as long as he is deserving of it."

"What is so deserving of respect about him, Katy? Is it because of his clerical collar? Is that what earns your respect? Is it that he knows his Bible from front to back? Yes, then he is an honourable man, but surely there is something more to honour."

Katy wheeled on Josh. "Well, at least he can afford to support a family."

Josh's jaw dropped. He gapped at her, his entire face downcast. "If that is how you feel, then I am sorry I wasted so much of your time." He turned and began to walk with slouched shoulders back toward the smith's shop.

"Josh! Josh, I didn't mean it that way. Honestly, I was angry, and I said something I didn't mean."

Josh looked back at her sadly. "You don't get it, Katy. I like you a lot. But you don't like me. You have made that blatantly obvious. I am not going to waste my time chasing after you if I am never to have you. That would be useless. It's better that I don't get in any deeper than I already am." Slowly, he walked away. He did not look back; he just kept walking. Katy fought it off, but a tear ran down her cheek and dropped from her chin. Turning, she picked up her skirts and ran.

John stood back and stared at the post office door. He couldn't go in, yet he so wanted to go in. Why didn't he just walk through the door? He stepped forward, then stopped himself. She would say no. He was certain of that. She had for the past few days. What would make her say yes today? He could ask just one more time. What would it hurt?

He opened the door and stepped in. She was standing behind the counter. She looked so sad, it hurt him. She was always so sad, and he didn't know why. He watched her for a moment. She moved about quickly putting things away, marking letters to be sent out, stacking letters that had just come in. She looked at one letter, smiled, and marked it to be sent out. She had a beautiful smile. John liked it when she smiled.

He watched her for a while longer before he made his presence known. He cleared his throat. She jumped and he felt the usual blush colour his cheeks when she looked at him with those deep, unfathomable eyes. "How do you do, Miss Mede?"

"Quite well, Mr. Borden, thank you," she replied and went back to her work.

"Have I any letters, Miss Mede?"

"I am sorry Mr. Borden, but you have not received a letter today."

He knew that of course, but he needed something to ask. It was getting late. The mail carrier waited outside. Miss Mede picked up a small sack of letters, put them into a bag and carried it around the counter. John jumped to her side.

"Let me carry that for you," he said as he took the bag from her hands. She was left to stand in mute shock as he carried the post bag out to the mail carrier and then came back. "Does this mean that you are done for the day?" he asked.

Miss Mede nodded. "I only need to clean up."

"May I help you?"

Miss Mede shook her head. "That would not be appropriate, Mr. Borden. There is no mail for you, and the post just went out for the day. If you have no other business at the post office, it would be better that you leave."

John shifted uncomfortably from one foot to the other. "I would like to escort you home if that would be alright with you, Miss Mede."

This was her chance to deny him. She had before. Would she do it again, he wondered.

Miss Mede looked at him curiously. There was that look in her eyes again. It was a look that he had seen many times before; a sad look that could not be easily explained. "I don't think that would be wise, Mr. Borden," she replied and then turned away.

"Then, perhaps tomorrow would be a better time for you. I will walk you home then?"

"Tomorrow is Sunday, sir. I will not be at the post office tomorrow. You cannot walk me back from a place where I will not be."

"Then I could walk you home from the church. Would that be alright with you?"

"I might be sick tomorrow."

"Then it would be better for me to walk you home today, would it not?"

"Perhaps..."

"Is there a reason why you object to me walking you home? Have I overstepped my bounds in some way? Should I have spoken with your father first, before I asked you?"

"There is no need for you to speak with my father," Miss Mede replied sharply. "I will allow you to walk with me tonight, but you must turn to go your own way when I ask, and if you follow me, I will never allow you to come with me again."

John looked at her curiously. It was an odd request, but he could abide by it. "Very well, I agree to your terms." He smiled at her, and she scowled back.

"Sit over there, while I finish up." She pointed to the corner, and John did as she commanded. This would give him some time to study her. He watched as she went purposefully about her tasks. She was angry for some reason. He had probably stepped on a nerve and he should apologize. He would once they were walking.

John watched as she dusted off the counter and tidied up the already spotless office. Then, she blew out the candles, and it was time to go. John grabbed her wraps from the rack and held them up for her. She slipped under them and blushed. John smiled. It wasn't often that she blushed while he did not.

He held the door for her, and she stepped out. He exited, and she locked the door behind them. The night air was cool but pleasant. Spring was everywhere, and the birds were still chirping as the evening waned. "Which direction should we go?" John asked. Miss Mede pointed down the road. She started walking, and John kept pace.

"I believe I owe you an apology. I did not mean to act so offensively toward you. Will you forgive me?"

"All is forgiven, Mr. Borden. You have not offended me in any slight way." The conversation ended, and they continued to walk. John bit his lip, not knowing what to say. He pondered this for a while then decided to ask Elizabeth a little bit about herself.

"How is it that a young girl such as yourself comes across a job at the post office? It has been my experience that young men usually fill that position."

"True. But, I was looking for a job, and because I am not educated, the only fitting job I could find was at the post office. If I do not have this job, I do not have any job."

"Why would you want a job in the first place? Surely the members of the church would be willing to support you."

Miss Mede stopped and looked at him. She smiled. "Charity can only extend so far, and it was service enough that the church provided me with a job. Besides, it has been my experience, sir, that idle hands make devil's handiwork." She turned and continued to walk.

"I have heard such things before, but the church can't honestly expect you to keep a job as well as run a household. I know many a lady who tells me that running a household of any size is a full day's work. If the church supported you, wouldn't you be well occupied at home?"

"Perhaps those ladies haven't learned the lesson as well as I have," replied Miss Mede bitterly. "If they had, they wouldn't allow their hands to rest for one moment. And many of them would likely pick up a job to keep themselves more occupied."

"What dreadful thing has happened that has caused you to learn this lesson, Miss Mede? For, I see nothing wrong in resting my hands when I am tired."

"When you are tired you sleep, but if you are not tired, and you do not sleep, how do you occupy your time?"

"With many other things. I work, for one thing, and if I am not working, I go about other tasks, but I hardly doubt it is devil's handiwork when my hands are idle."

"Perhaps not. Even so, the first time your hands rest, the devil puts forth a temptation. You may ignore it. The second time, the temptation is a little harder to ignore, and your hands may start to fidget. The third time, your hands do not belong to yourself, and you go about the devil's bidding without thinking about it. I have learned that it is better not to put oneself in way of temptation."

"Perhaps," said John. "But, then there occurs just as many problems when one never rests. Didn't the good Lord also give us the seventh day as a relief? It would seem then that rest is a good thing. I would never take it from another soul."

"It is not necessary for you to take anything from anyone, sir. I was simply explaining why I have a job that keeps my hands busy."

"I suppose you were. I hope you enjoy your job. I am sure there are many pleasures in going through everyone's mail. I always wonder what people would think if they saw from whom I received letters and to whom I sent them. You could learn so much about a person."

Miss Mede laughed. "That is true. I don't think people notice how much they are revealing about themselves when they leave a letter at the post office. I mean, I'm not the only one who sees it. There are at least five people who see where the letter is going and where it comes from before it ends in its recipient's hands. How embarrassing that must be for some people."

John smiled down at her. "What is the latest scandal at your post office?"

Miss Mede smiled slyly and tried to hide the pleasure she was getting from this conversation. "The widow Hegler has an admirer that is sending her a letter once a week. He has been for the last three months. The amazing thing is that she sends a letter back just as frequently, to a Mr. Ronald Fretty. He was a traveler in town a couple months back."

John laughed out loud. "What a scandal that must be. When do you think the town will find out about it?"

Miss Mede thought about it. "Well, it has been three months, and some are already questioning the thawing of the old lady. It will be another two weeks, is my guess."

"I give it an entire month. We will have to see who is right."

Miss Mede smiled and looked about. They were nearing her house. "You must turn around now, Mr. Borden. I will not travel any farther with you."

John looked at her sadly. "Are you sure it must be this way, Miss Mede?"

"Mr. Borden, we have made a pact. You must turn around now," Miss Mede replied sternly.

John sighed. He gave Miss Mede one last, sad smile. "We will see how long widow Hegler's secret remains a secret. I am sure it will be another month."

Miss Mede laughed. "Go, Mr. Borden, or I may have to throw my shoe at you."

John laughed at the lady, then turned around. He sauntered off down the road. Miss Mede let out a sigh as he disappeared. She shouldn't have taken that chance. There would be talk if someone realized that Sir John Borden had walked her home. She sighed again. That would not be good.

She walked the rest of the way to her home in silence. Night enveloped her as she went about her chores. It was the regular routine. Nothing had changed. It was familiar. Familiar was good. Familiar couldn't hurt her. She tended to her father, and late that night, she crawled into bed. The dream would come. It was familiar. Perhaps just this once, it wouldn't hurt her so much.

THIRTEEN

JOHN SCANNED THE PEWS IN the church, but he didn't see her. People were lining up behind him, trying to make their way to their seats. He stepped out of their way and kept searching. The music started, and people stood to sing. John let out a sigh of frustration. He slipped into a bench and began to sing.

He tried to relax and enjoy the music, but he was frustrated and wanted to do something about it. He lifted his head and looked above the crowd. There were many benefits to being as tall as he was, but he still did not see her. She was not there. He would have to live with that. Perhaps she really was sick.

He sighed and turned his attention to the service. There was no point in bemoaning what he could not change. The music ended with one last note, and the curate stepped up to the pulpit. John took the opportunity to study him.

Caleb was a taller man, not as tall as himself, but in no way short. He was pale. His hair was blond, his eyes a grey blue. He looked sickly, and there were large bags under his eyes. He wasn't old, but he moved like an old man. Each step was first pondered, and then taken. Could this man really get through a sermon?

John took a deep breath as the first words left the man's mouth. He blew it all out in a sigh of relief as the baritone boom filled the room. Life snapped into Caleb's eyes and his entire being seemed to change. He became young and almost giddy. He used his arms, flailing them about with great expression. He pounded out his points and all in the audience were forced to take it upon themselves to consider every aspect of all he said.

He spoke about depravity. It was an odd topic. He spoke of the total and irrevocable evilness of man. There was nothing to be done to save mankind, he claimed, except for one thing. It was the cross, he shouted in a whisper. Go to the cross, he demanded. Repent of your evil ways, he urged. Tears dripped from ladies' eyes and even the elders bowed their heads in sad guilt.

John felt the guilt weigh him down, but he couldn't succumb. He was confused. He was a sinner, of that he was sure, but did he really have to continually review the evilness within himself? Was it so necessary that he bring his sorry evil self to the cross? *God*, he prayed, *I am sorry for my sins, but I know you have forgiven me, and you continue to forgive me. Is this curate really right? Do you still hold me accountable? Please, help me understand. Help me know what your truth is.*

John looked up in time to notice that it was time to stand and sing. He stretched his limbs and sang in a clear bass voice.

Alas! And did my Saviour bleed?

And did my Sovereign die?

Would He devote that sacred head

For such a worm as I?[1]

John didn't understand it. He didn't know entirely how it worked. All he knew was that he was forgiven, and that was good enough. His Saviour had died for him, and His blood had provided forgiveness. With this added assurance, John sang with more hardy satisfaction and peace.

Caleb listened as the congregation sang. He felt the strain of the sermon wear on his shoulders and back. He was exhausted. There was no other way to describe the weighted dread of walking down the aisle, of shaking all those hands, and, most of all, of greeting all those people. He needed to persevere. He was being selfish to want to curl up in a ball and sleep. It was Sunday, and his flock needed him. Now was not the time to be selfish.

The song ended, and Caleb gave the departing blessing. The congregation sang a benediction, and Caleb took up his post by the door. He prepared himself for the onslaught. First one lady, then a gentleman, then a young girl, another lady, and person after person after person. He smiled. He nodded. He did everything exactly as he should.

The last one passed by, and he was free to leave. He let out a sigh of relief and headed toward the pulpit. He picked up his notes, and was just about to leave when a throat cleared behind him. He jumped

1 Watts, Isaac. "Alas! And did my Saviour Bleed." 1707. Text is in the public domain.

in fright and lost his footing. He felt the floor beneath his bottom and had to fight to hold back the surfacing profanity. He looked up at who had startled him.

His eyes had to keep travelling up until they found John looking down at him lips pressed between his teeth holding back a chuckle. John held his hand out to Caleb, who accepted it. With a mighty heft, Caleb found himself back on his feet and swaying only slightly. The motion was terrifying, but he tried to ignore it. It would be far too embarrassing if he squealed like a girl in front of the man.

Caleb cleared his throat. "Thank you, Sir John," he murmured. "I did not know you were still here. You startled me. Now, how may I help you?"

John shrugged his shoulders. "I was just sitting here thinking, Curate. When I noticed you hadn't left yet, I cleared my throat to say a proper farewell. I didn't mean to startle you any. I hope you will forgive me for that."

"It is no problem at all, Sir John. If that is all though, I really should be going. There are many things that I have to do to prepare for tonight's sermon, and I won't be slacking on my duty now."

John nodded, but he didn't move from his spot, thus blocking the door. He just stared at the curate as if contemplating something. He cleared his throat again. "Are you alright, Caleb?"

Caleb felt his cheeks flush red. "I am perfectly fine," he clipped. "Now, excuse me, but I must be going."

"I meant no offense, sir. You are just looking a little tired. I was just enquiring about your health, nothing else."

"Well, I am perfectly fine, Sir John. You don't have to worry yourself one bit about my health. I haven't been sick for nearly two years now, and I plan on keeping up that record. Now, I really must be going." He pressed a hand to John's shoulder.

John stepped back and gave the curate one more concerned look. "Of course, Mr. Taylor. Whatever you need."

Caleb waltzed past, and took a deep breath of spring air. It was warm once again. It was a nice feeling, the warmth. He had missed it over the winter. Winter was always a depressing time. It was the hardest season to get through. It was in the winter that the nights were long and the light hours so very short. It was during the winter that the nights were especially dark and terrible. It was in the winter that everything hung dead and haunting. He hated the winter. Spring was so much better.

Caleb took another deep breath to reassure himself that it was really spring air he breathed in. He could smell the sweetness of the flowers. He could almost taste the dew drops that had formed that morning instead of the frost. It was a wonderful time. The road beneath his feet sucked at his boots and tried to tear them off with their muddy grasp. This was spring.

For one moment Caleb felt peace.

It didn't last. His sermon for the evening was not complete. There was mail sitting on the counter. There were house calls that needed to be done. His house needed to be cleaned. He closed his eyes and contemplated sleep. It would be so wonderful just to sleep. A shudder raced down his back. Sleep meant dreaming, and dreaming meant terror. No, sleep would have to wait. He had work to do.

FOURTEEN

THE KING AND QUEEN ARRIVED amid a flurry of men-at-arms, ladies-in-waiting and servants. It was really only a small retinue, but it provided more excitement than Emriville had seen in over a hundred years. Citizens waved their flags, and store owners posted banners to their shops. The innkeeper and his wife stood by the door and waited nervously as the royal carriage pulled up front.

A servant hopped down from the front of the carriage and opened the door. A foot appeared. It was a man's foot. It was the king's. He stepped down and immediately looked back into the carriage. He held out a hand, and a lady's hand reached down to it. Another foot appeared. It was delicate and wore a fine silk slipper. Ribbon and lace followed, and then the queen. Rose looked first at her husband with a quivering smile. Then, turning to the crowd, a more confident smile split her face, and a cheer erupted.

The Charade

The innkeeper and his wife greeted the king and queen. They bowed deeply and curtsied as low as they possibly could. The royal couple acknowledged them with a nod before being promptly led to their room where they could freshen up. The innkeeper's wife kept apologizing for the lack of finer things, but she was continually assured that the inn was quite charming and would do wonderfully well. Then they reached the room, and they were left alone.

Rose let out a nervous giggle. Henry chuckled back. "Alone at last," Rose sighed as she flopped down onto the bed. "I feel as if we have been travelling for ages."

Henry came up behind her and began to massage her shoulders. She leaned into his hands, and he kissed her on the cheek. She smiled. "You know, we only have a few minutes. If John's letter is accurate, we are to meet with Caleb immediately."

Henry sighed. "I suppose so, but can't we skip just this one appointment?" He gave Rose a pleading look, and she couldn't help but laugh.

"It really isn't all that bad. Besides, Caleb is our friend, and it will be good to see him again. I have missed him, and don't pretend that you haven't. You have been excited about seeing him again for the past week."

"Too true," whispered Henry. He kissed his wife. "Very well, I am ready when you are, dear wife. We shall make our rounds, and then we will have one blissful night of recuperation before it all starts again."

Rose smirked. "I'll have to get used to not being so spoiled again. Palace life has been wonderful, but I think it is making me soft."

"That's for sure, and slow as well. You better remedy that, though, because you also have a meeting with Josh on Tuesday evening, and I don't think he will be going easy on you. You're getting out of practice."

"Out of practice! I'll have you know, sir, I can still best you!"

Henry laughed and walked out of the room. Rose waited until the door was closed, then threw a pillow at it. It hardly made a sound, but Rose still heard Henry's guffaw as he walked toward the inn's entrance to wait for her.

With a deep sigh, Rose looked in the mirror and frowned. She looked tired. Travelling did that to her, and there was nothing that could be done about it. She splashed water on her face and pinched her cheeks. That would at least give her some color. With one last deep breath she stepped out into the hall to rejoin her husband.

Henry smiled at her, and took her arm. If they had been in Silidon, they would have immediately ordered a carriage, but they were not in Silidon, they were in Emriville, and they would take every advantage that offered. They stepped out into the streets and began to walk toward Caleb's house. They could feel eyes on them as they walked down the streets. The occasional person would walk up to them and bow or curtsy, and the couple would reply politely, but they kept walking.

They reached Caleb's house and stopped. "Are you ready to go in?" Henry asked.

"I'm not sure. It has been so long. So many things could have changed. He will be different, but then again, *we* are different too."

Henry sighed. "I didn't think that I would be this nervous. It's odd being nervous. We are the king and queen. People are nervous about meeting us, but do you think they ever realize how terrifying it is to meet them?"

Rose laughed. "That's why we smile and nod, and we do everything in our power to keep things normal. So, as long as you keep smiling, I'll keep smiling."

Together they stepped toward the door. Henry raised his hand and knocked. They waited. The door creaked open, and there stood Caleb before them with a look of astonishment. There was an awkward pause as everyone thought of something to say. "Welcome," murmured Caleb.

Rose laughed. "It is good to see you, Caleb. We have missed you so much. We should have stayed in better contact."

"Well, there is nothing to be done about that now. Please, come in. John said I should be expecting you as soon as you arrived. I must admit that I was quite astounded. I thought you would at least have visited the Monks first. I am honoured that you chose to visit an old friend instead."

They entered the parlour and took their seats. Caleb turned to Henry. "How are you, Your Highness?"

"Call me Henry, Caleb. You have always used my given name, and I will not have it any other way now."

"Very well, Henry," Caleb choked a little on the name but kept going, "how are you?"

"I am very well, Caleb. Life has been very good to us. God has blessed us far beyond what we deserve. I hope you can say the same. How have you been faring here among the ladies?"

Caleb laughed. "Fortunately, the ladies of the church have realized that there are other men available and most have set their eyes on other conquests."

"Most; that means there are still some who are chasing you. Please tell me that Katy isn't one of them!" exclaimed Rose. "I so thought that she had given up on you. No offense, Caleb, but I don't think she could possibly make you happy."

Caleb stiffened. "No offense, Your Highness. Miss Monks is in fact the girl, but I believe she will soon be smitten with the young Joshua Deplin. He has been pursuing her for quite some time now, and I think she is finally starting to take note of him." He didn't look at Rose. He refused to look at Rose.

Rose leaned toward him. "Caleb," she said calmly, "my name is Rose, and I would appreciate it if you would use it. I am no different than before. Perhaps I have grown older, and maybe I have been blessed with a little more wisdom, but that does not change the very essence of the person. I am Rose, and you are Caleb. Let us remember who we are."

Caleb smiled weakly, but he did not look at her. "Very well. I will have to remember that, Rose."

The conversation continued. They talked about the palace, and he talked about the parish. They talked about the various escapades they had been on together, and he talked about working steadily at the church and in the community. They spoke as two persons completely in tune with the other's thoughts. His words were singular and weak. They were together, and he was alone. They had changed. He had changed. And, the entire thing went miserably.

Hours passed. They shared a meal together. Then, it was time to go. Caleb wished them farewell, and watched as they left. They walked together down the road. They leaned their heads toward each other and whispered. They were together. He was alone. He was so alone. Caleb closed the door and walked to his room and lay on his bed.

Rose's words rang in his head. "Let us remember who we are," she had said. He shuddered. He remembered, and who he was made him unworthy of talking with the king and queen. He had called her Rose, and Rose had called him Caleb. He had called him Henry, and Henry had called him friend.

It was so false.

They should be calling him liar. That was what he was. They should be calling him traitor. That was what he had been. They should be calling him evil, pure evil. That was what his essence was. That was what made up his very being. They should be calling him Seth. That was who he was, and that was who he would remain no matter how much he loathed it.

Instead, they called him Caleb. They didn't know. How could they know? He was Caleb. People saw him as Caleb the curate. He was Curate Caleb Taylor. No one needed to know otherwise. He was a good man now, but even the best man was evil. He was depraved, and they should know that about him.

He closed his eyes and groaned. He called out in a whimper to a God who didn't seem to hear him. Don't you see, Lord, he seemed to call. Don't you see how I am trying? I cannot do it. I cannot be all that you want me to be. I am weak. I am empty. Why don't you just let me die? I want to die, Lord Jesus. Why don't you let me die?

There was no answer. There was only pain, but that was normal. He was used to the pain. He closed his eyes. He tried to ignore the dream, but it was there. It whispered in his ear and taunted him. He wasn't truly asleep, but it was still there, telling him to reach out and grasp at what he could never have.

He groaned and rolled onto his stomach. He didn't have the strength to reach for it. There was nothing left in him that would allow him to keep fighting. Perhaps in this way he would die. If he just quit trying. He could lie there, and he would be dead. Then he would be done. He would be cursed to eternal damnation, but at least he would know that there was nothing else he could do about his demise. The thought was tempting.

With a quick rap it beat against his skull demanding him to keep trying. With a low moan he reached out and grabbed at it. Perhaps he would die another day.

"He's different," whispered Henry.

"We knew that we couldn't expect everyone to remain the same," Rose whispered back.

"He looks old, very old." Rose thought about this for a moment, but didn't reply right away. She had noticed the same thing. Caleb had looked awful. The bags under his eyes were dark and worn in. His skin was pale and sickly, and his entire being seemed dead.

"He didn't look at me once. Did you notice that?" she asked.

"Yes. He seemed to be scared to call us by our given names as well. He stuttered every single time. Do you think that we made him that nervous?"

Rose sighed. "Perhaps we did, but I don't know. He didn't seem nervous. At one point I thought he was angry, but then again that doesn't make sense at all. Why would he be angry?"

"I don't know. He is not the same person, but that is a first impression. Perhaps it has just been a long day. We'll see him again soon. It will be different, and we will wonder what all our worrying was about."

"I hope you're right, Henry, because I don't know what I would do if I had to sit through another conversation like that one."

They walked the rest of the way in silence. The night was getting dark when they arrived back at the inn. The dining room was filled with men-at-arms as they took their first break in a long while. Henry greeted each of them by name. Most of them were older than he, but all of them gave him the same respect they had his father.

Sir Eldon Shoals was the eldest of all the men present. He was fifty years old, but didn't look it. He was as strong as ever and could easily defeat any other soldier, younger or older. He came up to the royal couple and bowed. They bowed and curtsied back. "Highness," he said to Henry, "everything is in place. The trunks are in the rooms, and all my comrades have a place to bed down. I think all of them are excited about spending some time away from any trying tasks."

"Very well," replied Henry. "You are free to go about as you please as long as you stay within the vicinity. I know it is a bother, but there are always dangers in travelling, and I will not put the queen at risk." Rose jabbed him in the side, and he smirked. It was unlikely that any man would be able to get past the queen if she had a sword.

Shoals wavered back and forth on the spot. Henry gave him a questioning look. "Sir," Shoals finally began, "please do not think this an impertinence, but I was wondering..."

"What is it Shoals? Speak up."

"Well, I was wondering if it would be wise for the queen and you to walk about without at least one guard. Perhaps it would be best if I accompanied you tomorrow. I would not be in your way; I would just join as an escort—just in case."

Henry looked at the older man and smiled. Shoals was a good soldier, a brigadier general in fact, and he often thought of things that others would not consider. "I think that is a very wise decision. I don't like to think that any harm could come to us in Emriville, but it is always better to take care. Therefore, I will see you tomorrow morning. You are a good man, Shoals."

"Thank you, sir," Shoals replied, beaming. "It has been an honour serving you. You are a good king, just as good as your father, if not better." Henry laughed and waved the older man away. Then, taking his wife's hand, the two of them retired. It had been a long day, and the next one would be even longer.

FIFTEEN

KATY SAT IN THE PARLOUR and waited. It was early, but Rose and Henry were coming today, and she didn't want to be caught in bed. She clamped her hands together and tried to keep them from shaking. She bit her lip and pinched her cheeks hoping the colour would remain there. She stood and began to pace. The sun crept higher in the sky. She sat and began to read a book, but the words made no sense at all. She set it aside.

When the knock on the door sounded, it was so long anticipated that it startled her. She raced to answer it, but it wasn't the king or queen. It was a man she had never met before. He bowed to her, and she curtsied. "Presenting King Henry Arden and his queen, Her Majesty Rose Arden." The man stepped aside, allowing the king and queen to step forward as he disappeared from sight.

Katy felt her jaw drop. They just stood there on her front walk, as handsome as you please, as if it were the most natural thing to do. She tried forcing her mouth to close, but it was nonresponsive. She felt as if she was about to faint. She took hold of the door handle and let it support her. She let out a whimper of surprise. If only Josh were here, she thought. He would know what to do.

Rose looked up at Katy and smiled. Henry let go of her arm, and she quickly stepped toward Katy. "Well Katy," she grinned, "the day is finally here. It is so good to see you." She reached out and embraced the younger girl who wilted against her. Katy quickly collected herself, and Rose couldn't help but laugh. "Honestly Katy! It looks like you have just seen a ghost instead of a long-expected friend."

"Easy for you to say. You're not the one who has to look at an old friend, the new queen. You would be the same way if you were in my shoes." She stopped and looked up at Rose with large, startled eyes. "I didn't mean a word of that!" she cried.

Rose burst out laughing. "You're right," she said between giggles. "Here I have been thinking everything should be just like last time, but to you it is all different. Forgive me, Katy. But please, let's not think about any of that right now. I want you to tell me everything that has happened while I was away, and I don't expect you to be able to summarize an entire two years in one sitting."

The two women moved into the parlour, and Henry followed. He greeted Katy, but soon excused himself to find Mr. Monks. He didn't want to disturb the ladies' conversations. Within minutes they found themselves sitting alone in the room.

Rose took a sip of tea and let out a relaxed sigh. "It really is good to see you, Katy. I didn't realize how much I had missed you until I actually saw you."

Katy smiled. "I missed you as well, but it scared me something awful with you being introduced as you were. Who was that fellow anyway?"

Rose smirked. "That was Sir Eldon Shoals. He is a very faithful, overly protective man-at-arms, but a good man. He wanted to escort Henry and me today, and when he realized that we were just going up to knock, he deemed it necessary to introduce us, and we obliged him. He really is a sweet older fellow, but never tell him I said that, for he would be far too embarrassed."

Katy laughed as she pictured the man at the door as Rose described him. He was definitely older, but sweet was not a word she would have used to describe him. He was far too fierce. "Do you often travel with an escort of fighting men? I can't picture you liking being surrounded all the time."

Rose contemplated this for a moment. "I am never lonely, that's for sure, and if I want to step out of the palace gates, I must have at least one escort with me, and that usually means that I will have three men trailing behind me. But, they are never overwhelming. They are so polite and good. Henry and his father have chosen good men. You should meet them. Perhaps you will find a beau. I know there are at least five eligible young men with us in Emriville, and they are all at the very least a lieutenant."

Katy blushed and turned away. "I don't think that will be necessary. There are plenty of young men available in Emriville, and I am tired of those who are interested in war and such things. We have enough of that in our town."

"Oh yes," said Rose slyly, "I hear there are many young men around now. I have also heard of one particular man who has been pursuing you quite consistently. Is that not true?"

Katy rolled her eyes. "You cannot seriously be considering Josh a real suitor. He is a nice fellow, that is true, but he is so young, and he is only an apprentice, and he doesn't even make enough to support a family. Besides, there is another man that I would much rather wed."

"That's right. I forgot. You still think Curate Caleb Taylor would suit you. I am sorry to have to tell you Katy, but you should give up on the curate. I don't think he will ever realize that there are women in this world. Besides, Josh is a good fellow, and you never know how his lot in life will fall. Perhaps one day he will be rich. No matter the circumstances, of one thing you can be sure. He will always love you. That is one thing that is predictable about him."

Katy sighed. "I don't know if that is so true. I don't think he is pursuing me anymore either. At least, I haven't seen him for about a week now."

Rose laughed. "Why wouldn't he be pursuing you anymore? If a man doesn't see you for a week, it just means that he is busy. There is nothing to fret about in that. There are times when it feels like I don't see Henry for the entire week, but that doesn't mean he has given up on me."

Katy turned away. She felt a blush tinge her cheeks, but she tried to ignore it. There was no use talking about Josh at the moment.

"Katy," Rose whispered. "What happened?"

Katy's eyes welled with tears as she turned to Rose. "I think I have hurt him horribly bad," she whispered.

Rose sighed. "What happened, Katy?" she persisted gently.

Katy shook her head and sighed. "It really was just a mistake. I was angry, and Josh was teasing me about the curate. I just let my tongue take over, and I made a comment about how at least the curate could support a family. I haven't talked with him since."

"I see. I don't think you have to worry about that too much. Josh is a grown man. He will forgive you."

"I don't know, Rose. He was so hurt. You should have seen his face. It was like I had taken a knife and stabbed it right into his heart. I know I shouldn't have said it, but I was so angry."

Rose took Katy's hand and patted it. "Katy, what would it be to you if Josh could never forgive you? Would you really care all that much?"

Katy pulled her hand away from Rose's. "Of course I would care. Josh is my friend. I wouldn't want to have hurt him that much. That would be awful. If things could just go back to normal, it would be okay."

Rose thought for a moment. "Katy, do you think it is possible that you like Josh more than a friend, but you are just unwilling to admit it?"

"No! Josh is a friend, and that is all. He is a friend. Besides, I am going to marry the curate some day. You'll see. It will happen."

Rose sighed, but she didn't push the topic. "Very well. Now, there must be a lighter topic to talk about. How many weddings have you attended since I have been gone?"

Katy scrunched her face as she tried to recall the number, causing Rose to laugh. Smirking back, Katy began to tell the wedding tales and the two of them rambled on and on about life since Rose had left. Time passed, and soon Henry came back with Mr. Monks, and lunch was served. The afternoon was spent outside walking through the town. It didn't take Sir Eldon long to find them, and he kept close behind watching over his superiors until the evening ended and it was time for them to return.

John stepped into the post office and looked around. Miss Mede was standing by the counter as usual, and he took a moment to watch her. She was getting used to his visits, and it seemed as if she was becoming more aware of his presence. "What would you like, Mr. Borden?" she asked without looking up. John smiled to himself and stepped forward.

"Well Miss Mede, I was hoping that you would allow me to escort you home. It has been quite some time since we last walked together, and I was wondering if it would be okay if we walked again." He smiled at her, but she didn't smile back.

She looked up at him with those deep eyes that were always so serious, and he felt his stomach twist as he waited nervously for her response.

"Why are you so interested in walking with me, Mr. Borden?"

John looked down to his feet and stepped back and forth on the spot. "You are an intriguing young lady, Miss Mede. If you are not as of yet spoken for, I would like to, if at all possible, court you."

A crimson flush bloomed across Miss Mede's face. She looked down at the counter top when John looked at her. "I don't think that is possible, Mr. Borden. I am not spoken for, but sometimes, the consequences of the past prevent things in the future. Unfortunately, this is one of those times."

John gave her a confused look, and she tried to avoid his eyes. "I don't understand. What in the past could possibly keep me from courting you?"

"None of that matters," Miss Mede replied pertly. "What does matter is that I am in an entirely different social class than you are. It would be impossible for our two circles to match. Thus, it would be pointless for you to court me."

John smiled. "If this is about social class, it doesn't matter one bit. If you haven't noticed, the king married a lady from one of the lowest of the social circles, and he is in the highest. I am the same way. I could not care less which social circle my wife-to-be came from."

"You may not court me, Mr. Borden. You and I would never form a compatible relationship. It is better that we don't try. That would only cause trouble for you."

"Is there a reason why you are trying to push me off? How bad could it be for me to court you? I will talk with your father tonight, and if he gives his permission, we could go out riding tomorrow. Perhaps the king and queen could come along, or if that does not please you, I could find another escort."

"We will not go out riding, because you will not talk with my father, and even if you did, I have to work. The post office cannot be closed tomorrow. It will be Saturday, and Saturday is the busiest of all days."

"Couldn't someone else watch the post office for you? Surely there are others trained in case you are sick." John was being pushy. He knew it, and he felt bad about it. But, he could not help it. He wanted her to accept. He needed her to accept. He did not understand why she wouldn't accept.

"It is not possible, Mr. Borden, and I would appreciate it if you quit pestering me about it." Miss Mede turned from him and began to busy herself with checking mail slots.

John bit his lip, but he couldn't keep himself from asking one last question. "Is there another person in your life that I should know about?"

Miss Mede turned back to look him in the eye. Her gaze was steady and certain. "No. There never has been, and there never will be."

John decided not to press the point any farther, but he was still determined. "Then, will you allow me to walk you home just this once?"

Miss Mede let out a sigh of frustration. "If I must; but if I discover that you attempt to talk to my father about courting me, I will never speak to you again. Do you understand me?"

John was about to reply when the door opened and Mr. Walters walked in. Mr. Walters stepped toward the counter and tossed down a letter. Miss Mede dropped her head and refused to look up. She accepted the letter and the coin that was tossed on the counter and smiled a polite farewell as Mr. Walters exited the building.

John watched as the man left and looked at Miss Mede. "Is he always that angry-looking?"

"Mr. Walters is an elder in the church. He acts as he sees fit," replied Miss Mede without looking up.

"What does being an elder have to do with anything? He looked as if he had swallowed an entire bottle of cod liver oil."

"Perhaps," replied Miss Mede, and turned toward the back of the post office to deal with the letter. John waited in front. It was almost time for closing. The mail carrier would be coming by soon. Then, he would walk Miss Mede home.

Miss Mede appeared again carrying a bag of letters for the carrier. John took it from her hands and brought it outside to wait while she cleaned up. The carrier took the bag as Miss Mede locked up the building.

They began their walk in silence. The air was warm and blew gently against their faces. It was nice just to be outside. John sighed contentedly and turned to Miss Mede. "Tell me about your family," he said.

"There is not much to tell. I am an only child, and my mother died when I was four years old. I hardly remember her."

"What about your father? Are you close with him?"

"Hardly. I feel as if I barely know him. Tell me about your family, though. I am sure it is much more interesting than mine."

"Perhaps. I am an only child as well, but I grew up with my cousin Rose who most people know better as the queen of Samaya. My mother was a horrendous person. Perhaps that is horrible of me to say, but she was very bitter her entire life. It really is quite a sad thing, actually. She never could forgive her sister for stealing her beau, but that is a story in itself. Anyway, I love her all the same.

"My father was a businessman of sorts. He was always busy doing something, and he had a kind soul. He always saw the best in people.

But, a couple years back he fell ill, and he passed on. I think that was the most tragic day of my life."

"What about your mother? What happened to her?"

John gave her a sad smile. "She went insane, quite literally. After my father died, she thought she had control of all the assets, but when she realized that I did, she lost control of herself, and she has never quite been the same again."

"I'm sorry. That shouldn't happen to anyone."

John looked down at her and smiled his thanks. "It probably shouldn't, but the Lord has blessed me through it. Just look at me now. If my mother hadn't been such a despot, Rose would never have met the prince, I would never have gone to Samaya, and life would not be as it is now. I am now a member of the court. This never would have happened if she had been a loving mother."

"Perhaps not, but I still think that I would want to have a loving mother."

"I don't know. I mean, it would have been nice if my mother could have loved me as she ought to have, but I was never deprived of anything. I am content with the mother I have. I love her, and that is all that matters, I think."

Miss Mede looked up at him with round, unfathomable eyes. "I don't understand you, Mr. Borden. You don't make any sense to me."

"I share your sentiment, Miss Mede. You have me completely bewildered."

"What a pair we make," she laughed. "I think this just emphasizes the fact that we should not associate with each other."

"You may believe that, Miss Mede, but I think this gives us all the more reason to spend more time together. If we speak more, we will understand each other more. The more we understand each other, the better it will be, don't you think?"

"No. Some people are better not to know. I am one of those people, Mr. Borden. It would be better if you did not know me."

"Perhaps, but I would like permission to find that out for myself."

"Don't you think that would be a little bit foolish? If you come to know me, and discover that I am better left alone, then you will have wasted your time when I already told you that I am a person that you would not want to associate with."

"Then allow me to be foolish, at least for a little while."

Miss Mede sighed. "I thought you said that we would not talk about this anymore."

"I don't think so."

"Well, I think it is best that we don't. I am weary of this conversation."

"What would you like to talk about?"

"Perhaps you could tell me what it was like to grow up with the famous Rose Wooden. That would be interesting enough to hear about."

John laughed. "Now you are just avoiding the issue, but I will oblige, just because I love the topic so much." They continued to walk down the road as John told stories about growing up with Rose. He told stories that he hoped would make her laugh, and smiled whenever he succeeded.

The night grew darker, and they came to the spot where they had parted the first time. Miss Mede turned to John and smiled. "You must leave me now," she whispered. John bowed, and without hesitation left her side. Miss Mede sighed as he left, then turned and continued on her way. She was running late, and the chores would not wait any longer.

John walked briskly toward the inn. Two days had passed already since Rose and Henry had arrived, and he hadn't yet seen either of them. He was anxious about seeing them, but he also wanted to spend more time with Miss Mede. There was something more to her story, and he wanted to know what it was.

The night breeze began to stir up. It was no longer warm, and the wind had a bit of an edge to it. He picked up his pace a little. When the inn came in sight, he was tempted to sprint the last few yards but thought better of it. He would arrive soon enough. He blew through the doors and into a group of royal guards. He acknowledged the ones he knew, but he did not stay to chat. He wanted to find Rose.

He walked down the hall. He had planned it out perfectly so that the king and queen would be surrounded by protectors on all sides, but they wouldn't be disturbed. He had also booked his room across the hall from theirs. He knocked on their door and announced himself. It was flung open, and he found himself in Rose's embrace.

"I missed you, John!" she laughed. "You have been gone far too long, and now I expect you to spend some time with me."

John laughed at her. It was so good to see her so happy. He couldn't remember a time before Henry had come into her life that she had been this happy. They were good for each other. Henry had made her happy, and she had made him grounded. John hugged her back and extended his hand to Henry who was standing in the door.

"It is good to see you too, cousin," John said to Rose. "I thought you had totally forgotten about me."

Rose shook her head. "There is no possible way that I could have forgotten about you. If you weren't there, who would have planned my schedule? I would have been entirely lost!" Rose said with mock excitement.

"How have you been, John?" Henry asked.

"Good, good. I've been really good. I think that Emriville is just the place I need to rest for a while. It really is a nice little town. I can see why you chose to stay here, Henry. I would have been easily motivated to stay in a place as pretty as this."

"He had other motivation besides the scenery," Rose said.

"Perhaps John has other motivation besides the scenery as well," stated Henry. The comment made the blush appear before he could do anything about it. John tried to hide it, but it was no use. Rose saw it immediately.

"There is, isn't there?" she exclaimed. "What's her name? We will most likely know her. You must tell us immediately, or I'll duel you over it."

John held up his hands in a sign of truce. "Her name is Miss Elizabeth Mede, and if I find out that you have interrogated her, I'll make sure Josh wins the duel on Tuesday."

Rose scowled. "I wasn't planning on interrogating her," she muttered. Henry kissed her cheek, and she leaned toward him.

"We're happy for you, John," Henry said. "Truly, we are."

John sighed. "Well, there is nothing there yet, so we will just have to wait and see."

Henry laughed. "What man hasn't waited for a woman before? When you marry one, it gets ten times worse!" Rose swatted at him, but he dodged it and kissed her again on the cheek. John took this as his cue to excuse himself. He was tired and hungry. He needed food and sleep, and he preferred to have them before the night was out.

SIXTEEN

CALEB WAITED IN THE PASTURE for Miss Mede. He wanted to tell her the rest of the story. He felt that he needed to tell her the rest of the story. She didn't judge. She just listened. No one had ever just listened before. He liked that about her. He didn't know why she didn't judge, just that she didn't.

He heard her come up behind him, and he turned to look at her. He smiled at her, and she smiled back tentatively. He turned to the grave, and she followed his line of vision. "Can I tell you the rest of the story?" he asked. She nodded.

"If I frighten you, you can ask me to quit, and I will. I won't speak another word of it if you don't want me to."

She looked at him, and he knew she wasn't afraid. "Please, tell the rest of the story," she whispered.

Caleb closed his eyes and pictured where they had left off. He could see it now. Sarah was standing there before him. She had that smile on her face that made him want to smile back. He felt himself letting go. He was no longer Caleb. He was Seth, and the entire world saw him as Seth.

"Sarah's parents were very angry when they found out she was talking to Seth. Her daddy confronted Seth, and told him to leave his little girl alone or he would hunt him down and, well, kill him; '...tear you to pieces,' I believe were his words. But, Seth couldn't leave that girl alone, and she wasn't afraid of him.

"If ever Seth did something wrong, she would confront him and tell him to do right. Most often he would listen to her, and he would do right. People began to think Seth would change. They were less wary of him, but that didn't mean they liked him. They still spat his name and cursed when he was around. He was still the son of a no-good lout.

"One day, Bill upped and told his pa about Sarah. Seth was so angry, and he beat Bill so hard that he didn't wake for a while. That didn't help any. When his pa found out, Seth was told to bring Sarah home."

Caleb looked at Miss Mede with an expression of desperation. "He didn't want to. You have to know that now. He didn't want to bring her home." She nodded, and he closed his eyes again.

"Seth brought Sarah home, and it went bad. It went so horribly bad, and Mark just watched. They took her into a corner, and they disgraced her. First Seth. He was told he had to. He was told that was the only way to prove he was a man. After that, his pa, then Seth again. Mark just sat there with Bill. They just watched. Sarah screamed and they just watched. Mark could have done something, but he didn't. Do you understand why I can't forgive him? He did nothing.

"Anyway, Seth took Sarah back to her parents and left. Her daddy saw him running off and shouted that if he ever caught Seth, he would kill him. And I don't doubt that man's words one bit. I don't know what happened to Sarah. I think she died. I don't think there could have been anyway that she survived.

"Mark stayed at home. A year later, he watched as his pa beat his mom to death, then he left. He joined the army, I think. He found Bill as well when he was on leave a couple years back. Bill told him that Seth was here, so he came to find Seth. He died in the hospital and was buried here. That is the story of his life. There is nothing more, nothing less. He was a coward. He could have done something, and never did. That will be his legacy. The boy who could've but didn't."

He paused. The story was ended, and neither of them knew what to say. "Why do you keep coming to his grave?" Miss Mede asked. "I mean, if he has such a horrible legacy, why would you keep coming here?"

Caleb sighed. "Because, no matter how much I try, I cannot find what he had when he died. I keep thinking that the answer is here at his grave, but I never find it. I try to find it. I dream about it. I grasp at it, but it laughs at me and disappears."

Miss Mede shook her head sadly. "I think I would have liked Mark," she whispered. "He didn't do anything, but what was he supposed to do? Seth made his own choices. Seth could have just as easily stopped what happened."

"You blame Seth entirely, then?" Caleb demanded. She wasn't supposed to judge. She never judged. Why would she judge him now?

"No," she whispered. "Seth did some horrible things, but we all do horrible things. One could just as easily blame his father, or his upbringing, or fate, or chance, or whatever it is that rules this life. Perhaps they could blame God. I don't know, but I don't think that they can blame Mark. He was young. He didn't know what to do. He couldn't know what to do."

Caleb felt himself relax. She wasn't judging him. He looked at her carefully. "Do I frighten you, Miss Mede?" he asked.

She looked back steadily. "Not one bit, Seth," she whispered.

Caleb stepped back, turned, and began to run. Miss Mede watched him run in shock. She hadn't meant it. She wasn't going to say anything, but then for just one moment, she had thought perhaps he was Seth. But she didn't think she would actually voice it. She felt weak in the knees. She wasn't frightened, but she didn't know what to do. She stumbled toward the post office. She had work to do.

She fumbled with the key in the door and nearly fell in. She made it around the counter and rested her head on top of it. She inhaled deeply and tried to calm herself. He would never come back. Of that she was sure. There was no way he would come back. He would be long gone by now. Surprisingly, the thought of this made her sad. She wanted to speak with him. She needed to speak with him.

The door creaked open and John walked in. She tried to fight back a groan. He wasn't supposed to be here. He never came in the morning. Why did he have to come this morning of all mornings? She tried to make herself appear busy, but her motions were jerky and unsteady. She could feel his eyes on her. She tried to ignore him, but she could not.

"May I help you, Mr. Borden?" she whispered. She didn't mean to whisper, but there was nothing she could do about it.

"Are you alright?" he asked. There was a splat outside, and Elizabeth ignored him as she raced to see if she could undo the damage she feared had occurred. It was no use. The letter bag sat in a puddle of mud that was quickly seeping through the threadbare haversack. She picked up the bag with a moan and tried to wipe the mud off, but it just got on her dress and all over her hands.

John took the bag from her and nearly dragged her inside. She snatched the bag back from his grasp and took it behind the counter. John tried to follow, but she refused to let him into her territory. He stepped back and allowed her her space. She tore open the bag and looked in. A soft whimper escaped her lips as she saw all the ruined letters.

"Can I help you, Miss Mede?" John asked.

"Get out," she whispered hoarsely.

"What happened, Elizabeth?" John didn't think it was time for formalities. He was sick of formalities. "Please, tell me what happened."

She looked up at him angrily. "What happened is idle hands, Mr. Borden. Do you know what idle hands bring? Devil's handiwork: that is what they bring. And now, I will pay for it. So, if you will leave me, I will enjoy the misery of it."

"I don't think I should leave. I would like to stay and help you."

"Get out, Mr. Borden," Elizabeth stated calmly. "Get out before I call the authorities. There are plenty of people to help me right now, and I will not be afraid of calling on them."

John looked at her with a hurt expression, but there was nothing he could do. He ducked his head and walked out of the post office. It didn't matter what he wanted. She wanted him out, and he would listen to her.

Elizabeth heard the door bang shut. She closed her eyes and let the tears fall. The letters were ruined. There was no way around that. Mr. Walters would be angry. She would lose her job. She wiped at her tears. She would not let them see her being weak while they did it to her.

With as much dignity as she could muster, Elizabeth looked into the sack and took out the letters one at a time. She cleaned them off as best as she could, and began to sort them. Mr. Walters came in. He took one look at his letters and, looking her in the eye for the first time in his life, dismissed her. With a quick nod of assent, Elizabeth dropped the bag onto the floor and left the post office. For the first time in ten years, the post office was closed on a weekday.

As soon as Elizabeth was out of the town's view, she let the tears flow freely. They were silent tears. There was no use in wailing like a madwoman. No one would listen anyway. She would only strain her voice. She thought of all the work she had done at the post office, and the time it had taken to do it. She thought of the stipend that she had earned to pay for necessities. It was all lost.

Her father was sleeping when she came home. He was barely living anymore. Sometimes she wished he would just die. If he were dead, she would be free of this place, and she would leave it all behind. These thoughts never lasted. He was a good man. He had done much for her. She would do whatever she could in return for that, even if it meant nursing him until he died.

Elizabeth looked around the house. It was a mess. She hadn't had time to clean lately. She began to work. She had all day to do it now, and there was no use keeping her hands idle. She shuddered at the thought of it. When the house was clean, she could move onto the barn, then back to the house, then perhaps the yard. There would be work to do. She would keep herself busy.

In the mornings she would go to the grave. There was nothing keeping her from that now. She could stay as long as she liked. She wouldn't be able to share that time with Caleb anymore. She stopped her thought. It wasn't Caleb. It was Seth. He was Seth.

She could read the letters now. Seth wouldn't care. Why would he care if she read the letters? What more could they say than what she already knew? Maybe they would say more about Sarah, or maybe they would hold death threats or something like that. She didn't care. She would find out.

The tears kept coming for the rest of the day, but by evening's light, she was done with them. There was nothing left to cry about, and she had nothing left in her to give. She would make it through. She didn't know how, but she would make it, and fie on anyone who said she couldn't.

John was miserable. Elizabeth was angry with him, and there was nothing he could do about it. He didn't even know what he had done wrong. He went over in his mind all that had transpired between them, but he couldn't think of anything that would have been so offensive. He considered going back to the post office, but decided to leave her in peace. There was no use pressing her. Besides, he still needed to figure out what she meant by devil's handiwork.

He let out a sigh of frustration and went in search of Rose and Henry. They were supposed to meet with Mrs. Jennings today, and he wanted to be the one to tag along. There was nothing else for him to do, and it wasn't like he would be in the way. He would play with the children while the 'grown-ups' talked.

Rose and Henry were just setting out when he found them. Sir Eldon was following them, so John relieved him. There was no need for both of them to be there, and there were plenty of useful things Shoals could probably think of doing.

When they reached the orphanage, Rose invited John to join them, but he declined. She gave him a sad sort of look but let him be. He went in search of the children. They weren't that hard to find. There were only a few of them, but children always know how to make noise when they want to. John sat and watched them while they played.

He recognized Lisa, the little girl from before, but he had never met any of the others. One of the boys looked over at him and stuck out his tongue. John stuck out his tongue back, and the boy scurried away in fright. Lisa giggled and walked over. She stuck her tongue out at John, but he didn't respond.

Lisa gave him a frustrated look, then, balling up her fists, she pushed them into either side of his face. John allowed his tongue to pop out and couldn't help but laugh at the little girl's amusement. Soon, the two of them were entertaining each other with hand gestures and childish games. The time passed and before he knew it, the door was creaking open behind him, and Rose was peeking in.

"Are you okay, John?" she asked.

"Perfectly fine." There was a noise from outside the room and Rose disappeared. Henry took her place. He stepped through the door and sat down beside John. Lisa snuggled up against John's chest, closed her eyes, and promptly fell asleep. Henry smiled at her, and for a while the two men were just content to sit.

"Are you okay, John?" Henry asked.

John sighed. "I'm fine."

"Are you really? Because if you aren't, I would like to know. You are my friend, and I don't want to leave you sitting alone."

John groaned. "Did you have any trouble when you were first courting Rose? I mean, did she ever yell at you or tell you to get out?"

Henry laughed. "Is that what this is about?"

John gave him a look and Henry sobered.

"Well, I would have to say that Rose was a master at throwing me out. When I first met her, she accused me of being a liar and said she didn't trust me. Of course, she had every right to say those things. Then, when I first started pursuing her, she dressed so severely, and was so cold, you could have picked ice off of her, though I don't think she will admit that to anyone."

There was silence for a moment as Henry considered his next words. "If that doesn't convince you, you can also consider the time she held a sword to my throat." Henry didn't say anything more. Nothing more was needed.

John looked at Henry. "Have you ever forgiven yourself for that night?" John had never asked this question before, but he was incredibly curious.

Henry sighed. "At first I thought I never would be able to. When I saw Rose's scar for the first time, I about vomited, I was so disgusted with myself. But lately, slowly but surely, I have realized that if God has forgiven me, then I must also forgive myself. Besides, I know Rose doesn't hold it against me, and she will only feel horrible if she thinks that I hold it against myself."

John nodded. "That makes sense. Would you have been able to forgive yourself if she had died?"

Henry gritted his teeth and John felt bad for asking, but he wanted to know the answer.

"I think, that if Rose had died, God would have given me the grace I needed to forgive myself. I don't know how he would have, but I know that he is good and all powerful, and somehow that would have sufficed."

"Thank you, Henry. You were very honest, and I didn't deserve that. I know I pried a little in something that wasn't even my business. You are a good man, and a good king."

Henry laughed. "You should wait before you make assumptions, cousin. For all you know, I could be a horrible king. I just haven't been tried yet. Wait and see. I have a lot to live up to in my father."

John shook his head. "No, I don't assume. I know you are a good king. Even if you are not tried, any man can see that you are good. It is your character that proves you. If your character were different, I would not have said you are a good king, but it isn't. You are a good king, Henry. Don't let anyone tell you otherwise."

John reached out and shook Henry's hand as the door creaked open. Mrs. Jennings and Rose walked in and looked down at the men. "Now would you look at that," said Mrs. Jennings. She pointed to Lisa who lay sleeping against John. "Perhaps you will have one of your own soon, Rose," she said.

Rose felt herself blush, and she turned toward Henry who just laughed. "Soon," he said out loud, and Rose thought she might perish from the embarrassment.

"I think that it is time we are going now, Mrs. Jennings. It was so good to see you again. I have missed you terribly, but there are other people we must meet with today." The two women embraced. "We'll meet again soon," Rose promised.

Henry stood and helped John to his feet. John handed the sleeping girl to Mrs. Jennings, who whispered her farewells as she walked away to put the child in a bed. Rose smiled after her and turned to leave. Henry squeezed her hand gently. She looked up at him and smiled. He winked down at her, and she couldn't help but giggle a little. John rolled his eyes at the two of them, which only made them laugh more.

They tried to compose themselves, but it wasn't until they were halfway back to the inn that they finally gained control of their emotions. It didn't matter. They were young, and they were enjoying life. It was a blessing God had given them, and they would enjoy it as much as possible.

Seth was running again. Why he always ended up running, he didn't know. He thought of her face. It had been a face of horror. She hated him. She loathed him. He couldn't go back. By now half the town would know. There was no way he could go back. They would hang him. He would sway back and forth, back and forth.

He shuddered at the thought of the noose. It terrified him. It was a curse, and he would not die under the curse. He refused to die under the curse. He knew what a hanging looked like. He had seen one once when he was younger. His father had brought him two counties over to watch it. His father had told him that was what they did with the weak criminals, the ones who allowed the law to take them.

Seth could still picture the bloated blue body. The head had lolled to the side. Its tongue had stuck out blue and swollen. The corpse's eyes had bulged from their sockets. It had been repulsive, detestable. The man who hung was under the curse. He had known it then. He knew it even more now.

Seth didn't know where he would run to. There was no way God would forgive him after he ran away from being a minister. He was running out on his flock without notice. That was evil, and God would add that to his side of the scale. There was no way of beating that side of the scale. Why did he even bother?

Other people perhaps could beat that side of the scale, but not him. He was Seth Hepton after all, and all Heptons were vile people. No, that was a lie. All Heptons were a vile people except for Mark. Mark had been good. Seth knew that now. That was what made Mark different. Mark's side of the scale had been heavier than God's. How he had done that, Seth didn't know, but Mark was good.

The wind began to blow with chilling gusts, and Seth wondered what to do. He couldn't go back. Or, could he? What would Miss Mede have told the town? *Caleb Taylor isn't Caleb Taylor.* Who would believe her? Who would know anything about Seth? No one would know the truth. It would be her word against his. He could go back. He would be safe.

He felt his feet stumble to a stop. There was no need to run. What was he even running from? Miss Mede hadn't been scared. And, hadn't she promised not to tell? That first time they had spoken. She had promised, hadn't she?

Seth was trembling. He didn't like trembling, but it was okay for now. He turned around. He was a long way from Emriville. He had been running for a long time. He was hungry. Slowly, he started walking back. He was limping. His muscles were seizing up, but he kept walking. He needed to make it back before dark, and that didn't leave him much time. He would get back, though. He must.

SEVENTEEN

WHEN ROSE AND HENRY MET with Josh, it was simple. There was no need for formalities, and the conversation flowed easily. Josh hadn't wanted to visit in his house because of the cramped conditions, so they decided to take a walk, to visit the pasture. John tagged along.

The pasture was in full bloom. Spring flowers displayed their colours for all to see, and the sky was clear of clouds. Rose fanned herself gently with her hand as the heat began to get to her. Henry led her over to the rock in the middle of the pasture, and she took a seat. Pulling out his sword, Henry smirked at Rose and turned on Josh. "Now Josh," he boomed, "what say you we show the fair damsel how men fight?"

Rose laughed and retorted, "Give me a sword, and I will put you boys to shame even with these clumsy skirts."

Henry laughed. "I think a challenge has been posed, Josh. What do you think?"

Josh gave the queen a look from head to toe that made her blush, and replied, "I definitely think that she has us beat in that dress. I don't know about you, but silk just doesn't match my figure."

Henry wacked at Josh playfully with his sword. "That is my wife you speak of so brazenly, man. I should have your head for that."

Josh drew his sword and prepared himself. "Then fight for her honour like a real man. Unless you are afraid. It would then be a pleasure to lay my head out on that rock over there as you decapitated me."

Henry laughed, and the two went at it. Rose allowed herself to study her husband. He did move much better than when they had first met, and it was nearly impossible for her to beat him now. She was getting much too slow. It didn't matter now. Though she found the sport amusing, there were many other things that now occupied her time.

"I say the victor receives a kiss!" Rose heard Josh exclaim.

"Are you so sure of your skills, young man?" asked Henry. "A prize such as that is sure to motivate me tenfold. I will definitely overpower you now!" True to his word, Henry feinted right, and quickly disarmed the young man who could only gape as his sword went flying. Rose let out a cheer as Henry bowed.

"Now, I believe I get to claim my prize," said Henry as he sauntered over toward Rose. He stooped down over her and, placing his hand behind her head, pressed his lips to hers. A throat cleared behind them, and the two quickly separated. Rose could feel the blush on her cheeks, but Henry only grinned. He gave her a wink, and her blush deepened.

"Bother," grumbled Josh. "I'll win next time. Just wait and see. I was simply being easy on you because it is polite, you know. You wouldn't want to humiliate those in authority over you."

John snorted and yanked Josh down onto the grass where he was sitting. "Learn to know when to keep your mouth shut. Now when you are beat next time, you will only look like more of a fool," he said.

Josh gasped in mock offense. "Sir John, you don't honestly think that I am so easily beat, do you?"

John gave the boy a quick once-over and smirked. "I bet that Rose will beat you this evening when the two of you duel."

"How much?" Josh asked with a smirk.

John thought for a bit and then smiled. "Since you are so fond of kissing, I suggest that the loser must kiss old widow Needler." Josh's face contorted into a look of disgust as a shudder travelled down his spine.

"Uh-uh," cut in Rose. "There will be no betting. I will not have one of you going up and kissing a poor unsuspecting old lady. That would be horrendous."

"I know what you mean," muttered Josh.

Rose glared at him. "I didn't mean it would be horrendous for you. I meant it would be awful for that old lady. She would probably die of shock on the spot. I will not have that hanging over me. If you must kiss something, go kiss a pig or toad or some such animal."

"The Kriddens have a dog," said Josh happily.

"I hardly think a dog makes much of a bet," replied John.

Josh grinned wickedly. "When you see this dog, it will be a bet."

Rose groaned softly to herself, but Henry squeezed her hand. She smirked back. She could picture the Kriddens' dog clearly in her mind. The beast was as despicable as a large rat and as treacherous as a mother bear protecting her cubs. She only pitied the fool that would have to try and kiss the animal.

The rest of the afternoon passed by slowly. There was nothing that needed to be done, and it was relaxing to walk out in the sun. They left the pasture as the sun began to set and decided on a time to meet later on that night. Josh went on home, and the other three walked back to the inn.

As they passed the post office, John suddenly stopped and raced toward the door. He grabbed a sheet that was posted on the door and moaned. Reading it through once more, he tacked it back up on the door and walked toward Henry and Rose who were now waiting for him.

"Is something wrong?" Rose asked, concerned.

"They are looking for someone to work at the post office."

Henry and Rose looked at each other, not sure what the importance of this was.

"Is there a problem with that?" Henry asked.

John looked at him as if he had a dunce cap on his head. "There is only one job at the post office, and the last time I checked it was already filled. If they are looking for a new worker, that means something must have happened to the last employee."

Understanding dawned on the royal couple's faces. "You are thinking of Miss Mede, are you not?" Henry asked. John nodded, but didn't look up. "Cheer up, John. You never know what could have happened. Perhaps Miss Mede decided that the job was no longer to her liking. She may very well have resigned."

John shook his head. "She wouldn't have quit. She liked her job. There is no possible way that she could have quit."

Henry tried to think of something comforting to say, but was at a loss. "Perhaps you should go visit Miss Mede tomorrow. There is no harm in checking in on a friend to make sure that everything is okay."

John tried to smile. "How long has it been since you have seen the young lady?" Henry asked.

"A couple of days. She sent me out of the post office the last time I visited, so I wanted to give her some time to forgive me for whatever I had done. I was planning on goingthere again tomorrow."

"Well, you shall certainly visit her again tomorrow. It just won't be at the post office," said Rose cheerily, and they continued on their way.

Josh was at the pasture early. He was already warming up when John, Rose and Henry arrived. Rose was dressed in a pair of inexpressibles and was much more comfortable than she had been when covered in lace. She donned her mask, and then, drawing her sword, she began to rotate her shoulders.

"Do you think you can beat him?" Henry whispered in her ear.

Rose shrugged her shoulders. "Perhaps. I think I will be relying more on speed than power. Josh has become a brute while we were away. He is no longer a boy. That is for sure."

Henry kissed her gently on the top of her head. "You will do fine," he whispered. "You are still very talented, and even if he wins, I won't regret seeing John kiss the Kriddens' dog." Rose laughed.

"Are you going to stand there all night, or are we going to fight!" Josh called.

"Are you so anxious to be beat once more!" shouted Rose, but she stepped out of Henry's embrace and moved toward Josh. The two held up their swords, and the duel began.

It was like old times. Rose felt herself fall into the familiar rhythm of the steps. She clashed swords with Josh and then would draw back. He was stronger than she had thought, and after some time had passed, she could feel her strength waning. Instead of allowing full frontal attacks, she started to fight more defensively, only meeting Josh's sword when absolutely necessary.

The fight went on, neither of them getting a lead, and neither of them wanting to give up. Josh pushed harder, and Rose knew she could not hold out much longer. She saw an opening, and she went for it. With a quick feint and a lunge, she took Josh by surprise and sent his sword flying. He let out a slight groan then slumped to the ground. John let out a hoot of laughter.

Rose heard none of this. She felt a bit dizzy. Leaning down and placing her hands on her knees, she began to pant. Henry was by her side almost immediately. Taking her mask from her face, he looked her over carefully. "Are you alright?" he asked.

Rose smiled weakly at him. "Just a bit winded, I think," she said, and stood up straight. Henry didn't feel comfortable with that answer.

He placed his arm around her waist and allowed her to place most of her weight on him.

Josh looked up from his slumped position on the ground. "Is everything alright?"

"Fine, fine," Rose assured him. Henry cut her off.

"I think this is all the fighting that will take place tonight. At least, Rose and I will be retiring, but if you two want to continue, you may."

"I think my pride has been wounded enough for one day," grumbled Josh. "I will retire as well, I think." He looked over at Rose nervously, and she tried to smile reassuringly. It came out more as a grimace.

The group separated, and they each made their way to their respective places. Back at the inn, Henry tucked Rose into bed and watched as she fell fast asleep within minutes. That was abnormal, and he felt himself become a bit nervous over the fact, though he tried to ignore it. It had been a long week. Perhaps it was just as Rose said. Perhaps she was just a little winded.

John was up early. He wanted to visit Miss Mede, and he didn't have the patience to wait. He dressed in anything informal he could find, and began walking in the direction he had gone with Miss Mede only twice before. He didn't know exactly where he was going. He only knew up to a point beyond which he had never gone. Now John wondered where he would have to go once he reached that point.

Not knowing, John decided to just keep walking in the most logical direction. He followed the road away from the town and deeper into the woods. He continued to walk as the trees thinned out, and up ahead, all he could see was field. Not far down, he saw a house. He did not know whom the house belonged to, but he decided to knock and find out.

He walked up the lane and down the path to the front door. The outside of the house was falling to pieces. There were cracks in the wood where it had begun to rot away, and the ceiling sagged at one end. The door creaked back and forth in the slight breeze, and John began to wonder if the house was even inhabited.

He knocked. The door creaked open, but there was no response. He called out, but there was no reply. Curiosity got the best of him. He stepped over the threshold and moved farther into the house. It was obvious that someone occupied the place because it was well swept and cleaned on the inside.

John moved farther in and tried to distinguish who the occupants might be. He heard a cough from an attached room. He followed the sound. Looking into a room, he saw an old man lying as if dead on a mat on the floor. Every now and then a moan would escape past the man's lips, but no one would respond. John went to move in closer when a door opened somewhere else.

"I am back, Papa," a voice said. "The cow has given us our break-fast this morning. Oh, I hear you. I'll be there in just a moment." John looked around for a place to hide. He stepped into the next room. He felt himself blush when he entered it, because it was very obviously a woman's room. He shouldn't be in it, but he had nowhere else to go.

He heard the murmur of voices in the next room and, finding a crack in the wall, he looked through. Miss Mede sat by her father, soothing his moaning. She held him gently in her arms and, when he was calmed, poured some milk down his throat. *Milk? Was that all she had?* John watched to see what she would do next.

When her father would drink no more, Elizabeth laid him gently down on the mat and took the bowl away. John crept behind her as she made her way toward the kitchen. There really was no place for him to hide, so he tried to make himself inconspicuous. Elizabeth didn't notice him. She began looking through the kitchen for something to eat. There was nothing.

John could see the sunken look of her cheeks as she drank the remainder of the milk. He could feel his stomach gurgling in contempt at the thought of someone going without food. With a sigh, Elizabeth looked around the kitchen. Slowly, she turned and left the building. Where she went, John didn't know. As soon as she was out of sight, John left the house and went back to town. He had a lot on his mind.

The job at the post office had obviously been supporting Elizabeth and her father, and now they did not have that income to sustain them. Knowing the type of pay she was getting, she was most likely just making enough to buy the food that they would need, and knowing the season, they were most likely out of any canned goods.

John clenched his fists as he thought of the look on her face as she bent over her father and tried to sooth his moaning. It was evident that the man was dying. Then where would Elizabeth be? She would need someone to look after her, though she was already doing that for herself. She needed a man in her life. She needed a husband.

John wiped his hand roughly across his face and tried to gain control over his emotions as he re-entered the town. There were so many things that he needed to accomplish, and that wouldn't happen if he couldn't keep himself in check. Taking a deep breath, he walked toward the most important place first.

The mercantile had all the basic necessities. He bought flour, sugar, yeast, and ground oats. He then went from one stall to the next finding eggs, meat, and anything he could think of that a cupboard might need. The final thing on his list was a basket that would fit it all. Then, taking the basket, he began to walk.

The walk did not take near as long as the one in the morning. John was sure of his destination, and his task weighed heavily on his mind. He wanted to deliver the food. He wanted to make sure that Elizabeth's sunken cheeks would again be rosy. He quickened his pace.

When the house was in sight, he held back a little. He didn't want to be seen. Elizabeth hadn't wanted him to know about her family, and he had broken that rule. He would try to make that up to her by not letting her know that he knew. Perhaps his logic was backward, but it seemed to make sense to him, and so he moved toward the house with caution.

When he was sure the area was clear, he creaked the door open, stepped toward the kitchen, and set the basket on the table. There was no one around, but he moved quickly regardless. When he was out of the house, he ran toward the woods. Elizabeth would find the basket, and she would have food for now. He would come again in the morning with something else.

John walked back to town. He felt he needed to do something. There had to be something he could do. He tried to think, but nothing came to mind. He allowed his shoulders to slump and his feet to drag. Perhaps he would come up with something later on in the day.

Seth sat in his room and shook. He quivered from head to toe, but he couldn't control himself. He was dreaming, and *it* was taunting him, only it was different than normal. He tried to fight it off, but it screamed at him. He was hiding, and it didn't want him to do that. It wanted him out in the open. It wanted him to go back to the grave.

"No, no," moaned Seth. He covered his ears and sobbed. "Go away," he whined. "Just go away." It didn't want to listen. He grabbed his legs to his chest and began to rock.

So, she knows your story, does she? So what! It yelled. *You're a coward, a lily-livered coward. I shouldn't waste my time with you. Go die in a corner. I don't care. Just, die!*

Seth began to hit at his ears, but the noise wouldn't leave his head. It kept talking to him. It kept yelling at him. He tried to scream over top of it, but it just gave him more of a headache. The voice was inside his head, and it couldn't be drowned out. He had to listen. He was forced to listen.

Go to the grave, unless you are scared to go. It takes a man to actually go to the grave. But, you aren't a man, are you? You never were a man. Just look at how you handled Sarah. You gave her up. You beastly little coward! You couldn't handle her, could you? That is why you let her go. You couldn't handle a wee little girl.

"I didn't want her to die," Seth replied. "She would have died if I didn't let her go."

212

But she died anyway, didn't she, and it is all Mark's fault. Go to the grave and see what happened to him. He's dead, and you are alive. Go to the grave and see what happened to weak little Mark. He wasn't good for anything, was he?

"No, no he wasn't good for anything. I'll go. I'll see. I'll see the grave. I'll see that he wasn't good for anything at all. But, I don't want to see her. She knows too much. She knows much too much."

It growled at him, but he didn't care. Seth was going to the grave again, and he felt much better about it. He would see Mark. He would see what had happened to Mark, and know that he was better off.

It let out a wild scream that tore through Seth's head. Seth felt the pain and began to moan. He grabbed his head and fell to the ground. "No, no," he whimpered. Then all went silent. There was no more voice in his head. The dream was over.

Seth woke with a start. Exhaustion coursed through his veins. His eyes sagged, and he tried to keep them open, but they wouldn't listen to him. His body was curled up against the wooden walls of the corner of his room. Picking himself up, he stumbled toward his bed. Falling on top of his covers, all was lost to unconsciousness.

Seth did not dream. There was nothing more to dream about. It had visited him already and had gotten its way. It did not need to visit him again that evening.

Seth no longer yearned for it. His dream had shown him what it was really like, and though he thought it was what Mark had had, it wasn't. This only made him angry. What could it have been that Mark had? He didn't think he could find Mark's *it* at his grave, but he had no choice but to go. He feared what would happen if he didn't go.

For now, though, he slept. He slept deep and long. When he woke in the morning, he was not rested. He could feel the bags under his eyes, and he wondered why they lasted. He felt his feet drag heavily as he went about his daily tasks. The only explanation he could come up with was that God's side of the scale seemed to be weighing heavier with each day, and the burden of it was resting on his shoulders. But, this didn't make any sense, so Seth went about the rest of his day and decided to go to bed early. Perhaps that would get the rest of the sleep out of his eyes.

EIGHTEEN

ELIZABETH SCOWLED AT THE BASKET on the table. It was the second she had received, and she didn't like it. It was charity, and she hated charity. She set it next to the first one and tried to ignore the sweet honey scent coming from it. Her stomach growled, but she pretended it hadn't. Her father started coughing in the next room. She raced to his side.

He was getting worse. It would only be a few days, or maybe a few weeks, and he would be gone. She had no doubts about that. When he was gone, she would sell the land and the cow, and she would move. She would move as far away as she could. She would find a job in some far-off city and support herself. Perhaps she would get a job as a servant in some fancy house. It wasn't like she was afraid of work.

Her father was resting again. Elizabeth had dug in the first basket to find food for him, but she refused to take some for herself. Perhaps it was pride, but it was her own fault that she had lost her job at the post office, and she would not allow others to support her when she could have supported herself.

She left the room and went outside to work at some chores. There was only so much that could be done. Everything was easily kept now that she wasn't required to leave the farm all day. It was spring though, and she now had time to plant a garden. She didn't know if she would be there to reap the reward of it, but perhaps a garden would bring a better price to the land.

Finding a patch of earth, Elizabeth looked it up and down. It needed to be hoed and broken up. That would take much of her time. She looked in the barn for some tools, then went at the ground with a vengeance. It felt good to work. She hacked at the grass and weeds and shook them out so that only dark brown soil remained.

The sun made its way higher in the sky. Elizabeth continued to hoe the ground. Her muscles began to ache, but the work was such a wonderful distraction, she didn't want to stop. She pushed herself harder and harder. The sun switched directions. It grew darker.

Elizabeth dropped the hoe on the ground and looked around her. The patch had transformed into a large garden with plenty of room for many different types of vegetables. Elizabeth looked down at her hands. Blisters had formed, and they were beginning to smart from all the dirt that had clogged them up.

She dropped her hands to her side and walked back toward the house. She would get cleaned up, and then she would have to do the chores. There were things that needed to be done. She walked into her room and saw the two letters addressed to Seth. She smirked. There was no need to read the letters now. Perhaps she would, though. Perhaps she would just take a peek to see what they said.

She stopped herself. There was work to be done. The letters would have to wait.

Seth walked into the pasture. She was standing at the far end by the grave. He stopped. He didn't want to go further. If he went further, she would see him, but if he didn't go further, it might be angry with him. He stumbled forward, fearing it was his only choice.

Elizabeth turned and looked at him curiously. He waited for her to say something, but she chose not to. Instead, she turned back to the grave and just waited.

Seth tried to calm himself, but his heart pounded in his ears, making his entire head throb. He pulled himself up straight, but it didn't stop the trembling in his hands. He had dressed properly, but he still felt ruffled and unkempt.

He pushed the thought out of his head and looked at Elizabeth. "Are you afraid of me?" he asked in as clear a voice as he could muster, though it sounded as if he was talking around a mouthful of sawdust.

Elizabeth stared at him. "No," she said and turned back to the grave.

"Why not?" Seth asked incredulously.

Elizabeth sighed deeply. "Because," she whispered, "if you were such a bad person, why haven't you done something like that again? Why didn't you kill Sarah, for that matter? No, I really don't think there is anything to fear in you. You are different now than you were back then."

Silence fell. Seth wasn't sure what to say. It didn't seem to make any sense that she wasn't afraid. "Are you sure that you aren't afraid of me?"

Elizabeth laughed. "Seth, there are things far more terrifying in life than you. You are a man. What can you do to me? Kill me? Fine. I will die then. In a way, death would be a welcome relief."

Seth slumped his shoulders and allowed himself to relax. Nothing had changed. Everything was just as it was before. "I know what you mean. Death would definitely be a relief."

"Why do you say that? You have so much to live for. You have a church, a congregation. You have people who love you, and you have a chance to be someone. What good would death do you?"

"You are mixing me up with Caleb. When I am Caleb, I can be whatever I want to be, but I'm not Caleb. Oh, how I long to be Caleb, but even you could see through that. I am a fraud. You know that, I know that, it knows that, and soon everyone in the congregation will know that."

"Are you going to tell them?"

"No," sighed Seth. "I couldn't do that. That would be stupidity there. I may want to die, but I don't think that I want to do it at the hands of an angry mob. Besides, no matter how much I want to die, I cannot before I find it."

Seth stopped, and Elizabeth tried to figure out what *it* was.

"You know, I tried to take my life once; more than once, actually. Each time, I came so close. I was mere seconds away from my death, but something stopped me. I thought it was the thing from my dreams, but, truthfully, that thing is something totally different. That thing is terrifying. Something else is keeping me from dying, and I can't die until I find out what this thing is."

"What is *it*?" asked Elizabeth. "You keep referring to *it*, but you never say what *it* really is."

Seth shuddered. "It is terrifying. It haunts my sleep, tormenting me and laughing at me. It told me I had to go to the grave to see what happened to Mark the coward. So I came as it told me to, but I don't know why it wanted me to come. There really is nothing good or horrible about this place. It is just a place after all."

"So, *it* is a ghost?"

Seth shook his head. "I don't think so. It has to be something else. I don't think it is a ghost or anything like that. I just don't know, though. I have no idea."

Elizabeth nodded and turned back to the grave. "I have nightmares sometimes as well," she whispered. "In them, something laughs at me and forces me to do things I don't want to do. Most of the time, this thing comes to me in the form of the wind. Does your *it* come to you as the wind?"

"No," whispered Seth. "It has always just been *it*. It has never come as the wind or anything really, just a voice."

Elizabeth sighed, and everything went quiet.

"When did you start dreaming?" Seth asked.

Elizabeth gave a half-hearted smile. "When my mother died. I was four then."

"What happened to your mother?"

Elizabeth looked at him reluctantly. "You don't know?"

"No."

Elizabeth laughed. "And here I was thinking that everyone in town knew the horrid story of poor little Miss Mede." She shook her head. "I guess I owe you my story, though. You did tell me yours."

"You don't have to. I don't need to know if you don't want me to know. Besides, I never told you my story. I told Mark's story."

Elizabeth gave him a look of gratitude that soon faded. "My name is Elizabeth Mede, though the name Mede was given to me as a pittance, I guess you could say. I am twenty-three years old. This of course probably matters little to you, but it is important if I am to tell you my story."

Elizabeth looked off into the distance and sighed. "I don't know exactly where to start, but perhaps the best place would be even farther back than my age. So, I will begin twenty-six years ago, when Miss Tanya Genaux met Mr. Gerald Mede. Perhaps it could be described as love at first sight, I am not sure exactly, but months later they were wed. He was thirty-three. She was seventeen."

Seth looked at the rising sun. "Perhaps you should tell me the rest of the story later. It is getting to be morning, and they will need you at the post office."

"I no longer have a job at the post office. But you probably have not been to the post office to notice. I believe a Mr. Hectors has taken my position. So, if you please, I will finish my story, or I may never get out with it all."

"Okay," Seth replied, and found a comfortable seat on the ground. He didn't have anywhere to go.

"The couple spent a year in marital bliss which was soon ended. There were skirmishes along the border, and Gerald was forced to leave his bride to fight. He was gone for a long time, and Tanya began to get lonely. She could no longer remember his laugh or his smile or anything else like that. So, when a tall, handsome stranger passed through town one month, she became infatuated with him.

"They tried to keep it from the town, but when Gerald returned nearly two years after being sent away, he found his wife just beginning to show. The entire town was in an uproar. What should they do with such a lady? Many people gave her dirty looks and spat on her as she passed in the streets. Some called her names, but everyone condemned her.

"Gerald did not want to believe it. He reminded the town that he had had some leave time, and the child could have been conceived then. This split the town. No one knew for sure what to believe." Elizabeth was cut off by the sound of feet tramping through the woods behind them.

Seth looked at her with pleading eyes. "I must go now. You see the necessity don't you? I am Caleb. Perhaps I have a chance yet."

"Alright, Caleb, go," Elizabeth whispered. He smiled weakly and raced off into the bushes. Elizabeth sighed as he disappeared. What would he say when he knew the rest of her story? Perhaps then he would understand why she didn't fear him. She turned to leave.

John stood at the far end of the pasture looking at her. He walked toward her, and she tried to hide her frustration. "Good morning, Miss Mede. I must say that I am surprised to see you out here this early in the morning."

She smiled at him. "It is a good morning, and it would be useless to waste. Besides, I could not sleep, and idle hands make devil's handiwork."

"Yes, I have heard that one before," muttered John. "Well, since you are up, perhaps you will accompany me to breakfast. I am supposed to join Henry and Rose, but they are miserable to be around at the moment. Henry doesn't seem to want to let Rose out of his sight, and Rose has threatened to have him thrown in prison for being overprotective. It really is quite amusing actually. You might enjoy it."

Elizabeth smiled as she pictured the king and queen bantering back and forth, but she caught herself in time to reply. "I don't think that would be a good idea, Mr. Borden. I have much to do today. I am starting a garden, and I need to find some seeds to plant. Also, I have baskets full of laundry that need to be washed. In fact, I should be leaving for home immediately. Good day, Mr. Borden."

John reached out to grab her hand, and she tried not to scowl in frustration. "Are you sure that you won't stay? I believe Josh Deplin will also be attempting to kiss the Kriddens' dog today. If not for breakfast, you should stay to see such a thing as that?"

"I am afraid that can never happen. Though, I am sure it will be a very amusing pastime, I really must go."

"May I at least walk you home?"

"You would be missing out on your meal with the king and queen then," Elizabeth said as she walked away. "Besides, I am needed to make a meal for everyone at home. Now, I really must go."

John watched as she left. "Fine, go," he muttered to himself. "Go make a meal for your father, but when are you going to eat something yourself?" With slumped shoulders, he turned and left to go have his meal with Henry and Rose.

"Honestly, Henry," Rose said, "I am perfectly fine. You don't have to worry so much about me. I was just a little sick, that is all. I am perfectly fine now, truly."

Henry gave her a pointed look but allowed her some space. She sighed and moved to her trunks to find something to wear. There were so many options, half the time she didn't know what would actually be suitable. She bent over and felt the nausea take hold. She bolted upright and went for the chamber pot. Henry held her hair back as she lost the rest of her breakfast. "Bother," she muttered.

When she was done, Henry handed her a cloth for her face, then, picking her up into his arms, placed her gently on top of their bed. "You are not going anywhere today. You are sick. You need to get better, and you will do that right here."

Rose groaned. "I am never sick, though. I have always been healthy. I hardly even get a sniffle when others are being put out for weeks from illness."

Henry climbed up beside her. "Perhaps it is from all the travelling. We have been doing an awful lot of it, and now that you aren't moving, your body is reacting."

"Maybe," sighed Rose. "But, I don't think that is it. I really honestly do feel perfectly fine except when, well, when my food doesn't want to stay in my stomach. It really can't be something that severe. Perhaps it is nothing at all, and we are making a bigger thing of it than it really is."

"Perhaps. I would still feel better about it if you stayed in bed today."

Rose sighed. "Will you stay with me?" she pleaded.

"I think that should be okay, but if you don't mind, I will have to tell John that he will need another officiator for when Josh kisses the Kriddens' dog. I said I would act as witness."

Rose laughed. "Please, don't tell John that you won't be there. Go and be officiator of this event, then come back and tell me all about it. I believe I could use the extra humour."

Henry smirked. "It will be quite amusing, won't it?" Rose laughed as she pictured the possibilities. Henry leaned over and kissed her forehead. "I'll be back soon," he whispered, then silently left the room.

Katy stood at Josh's door. It was awkward to be there, but she felt she owed him an apology. She tried to think of what she could say, but nothing would prepare her for when he opened the door. She knocked and waited.

There was a stumbling sound coming from inside, then the door burst open. Josh looked down at her with a look of shock, the sleep still evident on his face. He wiped at his jaw, which was still covered in morning stubble. Slowly he closed his gaping mouth. "Good morning," he said with a hint of curiosity.

Katy felt the blush at the roots of her hair. She tried to respond, but no words would come to mind. She turned her face away and tried to hide herself. It was foolish, she knew, but she didn't know what else to do.

"Umm, I would invite you in, but I don't think that decorum allows for that. Unless, of course, you have a chaperone with you." Katy shook her head. "Well then, I guess we will just have to speak in the doorway. If that is okay with you at least?"

Katy shrugged her shoulders in a sort of agreement.

Josh looked down at her and started to dance uncomfortably on the spot. "There is a reason why you came, right? You aren't just here to bother some poor guy early in the morning."

"It's not early morning anymore."

"Oh, well then." Josh cleared his throat. "About how late is it?"

"It is nearly mid morning already."

"Mid morning!" Josh exclaimed. "Bother, I slept longer than I thought." He looked down at her and cleared his throat again. "Um, is there a reason that you are here, Katy girl?"

She looked up at him and tried to prevent the quivering in her jaw. "I wanted to apologize for my behaviour the other day. I was entirely rude, and you have every right to be angry with me. I hope that you will be able to forgive me for what I said."

"Not a problem, Katy girl. I've already forgotten what you said." He was still dancing on the spot, and it was making Katy angry.

"Is there somewhere you have to be, Josh? Because if there isn't, I would appreciate it if you stood still while I try to apologize to you."

Josh looked at Katy with a half smile. "Sorry, Katy girl, but I did make plans with a 'friend' of mine, and he should be here any minute now."

"What do you mean you made plans with a 'friend,' Josh? You seem far too nervous to just be visiting with a friend."

"Oh, it is nothing that you should concern yourself with, Katy. It is just a small bet we have. That's what has me nervous. It is nothing that big at all, really."

"Josh, what is your bet? Please tell me."

Josh bit his lip and looked down at her and then looked away. "I already lost the bet. It is the aftermath I am worried about."

"Well, obviously, but what did you bet? Is it something to do with money? Because if you owe someone money that you can't pay, I will be forced to tell someone about it."

"No! It is nothing like that at all. I wouldn't bet money I didn't have. That would be stupid now, wouldn't it be?"

"Josh?" Katy began to tap her foot impatiently.

"Do you promise not to be angry?" Katy raised her brow with an ill-humoured glare. "Alright, well, you see, John and I had a bet, and whoever lost the bet, which just so happened to be me, has to kiss the Kriddens' dog. You see, it really isn't anything all that bad. I just have to do it."

Katy's eyes widened in shock. "Are you crazy! You will get yourself killed before you get anywhere close to that dog. You might as well talk with the curate before you go about this. Then at least your funeral will be in order and others won't have to deal with it."

"Oh, bother! I'm not going to get myself killed. It is just a dare. I will do it, and I will be perfectly fine. You will see. I will be perfectly fine."

"Boys," muttered Katy. "Do you really have to do something so stupid?"

"Well yes, Katy girl, I do. I am glad you are so concerned about my wellbeing, but I will be perfectly fine. You will see. In fact, if you want, you can watch as I go about this dangerous feat. If you head over to the Kriddens' now, I am sure John will already be there, and Henry as well. I will be there in a bit as well, but I believe I must get ready before I leave."

Katy looked him over from head to toe and blushed again when she recognized the total indecency of their conversation. "I am really not that concerned about you, but perhaps I will go, just to make sure you boys don't do anything else stupid."

Josh smirked. "I am sure you are not concerned at all. But, it is nice to know you don't want me dead. I'm not sure that every lady would be so gracious."

Katy glared at him. "Perhaps I will decide I don't want to be so gracious after all. You never do know. Perhaps I will set the Kriddens' dog loose on you as you go to kiss it."

Josh grabbed at his chest in an overdramatic act of pain. "That hurt me, dear Katy. Right down in the depths of my heart. It is as if you have taken an arrow and shot me. Now, I lie bleeding."

"You're pathetic, Josh," Katy yelled as she walked away. "I will see you at the Kriddens'." Josh laughed and watched as she disappeared.

NINETEEN

JOSH LOOKED AT THE BEAST before him. It was repulsive. It growled and grunted, pulling against its chain, trying to get at the people who looked on. He shuddered as he pictured himself going toward it and kissing it. He felt his stomach churning, and he told himself not to be sick. It really couldn't be all that bad. It was, after all, just a dog.

"I see why you made this the bet now, Josh," laughed John. "That certainly is a horrendous thing to have to kiss." Josh made a face at him. John only laughed.

"Can't you boys just forget about this bet?" asked Katy nervously. "It really is rather stupid."

"Not at all, Katy girl," stated Josh with as much gusto as he could muster. "We made a bet, and now I must hold to my end of it."

"Exactly!" laughed John. "I really am finding this quite amusing. Aren't you, Henry?"

"Of course. I must say that Josh had it coming. He was sure to lose. Besides, Rose is waiting anxiously to hear the outcome of this all. She regrets not being here to see it happen."

"Where is Rose?" asked Katy. "I thought she would be here."

Henry's face darkened. "She would have been here, but she is not feeling well. She is sure to be back on her feet by tomorrow, but she thought it best to rest for the day."

"Oh," replied Katy as she returned her attention to Josh.

Josh looked at the dog, and began to take small steps toward it.

"Come on!" yelled John. "The dog will be sure to bite you if you move that slowly. Come on man! Be done with it."

Josh turned on him. "If you are so anxious to see this dog kissed, then why don't you come and do the task yourself? I am sure the critter wouldn't mind a peck from your rosy lips!"

John laughed. "Ah, but too bad that was not the bet. Now, pucker up boy! Your lady waits."

Josh scowled and moved forward. The dog growled, and Josh grimaced. He took another step, then decided to get it done and over with. He sprinted toward the beast, pecked its head and bolted away. Unfortunately, he wasn't quite quick enough. He felt his pant leg tear, and some pain as he slipped past the grasp of the dog.

He let out a cry of shock, and Katy was immediately by his side. "Let me see," she gasped and began pulling on his arm. "Stupid boys," she muttered when she saw where the dog had gotten its teeth into him. Josh winced when she touched it. John was busy rolling on the ground laughing.

"It really isn't that bad," said Josh with much bravado. "You should try it, John. I'm sure you're brave enough to."

"Brave, yes, but stupid I am not. You should have seen your face as you ran back. Then that brutish dog bit you, and I thought you were going to faint right there. What a mess that would have been. I think you insulted your beastly lady. Look, that dog is almost pouting."

Josh scowled, but had to stop and gasp in pain when Katy poked him a little too hard where the dog had bitten him.

"Bother," muttered Katy. "I am going to have to do something with this gash. You'll have to come with me, Josh. There is no way I am going to let you leave it to sit and fester. It will probably be the death of you."

"Yes ma'am."

John hooted with laughter as he watched Josh take up a position behind Katy and follow her back toward town. Josh didn't mind. As far as he was concerned, he had the best nurse in the entire town. He wouldn't turn the opportunity down.

He followed Katy all the way back to her house. By that time, the bite was starting to smart and he was beginning to wish he had never made the bet. Katy had him sit on a chair and raise his leg so she could tend to his wound, but it was just behind his knee, making it difficult to clean and bandage. She tried for a while, then, with a sigh of frustration, she began to look around the room for a better way of going about it.

"Alright Josh," she said carefully, "I am going to need you to lie down on your stomach on the sofa over there, and I am going to have to rip a large hole in your pant leg just bellow your knee. It is in my way."

Josh shook his head. "That won't work. I need these." Josh considered her for a moment, then without any further hesitation, he pulled off his shoe and rolled his pant leg up past his knee. Katy tried to hide her blush, but she couldn't help it. The entire situation was completely inappropriate.

"Alright," she muttered, "go lie on the sofa."

"Yes ma'am."

Taking a cloth, Katy began by cleaning the wound. It wasn't deep. The teeth had just been able to graze his skin, but it had bled a lot and it needed to be bandaged. Taking out her sewing kit, Katy found some extra scraps of material and began to bind the wound. Josh took a sharp intake of breath when she pulled too tightly, and she apologized.

"There," said Katy as she finished up. "You are as good as new." Josh smiled and reached down to unroll his pant leg and replace his shoe.

"Wait," said Katy. "Why don't I fix that before you go? I have all my stuff out, and it really will only take a minute. It's the least I could do."

"I would appreciate it, but how will you fix my pants while I'm still wearing them?"

Katy felt herself blush as a tiny 'Oh' escaped past her lips. "Well," Katy collected herself, "bring them by later, and I will fix them for you."

Josh smiled his thanks. "I appreciate that, Katy. I guess I should be going, though. John will be wondering if I have bled to death."

Katy walked him to the door and waved as he walked down the path to the road. Josh was a good friend, she told herself. It was good to have friends like Josh. With a contented sigh, she turned and walked back into the house.

John had picked up what he needed from the mercantile the previous afternoon. It had been quite simple. He had asked what seeds were planted in most vegetable gardens, and the store clerk showed him a selection of various beans, carrots and other such things. He had taken one packet of nearly everything. Elizabeth would have all the seeds she needed.

It was early morning now. Very early, in fact. John planned to do some chores when he stopped by, and he didn't want to disturb the house's occupants while he worked. First on his list was to pull the weeds from the plot of dirt out back. If Elizabeth was to plant the seeds he had bought her, she would need a weed-free area of land, and even though the area had been clean just a day ago, weeds had already made their presence known.

Then, there was wood that needed to be chopped. Winter had nearly consumed the pile of kindling and logs that had once been stacked up against the wall of the house. And though summer was soon to come, wood would still be needed for cooking and warming the house during the spring. This could be done away from the house so as not to disturb its occupants.

By the time he finished those tasks, it would most likely be late enough in the day to move on to fixing the actual house. The first thing to be mended would be the door. It was barely on its hinges, and was sure to come right off one of these days.

John would start there, and then he would see what he could do beyond that. It would be a little difficult to fix the roof without any other help, and he didn't know what else needed to be done. All the moderately simple tasks were well taken care of.

John dropped the basket off in the kitchen and noticed that not much more of the food had been eaten. Elizabeth seemed to refuse to eat, and it was evidently taking a toll on her. She was getting thinner and thinner, but she didn't seem to notice at all. She would have to eat soon if she wanted to stay alive.

John moved out to the backyard and took his anger out on the weeds; then, picking up the axe, he walked far from the house and began to swing. When a moderate pile had been created, he began carrying it to within easy distance of the house. By that time, it was a reasonable hour for a person to awake, so John decided to work on the door.

Picking up his hammer, he began working on the hinges. When the rusty contraptions finally released their grip, John replaced them and made sure the new ones swung quietly. Then, taking some new boards he had brought with him, he replaced a few on the front step that were rotting away. There was a noise from in the house. John picked up his tools and silently slipped away. Now was not the time to get caught. He raced toward the woods and headed back to town. He would be back the next morning to check on Elizabeth.

Elizabeth stumbled her way toward the kitchen. She could have sworn she heard the door opening and closing when she woke. Of course, it could easily have been part of the dream. She shuddered as she remembered it. She looked into the kitchen. It was empty, but on the table next to the baskets sat a cloth bag.

Elizabeth stepped forward and looked inside. There were seeds of every kind. She could see some for carrots, beans, strawberries, cucumbers and everything else she could think of. She closed the bag and tossed it aside with a glower. The charity had evidently come while she was sleeping. Whoever had left it was annoying her. She did not need their help. She could figure things out on her own.

She grabbed a shawl and headed outside. The door swung smoothly on its hinges and gave her a start. She looked at it carefully. It was different. It was in good condition now. Apparently the anonymous 'helper' did not think her capable of caring for her own property. She scowled and began to move toward the woods. She wanted to go to the grave, and she had slept longer than normal.

She walked toward town and tried to keep her anger at bay. There really was nothing to be angry about. Someone was just trying to be nice. It was better than someone stealing. Perhaps they didn't think of it as charity. Maybe they had good intentions. She would not fault someone for good intentions, but neither would she live off of them. Besides, good intentions eventually faded, and then where would she be?

Elizabeth followed the road into town and past the post office. It was in total disarray. Through the window, she could see an older man moving slowly about. Customers were waiting for him, but he was clearly overwhelmed. There was a mess all over the floor, and bags of letters rested unsorted behind the counter. Elizabeth couldn't help but laugh.

She walked toward the pasture. Nothing drew her this morning except habit. She knew Mark's story, and it hadn't helped her any. What use was there in still going? She would have given it up except for Seth. Something about him interested her. He knew pain, and he understood her. That was more than she could say about anyone else.

Seth wasn't at the grave today. She was late. He may have been there earlier, but perhaps not. There was no reason to stay if he wasn't going to be there. She might as well go back.

Her stomach growled. She was hungry, but she was getting used to that. It wasn't the first time she had gone without food, and she could last much longer if she had to. She ignored the pains that reached out from her stomach, and she walked out of the pasture back to town.

As she stepped out of the woods, she was greeted by a group of young men. They looked her up and down, and one of them let out a cat call. "Well, I'll be. It's little Miss Mede. I wonder what she was up to in the woods. What do you think, boys?"

The group of young ruffians started laughing and hooting at her. She tried to walk past them, but they wouldn't let her by. She tried to push them aside, but they were much stronger. "Why are you being so vexatious now, little girl?" one of them sneered. "Are you not as easy as your mother? She was a slut too, wasn't she?"

"Please let me by," whispered Elizabeth. She tried to keep the tears back, but it was impossible. The man just laughed at her.

"Did you hear that, boys!?" he shouted. "The daughter of the slut asked us to please let her by. Can you believe that?" There were a bunch of fake awws and poor child's, but no one moved. "I don't think I want to move right now. I think I will stay right where I am," the ringleader sneered.

"That would not be wise," stated a voice from behind the man. He turned and laughed.

"What's this?" he shouted, "the king's brigade to come save the daughter of the slut." He continued to laugh. Elizabeth felt the tears fall across her face as fear turned to relief. John stepped past the young men. He towered over most of them, and they stepped away, intimidated by his stature. Four men-at-arms followed suit behind him.

"I think it is time that you young hooligans head home. There is no room for this type of behaviour here. If you don't disperse, we'll have to make sure that the king is involved." John looked at the leader of the group pointedly. The man shrank away from his gaze. The group skulked away, and John turned his attention to Elizabeth.

"Mademoiselle, are you alright?"

Elizabeth looked at him with shock. *Had he not heard what they said? Did he not understand?* "I am fine, thank you. I believe you have rescued me, and for that I am grateful. Now, I think that I will be on my way. Good day, gentlemen."

Elizabeth stepped past the men and hurried away. She rubbed at the tears as she went. Enough people had seen her crying. She didn't need the rest of the town seeing her tears. She took a deep breath and moved on. She had a lot to do. She had to go into the cellar and find the seeds. She would not live on the seeds bought with good intentions. She would go into the cellar that very day.

John watched as Elizabeth left. He tried to think of a way to detain her, to ask her all the questions he now had, but he had to go about his own business. He was to go with the group of men to find a suitable place for the soldiers to get rid of some of their extra energy. Too many of them were getting restless. It wouldn't be a hard task if they all agreed on a spot. Unfortunately, it was unlikely that they would. Thus, he planned to spend the entire day trying to find a spot that all would consider suitable for fencing, jousting, and whatever else they wanted to do.

John sighed and allowed Elizabeth to disappear. He would go back to her place in the morning and begin to fix up her house. That was the least he could do for her. Perhaps he would get answers some other time.

Elizabeth looked down into the cellar. It was dark and it smelt bad. She considered not going down. She could live off of good intentions at least this once. She shuddered and fought back the urge to run. Slowly, she slipped her first foot down into the hole.

The darkness enveloped her. It closed in on her on all sides. She took deep breaths and tried to calm herself. She focused on the light. The light was behind her. The hatch was still open. She knew where she had to go. She hurried toward the shelf and grabbed the bag. They should all still be in there.

She turned toward the hatch and bolted out of the cellar. There was no purpose in staying in it any longer than she had to. She shuddered again as she sat down in the kitchen. She had no intentions of ever going back down there. For all she cared, they could fill the cellar in and destroy it. She had no use for it.

Elizabeth took a deep breath to get rid of the rest of her jitters. Taking up the bag of seeds, she looked into it. She let out a soft moan and dropped the bag on the floor. It had all been useless. She had wasted her time. She could have avoided the cellar. The seeds were mouldy. Every single last one of them had gone bad.

Elizabeth groaned. Her stomach growled at her, and she wanted to shout. She wanted to fall on her knees and shout at the God who had never once looked down at her. But what was the use in doing that? He wasn't looking. He wasn't listening. He wouldn't hear or see her no matter what she did. It was better to keep going on.

Elizabeth went about the rest of her day haunted by a bewildered sense of loss. That night, instead of dreaming about the dead, bloated corpse, she dreamt of the cellar.

It was early morning again, and John was busy pounding nails into the side of Elizabeth's house. Perhaps it was a stupid thing to do. She would most likely wake up, but he could think of nothing else. Many of the boards were rotting off, so he had decided to replace them. It really wasn't all that difficult, but it did create a lot of noise for the occupants inside.

He worked steadily, but he hadn't gotten very far when he was finally caught.

"Good morning," Elizabeth whispered with a sour look on her face.

"Good morning." John picked up another board and moved to the other side of the house. Elizabeth ignored him and walked toward the barn. John watched her as she disappeared. She was angry, but what else could he expect from her? He randomly showed up at her house and started tearing it apart. She had every right to be upset.

When Elizabeth came out of the barn, she looked even more furi-ous. She stomped toward John. "Is there a reason why you are here?"

John dropped his hammer to his side and shrugged his shoulders. "I was fixing the house up. I saw there were some boards that needed to be switched, so I went about it. I was considering doing the roof as well, but that will require some work. It could take up to a day or two, if I have some men with me. That is if you don't mind going without a roof for that long."

Elizabeth glared at him. "You've been leaving the baskets, haven't you?"

John nodded. "Yes ma'am, I have been. I saw that you were hungry, and I thought it best that you had food so you don't starve to death. That would be a tragedy."

"Well, you can stop now. I am not going to starve. I will be perfectly fine. I do not need to live off of your charity." She turned to walk away.

"Are you too proud?" John called after her.

She turned on him and laughed. "Do you think that is what it is, Mr. Borden—pride?" She laughed again. "Did you not listen to what was being said yesterday? I am the daughter of a slut. This refusal to live off charity is not pride. It is the only dignity that I have. If you have anything against that, speak up or keep it, and the rest of your good intentions, to yourself."

John did not reply right away. He looked down at his feet and just stood there for a moment. He sighed. "Why does it matter who your mother was? What does it matter if your mother was not the most righteous person? What sin can make one sinner worse than another?" Elizabeth looked at him quizzically. He smiled.

"You know, I am probably the worst sinner out there. I have been jealous. I have wanted what is not mine. I have hated and destroyed people with my words. And there is much, much more that I have done. Perhaps my only dignity then is that I have enough money to try to help someone. Would you deny me that dignity by not accepting my gifts?"

"That is unfair. You are not a horrible person, and you do not have people mocking you. You do not have people sneering behind your back and avoiding you. You have dignity in other things. People treat you with dignity. I don't have that. People treat me as I should be treated."

"That is the only difference between us, then. You see, at least people treat you as you deserve. People don't treat me as I deserve. If they did, they wouldn't hold me in such high esteem. They would throw me out to the streets. They would call me names. They would throw me in prison. I deserve all these things. Unfortunately, others have not noticed that I deserve all these things."

Elizabeth balled her fists. "You're being silly. No one would treat you that way. You are next to the king. He would stand testimony for you. Who do I have to stand testimony for me? Do I stand next to the king? No, I am the daughter of the slut, the lowest of the low."

John gave her a look of confusion. "I don't understand. Don't you know?"

"I know a lot of things," Elizabeth replied, exasperated. "But I haven't a clue as to what you are talking about."

"Well, the King has come and has claimed all the poor and lowly as His own. He even claimed the lowest of the low. He wants them all to share in his kingdom."

Elizabeth groaned. "Mr. Borden, I know you believe this about God, but God has denied me that privilege. There are some things that don't belong in His kingdom, and I am one of them. So, unless you have something reasonable to say, I believe I will continue on with my morning alone."

"I don't get it. What could you have done that would turn away God? What is so horrible about yourself that not even God can stand you?"

Elizabeth laughed without humour. "Don't you see, Mr. Borden? It is not what I have done. It is what I am. I am the devil's handiwork, and that is why I will never be allowed in the kingdom you speak of."

John stood back in mute shock. What was he supposed to say to that? Nothing came to mind. Taking up his hammer, he pulled out a rotting board and began pounding a clean one into place. He had all the time in the world. Why not work it all out on the house?

TWENTY

ELIZABETH SAT IN THE MIDDLE of her room trying to ignore the pounding of the hammer on the wall. It was getting annoying, but John refused to quit and go home. At first Elizabeth had busied herself with re-cleaning the house. Then she had read to her father while he gazed blankly up at the roof. Finally, she had begun stitching up ripped clothes. This only lasted for a short while before it was all done, and she was left with nothing to do.

Elizabeth gritted her teeth as she listened to another nail go in. Wouldn't he ever leave? It was well past noon. He had to be hungry. She felt her own stomach gurgle. She ignored it. She was not going to give in. Not when she had made it this far. She looked around for something to distract herself. Her eyes fell on the letters addressed to Seth.

Elizabeth stared at them. They sat there tempting her. What would she do with them? She could read them, but she already knew his story. She could burn them. The rules of the post office were still well ingrained in her, and the thought of burning a letter left her feeling guilty. Besides, they could contain something new, something important. Elizabeth picked up the top letter and began to turn it over in her hands.

Slipping her finger under the seal, she broke it. Elizabeth inhaled sharply. This was the first time she had ever opened another's mail. She felt as if she was breaking the rules, destroying someone's trust. Then the truth of the matter finally came to her. She was no longer working at the post office. She didn't have to worry about breaking the rules.

Elizabeth slid the papers out and began to read.

> *Deer Seth,*
>
> *So's I dont no if ya got my last letter but Ill pretend thet ya did. I no ya probably dont wanna see me but I dont have anywhere else t'go. Ive bin eevicted frum my house cause I couldnt keep up the rent. It's a tough thing t'do what with it bein so hard to find a job.*
>
> *Well any ways. I was wonderin if you would be willin to take me in. I no that it would be a great inconveenience to ya but I no that yer a good person now and I was hopin you could tell me more bout thet. I no it is a weird thing t'ask but I want to do things rite now. I can be a better person if I have t'be. Ill show ya. Just give me a chance wont ya Seth.*
>
> *I gess I dont have thet much more t'say. I said it all in the last letter. Send a letter if yull allow me ta cum. Ill wait until then.*
>
> *Sinseerly,*
>
> *Bill*

Elizabeth felt her hands shaking. Bill was a real person. That meant Seth's story was true. That meant everything was true. She felt herself shudder. It hadn't seemed entirely true until now. She felt a little dizzy. She reached out a hand to steady herself. Taking a deep breath, she calmed herself. This didn't change anything. She reached out and grabbed the next letter. It was much like the first.

Holding the letters to herself, she closed her eyes and breathed deeply in and out. Seth was Seth. He wasn't Caleb. He was Seth. She had known that. She could handle that. But now this truth was a part of reality and not just part of her dream-like life in the pasture.

The hammering outside stopped.

The door opened.

"Elizabeth!" John called. She didn't reply. "Elizabeth, I know you're in there, and I know that you probably don't want to talk to me, but I want to let you know that I am going to get something to eat. You are free to come with me, but if you don't want to, I guess that is your choice. I'll be gone for about an hour, then I will finish what I started." There was quiet and Elizabeth wondered if he was gone.

"Elizabeth, if you come out while I'm gone, please don't get too upset. I promise I will be back to finish the job tonight." He paused again. "Maybe it's best if you don't come out."

Elizabeth heard the door close with a bang. She counted to ten before curiosity got the better of her. She picked herself up off the floor and tossed the letters aside. Creaking open her door, she stepped out. She quickly stepped back into her room and closed the door. Closing her eyes, she took a deep breath. Once more she opened the door.

The horror washed over her as she looked at the wall. What once had been their kitchen wall was now a great gaping hole. Broken, rotten boards littered her yard. Elizabeth let out a slight groan and sank to the floor. It was a mess. Everything she had worked to clean up was a mess, and John was determined that she would live off of his charity. She scowled and brought her hands up to her face to cover her eyes.

Taking a deep breath, Elizabeth picked herself up off the floor and went through the hole into her yard. There was wood everywhere. Looking over the pile, she began to work. She stacked the moderately good boards in a neat pile, and any of the rotten boards were thrown into a pile of firewood. That would save her from having to split any more.

Despite the fact that she had a hole in her kitchen wall, Elizabeth found that the work felt good. It was something that she could do besides moping, and it kept her mind off of her growling stomach. She smiled as she continued to work. She even considered singing, but thought better of it. It would be embarrassing to be caught singing.

The sound of a buggy coming down the road caught her attention. She looked up and saw John coming with a wagon full of wood. She scowled. Apparently he would have his way no matter what she wanted. The buggy pulled up to the house, and John jumped down. He smiled at her, and she scowled back.

"You don't have to do that," said John. "I'll clean it up once I am done with fixing the hole." He looked at the hole and blushed. "I'm sorry about that, by the way. I was just a little frustrated, and I was pulling out boards, and then, well let's just say I got a little ahead of myself."

Elizabeth rolled her eyes and continued at her work. She was not going to give it up as long as John insisted upon being there. Besides, she wanted to make sure that the hole actually got fixed. "You know, you really don't have to be doing that," said John.

Elizabeth turned on him. "As long as you are here, Mr. Borden, I will not allow you to do charity work on my house while I sit inside and do absolutely nothing. Now, you can either live with me working beside you, or I will have one of those soldiers come down here and arrest you for destroying my house and trespassing. Do you understand me?"

"Yes ma'am," muttered John, and he turned back to his work. They worked silently the rest of the day. Sometimes John would try to start up a conversation, but Elizabeth just scowled at him until he turned back to his work. When all the boards were cleaned up, Elizabeth took up a hammer to help John on the house. He protested and was about to forcibly make Elizabeth leave him be, but Elizabeth reminded him that he promised to have the hole fixed before he left, and she wouldn't quit working until he left. This time John scowled at her, but she just smiled back.

It wasn't until late that evening that the hole was finished. Elizabeth was hungry. She couldn't recall the last time she had eaten, and the hard work had taken a lot of her energy. She clamped her jaw to try to ignore the pain in her stomach. John's stomach growled beside her. "Hmm," he murmured. "It appears as if it is time for some dinner. Would you like to join me for a meal in town? I would appreciate the company."

Elizabeth scowled at him. "You don't give up, do you, Mr. Borden?"

He smiled down at her. "Please, call me John, and no, I don't give up. I am told that I am quite stubborn, but that is only Rose who says that. She's worse, I personally think."

Elizabeth sighed. "For once, won't you just give up, Mr. Borden? I will not eat a meal with you in town. This just can't happen, and I will not encourage it. Now, I have chores that need to be done." She turned and left John standing there.

Elizabeth did not sleep that night. Her stomach gnawed at her. It ached so badly, she couldn't help but toss and turn. She tried to ignore it. She tried so hard to act as if it wasn't even there, but it would not be ignored. Finally, she got out of bed and walked to the meadow.

Seth was waiting there. It was unusual for him to be there before her. She walked up beside him and immediately sat down by the grave. "Did you have to come this morning?" Elizabeth asked.

"No," murmured Seth. "I have not been dreaming lately."

"Then why are you here so early?"

"Because now I want to know why I don't dream." He laughed bit-terly. "It's ridiculous, isn't it? I hated the dreams so much that I would have given almost anything for them to stop, or for it to come so that I could have it, but that has changed so much now. I had it for one brief dream, and I decided that I didn't want it. Now it is gone, and I feel so, so empty. Isn't that just so ridiculous?"

"Consider yourself blessed," muttered Elizabeth. "For years I have been empty while I still dream. At least you only had to experience one at a time."

Seth turned to her and sighed. "Do you ever get used to it?" he asked, his voice so sad, it brought tears to Elizabeth's eyes.

"Never," she whispered. "It haunts you forever and always. There is no escape from it, and it is lonely, so miserably lonely. No one understands how lonely it is until they experience it. No one cares for you at that point, not even God."

"Why did God abandon you?"

Elizabeth laughed softly, bitterly. "I guess I owe you the rest of my story, don't I?"

"I would appreciate it."

"Alright, then. I'll begin where I left off." Elizabeth lay back on the grass and looked up at the dark sky. She pictured the time and the place of her story and began to speak.

"Tanya was receiving a lot of ridicule as she walked about town. She was often called slut or whore or any other such name. Sometimes she would come back home and she would be crying, and Gerald would be so angry about it. He went to the preacher once to ask him to do something about it. The preacher refused, because he himself was unsure about the legitimacy of the child.

"Of course, there were a few people who believed Tanya and Gerald, but that all changed when they saw the child. You see, the child was born late one night in the dead of winter. The neighbours came from all around to see the baby. This isn't a normal thing to do, but most of them wanted to see if the child was legitimate.

"Some said that she looked liked Gerald, but others said there was no resemblance, but that didn't matter any. There was one thing that set her out from both her parents, and that was her dark black hair. You see, both of her parents had honey blond hair, the colour of spun gold.

"This decided it for many people. They said that the traveler had black hair. He had to be the father. But then there was an old wise lady in town who said that sometimes a babe's hair changed colour. They wouldn't know for sure until the fourth birthday. So, all of the town's folk went home. They all thought to themselves that they would be back in four years to see about this child.

"So this child, which you have probably and rightly conjectured to be me, grew up to be four years old. Of course, the town's folk watched constantly to see if my hair would change colour, but the most it did was turn to a dark brown. Never did it go blond. So, I was a marked person.

"No mother in her right mind would let me come in and play with her daughter. What horrendous things might I teach their daughters? Gerald lost credibility in the town because he refused to leave his wife. Tanya became more depressed and miserable, and I lived through it all, alone.

"I can remember my mother muttering all the time under her breath. 'Idle hands make devil's handiwork.' Then, she would look at me with sad eyes and shake her head. Eventually the town gave up on being nice to Tanya. They were outright cruel in their comments to her. It was too much for her."

Elizabeth could feel the tears coming, and she tried to push them off. There was no use in crying about it now. "Gerald had to leave for a week. I don't remember why anymore. He left me and Tanya to fend for ourselves. Tanya took advantage of this time alone. As soon as Gerald was out of sight, she found some bed sheets. She twisted them into a knot, and she hung herself.

"I sat there and watched as my mother hung. I can remember her gasping for breath, and I couldn't do anything about it. I just watched. I didn't even call out. I didn't scream or cry. My mother's dead body hung there for quite some time, and I just sat there watching it, never moving. Finally, I got hungry enough to move. I had gone a few days without food, and I wasn't steady on my feet. I fell into the cellar and I couldn't get out.

"I remember sitting on the floor and crying because I couldn't see anything to get any food, and I was so thirsty. When Gerald came home, he found me there nearly dead. He took me to my room and called the doctor. The doctor didn't come for over a day. Why should he care if the illegitimate child should die? When he finally did come, Gerald was so distraught and angry that he nearly came to blows with the man.

"No one has ever understood that. Anyway, I got better. I was four, and I was resilient. But, from that day forward I always dreamt. I dreamt of my mother's dead body. I never want to look, but the wind always tells me to, and when I finally do look, I scream.

"At first, Gerald came running every time I screamed. After a while, he just left me to scream. He was even able to sleep through it after some time. This kept up for nearly ten years. Then, one day,

Gerald didn't wake up in the morning to go to work. I called the doctor, but again he didn't come right away. When he did, he said my father had had a stroke, and it was only a matter of time, and he would die.

"You should have seen the look of pity he gave me as he walked out. But he didn't want to do anything about my situation. I was the devil's handiwork after all. Anyway, we eventually ran out of money. I got the job at the post office. Gerald didn't die. He just kept pushing through. I don't know on what strength, but he is still alive today for some reason. He's lived through pneumonia and such, and it hasn't killed him, but lately it's been getting worse. It will be any day now, and he will be gone, and then it will be just me, the illegitimate child of the slut."

Elizabeth ended her story and just stared up. Seth didn't say anything. He just stood there. Elizabeth didn't care. She wasn't sure she wanted to hear what he had to say. He probably wasn't too fond of her anymore.

"I don't get it," he finally said. "What did you do wrong? Why would God leave you? What did you do?"

Elizabeth sighed. "You don't *get* it? I'm an illegitimate child. My mother slept with another man while she was married to Gerald, and I am the result of that. I am a bastard child."

Seth looked at her incredulously. "So what does that matter?"

"I am the result of something evil. That is why God cannot accept me. I am evil. I am dirty and disgusting. Don't you get it? Can't you understand?" Elizabeth was shouting now. "I am worthless to God."

"You think you are worthless to God? What about me? I'm a rapist. I killed someone with my own two hands. I destroyed someone's life. If you are evil, I am monstrous. As far as I am concerned, there is no reason why you should be far from God."

"Hah. What you do doesn't make you who you are. We all make mistakes sometimes. We all can be forgiven for mistakes, but me, I am the result of a mistake. There is no forgiveness for the results. I am disgusting to God. I am sure of that."

Seth sighed. "Perhaps. Who am I to say?" He looked at the sky. "I should go." He turned and left her there. She watched him leave, then she walked back to her house. Chances were John would be there, and she would not have him working on her house if she was not present. She sighed. What was she to do about him? He was really starting to become obnoxious. She scowled. Perhaps she would have him arrested for putting a hole in her wall after all. It would certainly keep him away from her house for a while.

John was at her house again, as expected. What she hadn't expected was for him to have five other men with him and her roof completely gone. Perhaps that was a bit of an exaggeration. Her roof was not completely gone. It lay in pieces on her once-neat yard. Elizabeth could feel rage boiling underneath her skin.

She walked toward the house and into the barn where the cow waited. Methodically, she milked the cow and counted to ten repeatedly, hoping to calm herself. She inhaled deeply and exhaled slowly. When the milking was done, she picked up the pail, walked into the roofless house and tended to her father as best she could. She could hear the shouts of men working and the pounding of hammers, but she ignored them.

Finally, she got up and went to find John.

"I see that I have more than a just reason to have you arrested," she said to him in a sickly sweet voice. "You have gone far beyond putting a hole in a wall. I must say, it is quite rude to destroy a roof and invade a person's privacy without permission. And, to think, you invited these innocent soldiers to join you in your escapades."

John smiled down at her. "It has been my experience that it is better to beg forgiveness than to ask for permission. I have enough men here that the roof will easily be done by the end of the day. We'll come back tomorrow to clean up the mess."

"Give me a hammer!" demanded Elizabeth. John shook his head. "Give me a hammer now," growled Elizabeth, "or suffer the consequences. I can guarantee that I will not be held responsible for my actions."

John couldn't help but laugh. He handed over his hammer, and Elizabeth turned to go to work. The men present gave her odd looks, but they didn't say anything. John took charge. With a new hammer from his pile of supplies in hand, he directed every person there effortlessly and flawlessly. With his leading, it was only noon by the time that they were finishing up.

Elizabeth sat precariously up on the roof and pounded nails into the new shingles. She was feeling light-headed. It was hot outside, and it had been a while since she had gotten anything to drink, let alone eat. She wiped her brow and considered going to the well. She stepped toward the ladder and felt the roof slipping out from under her feet. The ground was a long way off, but at that moment she could not have cared less. She closed her eyes and let herself fall.

John let out a shout of horror as he watched Elizabeth fall from her perch on the roof. He saw her land and waited for her to get up. She didn't move. He raced to her side and scooped her up in his arms. "What happened?" he growled at the nearest lieutenant.

The young man stepped uncomfortably. "She just fainted, sir. There was nothing I could do. There was no one down by the ladder to catch her." John glowered at the young man, then, cradling Elizabeth in his arms, he carried her toward her room.

Elizabeth moaned softly as he set her down on her bed, but she didn't stir. John took some water and perched her up into a sitting position. He began to dribble water into her mouth. She swallowed and began to cough. Shaking her head, she opened her eyes and looked up at John, astounded. He smiled down at her. She looked a little confused.

"Elizabeth, I believe that right before you fainted, you were agreeing to eat something for my sake. You told me that I should not leave until you ate a substantial meal, and that I should come back in the morning to make sure you ate another full meal. Do you remember this?"

Elizabeth scowled. "I said no such thing. Now, if you don't mind, my roof has to be fixed." She turned to get out of her bed. Her face went pale and she began to wobble. John steadied her and helped her back into her bed.

"As I was saying," muttered John, "I will not be leaving until you have completed an entire meal. And, I will be back in the morning to make sure that you eat another one."

Elizabeth scowled and turned away with a sigh. John laughed and went to find her something to eat.

TWENTY-ONE

ROSE WALKED TOWARD CALEB'S HOUSE. She wanted to talk with him, and she was rather bored. Ever since she had been sick, Henry had been keeping a close eye on her, and she hadn't been allowed to do anything. Of course, that had meant Henry had spent a lot of time with her, but he also had obligations of his own, and while he attended to those today, she had nothing to do but sit around. Visiting Caleb would give her something to keep her mind busy.

She walked up to the parsonage door and knocked. There was no response. She considered leaving, but decided she should try knocking one more time. There was a thud in response. She heard something fall, then the door opened. Caleb stood before her, tall, pale and gaunt. She smiled up at him. He frowned at her.

The look made her laugh. It was so like Caleb to be absolutely miserable. She reached up to his cheek and patted it. "It is good to see you, Caleb. I have been here for some time, and I feel like I have barely seen you. Would you mind if I came in briefly?"

He looked at her and glowered. "I think you know just as well as I do that that would be inappropriate." He wouldn't look her in the eye. Rose couldn't help but laugh harder.

"Yes, you are definitely the same old Caleb. So prim and proper, you set boundaries that are not even in existence." Rose laughed again. "Caleb, I am a married woman. You are the pastor of a small church. If we are visiting, no one in their right mind would think anything of it."

Caleb still did not smile. "You are the queen, and I am the curate. We are to be above reproach, and it is not above reproach to be visiting when your husband is not present. People will talk."

"And what will they say, Caleb? Will they say that the queen visited with an old friend while her husband was about being the king of the country? Will they say that Rose visited Caleb, and they enjoyed each other's company and then parted ways? Will they conjecture that something unscrupulous occurred because there was no chaperone present? Honestly, Caleb, you are far too upright for your own health. The stress you put yourself through will put you in the grave early."

Still, Caleb did not smile. "I am afraid, Your Majesty, that I cannot let you in."

Rose gave Caleb a pained look. "I'm sorry that I have to do this to you Caleb, but I fear that I am at my last resource." Caleb's serious face twisted into a look of curiosity, and Rose grinned. "I hereby enforce by the power given to me by this wonderful country, a de-

cree that states you must let me into your house, or suffer the consequences. Now, I would suggest that you let me in before I force you
to do so."

Caleb scowled at her and stepped out of the way. "You didn't have
to make a decree to force me to give in. All you needed to do was find
a chaperone."

Rose laughed as she made her way toward the parlour. "I would
have found a chaperone, and you would have clammed up like an oys-
ter. You never do have anything to say when others are around. It is
like it is a curse to say too much when you have company over. But,
today you will talk with me because I am sick and tired of hearing
nothing at all from you."

Caleb sighed and looked at Rose. "Why did you have to come,
Rose? Why can't you leave me alone?"

Rose looked hurt. "I thought we were friends, Caleb, and that is
what friends do. They visit with one another. Now, if you can honestly
say to me that I am not your friend, then I will leave and never return
again."

Rose looked at Caleb pointedly, and he stared back at her. He
looked away, and Rose smirked. "That's what I thought. Now, I know
things are different than when I first lived here. I understand that. But,
truthfully, I am the same person. I am still your same old friend, and I
still love you just as much as before."

Caleb inhaled sharply. "You shouldn't say such things, Rose,"
whispered Caleb. "People will think badly of you if you say that you
love me. Especially when I know that you don't mean it."

"You don't get it, do you Caleb?" Rose asked. "You were always like that. You never understood that I loved you as a very dear friend, and there is nothing wrong with that, and there is no lie in saying it."

Caleb shook his head. "You were wrong before, Rose. You said you are the same as before, but you are entirely different. Before, you would never have used the word love. You didn't love before. Before, you liked people, and you enjoyed their friendship, but you did not love. Even you know that is true."

Rose smiled sadly. "Perhaps that is true, but is it so bad that I have finally opened myself up to love again? I personally do not find anything wrong with it. If that displeases you, please explain to me why, so I won't further offend you."

"There is nothing wrong with it," muttered Caleb and he turned away. They sat in silence. Rose watched Caleb. She studied him to see what the matter was, but could read no clue as to what his problem was. He just looked incredibly tired.

Caleb in turn did everything in his power to avoid looking at Rose. She shouldn't be in his house, and he shouldn't be thinking about how good she looked and how cheery and wonderful she was. He tried to ignore her presence, but it wasn't easy.

"Why are you so sad, Caleb?"

Caleb jumped to his feet and began to pace. "I am not sad. I am just tired. I haven't been sleeping well. That is all. I'll be fine come tomorrow morning."

"Why aren't you sleeping, Caleb?"

Caleb glared at her. "I think it is time that you leave."

Rose scowled back at him. "If you want me to leave so badly, then kick me out. Tell me right now. Look me in the eye, and tell me to get out of your house and to never return."

Caleb glared at her, but his expression soon changed. His squinted eyes soon turned wide, and his stiff jaw loosened and fell agape. "What's the matter?" demanded Rose.

"Why didn't you tell me you were pregnant?" he shouted, and then slumped back onto the seat.

Katy walked down the road trying to sort through all the feelings in her head. Her brain battled back and forth. At one point it sided with Caleb. Then, on the other hand, Josh was a pretty good option as well. It was silly, really. Why she should even worry about it, she didn't know. It was childish and would work itself out. Wouldn't it?

Katy scowled at the sky. Why couldn't God make life easier for people down on earth? Why couldn't he just say do this, go here, don't go there, leave this person, marry that person? It would be especially helpful if he said whom to marry.

What would God say to her choices for marriage? On the one hand, she had Josh. He was kind, courteous and handsome. But, he did have some downfalls. He was young for one. He was hardly a year older than she was. Also, he didn't have a career. He could hardly afford to pay for a one-room dirt floor hut. How would he support a family? But, he was a good friend.

Then there was the curate. He was handsome, respectable, and had a good career. He could support a family. Of course, he had downfalls as well. He was severe and hardly ever smiled. She would be required to live a very righteous life. But, she loved him, *didn't she?*

Katy scowled again. How was she supposed to know what to do? It would be so easy to just go to Josh and say she would be his girl, but would she then live in regret? It was almost just as easy to leave Josh out of the picture and only focus on the curate. Caleb was softening toward her, and it wouldn't be long, and he might very well see what she had to offer him. Then again, he might never realize that she could be his bride.

Katy sighed and continued walking. There was no use in mulling it all over. It would only give her a headache. She had enough things to worry about as it was. She should be concerning herself with visiting Rose or planning a ball while all the soldiers were still with them. That would be much more fun than thinking about marriage. Marriage would just have to wait until she was sure her head was on straight. Then she would think about it.

Rose laughed. "I'm not pregnant, Caleb. You must be imagining things. I would have told you if I were pregnant. It would have been mean of me not to tell you if I was; but I'm not."

"You are," whispered Caleb hoarsely. "If I hadn't been so concerned about other things, I would have seen it the moment you walked in. You are definitely pregnant."

Rose shook her head and blushed. "I am not. I would know if I were pregnant. There would be signs." Rose felt herself become beet red and she tried to hide the embarrassment. Caleb gave her a look, and Rose tried to think whether or not he could be right. She counted back the months and felt all the blood drain from her face. She slumped down on the couch.

"But it can't be true," she muttered. "I would have known. I should have known."

"Would you like a glass of water?" Rose nodded, and he disappeared. Slowly, she counted in her head over and over the months that had passed. They had been travelling. She had thought it was due to stress. It wasn't uncommon for her to miss her monthly, but for this long?

She counted it again in her head. Four months. It had to be at the very least four months, perhaps even getting close to five. How could she not have noticed? Her baby would be kicking soon, and she had just found out it existed.

Other things started making sense. The nausea when she never before had been sick. The tiredness when they had been staying in one spot for so long. The strange stomach flutters, the extra weight and so much more. How could she not have known?

Caleb handed her a glass of water and she thanked him for it.

She was going to have a baby. Henry would be so excited. He wanted children. At the beginning of their marriage, he had been very vocal about it. But, when two years had passed and none had come, he stopped mentioning it. Rose smiled as she pictured what his reaction would be.

"You're getting your colour back. You should go see your husband. I'm sure he will want to know the news. Let him know I offer my congratulations." Rose turned and looked at Caleb.

"How did you know? If I didn't even know, *how* did you?"

Caleb looked uncomfortable. "I've seen a lot of pregnant women in my lifetime. You begin to be able to spot it when you see it." Rose gave him a look of disbelief, and Caleb blushed. "You just looked different, and that was the first thing that popped into my mind."

Rose raised an eyebrow and gave him a long look. "If that is the only explanation you can give me, I'll take it, though I don't believe you for a minute." She moved to make herself comfortable in the chair. "Well, just because we've discovered I'm pregnant, doesn't mean that I have to up and leave. Henry won't be home for a few more hours, and I refuse to go back and pace while I wait for him. So, you will be blessed with my company for a while longer."

Caleb blushed. "What if I think it is entirely inappropriate that you are here while being pregnant? It would be best that you leave then."

"Perhaps. But, we've already gone over this. I am not leaving until you can look me in the eye and tell me that you don't want to see me again."

Caleb sighed. "Why do you have to be so dramatic? I may think it is best that you go now, but that doesn't mean I want you to go forever. I just think it would be more appropriate if you had a chaperone. It is entirely inappropriate for you to be alone with me."

"You know what, Caleb? I think you are pulling excuses out of the air because you don't actually want to have a good conversation with me, but I will not live with that. Everyone knows it is entirely appropriate for a married woman to converse with whomever she wishes.

Well, I want to talk with you, Caleb, and I will not give up until you give me a week's worth of intelligible conversation."

Caleb scowled at her, and Rose smiled. "I have lots of time on my hands now," smirked Rose. "So, if you don't mind, I think we should start talking. I'll start us off. Hello Caleb. I am your old friend Rose. Do you remember me at all?"

Caleb couldn't help but laugh, and Rose smiled back.

"Yes, I remember you, Rose. If I remember correctly, you were the one fair lady I knew who had every young man in the county chasing after her but couldn't care less for any of them."

Rose laughed. "I cared about some of them. One of those men became a particularly good friend, and if my memory doesn't lapse, I am pretty sure that another of those fellows is my husband." The two smiled amiably and the conversation went on.

Rose stayed with Caleb until later that evening, and then she went home to Henry and told him the news.

Henry's reaction was exactly as Rose had pictured it. He picked her up and spun her in a circle. He kissed her, held her and laughed with such merriment that it was infectious. It was a memory Rose would cherish forever.

Katy walked toward the curate's house. She was going to visit him. She would talk with him, and if she could not hold a conversation with him, she would forget him. Her heart raced at the thought of it. What if she messed it up? Would she really be able to just drop the thought of marrying Caleb? He was such a good man. It was amazing that he was not married yet.

Katy stepped up to his door and knocked. There was no response. She knocked again. A low moan greeted her ears. She called out, but no one responded. She turned to leave, but the sound of whimpering stopped her. Katy looked at the door and pondered it. Finally, she reached out and tested the door handle.

It opened easily.

Once in the house, Katy called out again. Only the sound of sobbing met her ears. She followed the noise. It led her down the hall toward the bedrooms. She felt her heart pounding. What if it wasn't Caleb? What if it was a strange animal she was hearing? She moved forward cautiously and opened the door that led to the noise.

It was Caleb.

But it wasn't him, either.

Katy looked at the sobbing mass of flesh curled up in the corner. It looked like Caleb, but how could it be? Caleb was a strong, passionate preacher. This thing was a wretch, a weakling, a dejected waste. Katy stepped forward to get a better look.

"Leave me alone," it whimpered. "Can't you see?" it asked. "Can't you see what a wretch I am?" He pointed at himself. "Of course, you can see. You can finally see now, can't you? You know that I am repulsive. You see me now."

He turned away and moaned into the corner of the room. His tears came out in torrents, and a wail escaped past his lips. Katy couldn't help but pity him. She reached out a hand toward his arm. "No!" he shouted. He spun his arm around and knocked her to the floor. He got to his feet and glared at her.

"You must see. Everyone must see. I am no good. Everyone will see it soon. It is only a matter of time, but God will have his judgment. I am a wretch, and God will show the world. Just wait. You will see." The man laughed hysterically. "Don't tell anyone, though. That would ruin everything." He slumped down dejectedly on the bed.

Katy got up and stood on shaking legs. She walked toward the man and rested her hand on his shoulder. He didn't respond. She added a little pressure, and he lay back. Carefully she lifted his legs onto the bed. He moaned. Lifting up the covers, Katy tucked him in and watched as he closed his eyes. She turned to leave.

"Don't leave me," he whimpered. "I'm sorry. Just don't leave me. I couldn't stand it if you left me."

Katy sighed. "I can only stay for a while longer. Okay?" Caleb nodded. Katy held his hand and watched as he closed his eyes and drifted off to sleep. Then, collecting herself, she brushed off her skirts and walked out the door.

The tears came when she got outside. How could someone be so terribly haunted, yet keep it all inside? She pictured in her mind Caleb's broken face. He had been so miserable. She couldn't help but pity him. She didn't know what to think anymore. She had once thought that he was strong, but now all she could picture was how weak he had been. At first she had thought him entirely righteous. Now she wondered if he even believed in God.

Katy walked in silence. Her head was down and tears streamed down her face. Wiping them didn't help any; they just kept coming. She looked up to see where she was going just in time to prevent herself from running into Josh.

He looked her up and down with concern. "Are you okay, Katy girl?" She nodded. "Are you sure?" She shook her head and felt more tears rush to her eyes. Josh grabbed her into a hug and she cried into his shoulder. He murmured soft reassurances to her, and she soaked in all his words.

Finally, the tears stopped and Katy was able to look up at Josh without having to look through a layer of water. "Thank you," she whispered. He smiled down at her.

"It's no problem at all." His smile brightened. "In fact," he laughed, "my shoulder is yours any time you need to cry."

Katy couldn't help but smile. A blush crept up her neck and into her cheeks, and she looked down at the ground.

"Do you want to tell me what the matter is?" Josh asked.

"Not really. It's just that I finally realized that someone wasn't exactly who I thought he was."

"I see. Is that alright with you? I mean, can you live with who this person is even if he is different than you expected him to be?"

"I don't know. It's just a big change to get used to. I thought I knew him so well. I thought that he was someone that he wasn't." Katy could feel the tears coming again, and she blinked them away. Josh gave her a gentle hug. Katy took a deep, calming breath. "I will just have to get over it. It's probably for the better anyway."

Katy looked up at Josh and smiled. He smiled back at her. A thought came to her and she couldn't help but blush dark red.

"What are you blushing about?"

"Nothing."

"Oh, come on," laughed Josh. Katy felt the blush deepen. Josh hooted and Katy scowled at him. He quit laughing and just smiled. "Come on, Katy girl, you can tell me what you were thinking."

She gave him a look and he sobered himself. "I trust you, Josh. You promise that you won't make fun of me?"

Josh made an x over his heart. "I promise."

Katy looked down at her feet and used all her will power not to blush. "I was wondering," she muttered. She looked up at him and lost all her will power. Her face turned a deep crimson. "I was wondering if by chance you would still be willing to let me be your girl."

Josh was silent. Katy looked back up at him. There was no expression on his face. Katy thought she might faint.

"I'm sorry, I shouldn't have said that. It was far too forward of me. I'll go now." She turned to leave.

"Katy."

Katy turned dejectedly toward him. Josh took a step forward and, taking her face in his hands, he kissed her full on the lips. When he finally stepped back, he smiled down at her. She gasped for breath. "Katy girl, I have been waiting to hear those words ever since I met you. You will always be my girl."

Katy grinned back up at him and chuckled. "Perhaps it just took me a while to notice the truth."

Josh laughed. "Just a while." He leaned down and kissed her gently. Taking her arm, he leaned down and whispered in her ear, "I hope you don't mind if I escort you home. I think I need to speak with your father." Katy smiled shyly and wrapped her arm around his. Perhaps God did have a little bit to say to those on earth.

Rose woke early the next morning with a pain in her side. She tried to hide the fact from Henry, but she could not hide the evidence that was left on the bed sheets. Henry's face blanched when he saw the small stain. "Is this...?" The question was clear enough in his eyes that Rose didn't need him to continue.

She shook her head. "No, it can't be. At least I wouldn't think so. The baby is fine."

"I'm calling a doctor.".

When the doctor came, he had Mrs. Jennings in tow. Together they examined the sheets, then the queen, and after a short conferral, they went to speak with the anxiously waiting royal couple.

"The baby is fine," stated the doctor, "but there is some concern about the continued state of its wellbeing if you continue on with your travel plans."

"What do you mean?" asked Henry.

Mrs. Jennings stepped in. "Rose, you can't plan on travelling anywhere out of Emriville until the baby comes. Whether by carriage or by horse. Such travel is too dangerous when considering your condition and recent events. You would only be putting yourself and the baby at risk."

"But," stuttered Rose. "I have to travel. I have to make it back to the palace. The queen mother—she will want to know. She needs to know, and I need her here with me."

"Perhaps the queen mother would like to visit Emriville?" suggested the doctor.

Henry scowled at the doctor. "That's all the advice we need for now," Henry clipped. "You may go." Mrs. Jennings hugged Rose and left the room. The doctor bowed and followed in her footsteps.

"I have to go, Henry," Rose whispered when they had left. "Just think of the doctors that can be provided at the palace. And, think of your mother."

Henry scrubbed a hand across his forehead. "We can't leave, Rose." She was about to object when Henry cut back in. "I am thinking of my mother and what she would want. She would want to know that you and the baby are safe. Besides, I am a little more concerned about you right now. I can't deny what the doctor said. We will stay, and I will go as soon as possible to the palace and make sure those there are informed. Mother can decide after that if she will come to Emriville."

"I want to go," replied Rose stubbornly, "and I will go whether you like it or not. I am queen after all. That must be good for something."

Henry shook his head. "Queen you may be, but as your king, I forbid you to leave."

"You can't stop me."

"You want to bet? I will tie you to this bed and feed you three times a day if I have to. Though, I would prefer not having to do that."

Rose gasped. "You wouldn't!"

Henry smirked. Picking her up, he placed her gently on the bed. "Go to sleep, Love, and don't tempt me."

TWENTY-TWO

I T DIDN'T TAKE LONG FOR THE news to spread in small-town Emriville. The queen was pregnant, and Katy Monks had finally decided that Josh Deplin was worthy of her attention. For some, this seemed a worthy enough cause for a ball, and it wasn't long before the date was set.

It was a festive time. It was late spring, and everything spoke of fresh life and beauty. It was quaint to a point of being disgustingly sweet, but only to those who did not share in it. Among those people were Caleb, who watched from his window as the world went by; Elizabeth, who watched over her father as he moved closer and closer to death; and John, who watched Elizabeth struggle because of her refusal to ask for help.

As the day of the ball drew closer, John became more and more morose. He stopped talking. What was there to say? All the thoughts that filled his head revolved around Elizabeth, and she was miserable.

Therefore, he was miserable. At first, Rose and Henry ignored his mood, but Rose could last for only so long. Henry told her to leave him alone, but Rose could not. She decided to confront John.

He was sitting in a corner at the inn. Rose walked over and sat down. The baby kicked, and she couldn't help but smile. John turned away. "What is the matter, John?"

"Nothing," he muttered.

"Hah, as if I'm about to believe that! You yourself know how bad a lie that is. Now, I ask again, what is the matter?"

John turned on her and glared. "I do not have to answer you, cousin; now if you will excuse me." John placed his hat on his head and left. Rose sat and waited.

John didn't know where he was going, but he was going somewhere. He had to go somewhere. His horse took him through hills, over bridges, through towns, but late that night, it brought him right back to the inn feeling like a cur. Rose was still waiting at the table where he had left her. Henry had tried to convince her to go to bed, but she refused to move.

John walked over to her. He started to apologize, but Rose shushed him. Taking his hand, she led him up to her room and told him to wait in the hall. He obliged. When Rose reappeared, she was dragging a half-sleeping king and two swords. John smiled.

The three went for a walk.

When they arrived at the pasture, Rose threw a sword at each man and settled herself on the rock. She smiled up at John. "Once, when I was young, I was so angry, but you took me by the hand and led me to a pasture much like this one. You gave me a sword and said, 'beat me if you can.' Now, I would do the same thing for you. Only thing is, you're going to have to beat my husband, and I am going to watch two fine fighters go at it."

John smiled down at Rose, then, bowing to Henry, the two began to duel. John couldn't believe how good it felt. He felt the stress roll away in rivulets of sweat. His anger dissipated, and he was soon laughing and jesting with Henry.

He did not know how long they duelled, or why they stopped, but the next thing he knew, he was watching as Henry bent over his wife and kissed her cheek. John felt the jealousy coil in his stomach. Rose looked over at him and gave a half-hearted smile. She walked over to him and gave him a gentle squeeze. John could feel where her stomach was starting to bulge. He blushed.

"Sit, John," Rose whispered. "It's time that we talk."

John nodded and sat down near the rock. Rose took up her previous position and Henry took a spot close to her. "Now, John," said Rose. "I want to begin by apologizing to you."

John groaned. "Rose, you don't have to do that. I am the one who should be apologizing. I acted like a cad, and you have every right to be angry with me. I have just been a little stressed lately."

"And that is exactly why I must apologize. You have been stressed for more than a while, and I have been far too concerned with my own needs to even care about yours. I hope you will be able to forgive me for that."

John looked down at the ground. "On one condition," he whispered. Rose nodded in agreement. "I will forgive you, if you will forgive me for not sharing in your happiness. I have been so concerned with my own needs that I have not been able to find joy in the fact that I am going to be an uncle of sorts."

Rose smiled. "It is agreed. You are forgiven." John smirked. "Now, tell me what has been going on. I don't want to walk out on you, when I just now asked forgiveness for doing that very thing."

John bit his lip. "It is silly, really. You will probably laugh at me, but I guess I can live with that."

"It's a girl problem, isn't it?"

John blushed. "Rose, my dear," whispered Henry, "perhaps you should let John finish without cutting in. I have a feeling this is hard enough for him." John gave Henry a grateful smile. Henry smirked back.

"I guess you could say that it is a girl. You see, Elizabeth is different than most women. She isn't prim and proper, but she has manners. She is a hard worker, and she cares so diligently for her father. She truly is an amazing lady." John quit talking.

"What is the matter in all this, John?" Rose asked.

"She is poor, very poor. She used to work at the post office, but she lost her job, and I think that was partly my fault, and her father is dying. She can't even afford to buy food for herself, and she refuses to live off charity. She is angry with me because I have a tendency to destroy small parts of her house and then fix them."

Rose couldn't help but laugh. "I'm sorry, John, but I have been waiting for what seems like ages for you to find a girl, and now you have, and it is just so wonderful. She sounds like she is perfect for you."

"There is more to it than that."

"Go on telling then," said Rose excitedly.

"Elizabeth is an illegitimate child, and she blames herself. I asked around town, and it turns out that her mother hung herself when Elizabeth was four. The man Elizabeth is caring for is not her real father, though Elizabeth calls him that. He is in fact the husband who was cheated on. No one knows why he did not rid himself of her when he had the chance. He was legally allowed to."

Rose reached out and hugged John. "You should have told us sooner," she whispered. "How do you think that we can help?"

John shrugged his shoulders. "I don't know. What can be done? Elizabeth is dead-set that God hates her because of who she is. She nearly starved herself to death because she refused to live off charity, and even now she vows that she will pay me back for every morsel of food she eats."

Rose became thoughtful. "What if she had a job? Would that suit her well?"

John looked at Rose. "What do you mean?"

Rose smiled craftily. "I am going to become awfully big with the baby on the way, and moving from place to place is going to become miserable. This baby already kicks enough to be mistaken for a young stallion, and I think I'm only six or so months along. I could really use a maid who is good at nearly anything, and who will keep me company. Henry does seem to be overly protective, and I feel like I am cooped inside all the time."

John laughed at his cousin. "You really are a little weasel sometimes, you know."

Henry grunted. "You only know the half of it. If you haven't noticed, her little story there does paint me as the evil monster keeping her locked inside."

John laughed. "It may work, but it will take a lot of convincing. I don't think Elizabeth will take to being seen in public with the queen. She is often worried about other people's reputations being tarnished by being around her."

"Hah, sounds like another person I know," muttered Rose. John and Henry both raised an eyebrow at her. "It is nothing that I cannot handle. Besides, if I can't convince her, I will just have to be a little more creative."

Henry smiled at her. "My lady, I have no doubts of your skills of persuasion, but what are you going to do about your current maid? Elizabeth is sure to know that you have a maid with you and will not take to the job if she thinks it is unnecessary."

Rose pondered this for a moment. "Bess has been bothering me for a break for quite some time, and I unthinkingly gave her leave. We will not see her until I return to the palace, and now I am in desperate need of someone to replace her for at least a short while."

John couldn't help but laugh.

"What is that laugh for?" Rose asked.

"Nothing. I am just trying to picture you doing something without first thinking it entirely through. You would never do it. You are too methodical."

Rose smiled. "I'll blame it on my currently altered state and sleep deprivation. I'm sure that will do."

Henry perked up at the mention of sleep deprivation. "If I recall correctly, I was in the middle of a wonderful sleep before I was dragged out to this late night meeting. Is there any way I can return to it before the sun is up?"

"I suppose," sighed Rose. "But you have to help me up first. I honestly don't feel like moving." Henry helped her to her feet, and all three walked back to the inn.

John was there. Elizabeth knew it, and she was ready to throttle him. He had left her a box of chocolates. Food was one thing, but chocolate was something entirely different, and she would not be ridiculed in that manner. She looked around the yard to see if he was working on the house. That's where he usually was when she came back from the meadow. She walked around the building, but she didn't see him there.

That was odd. She saw the carriage, which meant that someone was there, but John wouldn't go into the house, or would he? Elizabeth went toward the barn and decided to milk the cow before she went in search of John. He could wait for her. It wasn't like she wanted him to be there. He was an unwelcome guest, and she would do anything she could to deter him.

It did not take long to tend the cow, and there wasn't much else to do. Hesitantly, she moved toward the house. She opened the door and looked in. No one was in the kitchen, and nothing had moved since the last time she had stepped in. Moving further into the house, she listened to see what she could hear, but there was no noise.

Where could John be, she wondered? If he wasn't around the house, and he wasn't in the house, where could he be? Elizabeth moved further into the kitchen and began to make a meal for her father. It was the same as always, porridge. She walked to his room with it.

Her father wasn't alone, and it wasn't John who was with him.

The lady was elegant and very beautiful. Elizabeth recognized her from two years ago. Of course, two years ago she had seen her in the post office sending letters to John. Now she was much different. Now she was a queen and it showed in all aspects of her being, even if she was pregnant. Elizabeth didn't know what to do. She decided to bow, and when this gesture was complete, she went immediately to her father's side. Lifting him up into her arms, she spooned the porridge into his mouth. Half of it was spit out, but Elizabeth very gently went about getting it all into his mouth and down his throat. Before the bowl was half done, the man refused to eat another bite. Elizabeth sighed and placed the bowl on the side table.

She turned and jumped when she saw the queen sitting right next to her. The queen laughed. "Sorry, I am being terribly rude. You are probably wondering why I am even here. But, I was so fascinated with the gentle way you cared for your father that I completely forgot my manners."

The queen smiled, and Elizabeth smiled politely back. "Now, to introduce myself. I am Rose Arden, and if I am not mistaken, you are Elizabeth Mede, correct?" Elizabeth nodded. "Good. I have a proposition for you."

"Excuse me Madame," Elizabeth cut in, "but I must know. Did Mr. Borden send you here?"

Rose laughed. "John has nothing to do with this. Unless that will change your answer. If John having something to do with this will make you reply agreeably, then John has everything to do with this. Now, will you listen to my proposition?"

Elizabeth bit her lip. "I have a lot of things to do. If you haven't noticed, Mr. Borden left my yard a mess when he decided to rip off my roof and repair it. I must say, he does not always think things through."

Rose sighed. "So, you would rather clean your yard than listen to my proposition. I guess I will have to leave you to it then. Though, I must admit I was hoping you would hear me through. Anyway, good day Miss Mede." Rose turned to leave.

"Forgive me, Your Highness," whispered Elizabeth. "I do not want to seem rude. Please tell me your proposition. I will hear it out."

Rose couldn't help but smile to herself before she turned back to Miss Mede. "Very well," she said with a sigh, "if you truly wish to hear it, then I will tell you." Rose made herself comfortable.

"Yes Madame," replied Elizabeth politely. "I would really like to hear your proposition."

Rose could tell she was lying through her teeth, but she wouldn't say anything. Elizabeth was being polite, and that was the first step. They would get through that step and then move onto the next.

"It is really only a result of my own foolishness, but I find that I am currently out of a maid. Now, this wouldn't have been such a great matter if it weren't for my current condition. I find myself completely at a loss as to what to do. Anyway, I was hoping that you would help me out by filling in as my maid for some months."

"Excuse me, Madame. I am not sure I understood that at all."

"Oh, I suppose you wouldn't have. I'll have to start at the beginning. Well, a couple of days ago, I was not thinking, and I allowed my maid a time of leave that she has been asking for, for so long. Now that Bess is no longer with me, I realize how much I need her in my current condition. Seeing as it is much too late for me to call Bess back, I thought I would hire a completely new maid while she was on leave.

"Now, finding a maid in Emriville is not an easy thing to do. There are plenty of willing young girls, but not many of them have the tenacity to do the job. That is when I remembered you. You used to work at the post office and you did such a splendid job, and then John told me about how you worked so well and so hard, and I thought that perhaps you would be willing to take the position as my maid." Rose looked at Elizabeth hopefully.

Elizabeth sighed and looked down at the floor. "I don't think that would be appropriate, Your Highness. I am truly grateful for the offer, but I am the least qualified for the job. There are plenty of girls in town more qualified, who you would be much more pleased with."

"I am not entirely sure of that. Sure, many of the girls are nice young ladies, but there are so few who actually know how to work, and who I would enjoy talking with. You see, there is more to this job than just working. I am looking for someone who is companionable, because otherwise, I am sure to be driven insane by the four walls that will keep me cooped inside."

"I am not the person for you," whispered Elizabeth. "I don't think I could be very good company. I do not hold conversations, and it is rare that I speak."

"So, you are a good listener! That is very good. Bess is such a babbler, and she has already heard all my stories. If you took the position, you could hear the stories and they would be fresh in your ears even if they are becoming very old news."

Elizabeth squirmed uncomfortably. "I don't think that this will work too well, Your Highness. I really think you should find someone else. I won't be able to care for you, or tend to your needs. I am not trained to do that. I don't even have any formal education."

"But you tend your father so diligently," whispered Rose.

Elizabeth turned away. "Why are you so insistent that I be your maid? Why me?"

Rose thought for a moment. "Because, I think you are interesting, and that there is more to you than meets the eye. I am hoping that by having you as a maid, I will get to know you, and that we can become friends."

Elizabeth looked down at her hands. "I have things that need to get done at home. The yard is a mess, I have a cow that needs to be milked; my father needs to be cared for. There are so many things that need to be done right here."

"If that is the way you feel," sighed Rose. "It is too bad. John said you wanted a job. I was hoping you would take this one, but I guess you really don't want a job so badly."

Elizabeth shook her head. "Your Highness," she said nervously, "I truly do want a job. It is just that this one would be inappropriate for me to take. I would be putting on airs if I took this job, and everyone would know it. It is better that I not take it."

"What would be inappropriate about it, Elizabeth?"

Elizabeth sighed. "It would just be inappropriate. The people in town would not understand, and they would think badly of you because of it. That would never do. I will not have the entire town thinking badly of the queen because of me. No, I cannot take the position."

Rose looked at Elizabeth sadly. "Elizabeth," she whispered. Elizabeth looked up at her. "Is this because of your mother?"

Elizabeth blushed and looked down at her hands. "You know my story, don't you?"

"Brief bits of it."

"Then you know why I cannot be your maid," whispered Elizabeth.

"I think, that, that is a very poor excuse. If you think people will look down on me because of you, then you are wrong. If people judge you because of your mother, they are wrong. And, if I did not ask you to be my maid, I would have been in the wrong."

Rose smiled at Elizabeth. "I know you may think it is inappropriate, but I would appreciate it if you would be my maid, no matter what the people in the town think. None of that matters. Would you do it then?"

Elizabeth ignored the stutter in her voice as she answered. "I-I don't know if I should." She turned and tried not to look at Rose. She needed to think. This offer seemed too good to be real. Could it be possible that the queen was with her now asking her to be her maid? It had to be impossible. "I still don't feel worthy of the job."

Rose smiled. "That doesn't matter one whit now, does it? All that matters is that you say yes to becoming my maid."

Elizabeth closed her eyes and took a deep breath. "Very well," she whispered. "I'll do it."

A smile covered Rose's face as she reached over and embraced Elizabeth. "Thank you," she laughed. "I am looking forward to the next few months now. I am sure we will have a great time together."

Elizabeth looked at her with round eyes. How was she supposed to respond to this lady? She was different than anyone she had ever met. Elizabeth bowed her head and blushed. "I hope you won't regret asking me."

Rose laughed. "I think that is impossible. Now, you can take the rest of the day to collect yourself, and I will see you tomorrow morning. I think your hours should be from nine in the morning until dinner time. You will not leave until after you have eaten your dinner. It shall be part of your pay. And I will make sure there is someone here to tend to your father. I am sure I can find a suitable man-at-arms or servant for the task. If not, Shoals will know of a person. Are we agreed?"

"Yes ma'am," Elizabeth replied and began to shake her head. She was sure it all had to be a very strange dream.

TWENTY-THREE

THE NEXT MORNING, ELIZABETH MADE her way toward the inn. It had been odd getting back into the routine of working. It had started with getting up extra early to tend her father and the cow. Then, she had made her way to the pasture, but by that time she was running late and needed to leave immediately to make her way to the inn.

It felt good to have purpose again. It felt good to know she wasn't going to be living off charity. She would be earning her keep. She could at least hold up her head again.

The inn was quiet. The only people awake were the men-at-arms who seemed restless even at such an early hour. Many of them were chewing on their breakfast. Their faces were unshaved and their hair tussled. Sleep was still in some of their eyes. Elizabeth felt her cheeks glow red when she realized she was the only female present.

She wasn't sure where to go. It was unlikely that the queen was awake, and it was even less likely that she was needed to do anything at the moment. Looking around cautiously, she took a seat in the corner and waited. The innkeeper saw her sitting there and glared. She saw him walk over to one of the men and start whispering. The two men looked at her, and she blushed. She turned and looked at her hands.

A throat cleared behind her.

Elizabeth turned and looked up. The man was tall and broad. He had dark brown hair and eyes that burned with a terrible fire. Elizabeth felt herself shrinking away from his presence. He just stared at her. "Is there a purpose for your presence here, mademoiselle?" he asked.

Elizabeth bit her lip. "I am the maid the queen hired yesterday. I was told to report to the inn at nine." Her cheeks were red. She could feel them burning. What was this man thinking? He just kept staring at her. She tried to avoid his attention.

"I had not heard about the queen hiring a new maid. You must be mistaken. Perhaps you should come back at a more seemly hour."

Elizabeth could feel her stomach coiling up inside her. It twisted in a knot and pulled hard. She must have been mistaken. It was a dream. It had always seemed too good to be true. She had had a foolish dream and now she would pay for it. "I'm sorry sir. I'll go now."

Elizabeth turned to leave, but the man reached out and grabbed her arm. She froze. She could feel herself trembling with fear. Who knew what this man was capable of? Elizabeth looked up at him with wide, terrified eyes. He looked away and dropped her arm. "I'm sorry," he muttered.

He kicked his foot into the wood floor and looked back up at her. "Do I know you?"

Elizabeth looked away. "It is unlikely, sir. I have lived in Emriville all my life, and I have not once ventured past the town limits."

The man rubbed his eyes. "I'm sure I have seen you before."

Elizabeth turned away. "Perhaps I only remind you of another person you know."

"Perhaps," the man muttered as Elizabeth turned to leave.

"Sir Shoals!" a woman's voice shouted across the room. "What have you done to send my new maid scurrying away? That will never do at all. I have great need of her today."

The man turned and looked at the lady. "I'm sorry, my Queen. I did not know you had hired a new maid. I am afraid I have nearly scared that young girl out of her wits." He turned to Elizabeth. "Forgive me," he murmured.

"I am sure all is well. It really is my fault. I find I have quite overslept. I am doing that much too often these days." Shoals smiled politely down at the queen. "Now," Rose continued. "It is time that we make introductions so we don't have to deal with this mess again."

Rose turned to Shoals and smiled. "Sir Eldon Shoals, this is Miss Elizabeth Mede. Miss Mede is my new maid. Miss Mede, Sir Shoals is one of our most trusted soldiers. If you ever need anything, you can go to him."

Elizabeth smiled and bowed. Sir Shoals looked down at her and just stared again. Elizabeth could feel herself blushing. *Why wouldn't he stop staring?* She turned away from him to look at the queen.

"Sir Shoals," laughed Rose, "you are being perfectly rude by staring at Miss Mede. It is very clear that you are making her horribly uncomfortable while you're at it as well." Shoals blushed and turned away.

"I have to go," he muttered. He bowed to the queen and disappeared.

"Well, that was odd," said Rose with a shrug. "I have never seen the man so uncomfortable before. He is usually perfectly amiable. A touch protective perhaps, but he is always kind. I wonder what has gotten into him."

Elizabeth shrugged and averted her eyes to the ground. Rose gently grasped her arm and pulled her toward the hall. "There is so much I want to do today, and I am hoping you will be able to help me. I don't exactly know what you are all capable of, but I am hoping you know how to sew. I have an entire wardrobe that needs alterations, and I don't know how I am to get it all done."

Elizabeth followed the queen, a little overwhelmed with everything that was going on. She felt as if she was riding a wild horse; one moment she thought she was mistaken about everything, and the next she was following the queen to her room talking about sewing. "Anyway," continued Rose amicably, "I have no problem sewing myself, only there is to be a ball soon, and I have no idea how I am to alter a ball gown. It is going to be downright miserable."

Shoals drew calm, steady breaths as he walked toward the stables. He didn't look at anyone; he didn't speak to anyone; he kept walking straight and breathing steadily. The stable was crowded with soldiers and their horses. Shoals flinched at the noise. He found his mount quickly and disappeared out of the mayhem.

As soon as the country air hit his face, he could breathe. He set his horse to a gallop, and the two of them enjoyed the freedom, the speed and the wind in their faces. Despite all this, Shoals could still feel the stress mounted on his back. He needed to shake it off, but how?

He slowed his horse, and looked around at the countryside. Up ahead, a small, dilapidated house sat on a small hill. It was surrounded by scrap pieces of lumber and rotting boards. The sound of a solitary hammer pounding resonated across a field of knee-high corn. Shoals made his way up the drive to take a look.

The house was in better condition than he had expected. New boards replaced the ones that had been rotting on the side, and a new roof had recently been set in place. Shoals looked for the source of the thudding hammer.

Just then, the hammering stopped and a young man walked around the corner of the house. He looked up at Shoals and smirked. "Nice to see you, Shoals."

"You as well," replied Shoals stiffly as he looked at John. "May I ask what you are doing here?"

John laughed slightly mockingly. "I should be asking that of you, don't you think? After all, I am the one who was here first. So Shoals, what are *you* doing here?"

Shoals felt his face colour, and he turned away from the ornery young man. "I was looking for something to do. I heard the hammer and I was wondering if I could help. I didn't know it would be you here. I was hoping to encounter a stranger."

John smiled with a little bit of compassion. "Well, there is definitely work to be done here, and I'll keep my mouth shut if you keep yours just as silent. Is that good enough for you?" Shoals nodded and John tossed him one of the many hammers that still littered the ground from when the other men had helped with the roofing. Shoals dismounted, and John led him to the back of the house where there was a rather large hole in the wall. Shoals whistled at the size of it, and the two men set to work.

The sun rose higher in the sky and began to descend on the other side. The two worked side by side, the only noise the loud thuds of their hammers and gentle grunts when nails were nonresponsive. When the sun finally began to sink lower in the sky, John tossed aside his hammer and fell back onto the grass with a heavy sigh. Shoals followed suit.

"Thanks for letting me help," muttered Shoals. John grunted a response. "Whose house is this anyway?"

"It belongs to a Mr. Gerald Mede, though it is mainly his daughter Elizabeth Mede who benefits from this," responded John with very little emotion.

Shoals bolted off the ground and looked down at John in shock. John looked at him incredulously. "What's the matter with you, man? You look as if you've just seen yourself die."

Shoals took a deep breath and forced himself to sit down. "It's nothing," he muttered. "I just thought you said something entirely different. It just startled me, that's all." John gave him a look, then turned back to watching the sky. Shoals sighed and looked up as well.

"John, have you ever had the feeling that everyone thinks you are so virtuous, yet you yourself don't feel that way? For example, think of me. My entire life I have been living as or working to be a soldier in the king's guard. The guard is supposed to be the most honourable of all men, yet I am just ordinary. I am not exceptionally pure or good."

John kept looking at the sky. "I'm too young for all that, Shoals," he replied in a dead monotone. "I'm just getting to the point in my life where I am trying to be the virtuous person. Why else do you think I am here?"

Shoals shrugged his shoulders. "I figured it was just in your nature to do something like this. Besides, you've been awful depressing the past few days."

John smirked. "It's all this trying to be virtuous. It puts me in a bad mood."

Shoals rolled his eyes at the young man beside him.

John sobered and sighed. "Perhaps it's in my nature to want to work, but I wouldn't be doing this if it wasn't for a purpose."

"So, what is your purpose?"

"That is a very good question. At first it was because of a girl. I wanted to do something for Elizabeth that would make her smile for once, but that didn't work, and now I just stick around trying to be helpful, half the time getting in the way, and the other half making her more angry than a rooster with its dander up. I think the only reason I keep coming back is because if I stick around the inn, I might lose what self-control I have left, and I don't want to be around Rose when that happens."

"So you take it out on the house."

"Yup."

The two lapsed into silence and stared up at the sky where the clouds floated lazily about their domain. "You going to be back tomorrow?" Shoals asked.

"Most likely."

"Mind if I join you?" Shoals asked. John shook his head affirmatively.

The sound of someone humming brought the two out of their reverie. John looked around and sighed. He picked up the tools and looked around to find his horse. Shoals picked himself up off the ground and began to help. The humming stopped and a low, frustrated sigh sounded nearby. John bit his lip and made a motion toward Shoals, telling him to keep quiet. Shoals shrugged his shoulders and went to get his horse from where it was grazing.

Before he could get very far, a very angry-looking Miss Mede walked around the corner and glared at John. "Mr. Borden," she began with a forced calm, "you are not needed around this house. If my father and I required your assistance, we would have asked for it, but seeing as we haven't, it would be best if you did not come."

John smiled politely at the young lady. "It's good to see you as well, Elizabeth. I know you and your father did not ask for my assistance, but I have nothing better to do, and I am rather enjoying myself. Besides, I need to repair all the damage I have done, and I am not anywhere close to doing that." Elizabeth glared at him, and Shoals tried not to laugh when he saw the man blush.

"Very well, Mr. Borden, but if I see you add any more damage to my house, I will be tempted to have you arrested for damaging my property." Miss Mede turned and left the two of them standing there.

"She really doesn't like you, does she?" said Shoals.

John groaned and shook his head. Shoals couldn't help but laugh a bit at the young man's difficulties.

"It'll get better," he reassured him. "No woman can say 'no' forever." John gave Shoals a look. Shoals shrugged his shoulders. "Well, they could say no for a very long time, but maybe you will have better luck, and you will only have to wait for another few years. Cheer up lad," Shoals laughed. "You never know when your luck might change."

Rose enjoyed Elizabeth's company. She was sweet, quiet and always overly polite. Of course, it was sometimes hard to come up with conversation topics, because the young girl would never disagree with her; but it was a fun challenge.

Rose laughed when she realized that she thought of Miss Mede as a young girl. The lady was older than she was by three years. There was no way she could justify calling her a young girl, but she couldn't help but think of her that way. No, she was not young in the physical sense, but everything about her made her seem young, and in a way, vulnerable. Rose shook her head. It was a shame Elizabeth was determined not to like John. The two of them would be so good for each other.

Rose put her hand on her expanding belly. She could imagine her tiny child in her arms. Henry would be there beside her, and they would be caring for their little one together. She smiled at the picture, and wondered what it would be like not to have that picture. She shuddered as the image of herself standing alone with a baby in her arms came to mind. It just wasn't right when Henry wasn't there.

Rose wondered if that was how Elizabeth felt. Was she the child in the picture without the father? Rose shook her head. That couldn't be. Elizabeth had a father. What she didn't have was a mother, and that was almost worse for a young girl. Rose sighed. She didn't dare form a picture where it was just Henry and their child. It was terrifying to think of that being possible.

Rose looked around at the empty room. Elizabeth was not working today. She had wanted to work, but it was Saturday, and Rose knew she needed time to tend to her own home. Henry was also gone. He had decided that he had procrastinated long enough, and it was time for him to go back to the palace to bring his parents the news of the soon-to-arrive prince or princess. That left Rose all by herself.

Of course, she could easily go out and find John, but he was most likely working at Elizabeth's place with Shoals. Those two seemed to becoming better friends lately, which was a little odd, considering they had hardly ever talked with each other before. Men were odd that way. They always seemed to make friends at the strangest of times.

Rose sighed and looked around. What could she do? She could sew, but she had been working on that for days already, and she was really quite tired of it. She could read a book, but her supply had already been exhausted, and she did not really feel like re-reading any of them. There really wasn't much to do indoors.

With a frustrated grunt Rose picked up the edge of her dress and moved toward the door. She was weary of the indoors. She would go out, even if it took a royal decree to do so.

As soon as Rose was past the dining room, she had a trail of men following her. "Bother," she muttered under her breath. She turned with a polite smile. "Good afternoon, gentlemen. I am currently going into town to visit the curate. If one of you would like to accompany me, the rest of you can return to your previous activities."

They all turned and looked at each other. A few of them shrugged their shoulders. The other ones bolted off toward the livery and their horses. Two men stayed behind to escort the queen. The diminished numbers were a lot easier to deal with than the earlier crowd. Rose could let herself breathe with only two persons trailing her.

She turned and began walking again. She walked slowly, taking in deep breaths of air. The air in the rooms at the inn began to get stale after spending a couple of days cooped up in them. She would have to take a walk with Henry when he got back. It was such lovely weather out now.

Caleb's house came into view all too soon. One of the men rushed ahead of her and knocked on the door. Caleb answered it with a gruff hello. He tried to force a smile when he saw Rose, but she could tell he was in a bad mood. "Well, he will just have to put up with me for a while," whispered Rose quietly to herself.

She waltzed up to the door and curtsied in greeting. Caleb bowed his head, but he still stood in the door.

"Would you mind if I came in for a while, Caleb? It has been a while since I have seen you, and I was hoping you would have a few spare moments to share with an old friend."

Caleb nodded and stepped out of the doorway.

Rose stepped in and headed directly to the parlour. Taking a seat in the most comfortable chair, she smiled at the curate. "You look miserable, Caleb. Have you been sleeping at all?"

Caleb smirked. "You sound like a mother already, and you haven't even seen your baby's face."

Rose scowled. "Is that your way of avoiding my question, Caleb? Because I won't be ignored. You really do look miserable, and I want to know if there is some way I can help."

Caleb smiled. "I've just had a few rough nights, that is all. I am sure to look much better after a good night's rest. There is nothing for you to worry about." Rose gave him a quizzical look, but he ignored it. "So, how are you?"

Rose sighed. "I am fine. I'm bored out of my wits, but other than that, I am fine."

"That is good." There was silence. Neither spoke; neither moved. They just sat there doing nothing at all.

Rose raised her brow and looked around herself. "You haven't changed much since I was here last. I thought you would have changed the place a lot."

"No, I like it the way it is. You, on the other hand, have changed quite a bit. I never would have pictured you so happily married."

Rose blushed. "I didn't think I was capable of being as happy as I am. Life with Henry at the palace is so wonderful. I wish you would come and see the place, Caleb. It really is wonderful. There is so much to see and do, and you would love the church there. It is so big, and it has the most beautiful windows."

"I am sure that it is lovely."

Rose tugged on a curl and ignored the forced way Caleb spoke to her. "Are you happy here, Caleb?"

"Happy enough, I suppose," he muttered. "I have everything that I could ever want here. I have a house. I have a job, and I am well respected throughout the community. What more could I ask for?"

Rose looked at him sadly. "You could want love."

Caleb raised his eyebrows in a look of shock. "What would I ever do with love? I am too busy for that. Besides, there is no one out there who would ever want to be in love with me."

"You cannot honestly believe that. When I lived here, nearly every girl in the county wanted to marry the curate. Surely there are still some girls out there who would not mind being courted by the curate. You just have to ask them."

"That wouldn't be a good idea," replied Caleb with a dead voice. "Do we really have to talk about this, Rose? I think there are better things that we could discuss. Perhaps you should tell me the names you have picked out for your baby."

Rose sighed. "I suppose we can drop the topic for now, but I am coming again next Saturday, and I hope you are ready to talk then, because I will be even more bored than this week. I really need to find something to do with all my spare time."

"You could take up reading."

"Don't even get me started on that topic," muttered Rose, then she shrugged. "Maybe I'll just have to raid your shelf before I leave. You're sure to have plenty of great books and that will give me an excuse to come back." Caleb gave a mock groan, and Rose felt herself laughing for the first time with him.

TWENTY-FOUR

"I NEED YOUR HELP!" EXCLAIMED ROSE when Elizabeth stepped into the room. Elizabeth looked around the room, bewildered. Clothes were strewn everywhere. The trunk that normally stood at the end of the bed was open and overflowing. Yards and yards of fabric filled up every corner of the room.

"What happened here?"

Rose gave her a strange look. "Nothing happened here. Why do you ask?" Elizabeth gave the queen a look, then set about tidying up the room. "What are you doing?" Rose asked.

"I am cleaning up this mess."

Rose looked around the room as if seeing the disarray for the first time. "Oh," she muttered. "Bother. Well, that will just have to wait. I am in desperate need of your help right now."

"What do you need my help with?"

"Well for starters, there is a ball tomorrow and I am not anywhere near ready for it. I don't even have a dress picked out."

Elizabeth tugged on a sleeve and looked at the queen's slightly expanded belly. "Are you sure you should be going to the ball, Your Highness? I mean, won't it be a little dangerous for you and the baby to dance in your condition?" Elizabeth could feel herself blushing for being so bold.

Rose laughed. "Oh, perhaps it is a little risky dancing in my condition, but Henry promised me he would be back in time to escort me to the ball and dance the very first dance with me, as is appropriate. Besides, I am sure no one will say anything if we make the dress sit just right. My belly is hardly noticeable as it is." Rose looked around the room. "Now, where did I put that fabric."

Elizabeth looked through the piles of clothes until she saw the green silk peeking out of the corner. She moved toward it, and held it up for the queen to see. The queen smiled and nearly raced over to the fabric. "Perfect," she said as she held up the material to inspect it. Rose held it up to Elizabeth and sighed. "It matches, just as I had hoped it would."

Elizabeth stepped back. "I'm sorry ma'am, but I don't understand." She bit her lip. "That colour will suit you wonderfully." She turned her head down, not sure what else to say.

Rose laughed. "This isn't for me. I have a few dresses to pick from in the corner. They just need a few alterations and then they will be fit to go. No, this fabric is for you. I know you might have your own dress already, but I really would like it if you would let me make you one because I haven't been able to make a dress for anyone in ever so long a time."

Elizabeth stepped back shocked. "For me! But, I wasn't planning to go to the ball. I've never even been to a ball before."

Rose smiled in delight. "Oh, you will love it. There are always young men to dance with, and the dresses are just so beautiful, and people swirl around so gracefully as if they are floating. It is the most wonderful thing ever."

Elizabeth turned her head down. "I don't think I should go. It wouldn't be proper. You know it wouldn't be proper. People would be offended if I went. Some people might even leave early if I go, and that would never do."

Rose smiled. "Well, if people leave early, it will only be their loss. I will not have other people's opinions preventing a beautiful young lady from enjoying the ball. That is just wrong. Everyone has the right to go dancing."

"I don't think we should make a dress out of silk. That is far too expensive. I can't accept that. It would be better if it were made out of something else. There are plenty of other selections at the mercantile. Perhaps I should go there now and exchange this."

"Nonsense! We only have one day to make this dress, and I will not waste any of our time walking down to the mercantile. This material is beautiful, and the expense is of little matter. Besides, it will look beautiful on you, and any other material will be much too warm for the evening. Honestly Elizabeth, you have never been so disagreeable."

Rose looked around herself and shuddered. "I suppose we will have to clean up this mess before we get started. I got a little carried away looking at my dresses. I wanted to get some ideas of what to make, and then I had to find my own dress. I didn't realize I had done so much damage." She cringed and bent to pick up the first dress. Elizabeth raced to her side, and together they tidied the room and began making Elizabeth's dress.

Elizabeth looked at her reflection in the mirror and shuddered. The girl who stood before her was no longer a young girl. She was a grown woman; tall and elegant. Her hair was pulled up in a fancy knot with a few strands hanging around her face. Her slippers were new; another gift from the queen. They were soft, almost delicate.

The dress was what really grabbed her attention. It was dark green, and it was beautiful. There were no other words to describe it. It was fitted close to her waist, but it flared out at her hips, exaggerating them, and making her look much more feminine. Her shoulders were bare, and the neck of her dress cut lower than she was accustomed to. The queen had assured her it was still very modest. Now that she was wearing the dress, she wasn't so sure.

Elizabeth grabbed a shawl and threw it over her shoulders. It wasn't nearly as elegant as her dress, but it would have to do. She pulled her eyes away from the mirror and sat gingerly in a chair to wait for the queen's summons. The queen had told her to wait in the dining room for her while she finished getting ready. She had been the one to do Elizabeth's hair. She had practically begged Elizabeth to let her.

Elizabeth sighed and patted at the pins that were stuck to her head. There had to be at least twenty of them in her hair, but when she had looked in the mirror she hadn't been able to see a single one. It had to be a talent to be able to style hair so well.

The door slammed shut. Elizabeth jumped out of her seat in shock. John walked into the room and stopped suddenly. A bright red blush covered his face when he saw her. "You look beautiful," he muttered.

"Thank you," Elizabeth muttered back.

They stood staring at each other awkwardly. Neither of them knew what exactly to say, and neither of them had anywhere else to go. Elizabeth took this time to study John.

He was well dressed for the occasion. His boots had been polished until they shone, and matched his tan britches. His coat fit snugly against his broad shoulders, and was the same color as Elizabeth's dress. She clenched her jaw when she realized this. "The queen," she muttered under her breath.

"What did you say?"

"Nothing. I just noticed that your jacket looks very good on you. It is a very fine piece of clothing." Elizabeth could feel herself blushing as the words came out of her mouth. *A fine piece of clothing? What was she saying?*

John looked at the sleeves of his jacket and smiled. "Rose gave it to me. She has a very good sense of style. She only has trouble picking out clothing for herself. You should see how she agonizes over what colour each of her dresses should be. It really is quite humourous."

Elizabeth looked up at him and smiled. "She is a wonderful lady, the queen. She has so many talents. It is hard to believe a person could be so blessed."

"Talented she may be. Just don't get on her bad side. She has an awful temper." John bit his lip. "Don't tell her I said that. She may very well give me a good beating for saying that."

Elizabeth couldn't help but laugh at that. "I can't picture the queen giving you a beating. She is probably half your size."

"Small and mighty that one is," John muttered seriously, and Elizabeth found herself laughing a little bit harder. John grinned at her, and she smiled back.

"Oh good," exclaimed Rose as she walked into the room on the king's arm. "You two are ready to go. I think we may be late, so we will have to hurry. I did not think it would take this long to get ready."

Elizabeth sobered and stepped to the queen's side. She was only going to the ball to be of assistance to the queen. That was all. Besides, it wasn't like anyone would want to dance with her. John came up beside her and, taking her hand, he placed it into the crook of his arm. "I am the king's escort," he whispered into her ear, "and seeing as you are the queen's, we are to be a couple for tonight. If you want to get rid of me after that, I will be gone before you can say 'scat.'"

Elizabeth blushed and allowed John to escort her behind the royal couple. The hall was only down the road, and it did not take them long to get there. The crowd hushed as the royal couple stepped into the room. They were formally introduced by one of the colonels who had been asked to do the honours, and then the ball was begun.

Couples whirled about in masses of ribbon and lace. Young men grinned at the young ladies who blushed prettily, and the night went on and on.

Elizabeth watched, absorbed in the swirling rainbow and the mixed scent of rosewater and lilacs and the absolute joy that surrounded her. No one seemed to notice her. No one gave her a second glance. They were too caught up in their own happiness to care if she wasn't like them.

A throat cleared behind her. She turned to see John looking at her. He bowed, and she curtsied. "Would you dance the next dance with me?" John asked.

Elizabeth shook her head. "I don't know how to dance."

John smiled. "Then the next dance will be perfect. All you have to do is follow my lead. I will make sure that you get through the entire thing unscathed."

"I might step on your toes."

John grinned. He took her hand and pulled her closer to himself. He leaned down closer so that only she could hear what he said. "Look out onto the dance floor, and find Miss Monks and Mr. Deplin. What do you see?"

Elizabeth looked out over the dancers until her eyes rested on Miss Monks. The young lady was moving about the dance floor with unco-ordinated steps. She lacked any grace, and her feet fumbled about. Her partner, Josh Deplin, didn't seem to mind one bit. He flowed gracefully beside her with the biggest grin on his face.

"She cannot dance, and he doesn't seem to care. Is that what you are trying to say, Mr. Borden?"

John smirked and tried to keep the grin from his face. "Keep watching. You'll see it yet."

Elizabeth turned and continued to watch the young couple. She was surprised when a look of pain suddenly crossed Josh's face. It was quickly replaced by a grin, and the two continued dancing. "Watch their feet," John whispered in her ear, and Elizabeth had to fight the urge to shudder.

She turned her attention to the couple's feet. She really couldn't see Katy's feet, so she settled for watching Josh's. Then she saw it. She felt herself gasp. John laughed beside her. "You see," he said, "it doesn't matter if you step on my feet. I honestly couldn't care less."

"That isn't funny," muttered Elizabeth. "The poor boy is in pain because Katy is such a horrible dancer. Surely something should be done about that."

"What do you suggest, Miss Mede? I doubt that Josh would take a different partner, and Katy has been trying to learn how to dance for a couple years now. She just lacks all talent when it comes to dancing."

"Well, Josh shouldn't take her to balls then. It would be better if they entertained themselves otherwise."

"But Katy loves balls, so Josh will take her to them even if it means a few bruised toes. He is man enough to handle that. Besides, he loves the girl."

"I don't get it."

"Will you still dance the next dance with me?"

Elizabeth bit her lip and looked up at John. He seemed sincere enough, and it did look like it would be fun. "Alright," she whispered. "But if I step on any of your toes, it is your own fault. I will not be taking the blame for that."

"Yes ma'am," John replied with a grin.

The dance ended and it was time for the next one to begin. Elizabeth lined up across from John and took a deep breath to try to calm herself. She was going to mess this up. She knew she was going to mess it up, and John would look like a fool.

John smiled at her, and she smiled politely back. The music began. John took the first step, and Elizabeth followed suit. She kept her eyes on his feet, doing exactly what he did only opposite. Every now and then he would take her hand then let go. She let him take the lead, and she soon found that she could predict what move he would make next.

Elizabeth lifted her head to smile at John. He smiled back. Too late, she noticed her mistake. They were near the end of the dance, and there was a change in the step. She turned the wrong way, and she would have walked right into another lady if it weren't for John. He picked her up by the waist and spun her in a loop, making it look like a planned part of the dance. The couple behind them laughed cheerily, and the dance ended.

Elizabeth looked up at John in shock. "How did you do that?" she whispered, slightly awed.

He grinned down at her. "I told you I would lead you through it. I just made sure you got through to the very end safely."

Elizabeth looked down and blushed. "Thank you."

"You're welcome," John murmured.

"John, Elizabeth!" They turned at the sound of their names. The queen was waving at them to come. They responded immediately. Rose was smiling when they came up beside her. "Your dance was absolutely beautiful. I did not know you danced so well, Elizabeth. That bit at the end was just beautiful."

Elizabeth blushed and ducked her head. "It was Mr. Borden. He is more talented than I am. He led the entire way. All I did was follow."

Rose smiled. "John does a wonderful job of leading, and though I would love to see the two of you dance together again, I must ask both of you a favour." Rose gave each of them a look, and each of them squirmed under her gaze. "John, I would like you to dance with Katy the next dance. Josh's toes need a break, and Katy will be insulted if she is required to sit down for a dance."

John groaned.

"Man it up, John. You can handle it if Josh can," stated Rose with a smile.

"Josh has an advantage. He is in love. That helps him bear the pain. I, on the other hand, will have to handle the pain all on my own."

Rose rolled her eyes at him. "Elizabeth, I was hoping you would consider dancing with Curate Taylor. I know you don't know him so well, but he hasn't danced a single dance tonight, and I know he will refuse to dance with me. So, if you don't mind, he is just over in that corner there. Do you see him?"

"Yes, but..." replied Elizabeth, but Rose cut her off.

"Good. Now, where is my husband? He said we would dance the next one together." Rose walked away before Elizabeth could raise any more objections.

John smiled sympathetically at her. "Don't worry. It is the same dance as the last one. All you have to do is follow his feet."

"The music will be different. How can it be the same dance?"

John laughed. "Listen to the rhythm. It is exactly the same." He gave her one last smile, then went to take Josh's position dancing with Katy.

Elizabeth took a deep breath and walked toward the curate. How was she supposed to ask a man to dance? It was completely unheard of. She slowed her step, unsure what she would say. She took one last deep breath, and the last step was taken. He looked down at her, and she stared back at him.

"Is it a habit of yours to go to a ball and dance with no one, Seth?" she asked. He smirked down at her.

"It used to be that I had to fight off the ladies. They all wanted to dance with the only eligible man. Unfortunately, the war ended, and I was given competition. I guess I just didn't add up."

"So, you just quit asking ladies to dance, and now you sit there and watch as the couples swirl in front of you?"

"I figure there is no use in pretending I am interested in one of these girls. I am not worthy of any of them, so it is better not to let them think I might like them."

"Well, I know who you are, and I won't think anything of a dance, so why don't you ask me to dance?"

Seth laughed. "Rose sent you over, didn't she?" Elizabeth winced and nodded. Seth laughed again. "Very well then, Miss Mede, may I have the next dance?"

"As long as you make sure I don't run into anyone."

Seth laughed again. "I think I can handle that."

He held out his hand, and Elizabeth took it. He led her to the dance floor, and they took their positions. Elizabeth took a deep breath, but she wasn't nervous. She trusted Seth. She knew him, and she knew he would not let her run into anyone else. The dance began.

"How are we supposed to talk if you are watching my feet?" Seth asked.

Elizabeth didn't look up. "I need to know what to do. If I don't watch your feet, we'll end up in a big heap of silk."

Seth chuckled at that picture. "You know the steps already though, Miss Mede. You learned them in the last dance."

Elizabeth looked up carefully. "I still might mess them up."

"Nonsense. Just keep your eyes on me, and we will make it through this dance together."

Elizabeth looked at him sceptically, but followed his advice. At first she felt like she was fumbling her steps, but then it came more naturally. She followed the motion Seth made without once looking down at her feet. It almost seemed natural. She smiled, and he smiled back. "You see," he muttered, "it isn't so much about the steps made, as the motion they produce. I can make the wrong step here," he did a little tap, "but no one will notice, because the motion is the same."

Elizabeth smiled. "The only problem with that is you still made the wrong step. Just because others don't notice doesn't mean the mistake wasn't made. It just means that the others are blind to the fact."

"Then it is their own fault for not paying attention, isn't it? I did not deceive them in any way. They just chose not to see my fault because they weren't looking at my feet."

"Someone could have seen it."

The music ended and the dance was done. Seth bowed and Elizabeth curtsied. "It doesn't matter now," replied Seth. "The dance is over, and the fault was made. Now all they can do is critique my mistake.

They can't change the fact that it happened, and their criticism does little damage because the dance is over."

Elizabeth stared up at the curate. She wasn't sure she understood the charade that he proposed. She wanted to ask him about it, but there wasn't time.

"Good bye, Miss Mede," Seth muttered and he disappeared into the crowd. Elizabeth watched as he went. John took her elbow and led her off the dance floor. He handed her a glass of punch, and she took it unconsciously. She needed to talk with Seth, and she wasn't sure she could wait till morning.

TWENTY-FIVE

OHN SAT BESIDE ELIZABETH AS the carriage made its way toward her house. It was late. Actually, it was early—very early. The ball had gone longer than planned. It had been such a happy celebration that no one wanted to leave, but all good things must come to an end and eventually the crowd began to dissipate.

John watched as Elizabeth slept restlessly beside him. She was beautiful. Her hair was starting to come out of its pins, and a few dark curls fell softly around her face. He lifted them back into place, and Elizabeth squirmed under his touch.

The carriage came to a stop. John bent over and gently shook Elizabeth. She looked up at him with wide eyes. "We're home," he whispered. She nodded and began to collect herself. She patted at her hair and worriedly fussed with it. John smiled and, opening the carriage door, he helped her out.

"It was a wonderful evening," Elizabeth whispered.

"Yes, it was."

"I didn't think it would be so much fun. Everyone was dressed so beautifully, and everyone laughed and danced and it was just wonderful."

John took her hand and tucked it into the crook of his arm. "Shh," he whispered, and began to walk her toward her front door. "It was wonderful, but now it is time for sleep. We can talk about it more in the morning." Elizabeth nodded and blushed. John smiled and opened the door for her.

She turned and looked at him. She tugged on her sleeve. "I haven't thanked you properly for all that you have done for me. Thank you. I really do appreciate it."

John smiled. "Goodnight, Miss Mede. I will see you in the morning." He turned and left her.

John walked to the carriage and listened for the door to close behind him. He heard the gentle thud and let out a sigh of relief. Perhaps there was some hope yet. Perhaps Elizabeth would learn to trust him after all.

A high-pitched scream rang through the air.

John spun around and ran to the house. Elizabeth was weeping by the time he got there. He gathered her in his arms and tried to calm her. "It's all right. It's all right," he muttered. "I'm here now. It will be okay."

Elizabeth pushed away from him. "All right! How can it be all right? He's dead. Nothing can change that. He's dead." She started weeping again.

John looked around the room. It was Mr. Mede's room, but it was different. It lacked the shallow gasps that marked the life of Gerald

Mede, and the sick feel had vanished. Instead, death hung like thick black drapes. It darkened the room and suffocated all those who were near.

John pulled Elizabeth closer, but she pushed him away. "I have to go. I have to get him ready." She held up her hands, not knowing what to do with herself.

"Elizabeth," John said sternly. "It is late. Come with me to the inn. I'll get a room for you, and in the morning, you can attend to your father. He'll still be here in the morning."

"I can't just leave him," whispered Elizabeth.

"Yes you can. You have to. Just for now. Just for a little while." He pulled Elizabeth to her feet and led her back to the carriage.

At the inn, they were met by Shoals. "What happened?" he demanded when he saw them. "Is she hurt? Did something happen?"

"We just need a room for the night, for Miss Mede."

"What happened?"

John winced. "Miss Mede's father passed away while we were at the ball tonight. It wouldn't be appropriate for her to spend the night with a dead body, so I took her back here so she could have some sleep before having to deal with things."

Shoal's started to sway. His face was pale, and he looked as if he was about to faint. "He died?" Shoal's muttered. "I need to go. I need to..." He turned and ran out of the room.

The innkeeper must have been woken by the noise, because he was soon in the room. John gave him an apologetic look. "We'll need another room if that is at all possible," John whispered.

Elizabeth was shaking. John could feel her quivering, and he feared she might faint. The innkeeper led them to a room, and John opened the door for Elizabeth to enter.

"I'll be right back. Don't go anywhere."

She nodded.

John dashed down the hall to the king and queen's room. He took two seconds to calm himself, then he knocked on the door. Henry answered it. The king rubbed his eyes and looked at the man standing in front of him. "Is something the matter, John?"

"I need Rose's help for a minute," he whispered.

"She's sleeping. Can it not wait till the morning?"

"Not really. It's important." John felt like shouting but thought better of it.

"Surely I can help instead, John. Tell me, and if Rose is needed, then I will get her."

"I need Rose's help, Henry," growled John. "Won't you just get her?"

There was a soft sigh, and Rose peeked around Henry. "I'm awake now," Rose muttered. "You men make enough noise to wake the dead."

Rose was tired. John could see it. Her face was pale, and there were dark bags under her eyes. She looked as if she could barely stand on her own. John almost regretted waking her, but he needed her help.

He cleared his throat. "Elizabeth's father passed away tonight. I took her to the inn so that she could have some rest before she has to deal with the dead, but I think that she needs some..." John tried to think of how to phrase it. "She needs some things because she only has her ball gown." He could feel his face flushing red.

Rose perked up a little at the news. "Well, why didn't you say so immediately? Henry would you light another candle, I'm going to have trouble finding things in this dark. John, give me just a bit of time and I will come with you to Elizabeth. She is sure to be miserable. Is there anybody with her now?"

John shook his head. "Goodness," muttered Rose. "You shouldn't leave a girl alone when she has just lost a loved one. Surely you know that John. I'll be quick." Rose disappeared into the room, and John began pacing up and down the hall.

It seemed like ages before Rose came out of the room again with a bag of necessities and dressed in a fresh gown. "Lead the way," she whispered.

Elizabeth was sitting on the bed, staring off into nothingness. "You poor thing," soothed Rose as she went to the girl's side. She wrapped Elizabeth in her arms and hugged her tight. Tears again came to Elizabeth's eyes, and Rose was quick to wipe them away with her handkerchief. "You can go now," she muttered to John. "You'll be more useful after a night's sleep and a good breakfast, so go. We'll be fine."

John felt like arguing that point, but thought better of it. Rose was probably right, and he would only cause trouble by arguing. He left the two women to whatever it was they would do. Rose would know what was best. She was experienced in this area. She knew what it was like to mourn, and she was probably the best person to help someone through mourning.

John slumped into the bed in his room and sighed. He was tired. Maybe he would close his eyes for just a little while. He would get up early in the morning and would help Elizabeth with the funeral arrangements. For now he could sleep. It wasn't like the dead wouldn't be there in the morning.

Elizabeth woke with a start. The dream had been the same as always, but now there was an addition to it. Her dead father lay at the feet of the swinging, bloated corpse. It was the story of her life. Everything she touched died. It was only a matter of time. It was her curse. Sin was death, and she was sin. It only made sense that she brought death.

She was crying again. She didn't know why she was always crying. "Shh now," someone murmured. Elizabeth froze. Who was saying that? Who was in her room?

"Settle yourself down, it is just me. You're at the inn. We'll go back to your house later. Sleep now." Elizabeth looked up at the queen, who was leaning over her and gently patting her sweaty forehead with a cloth.

"It must have been quite a dream you had to have put you in such a dither. Do you want to talk about it?"

Elizabeth turned her face away. "You shouldn't be here. You must be tired, and I need to go back to my house." Elizabeth tried to sit up, but a surprisingly firm hand kept her down. The queen gave her a look, and she sank further down into the bed.

"That's better," Rose murmured. "Now, it is barely five in the morning. You've only slept two hours, and those hours were restless. Yes, you need to get back to your house, but not until later. Right now you need more sleep than anything else. I'll have plenty of time to sleep later, you need me more now."

"I've slept enough. I am ready to go back to my house now," said Elizabeth stubbornly.

"And, what will you do there? Will you sit with your father and grieve him, will you ignore the fact that he has passed on? No, you must wait," Rose said sternly. "Believe me. I have had much experience in this area. What you need more than anything right now is sleep because that is what you are going to be lacking in the next little while."

Elizabeth made one more attempt to get up, but Rose was too strong. "If you keep this up, Miss Mede, I will be sorely tempted to get a sword out and persuade you to stay abed that way. It really is your choice."

Elizabeth scowled, then, closing her eyes, she pretended to go to sleep. Surprisingly, it wasn't long before the darkness actually surrounded her, and she was lost to the world.

Death was one thing, and funerals were another. John let out a sigh and looked around him. The small churchyard was nearly empty except for a few black-clad mourners. Everybody in town knew about the funeral, but they all seemed to be too busy to attend. Mr. Clydes had a lame horse he needed to tend to. The Glossens were newly married, and it would be too depressing to go to a funeral. But the worst people were those who outright said no.

Oh, they said they had an excuse. They said it went against their Christian character to mourn over a man who was so far from Christ; especially when that illegitimate child of his would be present. It did not matter to them that Mr. Mede had been a faithful member of the community until he fell ill. All that mattered was that Elizabeth would be there, and they would not taint themselves with such filth.

So, the funeral was small. There were barely ten people. The king and queen were present, along with Shoals, Katy, Josh, Caleb, John and, of course, Elizabeth. Every last one of them was dressed completely in black. It was a sorry sight, but it was somehow comforting. These were the people who truly cared for Elizabeth, and that was what mattered.

After Caleb had made his closing remarks, John moved toward Elizabeth and handed her another handkerchief. She gave him a broken smile, and he tried to smile just as bravely back. Another tear slid out of the corner of her eye, and John brushed it away. She sighed, and pulled away.

"Everybody keeps saying, 'Why does she cry so much? He wasn't even her father.' But, I can't help it. I loved him. It doesn't matter that he wasn't my father. He cared for me when no one else would. He loved me even though he should have thrown me out, and then when he couldn't care for me, I cared for him." Elizabeth let out a shuddering sigh and moved toward the hole where the plain pine coffin had been lowered into the ground.

"He was as much my father as any other man. I don't care if we didn't have one bit of the same blood. He was my father."

John nodded. "There's no reason for anyone to say otherwise. They showed their Christian character when they didn't show up today, and now they have no right to say anything about this man. If you say he was your father in every sense, then I believe you. He's your father, and you're his daughter."

Elizabeth let out another sigh. "Now, if only everybody else would believe me."

"Give them time," murmured John. "People take time. They don't like to admit when they are wrong, and they especially don't like to change their ways."

Elizabeth shook her head. "I'm not staying here any longer. I'm going to sell the farm, and then I'm going to move. There's no use in me lingering here. Things will be better when I'm on my own."

John turned away from Elizabeth and looked at the grave. "If you think that is best, then I can't stop you."

Elizabeth bit her bottom lip. Looking up at John she asked, "You wouldn't try to stop me, would you?"

John concentrated on his boots. "I won't try to stop you if you really think it is best that you go, but I would suggest that you stay and listen to all your options before you leave. There are many people here who love you and are willing to do anything for you."

Elizabeth turned away from him angrily. "What do you think these people can do for me? People already think less of them because they attended this funeral, and I will not completely ruin their reputations by asking them to do anything more for me."

John looked at her, his face solemn. "You don't have to ask. We'll do it for you just because we care enough."

"Well, what if I don't want you to?" Elizabeth demanded.

"Oh, come on Elizabeth," John nearly shouted. "You at least need to listen to what we have to say before you totally turn that option down. You are so concerned about our reputations that you trample on our feelings trying to protect them."

Elizabeth froze. "I'm sorry," she whispered. "I didn't realize."

"No, you didn't, but now you do. So, now you are going to come back with us to the inn, and we are going to discuss our options. You may be surprised to find out that there are a lot of things that can be done."

"Okay," Elizabeth whispered, and followed John toward the inn.

The room they were given to talk in was crowded. Shoals sat in a corner barely moving. He would have looked bored except for the spark that was lit in the back of his eyes. Rose sat next to Elizabeth, who was trying her best not to cry, and Katy was not far away holding tightly onto Josh's hand. John and Henry were sitting by the table with their heads close together trying to keep their conversation semi-private.

"It could work," muttered John, "and you know it. We can give it a shot, or at least let Elizabeth decide for herself."

"I can't let you do that, John," Henry replied. "It is too soon. The chances are that you'll end up being miserable, but you will do the honourable thing anyway."

"It is not too soon. I will not be unhappy. Besides, this isn't about me. It is about Elizabeth."

"Hush John," scowled Henry. "We'll look at our other options first and then if none of those work, you can go about your harebrained plan."

"Fine."

Henry gave him an understanding smile and turned to the rest of the room. "Thank you, everyone, for coming today. I am sorry that the room is so crowded, but we couldn't find a more private area on such short notice. Hopefully we won't be stuck in here too long." Henry looked over the people in the room. Sweat glistened on their brows as the heat of early summer had hit, and the tiny room was poorly ventilated. Tugging at his collar, Henry cleared his throat and continued.

"Now, it is a sad business that brings us here. Death is an awful thing, but that doesn't mean we can't get through this. Miss Mede, I understand that you have no more living relatives and that you are considering leaving Emriville?"

"Yes," Elizabeth replied.

"Well then, there is one simple solution in the forefront, and that is you can stay on as a lady's maid for my wife and then possibly as a nurse maid for when the child is born. We are always looking for help at the palace, and your services would be greatly appreciated."

Elizabeth looked at the king with wide eyes and her mouth slightly open. "You would do that?" she whispered. Henry nodded. She bit her lip and looked down at the floor. "What about now?" she asked.

"What do you mean?"

Elizabeth fidgeted with her hands. "People don't think it is proper that I am living without a chaperone. They think I am like my mother." She cringed and tried to fight the blush that coloured her cheeks.

Henry sighed. "That's where this gets a little bit complicated. We have a few options as to what we can do. You can choose which one suits you best."

Elizabeth nodded.

"Your first option," said Rose, "is that you can go back to the palace by coach. We can send a letter back with you and some of the men-at-arms. The only problem with this is that you won't have anything to do once you are at the palace until I arrive. Also, I was hoping you would be able to stay with me in Emriville. It may be selfish, but that was what I was hoping."

"This brings us to your second option," said Henry. "You can live at the inn with us until the baby is born and then return to the palace when we do. I can't promise you that people won't talk, but it is an option to consider."

"My concern," began Elizabeth after a moment's thought, "is not for my own reputation. I have lived for many years with people saying horrid things about me. But, what I cannot accept is that they would say such things about others because of me. Especially when those people have been far kinder than I deserve. I think, therefore, that I will continue on as I had planned before. I will sell the farm, and I will leave Emriville. I will go someplace where no one knows me, and I will get a job. I think that will be best."

"Very well," Henry replied. "If that is what you think, we can at least help you along. If you entrust your farm to us, we can..."

John let out a slight growl. "Henry you promised," he snarled.

"Hush up, John," Henry replied firmly. "I said we must look at all our other options first. We've barely glanced at them so far."

"Well, it's better to have all the options on the table when you are considering something so big, and you are leaving one of them out." John crossed his arms and glared at the king who ignored him.

"Miss Mede," John said before Henry could continue, "if you are concerned about reputation, there is a way we can make sure that no one will say anything bad about you or the king and queen."

Dropping to one knee, John clutched at Elizabeth's hand. "Marry me, Elizabeth. No one can say anything bad about you if you are married. And, I will take you away from here. Away from the rumours and all this petty hypocrisy."

"Get out, John!" Henry thundered. John looked ready to fight it, but Henry's look told him it was better not to. Picking himself up off the ground, he slouched out of the room. The door closed with a bang.

Elizabeth sat stiff in her chair, unsure if she could move. Nobody spoke. Nobody moved. Everybody waited. Henry cleared his throat. "Mr. Deplin, would you please go check on John and make sure he isn't doing anything rash. Take him out to the meadow if you must. He hasn't practiced his sword in a while, and it will do him some good."

Josh raced from the room, only stopping briefly to give Katy a look of farewell. The room remained silent.

"I am sorry, Miss Mede. John had no right to impose on you in such a way. Especially so close to your father's death. That was very wrong of him. I hope you will forgive him. But now, it is time for you to make a decision. Please do not feel obliged to accept John's offer, and know that whatever you decide, you will have the monarch's entire support."

Elizabeth closed her eyes trying to ignore the swirling of her stomach and the spinning of the room. Everything was happening too fast. There was too much to think about. How could she know what to do? What if she made the wrong decision? She was just about to speak when a throat cleared in the back of the room.

"Excuse me, Highness," Shoals said, "but I believe that there is one more option."

Henry gave him a curious look. "You see," continued Shoals, "Miss Mede could very well go and live with her father." There was a collective intake of breath amongst the ladies of the room. "Not the one that we buried," muttered Shoals. "I was referring to the traveler fellow."

Henry cleared his throat. "Shoals, we don't know who that fellow is, and we have no idea if he is a man of ill repute or if he even knows about Miss Mede."

"He does."

"How do you know, Shoals?" Henry asked.

"Because I am very familiar with the man." Shoals shrugged his shoulders and tipped his chair back so that it balanced on two legs.

"Shoals," Henry said as steadily as possible, "who is Miss Mede's father?"

The chair landed with a *thunk*. Shoals looked at each person in the room individually until his eyes rested on Elizabeth. "I am."

TWENTY-SIX

THICK SILENCE HUNG IN THE AIR. No one moved. No one spoke. Gentle gasps came from Elizabeth's mouth as she tried to gain control of her quickly vanishing sanity. Shoals fidgeted a bit and got up from his chair. He walked toward Elizabeth and stopped.

"I don't know what to say," he murmured. "I know it is not every day that you find out who your father is."

Henry cleared his throat. "Shoals, a word with you." Shoals shrugged his shoulders and turned to leave with the king.

"Wait," rasped Elizabeth. She jerked up from her seat and walked on unsteady legs toward the men. "I-I want to hear what he has to say." She drew in a shaky breath, and Rose quickly led her back to a chair. Shoals looked at Henry, who nodded.

Shoals rubbed a hand roughly across his jaw and looked around at those present. "I guess this is going to change your opinion of me, isn't it?" he asked. No one responded. "I guess I deserve it," he muttered.

Elizabeth looked up at him with pleading eyes. "Please tell me how you know you're my father."

Shoals bit his lip again. "You are twenty-three, correct?" Elizabeth nodded. He nodded as well. "Around twenty-four years ago, I was travelling through Emriville. It was a bit of a ghost town, what with a war going on. The women were a little man-deprived, so I thought I would stick around and maybe do some courting." Shoals gave a little half smile as if he were picturing those days.

"Tanya Mede was the most beautiful lass I had ever met. Unfortunately, she was already taken. As time passed, that seemed to matter less and less. Then, one time, it went a little too far. I couldn't change it, so I justified it. Then her husband came home. I left then, and I never looked back."

"I need to breathe," Elizabeth gasped. She jumped from her seat and left the room. Rose gave Henry a look and followed after her. Katy wasn't far behind.

The king turned to Shoals with a grim look. "We need to talk, man," he whispered. Shoals only nodded.

Elizabeth ran from the inn and into the streets. She didn't stop running until she reached the pasture. She dropped down by the cross and pulled her knees to her chest. "You were supposed to have answers," she sobbed. "I was supposed to find answers here, and my life was supposed to become easier, but every time I come, I just get more and more confused."

Elizabeth rocked back and forth and tried to stop the tears. "Why did you get to die? What did you do that was so special that you got to die? You were even happy. That's not fair. I want to be where you are." The trees rustled nearby and Elizabeth jumped to her feet. Seth stepped out of the woods.

He looked at her with mournful eyes. "I have been thinking the same thing for nigh on forever," he whispered. "Yet, it never seems to help." He walked over to the grave and held his hand out to her. She took it and he helped her settle herself on the ground. Seth took a seat beside her and let out a heavy sigh.

"Maybe Mark didn't have anything to regret," Seth murmured. "That was why he could be so happy."

"Regret could be it." Elizabeth stared blankly at the grave. "Or maybe it's guilt. From what you've said about Mark, he was innocent. We don't have that."

Seth nodded. "That could be it." The two sat in silence. "What happened that you came here?" Seth asked.

Elizabeth buried her head in her knees and groaned. "I found out who my father is, and I have the chance to go live with him."

Seth reached out and squeezed her hand. Elizabeth sighed and let the tears flow. Her lip trembled. "Do we ever understand life? Does it really even matter? I mean, we are here for one miserable moment, and then we die. What is there to understand about that?" Elizabeth asked. Seth shrugged.

"Josh, what are you thinking, dragging me out here in the middle of the day?"

Elizabeth and Seth turned in time to see John and Josh bustling through the trees. John looked livid.

Elizabeth cringed. "Another reason why I needed to come here," she muttered.

"Good afternoon," Seth called, and John stopped dead in his tracks. He looked at Elizabeth and his face coloured a bit.

Josh looked nervously from Seth to John. "I take it there is something I don't understand," mused Seth. "In that case, it is probably better that I go." He tried to slip away but was nearly ploughed over by the queen, who was followed closely by Katy.

He backed away hastily, apologizing profusely. Rose panted and grabbed his arm. His eyes bulged in shock. "Sorry," she muttered. "I just need to catch my breath. I'm not as sprightly as I used to be." Rose took a moment and looked around. "Oh, everyone is here, aren't they?"

Rose stood up straight and acknowledged each person present. Seeing the cross behind them, her eyes misted. She moved to the grave and reached out to touch the small cross. "Hello Mark," she whispered. "I am glad you are here as well. You would have been a wonderful friend in this situation." She patted the small ornament and turned to face the group.

"Now," she said confidently. "We have much to discuss, and I think this is a wonderful place to do it." She reached out one hand to John and one to Elizabeth. She smiled when they each responded favourably. "Elizabeth," murmured Rose, "John has said some things that have probably made your head spin a bit, but I think that we need to give him a chance to explain himself. I trust you do not object?"

"Okay," Elizabeth whispered, and Rose smiled at her.

She turned to John, who was looking down at the ground. "I am sorry, Miss Mede," John muttered. "I did not consider your feelings before I spoke, and I know I may have startled you." He was blushing. He was trying not to, but Rose could see the red tinge crawling lazily up his neck.

John looked up and stared at Elizabeth. "If you want to, you can completely ignore everything I have said, but know that none of it is taken back. This may not make things easier for you, Miss Mede, but I think that I love you." John cut off short as his face turned a scarlet red. There was a hush in the clearing as everyone waited for Elizabeth's response.

"Mr. Borden, I need some time to think about this. In the meantime, it would be better for you to try to forget about me. It really does not benefit you to like me in any form or fashion." Elizabeth turned her head down. Seth shifted on his feet uncomfortably. John paled. Josh looked for an escape route, and Katy clung to his arm. Rose smiled as if the entire situation was very pleasing.

"Now that that is settled," Rose said cheerily, "on to the next matter of business. Elizabeth, what have you decided to do about Shoals? I know you haven't had much time to consider everything, but I think you should get to know him before you totally reject the idea. He really is quite a good man, even if he does have his flaws."

"What does Shoals have to do with anything?" John demanded. He looked at Elizabeth and she winced. Rose laughed prettily.

"I guess you wouldn't know, would you? You had already been dragged from the building. Well," said Rose, smiling, "Shoals has made it known that he is Elizabeth's father. Isn't that wonderful?"

John's jaw dropped. "He—he did?" rasped John.

"When you left, he told us all that we did not have to worry about the welfare of Elizabeth because she could live with her father, who just so happens to be him. Once he said it, I realized a person would have to be blind to miss how much they resemble each other. It really is quite remarkable."

John drowned out Rose's musings as he looked at Elizabeth. "Now you have to decide whether or not you want to accept him as your father?" he asked.

Elizabeth nodded. John let out a groan. "I need a good sword and a willing fencer," he muttered.

Josh's face lit up as he raced over to John's side and handed over a sword. The two of them walked away. John's shoulders were slumped, but Josh looked quite happy to escape the rather awkward situation. Katy followed close behind, willing to watch their sport if it meant she could leave the unpleasant conversation. Rose took this as her opportunity to speak with Elizabeth.

"Elizabeth, I think that you should talk with Shoals. A man can't wait forever after he makes a confession like that. Perhaps you will learn something about him that you never thought possible. He is a good man. He won't harm you. I can promise you that much." Elizabeth nodded. She gave one last look at the grave, and then dragged her feet toward the inn.

Rose sighed and turned to Caleb. "I didn't expect things to go that well. It has to be this meadow. It always seems to resolve conflicts."

Caleb snorted. Rose wrinkled her nose at him.

"You don't believe me?" she asked.

"I don't think this meadow had anything to do with it. I don't even think anything got resolved. Look, John is fighting with Josh, and you've just sent Elizabeth off to face her father all alone." Caleb shrugged. "There are still a lot of problems."

Rose smiled. "I guess it all depends on how you look at it. What I see is John and Josh working off their pent-up energy. The physical exertion will also relieve some of their stress and they will have clearer heads to deal with important matters. As for Elizabeth, she is not alone. She is in my prayers, and I would suspect that you pray as well. That being so, she is in the hand of our heavenly Father, and I am sure he is quite capable of protecting her from Shoals."

Rose let out a soft groan and tried to stretch her back. "I believe it is time for me to get back to the inn. Will you be so kind as to escort me, Caleb? As I said earlier, I am not as sprightly as I used to be." Caleb smiled and offered his arm. Rose took it gingerly, and they set off for the inn.

When the last person left the room, Henry turned to look at Shoals. "You certainly had a mouthful to say."

"I guess I did," Shoals replied.

"What I don't get, is why now? Why did you have to tell us all now? Why didn't you just keep it to yourself?"

Shoals took a seat and stroked his chin. "It's a good question. Why, is always a good question. The only problem is that there is rarely an answer. Why is the sky blue? Why do birds fly? Why did God create lice? There's always a why." Shoals appeared to seek answers from the ceiling. "For a long time I felt guilty over what happened in Emriville. I blamed myself, and I felt dirty and stained. I never came back here. I avoided the town at all costs even when it would have been easier to pass through. It seemed like it would be safer than having to face Tanya and her husband. Now I know that was all foolishness.

"Guilt does things to a person. It makes them angry. It twists their insides and makes them do and say things that they normally wouldn't do. Guilt terrorizes some. Others will consider themselves insignificant or unworthy of praise. They will allow themselves to be trampled over and pushed around. But guilt made me callous." Shoals closed his eyes, seeming to picture the time in his life. "One thing is for sure. Guilt haunts you forever."

"How does this have anything to do with my question, Shoals? Why did you come clean now? Why not years ago?"

Shoals opened his eyes and looked boldly at his king. "Guilt eventually needs a vent. I found God, and he forgave me my guilt. What I didn't realize until just recently, is that I need to make things right with the people that I hurt as well. Today I had that chance. I will make things right with Miss Mede if it is the last thing I do. She deserves that much from me."

Henry nodded. "I am giving you a time of leave, Shoals. This is not a punishment. I want you to take this time to learn about your daughter, and I also want you to use it to find a way to provide for her. This may mean that you buy a separate house for her. You may find work for her, or you may decide to care for her in your own home in Silidon. Whatever your choice, you will care for her. She is your responsibility now."

Shoals bowed his head. "Yes sir," he murmured.

"I know it is a large responsibility, taking on the wellbeing of another life, especially at your age, but you must realize that as soon as you opened your mouth you chained yourself to your daughter and her wellbeing," said Henry sternly.

Shoals looked up with tears in his eyes. "What if I fail at this?" he whispered as one of the tears broke loose from his glistening eyes and slipped down his cheek.

Henry felt his gut twist. "You won't fail. It was what we were made to do. You will be a good father, and you will do everything in your power to make up for the lost years. Wait and see. All will work together for good."

Shoals wiped at his eyes and stood. Henry embraced the man and turned to leave the room.

There was a soft knock on the door. Elizabeth entered. She looked terrified. "Can—can I talk with you?" she asked Shoals.

He nodded.

"I will be down the hall," whispered Henry as he slipped out of the room.

Elizabeth looked at the man standing across from her. Rose was right. They looked a lot alike. They had the same hair, the same shaped face, probably the same smile. She should have seen it. She moved toward him. He stood completely still. "Are you afraid?" she asked in a whisper.

Shoals barked out a laugh. "Terrified."

"Why?"

"Because, I don't know if I know how to take care of a daughter, especially one I have abandoned for so many years."

Elizabeth turned her face away. "You shouldn't have said any-thing. I'm not worth that much to you. If anything, I will make life miserable for you. You should have just kept quiet. No one would have noticed the difference, and I would have been cared for somehow."

"I would have known, and God would have known."

Elizabeth couldn't help but laugh sarcastically. "What would God care if you didn't acknowledge your illegitimate daughter? I mean, I am worthless to you. I am a thorn in the flesh. I'm a sore spot that no one wants to acknowledge unless they can get rid of me."

Shoals swallowed hard. The tears were welling in his eyes again. "But, I love you. I had to speak up."

Elizabeth stared at him wide-eyed. "You don't love me. You just feel obliged to say that because everyone knows that you are my father now."

"No," said Shoals more firmly. "I love you no matter if people know you are my daughter or not. It is just a simple truth."

"How can you love me? You don't even know me. All you know is that I look like you and that you are my father. How can you say you love me then?"

Shoals bit his lip. "I guess it is kind of like how God loves us. He knows who we are because he is our father, and he loves us because that is just what a father does. He loves his children no matter what."

"That doesn't make one bit of sense," replied Elizabeth angrily. "God knows everything, and you don't know one thing about me. Be-sides, God doesn't love me."

"How can you say that God doesn't love you? Do you not love God?"

"That's not what we are talking about right now. You said you loved me, and I said that was impossible, and you still haven't explained how it could be possible."

Shoals sighed. "I love you because you are my daughter. I don't care if you are stubborn or disagreeable. I don't care if you don't know how to sew or if you are a horrible cook. You are my daughter, so I love you."

Elizabeth sat down in a chair, stunned. "Now, my turn for a question," Shoals said. "Do you not know God?"

Elizabeth swallowed. "I know God," she whispered, head bent down.

"Then how can you say he doesn't love you?"

Elizabeth jumped from her chair and looked at him with her fists balled. "How could he love me? I'm the result of sin. How could God love sin? How could anyone love me? I'm sin. Don't you see?" she shouted. "I'm sin!" She ran out of the room. Shoals followed close on her heels.

They strode into the livery and past the stalls. Elizabeth began to walk faster when she realized Shoals was following. "What do you want?" she asked as she moved farther away from him.

"A chance to tell you the truth," he said as he lengthened his strides to keep up with her.

"What truth?" Elizabeth asked over her shoulder.

"The truth that God loves you." Shoals caught up with her. He grabbed her shoulder and she screeched in fear. Shoals let go of her instantly. She cowered behind a horse.

"Listen to me, Elizabeth," Shoals pleaded. "I know that people have said awful things to you about your mother, and about how you came into existence, but they are just people. Everyone sins. How can one person judge another person's sins? It is like one blind man telling another blind man about the beauty of the sea. Neither of them can really truly understand the enormity of it."

Shoals paused to think. Elizabeth hid her face into the side of the horse. "I guess what I am trying to say, is that you aren't sin. I made a mistake when I went to your mother, and she—and well, you came about as a result of my mistake, but that doesn't make you evil. You are far from evil. You are a blessing. You're the one ray of sunshine in all this guilt I feel over what I did."

Shoals waited for Elizabeth to respond. She didn't. He thought about reaching out and touching her hand. He decided against it. He shifted his weight from one foot to the other, hoping that Elizabeth would reply soon. But it was no use.

"I'll—I'll let you think about that," he said quietly, and turned to leave.

"Wait." Shoals turned around, his face lit with expectancy. There were tears on Elizabeth's face as she looked at him. She tried to wipe them away, but they just kept coming. Finally she gave up. "Do you really think I am a ray of sunshine?"

Shoals felt like laughing for joy. Instead, he just smiled. "You are my sunbeam, my little flower, my great joy in the misery of my sin." Tears filled his eyes, and he choked back a sob. "I love you, Elizabeth. I love you with all my heart."

Elizabeth stepped around the horse, and Shoals pulled her into an embrace. They held each other tightly and wept.

"Does God really love me?" Elizabeth asked between the tears.

"More than anyone else in the world." He kissed the top of her head and she shied away.

Elizabeth pulled out of his embrace and wiped at her eyes. "I don't get it. I don't feel like I'm worth his time. There are so many better people he could care about. Why would he care about me?"

"Because God is great and God is good. Beyond that, I may never understand why God loves as he does."

"I think I need some time to be alone. Is that okay?"

Shoals smiled. "Take whatever time you need, daughter mine," he whispered.

TWENTY-SEVEN

ROSE WALKED UP THE PATH to the parsonage and knocked on the door. There was no reply. She knocked again and waited. She was about to leave when the door opened and Caleb looked out.

"Good morning, Caleb, how are you?"

Caleb's eyes went wide with surprise and he tried not to gape. "It is only eight in the morning!" he exclaimed.

Rose couldn't help but laugh. "It is a perfectly respectable time to visit, Caleb. Besides, the afternoons have been so stuffy lately that it's impossible to get good conversation out of the best conversationalist. Now, are you going to leave me out on the stoop, or will you invite me in?" Caleb opened the door wider and allowed Rose to step through.

"I stopped by the post office and took the liberty of picking up your letters. The building is a mess since Elizabeth has stopped working there. That new fellow really has no idea what he is doing. There is one letter here that is addressed to you that is a couple of weeks late. Something really needs to be done before something dreadful happens." Rose held out Caleb's letters and he took them mutely. Rose smiled again and walked to the parlour. Taking his favourite seat, she settled herself down and waited for him to follow suit.

"Now Caleb, tell me what you have been doing lately. I have not seen you since the funeral, and that was over a month ago. So, I plan on staying until we are completely caught up." Caleb rubbed his jaw as he looked at Rose.

"Does Henry know where you are?"

Rose scowled. "Yes, Henry knows exactly where I am, and it was a bother persuading him that I did not need an escort. By the way he treats me, you would think I was a child." Rose tried to act angry, but the grin wouldn't be kept off her face.

"That's good," muttered Caleb. He sat there silently looking at the ceiling. Rose waited for him to say something more, but he just sat there.

"Oh, bother," she muttered. She got up off the couch and Caleb jumped to his feet.

"What are you doing?" he demanded as she walked toward the kitchen.

"I am fixing you coffee and breakfast. I want to have a decent conversation with you, and that is not going to happen with you being undernourished. Now, where do you keep your coffee?" Rose started looking around the kitchen humming to herself. When she finally found the door to the pantry, she let out a sound of disgust.

"Caleb Taylor! What have you been living on? There is hardly anything edible left in this place. I thought you had a housekeeper; what happened to her?"

Rose looked at Caleb expectantly. Caleb cleared his throat. "The housekeeper retired a year or so ago. She was getting old and really wasn't up to the job anymore. Retirement suits her well."

Rose let out an exasperated sigh. "A year ago, and you haven't gotten a new one. Well, no wonder." She shook her head and continued to look around the kitchen. Picking out a few items, she began piecing together a breakfast.

"You need someone to take care of you, Caleb. What's keeping you from finding a nice girl and getting married? I am sure there is someone around who would make you happy."

"Marriage isn't for me," muttered Caleb. "Besides, the only person I wanted to marry is already taken."

Rose blushed. "That was two years ago, Caleb. Surely you have forgotten all about that by now."

"You are a hard person to forget, Your Highness. When you left and married Henry, I realized that marriage wasn't for me, and that was quite all right. I am satisfied with devoting my life entirely to God."

Rose shook her head. "Even God says that it is not good for man to be alone. I am sure the good Lord knew what he was talking about when he said that."

"The world's greatest missionary was not married and he even advocated singleness," replied Caleb. "I believe I will follow his example."

"Paul was a great man, that is true, but you are not travelling halfway around the world and facing great persecution like he was.

I am sure that if he were here, he would find it perfectly suitable for you to have a wife. Besides, you can better minister to your flock with a woman by your side, don't you think?"

Caleb sighed. "I think we should change the topic."

Rose threw him a look and let out a breath of frustration. "Fine, but know that I won't give up on you. There has to be a girl out there for you somewhere."

Caleb groaned and Rose set a plate of food in front of him on the table. Caleb looked at the odd mixture of leftover suppers and some things he wasn't sure he could recognize. He turned to Rose, who just scowled back.

"Are you sure this is edible?" he asked.

"You need a woman," Rose muttered as she handed him a cup of coffee and left the room.

"Where are you going?"

"I am going to look through your selection of books while you eat, and when you have cleaned up some, you can come and join me in the parlour." She left him standing there mumbling something about her actions being entirely inappropriate, but she ignored him and settled herself beside his bookshelf in the parlour.

Caleb did not take long. His breakfast had turned out to be very edible and better than anything he had had in the past few weeks. But there was no way he was going to sit there and enjoy his food while the queen was waiting for him in the parlour.

When he finally did enter the parlour, Rose was reading a book she had pulled from his shelf, and she looked to be completely at ease despite her large stomach. Caleb took a seat and considered picking up his own book. He reached toward the table where he had last left the text he had been reading, when Rose snapped her book shut. "Don't you dare pick up that book if you value your life," she hissed.

Caleb raised his hands in surrender and sat farther back in his chair. "Yes, Madame," he said. Rose gave him a nod of approval before the smile creased her face. Caleb smiled back. "So, where is Henry today?"

Rose sighed. "He isn't too far off. He is actually just down the road. He is determined to practice with his sword today, and it is unladylike for me to join him, so I am stuck waiting back at the inn. He won't be too long, though. He promised to come for me here once he was done."

Caleb nodded. "Where is Elizabeth?"

"She is spending some time getting to know her father. They have come such a long way in the past month. I don't think I have seen Elizabeth or Shoals smile so much. It really does do my heart good to see it."

"That is good," muttered Caleb. "She must be very busy then. Where is she staying?"

"She is living at the inn for now. She would have gladly gone home, but it seems that John has put a larger hole in the wall that can't be repaired for the time being. He works occasionally on fixing it, but he spends most of his time following Elizabeth and Shoals around. So it will take him quite a while to be about the repairs. It really is for the better. The way gossip has been flying around, you would think that something terrible had happened."

"Word spreads that way in a small town. Has she been suffering from dreams recently?"

"Who? Elizabeth?"

Caleb felt himself blushing. "She once told me that she suffered from night terrors. Is that still true?"

Rose bit her lip to think. "On the night of her father's death, she had a dream, but I have not heard anything since then. She seems to be okay. I will have to ask her about that, though. I don't want her suffering if there is no need for it."

"Don't ask her. I shouldn't have mentioned it. She would be quite angry with me if she knew I had mentioned it to you."

"How do you know so much about Elizabeth?"

Caleb squirmed in his seat. "I'm her pastor."

"You're telling me that your parishioners tell you about their nightmares?"

"Not usually." Caleb shifted in his seat and tried to find a comfortable spot. "Forget I even mentioned this. It really wasn't important. I just have some experience with bad dreams, and I was just going to say that I am willing to talk with Elizabeth if necessary."

"Since when have you suffered from nightmares, Caleb? And, why would you want to talk to Elizabeth about it? And, when did you start calling Elizabeth by her given name? I thought you barely knew her, and you usually call everyone by their formal title until you have been told to call them by their given name."

"I used to go to the post office once every week."

Rose gave him another look, and he just sighed. "Come on, Caleb. Tell me what has been going on. Do you like Elizabeth? That's not a problem if you do."

"What! Where did you get that from?" He jumped up from his seat and started to pace.

"Well, what else am I supposed to think? Tell me the truth, Caleb. That is all I want to know."

Caleb scowled and continued pacing. "It really isn't such a big thing. I have had trouble sleeping recently, so I would go out to the pasture. I met Elizabeth there, and the two of us would talk. That is all."

Rose was quiet, and Caleb turned to look at her. She had pity written all over her face. He scowled at her and continued to pace. "Is that why you have been so tired lately, Caleb?"

"I haven't been that tired," he lied.

Rose stood and placed a hand on his shoulder. He stopped in his tracks. "Don't lie to me, Caleb. You have been tired lately. Has it been because of these dreams?"

"Maybe a little," he muttered. "Things are getting better now, though." He shrugged off her hand and slumped into his seat.

Rose remained standing. "What do you dream about?"

Caleb turned his face away. "I don't dream about anything. My dreams are about absolutely nothing, and that is what is so terrifying about them."

Rose sat down on the edge of her seat and reached out to Caleb. He ignored her. "So, why do you go to the pasture?"

"It is the only safe place so early in the morning."

Rose gave him a questioning look.

"Okay, it is comforting to be there, and it was nice to know I would meet Elizabeth there and we could talk."

"And what did you talk about?"

"Do we really need to talk about this?" Caleb sprung to his feet again. Rose leaned back in her seat and gave Caleb a long look. He began to pace. "It's just that I don't think this is really a part of catch-ing up. We can talk about anything else, but why this?"

Rose sighed. "Because, Caleb, you have been so distant lately, I think the only way I will entirely understand it is if you tell me about your visits with Elizabeth. Besides that, the more you talk about it, the more stress you relieve, and the better you will be able to sleep. Now, what did you two talk about?"

"We talked about all sorts of things. We talked about our lives and growing up and all the pain in the world."

"That makes sense. Has it helped you any?"

"Lots."

"That's good. I like going to the meadow as well. That is why I had Mark buried there. He would have liked it too, don't you think?" Caleb didn't respond. "You didn't really know Mark, did you?" Rose asked. Again Caleb did not respond. "Caleb?"

"I-I knew Mark better than most people. He would have loved the pasture. It was just like him."

"Caleb?" Rose reached out to him, but he pulled away.

"Let's change the topic, okay?"

"Okay. But just one more question. Did you know Mark's family?"

Caleb paused. "Why do you want to know about Mark's family?"

Rose sighed. "Well, it probably isn't that big of an issue, but be-fore he died, Mark was looking for his brother Seth. He said that his brother needed Jesus more than anything else. He wanted to let his brother know that he had forgiven him and that God had forgiven him."

"Did Mark tell you anything else about Seth?"

Rose blushed. "He—he told me about Seth and about what happened with a girl named Sarah. That is all he told me really."

"And you still want to find Seth, even though you know about Sarah?"

Rose shuddered at the dead, hollow sound of Caleb's voice. "Mark said that Seth could change. I believe that to be true. I think that if Mark believed in Seth, then God could easily forgive him."

"I reckon you are entitled your opinion."

"What do you know about Seth?"

Caleb's face twisted into a bitter mask. "I know Seth better than I know Mark. I know Seth better than I know anyone else. Are you sure you want to meet Seth, Your Highness? I could introduce you to him."

"I—I would like that, I think," replied Rose nervously. She tugged a curl, a little less sure than she had been moments before.

Caleb laughed. "Are you that unsure about God being able to change Seth, Your Highness?"

Rose turned red at the remark. "I am never unsure of God. I am only unsure of myself. I am not nearly as strong or as good as God, and I am afraid that I will make a mistake and let God down."

"I thought you said God is forgiving. Won't he give you a second chance if you make a mistake?"

"Of course,. I just don't like to make mistakes."

"Well then, are you still sure you want to meet Seth?"

"Yes, I am sure. You can set up a date when we shall meet."

"How about today?"

"I don't know. Isn't that a bit short notice? I wouldn't want to upset his day's schedule."

Caleb laughed.

"Well, it would be rude to do so," stated Rose.

"Seth is a criminal who, if sentenced, will be hung from the nearest tree, and you, the queen, are worried about upsetting his daily schedule."

Rose blushed. "That doesn't make it any less impolite to barge in on him," she muttered.

"You are something else, Highness," muttered Caleb. "But, you won't be interrupting Seth's schedule any more than it already has been interrupted."

"Very well then, I will meet Mr. Hepton today. But, Henry will want me to wait for him, I think. Besides, he probably won't be partial to this plan, but he will come along."

Caleb sobered. "Henry must not know," he said hoarsely.

"Why not? My husband knows everything I know. I won't keep this from him."

"You have to," barked Caleb, taking a step closer to her.

Rose was shaking. She pushed away from Caleb. "I am sorry, Caleb. Perhaps it is better that I don't meet Seth today, then."

Caleb sighed and wiped his face. "I am sorry, Highness. Besides, it is already too late—you have already met Seth."

"What are you talking about, Caleb?"

"My name...is not Caleb. My name is Seth Hepton, and I would appreciate if you did not tell your husband that."

Rose felt the tears coming to her eyes. She wiped them away, but they kept coming. She reached out to him, but he stepped away.

"It would be best if you didn't come visit me anymore. I'll understand if you want to leave now."

He turned to leave the room.

"Seth," whispered Rose. The tears were still streaming down her face. "Seth, don't go." He stopped just because she asked. "Do you know? Do you know that God loves you?"

He let out a hollow laugh. "I know that God loves the people who deserve it. As for me? I think God knows better than to waste his time on me. I'll pay my time, and I will tell others that there is salvation for them, but I will never be under the illusion that God loves me."

"You're wrong," whispered Rose. "You are so wrong."

"What am I so wrong about, Rose? Am I wrong to say that I have done something horrendous? Is it wrong for me to say that I am evil and that God is good? Tell me I am wrong if I am."

Rose wiped her eyes and stared him down. "You are not wrong when you say those things, but the conclusion you draw because of them is wrong."

"What, am I wrong to say that God could not love a rapist?" Rose flinched. "Because that is what I am, Your Highness. I am a rapist. Can you forgive me for that?"

"Yes. God can forgive you, and so can I."

"Don't lie, Rose," Seth hissed. "You know it's not true, and you know better than to lie."

"I am not lying, Seth, and I resent that you would even suggest something like that. I think that you are too afraid to think of what it means for God to forgive you, and that it really isn't God keeping you from peace. You have been so set on your own guilt that you haven't been able to forgive yourself!" Rose shouted back at him. She started crying again.

"How can I forgive myself? You weren't there. You didn't see her. You don't have blood on your hands. How can I forgive myself for those things?"

"I don't know. But, I know that you have to if you ever want to find the same peace that Mark had."

"Rose? Caleb?" Henry called from the front of the house. "Are you in there?" he asked, the worry evident in his voice.

"Your husband is calling," hissed Seth. "I think it would be best if you didn't come back again. I won't answer the door if you do."

Seth turned his back on Rose, so he wouldn't have to watch her leave, but he listened, waiting for her to leave him to his misery. She didn't move. He waited. She sighed. "You know I love you, Seth. Don't ever forget that, okay? I love you like you were my brother." With one last sigh, she left the room.

Caleb felt the tears slipping down his face. He didn't wipe them away. Instead, he let them flow, hoping they would wash away every last image he had of the queen.

TWENTY-EIGHT

KATY COULDN'T HELP BUT WATCH him. It didn't matter that she would never marry him or that they would never be a couple of any sort; there was still something about him that she watched. The curate had always intrigued her, and there was no use in trying to ignore it. She only wished she knew what it was about him that drew her attention.

"You know, if you keep staring at him, you will have people in town talking." Katy jumped at the voice that spoke so close to her ear. She blushed when she realized who it was.

"I'm sorry, Josh. I really didn't mean anything by it. It's just that I used to be so, so intrigued by him that it is hard to give up."

He reached out and took her hand. She leaned toward him and allowed him to lead her on a walk around the block. An early fall chill had set in, and Katy shivered. Putting an arm around her shoulder, Josh pulled her closer.

"Are you upset?" Katy finally asked.

"No."

"Why not?"

Josh stopped and held out his other hand to Katy. She took it and Josh looked down into her eyes. "How many years did you like the curate?"

"A few," replied Katy with a blush on her cheeks.

"And, what made you decide to give up on him?"

Katy tried to turn away, but Josh pulled her gently back. "He wasn't everything I thought he was. It just took me a while to realize that," she muttered.

"Katy," Josh said with a tender voice. "I know there are still things you like about the curate. He is a good man, and I understand that you are not going to just suddenly stop thinking about him. I am fine with that. Just know that I will never give up on you. So, if there is ever a time that you second-guess anything about our relationship, I will be able to prove to you that I love you more than anyone else. Do you understand that?"

Katy nodded.

"Good. You also know that it is not too late to back out, right?"

"Yes," Katy mumbled as a reply.

"Are you wanting to back out?" Josh asked hesitantly.

Katy's head jerked up. "I won't ever back out, Josh. I—" she glanced around to see if anyone was watching, "—I love you." Standing on her tiptoes, she kissed him on the cheek.

Looking around, Josh pulled Katy into his arms and kissed her soundly on the lips. "I love you too, darling," he said with a smile. She smiled back, but couldn't prevent the blush that crept up her neck.

"Now, have you decided on a wedding date?" Josh asked.

Katy sighed. "I don't know. I don't want to wait too long, but there are still so many things to plan. I don't even have a dress for the day. Besides that, there are so many other things going on. I just don't know when a good time would be."

Josh looked around thoughtfully for a minute. "How long would it take you to find a dress?" "I could probably make one within two weeks if I had all the supplies. Maybe in less time if I had some help," Katy mused.

"Okay," said Josh excitedly. "The wedding should be in two weeks then."

"Two weeks! There is so much that has to be done. I could never be ready in two weeks. We don't even have a house!"

Josh hushed Katy and pulled her into a quick embrace. "You handle the wedding dress, and I will handle the rest. Okay?" Katy hesitated, but thought it best to agree with a nod. "Good. Now, let's enjoy the rest of this walk before I have to go back to work."

Katy sighed and entwined her arm with Josh's. It would be nice to finally be married. It just seemed like two weeks was so soon. She shuddered with the thought of it. In two weeks she would be Mrs. Josh Deplin. The thought of it was only slightly terrifying.

John looked at the hole in the wall and sighed. He had done it now. He had gotten so distracted taking out the rotten boards, he had forgotten to pay attention to what they were attached to. It was amazing that the house was still standing. John groaned and tried to think of a way he could fix the mess. None came readily to mind.

Tossing his hammer aside, he flopped to the ground and pulled his knees up to his chest. A soft moan escaped past his lips. "Lord," he whispered, "could you have not kept me from doing something so stupid? I know you always have my best interest in mind, but I think she may kill me when she sees this. Don't you think living is in my best interest?"

John could picture God looking down from heaven and laughing at His foolish child, and the thought of it brought a smile to his face. "Okay Lord, I guess I did get myself into this mess all on my own, but do you think you could grant me a little grace and help me get out of this?" With a sigh, John picked up his hammer again and began tearing out more boards. He figured it couldn't get any worse, so he might as well make the mess look better.

"What are you doing?" John felt himself cringe at Elizabeth's voice. The blush crept lazily up his neck, proving his guilt before a single word was spoken. "I thought I told you not to work on my house anymore." The blush on John's neck deepened in colour. "Mr. Borden, I am waiting for an answer."

John turned around to face Elizabeth. "Well, you see," muttered John. "After I was done fixing the other hole, I noticed that there were still a lot of boards that should be replaced on the south wall. Unfortunately, I got a bit distracted." John fidgeted with his shirt sleeve, hoping she wouldn't notice the way his feet nervously moved back and forth.

"And? How come you are still here, then? You are usually gone once the day is through so that I can go back to living my life."

John cleared his throat. "Here's the thing. When I got distracted, I kind of pulled out a few too many boards, and I don't know if your house is safe to live in anymore." Elizabeth's mouth dropped open in shock and John tried to think of something to say to make it better.

"I promise I will have it fixed in no time, and you can go back to living in it if you want to. For now, I am sure that you can live at the inn with Rose again. I know that she would love that."

Elizabeth scowled and turned to look at the house. "I don't see why you don't tear down the entire thing."

John looked at her his mouth agape. "I thought you didn't want me working on your house," he stuttered.

Elizabeth glared at him. "That doesn't seem to have stopped you."

John chuckled and plucked nervously at his shirt sleeve. "I guess I decided I liked working on buildings. It has some real benefits."

"Like tearing holes in walls?"

John shrugged. "You should try it someday. It really is quite enjoyable. And, it is a lot safer than sword fighting."

Elizabeth just nodded and continued looking at the hole in the wall. "So, are you just going to tear the entire thing down?"

"It would be a lot easier," muttered John.

Elizabeth scowled at him again. John shrugged.

"Is there a reason for this change of heart?" he asked.

Elizabeth blushed. "I'm not going to be living here anymore."

"Is that so?"

"Yes," replied Elizabeth matter-of-factly. "My father," she blushed at this reference, "is taking me with him to Silidon, and I am going to take care of his house and he is going to look after my wellbeing."

John nodded. "So, you think this property would have a better chance selling with a new house instead of a repaired one?"

"No, I just think it is silly to do repairs on a house when there will always be rotting boards that you can't get to. It would be so much better to start from scratch to get rid of the old and to make something new and something better."

"I can make this house look pretty good if you give me the time."

"Who cares if the house looks good? It will still be the same house. It is like putting a pig in a costume and saying it is a courtier. No matter what you dress the pig in, it will always be a pig. It is better to use those materials to make something completely new and better."

John looked at Elizabeth and smirked. She smiled back. "Do you want to help tear this down?"

Elizabeth's eyes lit up. "Can I?" John laughed. "Of course; only be careful. If something happens to you, I think Shoals would have my hide, and I have no intentions of dying this young."

Elizabeth laughed as John handed her the hammer. He was about to give her some warnings when she gave the hammer a hefty swing. There was a crack as a board snapped, and John dove to push Elizabeth out of the way. The structure of the house shifted and began to fall. John covered Elizabeth with his body as the house gave one final groan and collapsed.

John lifted himself from on top of Elizabeth and looked at the dilapidated building. Holding out a hand, he helped her to her feet. "As I was saying before, the hole I made left the house unsafe and that board you just snapped was one of the main supports that was holding up the rest of the building. It must have been rotted a bit for it to have snapped like that."

Elizabeth coughed and wiped the dust off her skirts. She looked up at John and started to laugh. John couldn't help but laugh along. "I guess the courtier was a pig after all," Elizabeth gasped between laughs.

"And what a mess it made!" laughed John.

Elizabeth looked at the pile that was the house with satisfaction. "I think it is better this way. Do you think that we could burn it?"

John chuckled. "I think I need to go through it first to see what is usable, but whatever is left after that can be burned. Maybe we can host a bonfire with all the extra wood. What do you think?"

"I like that idea. Maybe it could be to celebrate the arrival of the new prince or princess. That would be fun."

"Perhaps. But maybe it could be to celebrate a wedding." Elizabeth gave him a startled look. "Josh and Katy are supposed to be getting married sometime soon," he explained, and Elizabeth went back to looking at the pile of rubble.

"Well either way, we will have a bonfire soon, and it will be a great time. How long do you think it will take you to go through it all?" Elizabeth asked.

John bit his lip and sized up the pile. "I'll get some men in, and we will have to see from there. Perhaps only a week, but it could take as long as a month if I don't get any help."

Elizabeth nodded her head. "My father will help. I am sure of that."

John couldn't help but smile at Elizabeth's reference to her father. "It is nice to see that you and your father are getting along so well."

Elizabeth blushed. "He has done so much for me that it is hard not to want to do just as much for him. He is a good man, and he is always so happy. It is just nice being around him."

John took her hand and gave it a gentle squeeze. "That is good. You deserve to have a father that can look out for you."

Elizabeth looked down at the ground and muttered, "No I don't."

"Why do you say that?"

"I still don't feel like I deserve any of this. What did I ever do? I've yelled at God for most of my life for giving me the life that I have, and I've thought terrible things about all those people who treated me poorly at the post office, and I thought poorly of you when all you've ever done is be kind to me. I don't deserve any of this."

John reached out and pulled Elizabeth into an embrace. She shied away, but he wrapped his arms around her and held her until she finally relaxed. "We have all done things in our life that we are not proud of," he said. "None of us deserve the blessings God has given us, so instead of being sorry that we don't add up, we should turn to God and thank Him. He has given us such grace that it is truly amazing. That is why we praise Him. Do you understand that?"

"Yeah, I think I do. I think it is starting to make sense, little by little."

"Good," sighed John. He held her for a while longer, not wanting to let go. When she started to squirm, he loosened his arms and she moved out of his embrace with a quick shrug. John smiled and blushed as he realized the impropriety of his actions. "Sorry," he muttered.

"I need to go. I told my father that I would meet him at the inn once I was done with some things around the house. He didn't want to let me go, but I told him I needed the time alone. By the look on his face, you would have thought I had stabbed him with those words."

John chuckled. "He is most likely rolling on a bed of glass wondering if he is being a good father to you. I can't imagine it is an easy job to just pick up so instantaneously."

Elizabeth smiled. "I will have to let him know that he is doing a good job. And, I will tell him that you need help tomorrow at the house."

John laughed. "That would be good." Elizabeth smiled and began to walk away. John watched her go, hoping against hopes that someday he would be able to run up beside her, take her hand, and walk her home.

Josh looked at his house and groaned. It would never do. It was practically a pig sty, and there was no way he was taking Katy home to live in a pig sty. Winter was also coming soon, and though the house had been warm enough for him, he couldn't expect Katy to deal with the same chill. He looked around for something to redeem the rather unredeemable features of the two-room dwelling. It was two weeks to the wedding, and Katy was right: they didn't even have a house.

With another groan, Josh left the building hoping that all his stress would disappear as he exited through the door. He had no such luck.

As he walked down the streets, each door seemed to be filled with a happily married couple. Their houses were in order, and their yards neat. Not one of them looked discontent. How in the world was he supposed to provide that for Katy?

There seemed no answer to that, and he had promised Katy that everything would be in order in two weeks. What was he thinking when he made such a promise? He was a fool. He was the fool of all fools.

The pasture was an inviting place. It was a lot better than the streets that seemed crowded with too many overly happy couples, and it was a lot safer than seeking out Katy and telling her about the house situation. Unfortunately, he wasn't the only one who had chosen to go to the pasture. Over in the corner by the grave stood Shoals and Elizabeth, their heads close together as they talked about who knows what.

The two turned when they heard Josh ploughing through the brush. Josh acknowledged them and went to take a seat on the rock that he had occupied so many times before. He hoped the two would hurry up and go away. He wanted the place to be free for him to mope. Such was not his luck.

Taking Elizabeth's hand, Shoals set it in the crook of his arm and they walked over to him. "Good evening, Josh," Shoals said.

"Evenin'," Josh replied. He looked away hoping they would take the hint.

"Is there something wrong?" Shoals asked. The man just didn't know how to leave a fellow alone.

"Everything is just fine. How are things with you?"

"Good. Elizabeth was just telling me about how she helped John tear down her old house. He is going to build a new house on the property, but he needs some help."

"Is that so?" Josh didn't really want to talk about housing at that point in time.

"It is. Elizabeth was also telling me that they were hoping to host a bonfire in celebration after your wedding in order to get rid of all the extra wood. They thought that would be fun; what do you think?"

"It would be wonderful, if we could actually have the wedding any time soon."

Shoals looked at Josh with his brow creased. "Why won't you be having the wedding any time soon?"Josh sighed. "Because we don't have a house to live in. We can hardly get married if we don't have a house to live in. What kind of a husband would I be if I can't even provide a roof over my bride's head? It hardly seems fair to me."

"So, you need a house. Is that all?" Shoals asked.

"Is that all? Yes, that is the entire thing. I need a house before I can get married, and the way things are going for me, that may never happen. It will be at least a year before I can get out of work at the blacksmith, and even after that, it will take me another couple of years before I can save up enough to buy a house and my own land to build a shop or start a farm. How would I provide for my family in the meantime? Are you suggesting that we cram into the two-room box I now reside in? I can hardly see Katy enjoying that!"

"Have you asked her if it really matters to her?" Shoals asked. "I mean, it would be nice to have a house right away, but perhaps your two-room box would be perfect at least for the first little while."

"Not Katy," growled Josh. "She deserves better than that. I want to be able to provide for her, and I can. I just need a house."

Elizabeth tapped Shoals on the shoulder and leaned over to whisper in his ear. He smiled and patted her hand. She shied away, but seemed to be glowing with pleasure at the small touch. "Elizabeth has just presented a very interesting solution that I think you may very well like," said Shoals happily.

"What's that?"

"Well, like I said before. John is looking for someone to help him build a house on Elizabeth's old property. The only problem is that once the house is finished, there will be no one to take over the property. Elizabeth will be leaving with me to go back to Silidon, and not many people are interested in property so far out, especially when it doesn't have much of a farm attached. It really is quite a problem."

"What does this have to do with me?"

"Elizabeth would like to give the house to you and Katy as a wedding gift, if you promise to help John finish up the house and agree to hold the bonfire in celebration of your and Katy's wedding."

Josh's jaw dropped open. "But—but that is—is awful generous. I couldn't accept that."

"Why not?" asked Shoals. "You will be working for it, and it really will be a relief to have the house off of our hands. Besides that, there is a small barn attached where you can set up a shop and put that filthy drunk of a smith you are working for out of business. It really will work out for the best for the entire town, don't you think?"

"I—I don't know what to say."

"Well then," replied Shoals, "say you accept and then head over to the house to talk it over with John. He'll want to know how you want to go about setting up the house. I'm thinking that you will want two floors, with at least three bedrooms on the upper floor."

Josh continued to gape and Shoals just smiled.

"You are going to tell Katy the news aren't you?" Shoals said.

Josh turned and ran out of the pasture leaving a laughing Shoals and Elizabeth in his wake.

TWENTY-NINE

KATY WALKED UP TO THE PASTOR'S door and knocked. There were a lot of things she was leaving up to Josh, but informing the pastor about their wedding was not one she could chance him forgetting. At least, that was her excuse. She also carried a basket meal just in case.

The door opened and the curate looked down at her. Katy stared at the step beneath her as she tried to remember what she was going to say. "I-I brought a roast," she finally stammered.

Curate Taylor just stood there looking down at her. Katy squirmed, hoping he would turn away. Finally he sighed and held the door open wider. "Come on in, Miss Monks. You can bring it into the kitchen."

Katy slipped into the house and hurried to the kitchen. She placed the roast on the counter and took a deep breath to steady herself. "I also wanted to ask if Josh had talked to you yet," she said a little louder, hoping he would hear her. She turned to find him standing right behind her. She blushed and turned her head aside, trying to avoid eye contact.

"Yes, Josh has come to talk with me. I will be taking care of the details for the ceremony, so you won't have to worry about any of that."

Katy nodded.

"Is that all you were worried about, Miss Monks?"

Katy bowed her head and tried her best to steady her voice before she spoke. "Are you okay?" she asked.

"I am fine. How are you, Miss Monks?"

"That's not what I was asking," replied Katy angrily. "Are *you* okay?"

Caleb scratched his head as if he didn't know what she meant. "Like I said, I am quite fine, Miss Monks, how are you?"

Katy scrunched her face in confusion. "But, what about the last time I came over? You weren't well then. You were—well—you weren't normal." Katy blushed and began to tug anxiously on one of her curls.

Caleb's expression went cold. "What was I like last time you were over?"

"You were sobbing and claiming what a wretch you were. I-I didn't know what to do. I stayed with you awhile, but then I had to go."

Caleb sighed, and slouched into a kitchen chair. "I was dreaming. It was just a nightmare. They come and go. Unfortunately, you were there during one of my episodes."

Katy bit her lip and thought about how to respond. "Is there a reason why you have nightmares?"

"Yes," replied Caleb, but he didn't elaborate.

"Do you want to talk about it?" Katy whispered.

Caleb turned to her and sighed. "Miss Monks, there are a lot of things that the people of this town do not know about me. I know this may upset you and a lot of people, but I promise they won't be kept secret for long. In fact, it all should come to light soon, and then you will understand the nightmare completely."

"You told me that already," replied Katy sadly. "You told me that in your nightmare, which makes me think that you are terrified of people finding out about you. In fact, I think you are afraid of a lot more things than that, but you don't have anyone to tell them to. Well, Curate Taylor, I am listening. Do you want to tell me?"

Caleb rubbed his face roughly with his hand. "You don't want to know. It would be better if you waited. I don't want to ruin things for you, and if I tell you my nightmares, it could very well wreck things."

"Why did you become a curate, when you don't know a thing about sharing your burdens?"

"What does this have to do with anything?"

"God tells us to share our burdens, and you as a curate should be able to exemplify that. Instead, you hole up in your house and let ter-rors overcome you. God says not to be afraid, yet you let fear rule you. I don't get it. *Why* did you become a curate?"

"I—Miss Monks, I—" Caleb tried to think of something to say, but nothing would come to mind. Instead, his mouth stood gaping as Katy stared him down.

"That's what I thought. If you ever do decide to talk to someone, you can come find me. Until then, I have a wedding to plan." Katy turned to leave. Caleb called out to her, but she didn't turn. She didn't want to hear his excuses. She had tried to help him, and he hadn't ac-cepted it. That was his fault.

She was ready to move on. He had taken too much of her life al-ready. It didn't matter to her anymore. If he finally decided that he wanted to talk, she would be there, but she didn't think that day would ever come. Some people were just too proud to let others know when they were weak. As far as Katy was concerned, that was their own problem.

Rose was crying again. It wasn't a good sign. She had been crying on and off for almost a month. Ever since the last time she had visited Caleb, and Henry was afraid of what that could mean. Perhaps it was just the baby, but he was still worried, and he was determined to fig-ure it out.

Slowly, gently, he took Rose into his arms and she sobbed into his shoulder. "Shh," he whispered. "It's alright now, darling."

"No it's not," hiccupped Rose. "It is horrible, terribly horrible. And, I handled it all wrong. I could have done so much more, and I didn't. Now he may never know." Rose turned her face into Henry's shoulder, and he felt her whole body shudder with the tears.

"Tell me, darling. Tell me what is so horrible."

Rose shook her head and Henry led her to their bed so she could sit down.

"Why won't you tell me?"

"I want to," she whispered. "But, I don't know if I can. It might just make things worse, and I don't want them to be worse."

Henry hugged Rose closer and kissed the top of her head. "How do you know that it won't make things better if you tell me? Maybe I already know, and together we can come up with a solution."

Rose wrapped her arms around Henry and sighed. "I don't think anything can make this better. Some things just never get better."

"Then tell me, darling, and we can bear this together."

Rose took a deep breath, and Henry smiled encouragingly at her.

Looking blankly into the distance, she began to talk. "Remember when I told you about Mark and his brother Seth?"

"Yes," Henry murmured. He remembered that quite vividly. Rose had told him one night in tears after she had had a bad dream about the entire thing.

"Well, I was talking to Caleb about Mark, and it turns out that Caleb is—" Fresh tears came to her eyes. She brushed them away. "Caleb is Seth," she blurted through a despairing wail.

Henry breathed a prayer for wisdom and pulled his wife onto his lap. "Love," he whispered, "does this change anything for you?"

"What do you mean?" asked Rose between the tears.

"Well, do you love Caleb any less now that you know the truth?"

"No," sighed Rose. Her tears were subsiding now.

"Then, what is so horrible about finding this out? Does it change who Caleb is? Does it change the fact that you love him, and that God loves him, and that he is our brother in Christ Jesus?"

"No," whispered Rose. "It doesn't change anything. It just hurts because he hurts. He doesn't know God. He preaches God, yet he doesn't even know God."

THE CHARADE

Henry brushed back the hair from Rose's face and began to twist a strand of it around his finger. "I think the best thing we can do is to keep him in our prayers, okay? I know it seems like only a little thing, but I think it is the best we can do for Seth right now."

"Okay," Rose whispered. "I think I can do that."

Henry squeezed her a bit tighter. "This isn't going to be easy. There is the possibility that someday he will be charged, and we won't be able to do anything about it. But, Seth is in God's hands now. We will just have to remember that."

Rose sighed and snuggled into Henry's shoulder. Then, looking up at him, she kissed him gently. "Thank you," she whispered. "I needed that."

"You're welcome. But, promise me that next time you will tell me something like this right away. It about broke my heart in two seeing you crying and not knowing what I could do to help. Agreed?"

Rose nodded, and Henry gave her another squeeze.

"I only have one question," said Rose. "How come you don't seem so surprised? I mean, most people would have been shocked when told news like that, but you just took it all in stride. Why is that?"

Henry mulled the question over in his mind before he replied. "I lived with Caleb for a few months, and I got to know him fairly well. When you told me about Mark, I had my suspicions, but I didn't think it was worth it to bring it up. It would have only caused trouble then."

"I guess," sighed Rose. "But, I wish you had been more surprised by it; that way I wouldn't feel so bad about how I reacted when he told me." Henry chuckled, and Rose made a face at him.

"Are you going to do anything about this?" Rose asked after a moment of silence.

"What do you mean?"

"Well, you are the king and you are committed to the law. What Seth did was against the law. Are you going to do anything about it?"

Henry groaned and rubbed the back of his neck. "I don't know. The law says that I need to do something about this, but I figure the law is for justice, and justice is not always served in the same way. In a way, Seth has already paid the penalty in the guilt he has felt over his actions." Henry sighed.

"I guess, if anyone wants to accuse Seth, I will allow them to see justice to completion. There is no way I can stop them. But until that time, I think mercy is the best route. I don't see anything wrong in letting Seth continue as he is. He is not a dangerous man. In a way, he is just as much the victim as Sarah was. Does that make sense to you?" Rose nodded her head.

Henry held her close for a while longer. He was glad she had told him what had happened, but he wished there was more he could do. Caleb needed help and all he had to offer was a prayer. What kind of help was that? If only he could make it all better, not only for Caleb's sake, but also for Rose's.

Seth tossed the letter aside and let out a growl. Bill was coming, and there was no stopping him. Seth had tried ignoring him, but despite the lack of a response, Bill had decided he was welcome in Emriville. His most recent letter said it all. The idiot of a brother had no sense.

What person barged in on his brother's life after over ten years and thought it would be okay? It was ludicrous. But that was Bill for you. He didn't have a scrap of wit in that over-sized head of his.

Seth paced back and forth as he tried to think of what to do. He was low on options. Anyone who saw Bill would know immediately that they were brothers. They had always looked alike, and even if a person didn't make the connection, Bill was sure to tell them. He was that dumb.

Even if he didn't tell them outright, he would do something stupid that would make it obvious. Or, worse yet, he would come knocking on the parsonage door and ask the curate inside where the harlot's den was. Wouldn't that be just like Bill?

Seth scowled and picked up the letter to read it again. If only he had dealt with the letters sooner, instead of having Elizabeth help him ignore their existence. If only he had gotten this particular letter sooner. He could have replied and suggested to Bill that the person he was looking for did not live at that address.

But the letter had not come earlier, and there was no way of changing that. If only that post worker wasn't so inept. How hard could running the post office be? It wasn't like it took a whole lot of intelligence. What could the man possibly be doing so horribly wrong?

Seth sighed and threw the letter into the fire pit. Bill would arrive any day, and when he came, Seth would have to be ready to put out the fires that would be created, and it wouldn't be pretty. Maybe it would just be easier to let people know the truth. What would it matter? There were already enough people who knew who he really was, and chances were that Rose would tell Henry the truth and he would end up in jail in any case. Why not just tell the truth before then? It would be that much easier.

"No," Seth muttered. It would *not* be that much easier. People would hate him. He would be thrown into the streets. He wouldn't have a job. God would be angry with him. Hah, as if that weren't the truth already. But, at least he was working on that. It would be best to keep working on that as long as possible. Besides, he had already promised to officiate at Josh and Katy's wedding. It would ruin everything for them if they didn't have a curate to read the vows.

Would they really want him as their preacher after they found out about his past? Maybe it would be fairer to let them have a better curate for their wedding. It wouldn't take long to get in a circuit pastor, and Josh wouldn't resent a few more weeks to plan the event. He was swamped as is.

No, that would never do. Katy was set on that date, and there was no way Seth could suddenly back out on them. He would just have to hold out and hope that Bill did not show up before then.

Besides, it could all be a mistake. What if Seth told the entire congregation the truth, and then Bill never showed up? No, that would never do. It would be better to keep the secret. People were happier that way. He was happier that way. The secret wasn't hurting anyone. The truth would hurt people—many people, in fact.

Seth went to the kitchen and picked at the roast that Katy had left him. It was good; better than anything he had eaten in the past while. He would have to remember to thank her and Mrs. Monks for the meal. The morsel went sour in his mouth. That wouldn't happen. They probably didn't want to see him. Katy hadn't seemed too pleased with him the last time she had come. He had tried to apologize as she left, but she would have none of it. She wanted the truth, and he had promised it to her in time, but he wasn't sure he could keep that promise.

Seth gave up on the roast and decided to write his sermon. It was on forgiveness. He was using a verse found in Colossians 3. It read, *"Bear with each other and forgive whatever grievances you may have against one another. Forgive as the Lord forgave you."*

He smiled as he read over the verse again. There were many people in the church who needed to practice forgiveness, and this would be a good reminder for them. Maybe after the sermon he would be able to convince Mrs. Read to forgive her son for wanting to marry a young lady from another county. It was a long shot, but maybe.

Seth scribbled down some notes and continued to ponder the verse. It said to *bear with each other.* That was easy enough. Most people were willing to put up with others in the community. Of course, some of them had been a little hesitant to bear with Miss Mede, but that was already straightened out. Maybe he could suggest that the congregation should be willing to bear with people like Bill. It would help soften the blow his arrival would cause, and perhaps it would make people a little less judgmental. Maybe.

The verse continued with a call to forgive. Seth would remind everyone that it was their duty to forgive and not to hold grudges. Grudges never did anyone any good. They only created bitterness, and bitterness only made the grievance that much greater. It would be better to deal with the hurt before it festered and spread.

Seth read the last bit of the verse, and he suddenly didn't feel like writing anymore. It brought to mind Rose's accusation. She had said he was so set on his own guilt that he couldn't forgive himself and that was the only thing keeping him from peace.

She was wrong. She had to be wrong.

He didn't have peace, but it was because of what he had done. God could never forgive him for that, and that was why he couldn't have peace.

Forgive as the Lord forgave you.

The verse jumped out at him. Why should he forgive himself? God hadn't forgiven him, so he wasn't under any obligation to forgive anyone. What did it matter if he forgave anyone, for that matter? God didn't have to forgive anyone, and Seth was going to hell anyway, so why should he forgive anyone? Why should he even live as God would have him live, for that matter? What good was it doing him? It was just a burden, a chain that was keeping him from everything. What was the point in it all?

There had to be a point. There had to be a purpose to it all. He couldn't just wipe out his purpose on earth in one horrid action. Could he?

No.

He had purpose. His purpose was to make sure that no one else ended up like him. He had to make sure no one else was hurt like Sarah had been. That was his purpose, and he would live for that, and that alone. It didn't matter if God decided he would go to hell. As long as he stopped hurt; that was all that mattered.

Seth turned back to the sermon and smiled weakly. *Forgive as the Lord forgave you* applied only to those the Lord had forgiven. Rose was wrong in what she had said. He would find peace. He would find peace in knowing that by preaching God's word he was stopping sin; he was stopping terrible, horrendous sins.

When the sermon was done, he leaned back in his chair and read it over. Yes, it was a good sermon and it would stir the congregation. There would be some tears in some eyes. Some rifts would be mended, and the whole world would be set to rights. It would be one of those good sermons that he could add to his side of the scale.

He would show God yet. He would show just how good a person he could be; how good a preacher he could be. God would see, and maybe there was a chance that things would change for him. Maybe.

Looking at himself in the mirror, Seth straightened his collar and went out the door. The people needed their shepherd, and he would be there for them. He would be the best curate they ever had for as long as he was given. It didn't matter if he hated every minute of it. He would smile if it killed him.

Hell was a ways away. Seth would deal with the problems in front of him for now, and if God looked down on him to see what His worthless goat was doing, he, Seth, would be grinning and bearing it. He didn't need God's forgiveness. He would make it through on his own. God had forsaken him the night that Pops had invited Sarah over. He was done.

God could find another goat to kick. This one was ready to make it on his own.

THIRTY

THE WEDDING WAS HELD ON a Saturday. It was cool outside. Autumn had made itself known, and the leaves had already turned colour. Katy felt her stomach tingling as she prepared to walk down the aisle. She didn't have a clue as to what was going to happen. Josh had planned everything with only a little assistance from his mother and sisters, and chances were that everything would come to disaster.

Rose had assured Katy that everything would be fine, but every time Katy tried to get any details out of her, she clammed up and wouldn't say a single word about what Josh had done. "At least we have a house," muttered Katy under her breath.

"What was that, darling girl?" Rose asked cheerily. She was helping Katy with her hair and dress, and enjoying it a lot more than Katy was.

"Nothing," replied Katy sweetly. "I was just musing about the house. Do you know if it is done? Josh wouldn't show it to me, so I don't even know anything about it."

"Ooh, really? He is a bit of a romantic, isn't he? I still can't believe he planned this wedding. I don't know a single man who would have taken on that task. He really is a great man. You are the second most blessed woman in the world, Katy. You should know that."

"Second most blessed?"

"Of course. You see, I am the first blessed, because Henry is the most perfect husband and there is no woman that could have it better than I have."

Katy let out an exaggerated groan. "You still didn't answer my question about the house. Is it finished yet?"

"Darling," teased Rose, "you are going to be shocked at what a couple of men can accomplish when motivated by a wedding."

Katy felt a shiver run down her back. A wedding. Her wedding. She was getting married. Today!

Rose placed her hands on Katy's shoulders and squeezed. "It will be alright. I promise you."

"What if I don't do things right?" Katy whispered.

Rose laughed. "Katy, it is your wedding. It is pretty much expected that you will make some mistakes. As long as you get through the vows, it will be alright. People will laugh, you will blush, and you will barely remember a bit of it in a year's time."

Katy shivered with the thrill of the thought of a year later.

"Now, tell me what you think." Rose held up a mirror for Katy.

"It's amazing," gasped Katy. "How did you—?" she reached up to touch a curl and Rose slapped her hand away.

"I've worked an hour on that, and I will not have you messing it up. You don't have permission to touch your hair until later tonight. Promise me now."

"I promise," sighed Katy. "But will you tell me how you got it to curl like that? I want to be able to do it again sometime."

"Patience, my dear; that is how I did it, with a lot of patience," replied Rose. Katy smirked and stood up. She had been sitting for so long that she could feel the blood running back into her legs. She wobbled a bit, and Rose held a hand for her to steady herself.

"Thanks," muttered Katy.

"Not a problem. Now, where is your dress? Oh yes, I remember. We set it to hang in your mother's room. You stay here and I'll go get it. Don't move," she said as she scurried out of the room.

When Rose came back she was carrying the yards of fabric that were Katy's dress. It was a good thing it was a cooler day or she would have been sure to faint wearing so much fabric.

"I hope you don't mind," said Rose, "but I borrowed your dress the other day to add some embroidery. I knew you didn't have time to add all that you wanted to, and I had more than enough on my hands."

"Thank you. I appreciate that. You are so good at embroidery that I'm sure it will look fine."

Rose plucked at one of her curls nervously. "I hope you will like it. I tried something new, and it didn't turn out exactly as planned."

"Let's see," replied Katy. She wasn't worried about the dress. She didn't doubt Rose's talent. She knew whatever she had done would look wonderful, or at least it would be good.

Releasing the curl, Rose said, "How about you close your eyes, and I will help you into it. Then I will turn you to face the mirror so that you can see what it is supposed to look like."

Katy closed her eyes and allowed Rose to help her into the dress. She felt her doing up the tiny buttons at the back and then turn her toward the mirror.

Katy opened her eyes and gasped. "It's beautiful! How did you ever do this?"

Rose blushed at Katy's reaction. "It really is nothing. I have been practicing a bit, but I never knew when I would get a chance to use it." Rose shrugged, and Katy couldn't help but stare at the dress.

Rose had embroidered it, but she had also taken the time to add in tiny glass beads. The beads sparkled and made the dress look delicate despite its bulk. It was beautiful, and Katy didn't know how to thank Rose for all she had done.

"Thank you," she mouthed to Rose as tears flooded her eyes.

"Oh, don't start crying now, because if you start, I'll start, and we have a wedding to attend. Now, let me just make some adjustments here." Rose disappeared behind the dress and adjusted the bustle. She came back to face Katy and pinched her cheeks a little to add some colour.

"There. We are ready to go now. Don't you think?"

"Wait just a moment," exclaimed Mrs. Monks as she bustled into the room. "I've been looking all morning for these, and you will not be having your wedding without them." She held up a pair of earrings and Katy gasped. "They were your grandmother's. I had put them away and then I forgot all about them. But here they are to bedeck my lovely on her wedding day." She leaned forward and attached the jewellery to her daughter's ears.

With a contented sigh, Mrs. Monks looked at her completely dressed daughter. "Now you are ready to go."

Katy looked into the mirror and sighed. She was ready for her wedding. She was ready to become Mrs. Joshua Deplin. "Okay," she whispered.

"Good," said Rose. "Your father is waiting downstairs to escort you to the church. He knows when to leave. As for me, I must go now to make sure I am there on time." Rose went to leave.

"Wait," called Katy. Rose turned to see what she could want. "Will you be standing up with me as one of my maids? You never answered me before."

Rose let out a small laugh. "Katy, I'm not a maid. That would defeat the purpose. Elizabeth said that she would stand up with you, but I will be in the pew at the front of the church with Henry. You will see me there, and if you ever need any assurance, just look over. I will be there with a ready smile. Okay?"

"Okay," Katy whispered.

"Good, but I must be going now. I'm going to be late." With that, Rose left the room, leaving Katy with her mother.

It seemed as if only minutes had passed when her father came knocking on the door. It was time to leave. The carriage was waiting out front for them. Katy inhaled deeply and took her father's arm.

The churchyard was crowded with buggies and horses. It looked as if the entire town was present. Soft music came from the piano inside the building, and Katy felt her stomach start to squirm.

"You ready?" whispered her father.

Katy nodded, and he helped her out of the carriage. The door to the church opened, and the wedding march began. Katy looked straight ahead, putting one foot in front of the other. She almost stopped when she saw all the people, but the gentle pressure of her father's hand on her arm kept her moving.

And then she was at the front of the church and Josh was there. He was smiling as he took her hands, and she knew she was smiling back. It was perfect. Everything was perfect. She was marrying Josh, and that was all that mattered. She was going to become Mrs. Josh Deplin and at that moment she was the luckiest woman alive.

"I, Joshua Alexander Deplin, take you Katherine Lynn Monks, to be my wife to have and to hold from this day forward, for better or for worse, for richer, for poorer, in sickness and in health, to love and to cherish; from this day forward until death do us part."

"I, Katherine Lynn Monks, take you Joshua Alexander Deplin, to be my husband to have and to hold from this day forward, for better or for worse, for richer, for poorer, in sickness and in health, to love and to cherish; from this day forward until death do us part."

"I now pronounce you man and wife. You may kiss the bride."

Josh pressed his lips to hers, and they were man and wife. Katy felt like cheering, but didn't think it was appropriate. Josh let out a whoop and the congregation laughed. He pulled Katy into his arms and helped her down the aisle as the piano played. "I love you, Katy girl," he whispered in her ear, and in the very depths of her heart, she knew that it was the truth.

The house was huge. Katy hadn't been expecting that, but when they finally got to it she couldn't help but let her jaw drop. "But, there has to be enough room in there for ten people!" she exclaimed.

"Around there," replied Josh cheerily. "But, we will need lots of room if we are going to have children."

Katy felt a blush crawl up her neck at the mention of kids. Josh took her hand and squeezed it playfully. "There's lots of time to think about that later. Why don't we start with a tour? We have about ten minutes before everyone arrives. What do you think?"

"Can we?" Katy asked. Josh laughed and scooped Katy up into his arms. "What are you doing?" she squealed.

"I am pretty sure it is my duty to carry you over the threshold. Unless you have some objection."

Katy tried to hide her smile. "How are you going to open the door?"

Josh looked at the door and scrunched his face as if pondering the problem. "This calls for some creativity," he muttered. "If I set you down, do you promise not to run for it?"

Katy agreed. Gently Josh set her on her feet and turned to open the door. Katy waited obediently where he had placed her.

When the door was opened wide enough, Josh picked her up again and asked her to close her eyes. "Why?" she asked.

"I want to be able to see your face when you see everything. I promise I will make sure you won't hit anything. Just close your eyes and trust me."

"Okay," whispered Katy and closed her eyes. Josh started walking. Katy was so tempted to peek when she smelt the fresh wood and something else, something tangy and sweet. Finally Josh set her on her feet.

"Okay, Mrs. Deplin," he whispered. "Open your eyes, and welcome home."

Katy felt the tears sting at her eyes as she looked around the room. It was beautiful. The walls were freshly whitewashed, and the counter was sanded and stained. The stove crackled cheerily in the corner, and in the centre stood a table covered in a white linen tablecloth. To complete the picture, a vase of wild flowers sat in the very centre of the table. Their fragrance filled the entire room.

"Where did all this come from?" Katy gasped.

"Do you like it?" Josh asked nervously. "I can show you the rest of the house, but I thought it would be best to start with the kitchen so we wouldn't have to backtrack or anything like that."

Katy wrapped her arms around her husband and held on tight. "It's beautiful. It is more than I could ever imagine. I love it. I love you."

"Rose helped with a lot of things," replied Josh as he wrapped his arms around Katy. "Elizabeth was also a big help. They took care of decorating, and your mother and father provided the stove, along with a few other things. It was nearly impossible to keep it all a secret. So many people came out to help. Besides that, Henry banned his men from any swordplay until the house was completed. It was amazing how many willing hands there were after that."

Katy giggled as she pictured all the soldiers handing their swords over to the king and receiving hammers in return. "Josh?" she asked.

"Yes, Katy girl?"

"Do you think that you could show me the rest of the house before everyone shows up? I really would like to see it."

Josh took Katy by the hand and led her from room to room. In each room he would point out what people had given and things he had thought she might enjoy. By the time the tour was over, Katy knew she was the happiest woman in the world, and she couldn't wait for the bonfire so she could thank everyone and tell them all about the house—her house, her perfect house.

Rose walked through the crowd with Henry at her side. Almost everyone from town was there, and Katy was having the time of her life. Rose laughed at the way the young bride hung on her husband's arm and smiled up at him with adoring eyes. They would have a very happy life together. She was sure of that.

"Do you remember our wedding?" Henry whispered in her ear.

Rose laughed as she remembered the day. "I was so terrified. That entire church was filled with people, and I didn't know a single one of them."

Henry smirked at her. "Truth be told, I didn't know half of them either."

Rose smiled and continued thinking about their wedding. "I walked down the aisle on your father's arm. I was so happy when he suggested that. I don't think I would have made it down the aisle on my own."

"And then I saw you. It took you so long to get down the aisle I thought that you weren't coming," teased Henry. Rose pinched his arm in retaliation. He winced and rubbed his arm dramatically, making Rose laugh. Henry sobered and looked down at Rose. "You were so beautiful. You still are," he whispered.

"I'm a little on the fat side right now, if you ask me. I think this little one is long past due. What do you think?"

"I think that I can't wait to see you holding our daughter. She will look just like you." "How do you know we're going to have a girl? I think we are having a boy and he is going to love playing with his father and riding horses and sword fighting. And then one day he will take the throne. What do you think?"

"I think we will have to wait and see."

"Henry, Rose!" called John. He was sitting on a blanket next to Elizabeth and Shoals. "Come join us," he shouted.

Henry gave Rose an inquiring look, and she nodded her assent. She was getting sore and it would feel good to get off her feet. "How did you like the wedding?" she asked Elizabeth as Henry helped her take a seat.

"It was beautiful," replied Elizabeth. "There were so many flowers, and Katy's dress was gorgeous. You did a wonderful job with the embroidery, Highness."

Rose moved so that she could sit next to Elizabeth as the men started talking politics. She rolled her eyes at Miss Mede, who giggled. "Men," sighed Rose as she settled into her new spot. "It doesn't matter where they are. It could be a funeral or a wedding, and somehow the conversation will always turn to politics. You would think the world revolves around such things."

Elizabeth chuckled, and Rose winced as pain shot up her back. "Are you okay, Highness?"

"Fine," muttered Rose as she forced a smile on her face. "I am just a little sore, that's all." Elizabeth gave her an inquiring look, but Rose shrugged it off and the two continued their conversation.

As the night wore on, the pain increased until Rose decided it would be best to call it an evening. She took Henry's hand, and he escorted her to the carriage that took them back to the inn. Not long after that, the labour pains came in earnest.

Henry's face turned pale with shock when Rose reached out and squeezed his hand. "You need to get the doctor," she panted when the contraction ended.

"Are you sure?" he asked hoarsely.

"Positive," she replied giving Henry a weak smile. "Could you also get Mrs. Jennings? I want her to be here," whispered Rose nervously.

"I'll be right back." He kissed Rose on the top of the head and bolted out of the door. It seemed like an eternity before he came back with the doctor and Mrs. Jennings in tow. It had taken longer than normal because they had both been at the bonfire.

As soon as the older lady blustered through the door, she sent Henry out. "Och lad, this is no place for you. You best be leaving until

I come calling. Do you understand that? You'll be glad I sent you away in the end."

Henry looked at Rose, and she nodded in agreement. Giving her one last kiss, he left the room so the doctor and Mrs. Jennings could take over.

The dining room wasn't completely empty as Henry had expected. John was sitting in a chair looking worried. "Is she alright?" he asked when Henry entered the room.

"Mrs. Jennings is with her, and the doctor. They sent me out of the room," he muttered and began to pace.

Minutes ticked by. The men took turns pacing and sitting. Sometimes one of them would get down on his knees to pray, but no one said anything. Both listened for the one sound that meant it was all done.

When an hour had passed, Henry stopped his pacing and began rubbing his neck. "Shouldn't we have heard something by now?" he asked. John shrugged. "I mean, I haven't heard a thing. I haven't heard Rose or Mrs. Jennings. I haven't heard the doctor. You would think we could hear something." Again John just shrugged.

"I am going to check on them," said Henry determinedly. He strutted down the hall and knocked on the bedroom door. Mrs. Jennings opened it a crack and peeked out.

"Is everything okay?" Henry asked with a little less confidence.

Mrs. Jennings smiled. "Everything is fine. The queen and I were just taking a walk around the room, but I think that will be changing soon."

"Oh. But, it's been an hour! What is taking so long?"

Mrs. Jennings burst out laughing. "Lad, do you think these things just happen? All good things take a little time. Have some patience. You will hear it when the time is near. Now, get yourself back to the dining room. I have myself some work to do."

The door closed in Henry's face. He was left with no choice but to return to waiting and pacing.

A couple of minutes later, the screaming began. He shot out of his chair and tried to bolt down the hall. John tackled him to the floor and held him there until he quit struggling. "I don't think you want to be in there right now," whispered John hoarsely.

"That's where you're wrong," replied Henry tersely as he tried to pull out of John's grasp. John shook his head and dragged Henry back to the dining room where he sank dejectedly into a chair.

An eternity passed before they heard what they were listening for. It was the wail of a baby. Hale and healthy lungs screamed as they entered the world. Henry fell to his knees and let the tears fall. It was done. The baby was in the world. The baby was healthy. But Mrs. Jennings didn't come calling like she said she would, and Rose's screams continued.

John slipped down onto his knees beside Henry and placed his hand on Henry's shoulder. "Heavenly Father," he began, "we don't know what is happening in that room, but we place Rose and her offspring in your hand. Please keep them safe. Amen."

"Amen," echoed Henry. They remained on their knees waiting. They could hear the baby crying along with Rose's screams and Henry wondered what could be happening.

And then it happened.

A second set of fresh lungs joined the first. Henry wouldn't be kept back. He raced down the hall and barged into the room. Rose sat on the bed covered in her sweat. She panted, trying to catch her breath. Henry went to her side and took her hand. "Are you okay?" he whispered.

"It's a boy," Rose cried happily, "and a girl. A beautiful boy, and a girl," she whispered. "We were both right."

"Och," exclaimed Mrs. Jennings. "Here you are mooning over your babes, and you haven't even taken a look at their angel faces." Henry turned to the older woman, who was carrying over two cloth bundles. "Now," she whispered, "let's allow the young prince and princess to meet their parents."

Rose reached out her arms to take one of the bundles, but Henry hesitated. "Your son, Your Highness," whispered Mrs. Jennings as she handed over the second bundle.

Henry couldn't believe how small he was. He was barely the size of his two hands. How could something so small and delicate survive in the world? A tear slipped down his face as he whispered a prayer of thanks to his Father in Heaven.

"I think we should name him James, after his grandfather," Rose said. "What do you think of James Henry Arden?"

"It's perfect, but what about our daughter?" Henry asked as he turned to look at the two women that meant the most in his life. "Do you have any ideas for names for her?"

Rose scrunched up her face, and Henry took a seat beside her on the bed so that they could look at both infants at the same time. "I never really thought of a name for a girl. I was so sure we would have a boy."

"Is that so?" asked Henry. Rose nodded her head. "Well, I was so certain that we were going to have a girl that I think I have a name we could use."

"Is that so?"

"It is," laughed Henry. "What do you think of Rosalie Grace Arden?"

"I love it," whispered Rose.

The two would have gladly sat there for the rest of the evening staring at their children, but Mrs. Jennings had other ideas. "You will have to stand for a moment, Rose dear. I need to change those sheets, and once that is done, I will have to tuck you in and send in your cousin. He is about going crazy out there, the doctor told me, what with not knowing what is going on."

Henry helped Rose to her feet as Mrs. Jennings changed the sheets. He stopped to look around the room. It was a mess. Dirty towels sat in a pile by the door, furniture had been moved around to make things more accessible. It was amazing he hadn't noticed it all when he had come into the room.

"Now," said Mrs. Jennings, "Henry, why don't you hand over Prince James and go talk with John? Give us women about half an hour to get settled and then you can come in with him. Make sure you knock. I won't have any more of this barging into rooms. It's rude."

Henry thought it was best to obey orders. He would have liked to refuse, but he feared what the consequences might be if he didn't go and find John soon. So, he kissed his son's forehead and then his daughter's and then his wife's, and then he left the women and his son to get settled while he went to inform John of the good news.

The Charade

As he walked down the hall, he couldn't help but let out a chuckle. He was a father. He had a son and a daughter. Rosalie and James, his children. God was truly good.

THIRTY-ONE

WHEN HE REALIZED THE MEADOW wasn't empty, it was too late to turn back. Seth glared at Miss Mede's back and hoped she wouldn't turn. Such was not to be his luck.

She turned slowly, as if she had been expecting him. There was a smile on her face, and she seemed genuinely pleased to see him. She didn't say anything. She just stood there, smiling, waiting for him to say something.

"What are you doing here?" Seth grumbled as he walked past her to Mark's grave. He didn't want to see her face. It was too *happy*.

"You used to expect me to be here. Has something changed that I am no longer welcome, Seth?" She didn't turn. Her back was still to his, but he didn't have to see her to understand the hurt in the question.

"You're different now," he replied lamely. What else was he supposed to say? She was different, and he wasn't sure what the change meant.

"I suppose I am," sighed Elizabeth. "But I don't think the change is so horrible that you won't like me anymore." She came up beside him and folded her hands neatly in front of her. Seth scowled and crossed his arms.

"You used to understand me," replied Seth bitterly. "You don't understand anymore, because people like you now. You have a father now. God loves you now."

Elizabeth didn't reply for a long time. Seth was tempted to look and see if she was still there. "You missed one thing," she whispered. "People like me now, I have a father, I have God's love, and," she paused, "and I think I've found *it*."

Seth let out a hiss of breath. "How can you have found *it*?" he laughed sarcastically. "How can you have found it when I don't even know what it is?" He felt like shouting, but it would be pointless. Instead, he started kicking at the ground. Small tufts of turf dug up, leaving divots that scarred the ground.

"*It* was what Mark had," replied Elizabeth. There was no question in her voice. "And you've known exactly all along what it is. You just don't want to admit it because you think you will never be able to attain it."

"I know what *it* is?" mocked Seth. "What is it Elizabeth? If I know what *it* is, what is it?"

"Don't be cruel, Seth," replied Elizabeth coldly.

Seth groaned. "I am cruel though, don't you see. I am cruel. I am cold, vile, evil. I am all those things everyone expects me not to be." A strangled sound clawed out his throat. "I am so sick of it. Everyone thinks I am the perfect curate, but if they really knew me, they would spit in my face."

Slowly, carefully Elizabeth reached out and touched Seth's face. He flinched but refused to pull away. "I know you," she whispered. Stretching up on tip toes, she kissed his cheek.

"What is it?" Seth whispered hoarsely.

"Forgiveness; a clean slate, peace. It can be anything, but it all comes down to the lack of guilt. I told you once before, but I couldn't be sure then. I'm sure now, though."

"How? How can you be sure?" Seth's eye's begged for an answer, but Elizabeth wasn't sure she knew the right one. Taking Seth's hand, she pulled him down to sit on top of the grave, facing the cross.

"I think the answer was here all along." Biting her lip, she tried to think of how to continue. "You see this grave?"

"Yes," Seth said with a bit of a grumble.

"The grave represents death. I was dead in my guilt. I could do nothing, because it consumed me and ate whatever life I did have. Does that make sense?" Seth nodded.

"Fortunately, it doesn't end there." Elizabeth traced a line with her finger from the grave to the cross and hoped that Seth would make the connection.

"That isn't for me," muttered Seth. "I told you that before. God can't forgive someone like me. I'm the worst of criminals. I am cursed by God because I took someone's life."

Elizabeth bit her lip and tried to think of what else she could say. "Do you know the story of Jesus' death?" Seth rolled his eyes at her, and she shrugged. "Well, when Jesus was on trial before Pilate, and Pilate didn't want him to be crucified, Pilate gave the people the choice between Barabbas and Jesus."

"What does this have to do with anything?"

"Barabbas was a murderer, and Jesus took his place. Don't you think that he could stand in your place?"

Seth jumped to his feet and glared down at her. "What does this have to do with anything? Did Barabbas rape a woman? Did he steal what didn't belong to him? Did he brutally harm someone?"

Elizabeth sprang up as well and started shouting before he could finish. "The prostitute who anointed his feet. The thief on the cross. The soldiers who pounded nails into his flesh. 'Father forgive them.' That is what he said. Are you worse than that? Tell me. Are you so horrible that you are unforgivable, or are you so unforgivable because you hate yourself so much?"

There were tears in Elizabeth's eyes and she stopped to wipe them away. "I'm sorry," she whispered. "I didn't mean to get so angry."

Seth slumped to the ground and looked dejectedly at the cross. "Why don't you just leave me alone?" he cried. He pulled his legs to his chest and buried his face in his knees.

Elizabeth knelt on the ground beside him and wrapped her arms around him. "Because I love you, and God loves you, and for some reason you aren't able to love yourself. You're an honourable man, Seth," wept Elizabeth. "Maybe you weren't always honourable, but you are now, and despite your past, God can forgive you."

"I need to be alone," said Seth through gritted teeth. Elizabeth wiped at her eyes and got to her feet.

"I'll see you in church, Seth," she sighed. She fidgeted with her new lace sleeve and looked down at him. "I'll be praying for you, okay? Don't forget that." She turned and left him to think over what she had said.

"Why?" Seth wailed when he was sure Elizabeth was gone. The sobs racked his body, but he didn't want to stop them. For too long he had been holding it all inside. He had tried to be strong—first when his father told him how to handle his women, then all through seminary as he put on the face of perfection, and finally as the curate—but he had had enough.

"Why did you have to make me, me?" he whimpered into his knees. "I hate what you have made me!" Raising his fist to the sky, Seth cursed God. "You don't care, do you? You make us weak, useless critters, and then you sit back and laugh as we try to deal with what you throw at us."

Seth jumped to his feet and continued cursing. "Well this is what I think of you!" He kicked at the cross. He kicked and he kicked until it lay broken on the ground.

"You satisfied?" he shouted. "Are you satisfied with this messed up world? Well you created it, so you only have yourself to blame!" Seth turned to leave the pasture, but he couldn't.

With a sigh of frustration, he turned and picked up the now-broken cross. Fixing it as best as he could, he stuck it back into the ground. "I don't need you. I don't need it," he muttered, and turned again to leave. In his haste he didn't see the one remaining piece of the cross until he had tripped over it and was sprawled on the ground beside it. Blood spurted from his nose and he cursed.

"Do you want to laugh at me some more, God?" He wiped a hand under his nose and felt the warm, sticky blood as it seeped over his fingers. He lifted it to the sky as a twisted smile covered his face. "My blood, Lord," he chortled. "That is what you want, is it not? Blood.

Because you are sick. Blood. What kind of offering is that? It is pagan, heathen, vulgar.

"Do you enjoy our misery? I mean, why else would you inflict it so consistently? Or maybe you just like my misery. Well then, God, why don't you take my life now? Take my blood!" Seth shouted, shaking his bloody fist at the heavens.

The misery was too overwhelming. With one last oath, Seth collapsed into a bloody mass of tears. "Why won't you just accept my offering?" he whimpered. He knew the answer already. "So you only accept His blood, is that it?" There was no reply.

"But he doesn't like me," Seth whined. "I don't like me," he sighed. A shudder ran down his spine as the sobs subsided. His whole body rested, and was still. The only motion was that of his breath and the steady drip of his bleeding nose.

"Forgive as the Lord forgave you," whispered Seth. "Father, forgive me. Forgive me."

Seth dragged himself off the ground and started to crawl toward the road. Slowly he made his way to his feet. By the time he got to the street, he was able to stumble along on unsteady feet. The entire town was silent. It was still too early for any real activity. When his house was in view, the sun had just crested the horizon, sending beams of red light across every surface.

Seth's nose stopped bleeding. He took a deep breath of the crisp morning air. It tickled his lungs. It felt so good just to take another breath. Closing his eyes, he drew another deep breath, and then turned to walk up his pathway to his home.

He stopped in his tracks.

Standing on the front stoop was a man dressed in rags. Soiled and torn, the clothes were the last thing that identified the man as a beggar. His hair hung in greasy sheets down his back. His beard curled around dead leaves and stale bread crumbs, giving the man a look of wild insanity. Dirt smudged his forehead and his entire person smelled of alcohol.

"May I help you?" Seth asked.

"Well I'll be," muttered the man. "What happened to you? You look awful."

Seth couldn't help but smile at the irony in those words, but he chose not to comment. "I took a fall on my way home, which just so happens to be here. So, I ask again, may I help you?"

The man's hand went to his head, where he began to scratch. Small flakes of dandruff drifted lazily to the ground where they disappeared into the dirt path. "Isn't this the curate's house?""Yes sir. Do you need a minister for something?" The man rubbed his forehead where there was already a smudge of dirt and shook his head back and forth.

"No, nope," he muttered. "Do you know where the curate is?"

Seth took another look at the man in front of him and nearly lost his balance when realization finally dawned on him. "Why," he squeaked. He cleared his throat and tried again. "Why don't you come in and wait in the parlour while I clean up. The curate will meet you in a minute."

The man scrunched his face, trying to decide if he should accept. "I'll even make some eggs for a bit of breakfast while you wait," encouraged Seth. At the mention of food all doubt left the man's face and he was ready and willing to enter the house and sit in the parlour.

Seth didn't take much time cleaning up his bloody nose. He changed into a fresh outfit and put some eggs in a pan to fry. It wasn't more than ten minutes when he joined the man in the parlour with a plateful of eggs. Silently he sat and watched as the man devoured all that was in front of him.

"Is the curate going to be here soon?" the man asked uncomfortably when the eggs were gone.

Seth smiled and leaned back in his chair. "Do you really not recognize me, Bill?" Bill jumped from his seat and looked at Seth incredulously.

"It is you!" He rubbed his forehead again, and Seth understood why the dirt smudge was in that exact spot. "You look good. When I heard you were passing as a minister, I thought I would find you looking miserable."

Seth couldn't help but laugh. "The job has its perks. For one, I get to live in a nice house, and if you are good enough, the women from the congregation bring you food."

Bill's hand was back to his forehead. "Maybe I should get myself one of them fancy collars. I could go for getting fed."

Seth laughed outright when he pictured Bill as a curate. It could never happen. The man in front of him was more suited for a saloon than a classroom. The chances of Bill becoming a preacher were very near impossible. But then again, that was what most people had thought about him.

Bill shook his head to clear away his short-lived dream. "Well Seth, mind if I stick around for a while?"

Seth pursed his lips and studied the man in front of him. "How long will you be staying?" "Just long enough to get myself back on my feet. I promise I won't be here long, and I won't make one mention of being related to you. You can say that you are taking me in on charity or something. I promise I won't be a problem."

Seth rubbed his chin and looked his brother over. "Let's get you cleaned up," he sighed. "You can stay as long as I am here. I can't promise you that it will be long, but until then, the house is yours." Bill grabbed Seth around the arms and slapped him on the back in a sort of bear hug. Seth stiffened, not quite sure how to react.

"I always knew I could count on you, brother."

Seth reached out his arms and hugged his brother in return. It was awkward and stiff, but Bill was his brother. They stood there for what seemed like an eternity but was really no more than a couple of seconds. Bill released Seth, who went to prepare a tub of hot water. He had a lot of work to do in the next week. The thought of it all weighed on his shoulders, and having Bill present only seemed to make it more difficult by tenfold.

The church was crowded. Seth listened as the congregation sang a song of praise. He closed his eyes and hummed the tune. He smiled. The past week had been eventful. The king and queen had presented their children, Prince James and Princess Rosalie. Then the curate had presented a strange visitor. The community immediately adored the new royalty, but they weren't quite sure how to take the curate's guest. Most people kept their distance from the wild-looking man.

Seth smiled as he remembered when Bill had been told early that morning that he was expected at church. The poor man had never once graced the doors of a church, and he didn't quite know what to expect. Even now he sat at the back of the church looking uncomfortable in the formal clothes Seth had supplied.

The music faded and Caleb sighed. Duty called. As much as he would like life to continue as it was, some things needed to change. Slowly, heavily, he stood from his seat and grasped the sides of his pulpit. "For twelve years, I have been running from my past," he began in a near whisper. A hush fell over the congregation as they waited for him to go on. Lifting his head, Seth looked out at all the innocent, waiting faces.

"For six years I have served this congregation. I have baptized babies. I have witnessed weddings, and I have officiated funerals. All this time you have known me as Curate Caleb Taylor. What you haven't known is that I am an imposter, a fake." Seth waited for the gasp, but it didn't come. Everyone was waiting for the sermon. They thought he was making a point, but he wasn't. He was telling the truth, but they weren't listening.

"Listen to me!" he shouted. Some people jumped and a baby cried. "My name is not Caleb Taylor. My name is Seth Hepton. I have been living a lie for the past twelve years. I am a criminal, not a curate. I am a murderer. I killed a girl and left her in her father's arms as her last breaths faded from her lips."

Mothers pulled their children closer to their sides and fathers gaped up at the curate, everyone unsure what to do. Tears trickled down Seth's cheeks and he tried to gain control so that he could con-

401

tinue. "For years I have lived under the guilt of my own sin. I tried to reconcile myself with God by devoting my life to him. I tried to be perfect, but it didn't matter. I was still stained, still dirty." Seth wiped at his eyes.

"Recently, God showed me that I could not pay for my own sins—only his Son could do that. Jesus died for me, and I know that I am forgiven." Still no one in the congregation responded. Seth slumped into his chair and placed his elbows on his knees and his head in his hands, and waited.

It happened all at once. The congregation seemed to act of one ac-cord. "He needs to stand trial," shouted one man.

"Trial?" shouted another. "Let's hang him here. Why should we give him another chance to kill?"

"And to think we trusted him with our children," wailed a mother.

On and on the noise continued. Members of the church didn't know what was best. Should they kill him now? Should he stand trial? Babies cried and kids screamed as the mayhem continued.

"Silence!" someone shouted. All noise stopped and everyone turned to look at the king, who stood regally at the back of the congre-gation. Taking one step at a time, the king made his way to the front of the church, the people parting in front of him.

Placing a hand on Seth's shoulder, he looked out into the congre-gation. "Who condemns this man?"

There was a slight shuffling among the people. Then someone cleared his throat. "If no one is brave enough to, I will. He's a bloody murderer."

The king glared down at the man who shrank away. "Mr. Wal-ters." Stated the King. "You find fault in this man." It wasn't a question. "Then bring me two ropes."

"One's all it takes to do the job," snorted Walters indignantly.

"You misunderstand me, Mr. Walters. You see, when you con-demn this man, you condemn yourself. Does not the good Lord tell us to judge as we also would like to be judged?" Mr. Walters' face paled. "Unless you claim to be without sin, then bring me two ropes."

"That's unfair," blustered Walters. "I didn't kill anyone. Besides that, I've lived a respectable life. Who knows what this scum's done with his."

"You haven't killed anyone? What gives you the right to judge one sin more detestable in God's sight than another? Whether you call a brother a fool or take a woman's life, both are filth to God, and both are punishable by death. God has forgiven this man, but if you condemn him, then be prepared to stand condemned alongside him."

"You defend this man?" Mr. Walters said. "You're the king. You're supposed to be the one hanging him. What kind of king are you?"

"Stop." Everyone turned to look at Seth as he got up from his chair. Turning to Henry, he bowed low before him. "My king and my friend," he whispered. "You have been better to me than I deserve." Turning to the congregation, Seth found his brother and gave him a sad smile.

"I am going to Croden, to stand on trial before a judge there. That is where I raped and murdered the girl, and that is where I will face justice. If you want, you can follow me, but I will not stray from my path. I am determined." With this said, Seth slumped back into his chair.

"You don't have to do this, Seth," Henry whispered. "I can protect you."

The tears fell in earnest as Seth looked up at his friend. "God knew each detail of my life before I was even born," Seth whispered. "I am in his hands now. If he wills me to die, then I die in peace because I know that I am forgiven. But, if he gives me life, I will be ever more grateful, for the time that I will get to live in his love."

Henry grabbed the man into a hug and allowed himself to weep before these people. "Promise me one thing," whispered Seth. "Promise me that you will look out for my brother. He doesn't have anyone anymore."

"I'll take care of him as best as I can," whispered Henry.

"And another thing," Seth smiled around the tears. "Make sure Rose is happy. Don't let her cry too much over me. Tell her that I love her, and that I am going to be with my Father in heaven."

"I'll do that," laughed Henry. "But, promise me this in return."

"Anything."

"Promise me that you take the time on your way to Croden to pray. Pray hard, and if at any time you want to turn back, come directly to me."

"I'll do that. But I won't be coming back. God has a plan for me, and it comes to a close in Croden. I'll live whatever life I have left in prayer until I get to Croden."

THIRTY-TWO

THEY WERE FOLLOWING HIM. SETH had known that for the last couple of days, but today, as he drew closer to Croden, that fact became increasingly more annoying. He could hear them whispering and nagging at each other. They were deliberating what they would do once they reached the small town. They didn't know whether they should inform the mayor immediately of their arrival, or if they should just continue to follow Seth.

With the town in sight, Seth paused and waited for them to catch up. "Mr. Walters," he spoke loudly to the shadows behind him. There was no response. "I'll have you know that I'll be going directly to the girl's father. The last time he saw me he said he would kill me. If you are not satisfied of his intent after that, you can go find the mayor. I will willingly admit my guilt." Still the bushes remained silent.

With a sigh, Seth continued on his way. "Lord," he whispered under his breath, "I don't know if this is what you want from me, but it only seems right to seek reconciliation while I still have a chance. So I hand myself over to you and ask that your will be done."

Tears pricked at the corner of his eyes, but Seth kept walking. The sun set in the distance, bathing the town ahead in hues of red and orange. From a distance, it almost looked as if the entire place was burning. It reminded Seth of the Biblical pictures of hell. He wondered if that was what he was walking into. *"Even though I walk through the valley of the shadow of death,"* he muttered to himself.

He passed the town's first house as the last vestiges of sunlight tinged the horizon. The trees no longer hid Mr. Walters and his companion. They walked not far behind him. Their loathsome looks bored into his back, accusing him and sentencing him without a trial.

Seth felt his stomach flip and turn inside him as familiar sights met his eyes. He was almost there. The door was just ahead. A candle flickered in the window, inviting him in. He stopped at the gate and looked at the door. It taunted him, daring him to come and knock. With lead feet, he trudged up the path and knocked.

He heard the steps coming. They were a man's steps. That was for the better. He didn't know what he would say if it was Sarah's mother. He didn't think he was strong enough to handle that.

The door cracked open. "May I help you?" the man asked.

Seth studied his feet. "I..." he began, unsure of himself. He stopped. A tear trickled down his cheek as he continued to study the ground.

"Who are you?" the man demanded. "Are you one of those boys who have been up to the shenanigans I have been hearing about? Look at me." He grabbed at Seth's shirt and pulled him closer to the light.

Seth turned away, avoiding his gaze. The man released him with a disgusted grunt. "A grown man. What have you to say for yourself?"

Looking back down at the ground, Seth tried to compose himself. With a heavy breath he began. "Twelve years ago, I stood on this doorstep with a dying girl in my arms. I was carrying her back to her home after I had raped and abused her." Seth looked up at Sarah's horror-stricken father. The tears poured freely down Seth's face.

"Tonight, I come back to this very same door to beg your forgiveness and to put my life into your hands. You may do with it as you will."

Seth waited. The man gaped at him, unsure, or unable to say anything.

"Seth!" he shrieked in horror.

"Yes, sir," Seth murmured. He looked at his feet. He couldn't bear to look at the man in front of him. He knew what would be on his face: rage, hate, uncertainty, and, most of all, vengeance. What he wasn't expecting was the slap. The open hand met his cheek and sent him reeling. He collapsed to the ground in a heap at the man's feet. The spittle landed on his cheek close to his ear.

"How dare you come back!" the man screamed. He kicked at Seth, gashing his cheek and causing his nose to bleed. "Did you think that you could just come back here and ask for forgiveness and it would all be alright?"

Seth didn't respond. He lay at the man's feet and waited for the next blow. He groaned when the shoe connected with his chin, jarring his whole head. He felt the blood trickle out of the corner of his mouth. The earth swirled in and out of his consciousness.

He could hear Mr. Walters trying to convince the man to bring him to the mayor. He was dragged to his feet and shoved forward. He stumbled, trying unsuccessfully to catch his balance. The ground was merciless as it shredded his knees and hands. Bile rose in his throat and dribbled down his chin.

"Get up!" someone demanded.

Seth dragged himself to his feet and stumbled forward. He didn't know where to go, but sword pricks warned him of false direction. He tried to avoid the blades as much as possible but still they bit into skin, tearing at his clothes and piercing his flesh.

Finally they stopped. Seth collapsed to the ground and heaved in desperate breaths. The door opened and the mayor walked out. "What's this?" he demanded. His voice sounded shrill in Seth's ears. Seth buried his head in his arms, trying to drown out the sound, only to receive a jolting kick to the ribs.

"Tell the mayor what you came to say."

"My name," gasped Seth as he tried to catch his breath. Another kick cut off his breath, causing him to wheeze in pain.

"Stand up and show respect to those in authority."

Placing his hands on the spinning ground, Seth pushed up with all his might and tried to plant his feet beneath him. Impatience took hold of the condemning trio and they yanked him to his feet. Someone grasped him by the hair so that he wouldn't collapse.

"My name...is Seth Hepton. Twelve years ago I raped Sarah." The pain of it all overcame him and Seth began to weep. "Forgive me," he wailed. "Forgive the wretch that I am," he sobbed.

They shoved him to the ground and started kicking again. He quieted only because he could no longer breathe.

"I need a council," he heard the mayor whisper. "If we can call everyone together tonight, he will hang tomorrow." There was a lot of low muttering that Seth couldn't quite make out.

"Deal with it," was the last thing he heard before the whole world went black.

"It isn't right," Shoals said to Henry. "That man has been serving this community for six years, and when he says one thing they don't like, they send him to his death. You would think they would have a little mercy."

"How much mercy can you expect from them, Shoals? They were betrayed. They had been under the impression that they were being served by a faultless man, and when that illusion snapped, so did their ability to show mercy."

Shoals shook his head. "Well why don't you do something about it?"

Henry sighed. "There is nothing I can do. I may be the king, but I too am bound by the law."

"Surely you could make an exception. They have only been gone a day. You could easily overtake them and take Seth back to Silidon. He would at least receive a fair trial there."

Henry shook his head. "That's not how it works, Shoals. You know it as well as I do." Henry ran a hand roughly across his forehead. "Besides, that is not what Seth would want. I have thought about different options, but Seth made it clear the day he made his confession.

He is going to Croden to face his trial, and he is perfectly aware that he will most likely face his death there. Perhaps that is the best thing for him."

"So you are just going to let him walk off to his demise. You aren't going to at least be there to mediate or to comfort him. There has to be something."

A pained expression passed over Henry's face. "There is nothing I can do," he whispered. "I wish with all my might that I could change the events of the past few days, but I can't. All I can do is abide by the decision Seth has made, and wait and pray that he will come back to us alive."

"And what do you do in the meantime?"

"Prepare for his funeral," Henry stated as he walked out the door.

When Seth finally woke, it was to the stench of pig manure. It was still dark outside. The sun hadn't yet begun its ascent. Blood was caked around his mouth, and it hurt to move. He pulled himself into a sitting position. A startled pig squealed and ran into the opposite corner.

Seth groaned and clutched his side. It felt as if each rib in his body was disjointed and pointing in the wrong direction. Besides that, his face was swollen and his tongue was so chewed and bloodied that he doubted he could speak if he tried.

The barn door creaked open and a man Seth didn't recognize entered. His face was long and severe, and though he had never met Seth before, his lip curled up in a disgusted sneer. Seth guessed the man had already been informed about his sordid past.

"We'll be leaving soon," the man stated. "Make sure you're able to walk. I won't be carting you into town." With one last withering glare, the man left, giving Seth some time to find his legs.

Ignoring the pain in his ribs, Seth pulled himself to his feet and tried to balance. The world spun. He grabbed the side of the barn for support. He closed his eyes, hoping that would end the tilting. Slowly, the ground stopped moving. Leaning against the side of the barn, he took one unsteady step. The world started to spin again. He waited for it to stop before he took another.

The door banged open. Seth could see the sun just peeking over the horizon. "It's time to go," the man hissed.

They were out in the country. How far they were from town was hard to tell. Thick trees blocked everything from view. The man did not think it necessary to introduce himself or to slow his pace. He charged ahead, casting an occasional look over his shoulder to make sure Seth was following.

The road stretched on and on. Seth could feel the energy seeping out of him. Still, he pushed on. It would soon be over, he kept telling himself. Then things would be all better. It was coming to an end. He was sure of that. It would end today.

The town was just coming to life as they entered on the far side. They kept walking until they reached the central square where a circle of men, including Mr. Walters and Sarah's father, stood. All talking ceased when Seth stepped forward.

"Seth Hepton." The mayor stepped toward him. "As you may know, the council of the town of Croden met last night to determine your fate. After some deliberation, we have reached a decision and when the clock strikes nine, we will announce our verdict to the town. All verdicts will be acted upon immediately. Do you understand this?"

Seth nodded, not quite sure if his mouth worked.

With his speech delivered, the mayor disappeared into the town, followed by most of the council and Mr. Walters and his companion. Soon the only people to remain were Seth and his prison keeper.

Seeing that they were alone, Seth collapsed to the ground with a sigh of relief. There was no response from the prison guard.

As the sun crept higher in the sky, the square began to fill. Curious passersby stared at the slumped prisoner. Some who recognized him from twelve years prior spat on him. Others kicked him, enjoying his pain. Seth sat still through it all.

As soon as the clock struck nine, the mayor appeared on a hastily constructed platform. Looking out over the crowd, he smiled victoriously. "Today," he shouted, "we have the *privilege* to witness the demise of a wicked man. For twelve years, Seth Hepton has run free after committing a heinous crime. Assuming a false identity, he took a position in a church not far from here, but, as God would have it, today justice will be served!"

The mayor paused for effect. "Yesterday night, Seth entered town confessing his crime. He claims that twelve years ago he raped a young woman, leaving her at her father's doorstep, bloodied and dying. Because of his confession, the council has decided to be more lenient in our sentencing." The crowd booed and the mayor hushed them, wanting to go on with his speech. Condemning whispers hissed from person to person. Seth closed his eyes and prayed.

"For the crime of concealing his identity and wilfully deceiving honest Christian people, Mr. Hepton has been sentenced to thirty lashes. As for his other crime, the council could come to no other conclusion than death by hanging."

"Father," Seth whispered hoarsely. The mayor held out his hand and someone handed him a knotted cord. The shirt was torn off of Seth's back and he watched as the mayor walked vindictively toward him.

The first slash ripped into his flesh, leaving it ragged and torn. Seth screamed in agony. The crowd responded with cheers for more. Again the whip lashed out, pulling up more flesh, revealing bone and sinew. The crowd gloried in the blood. Lash after lash, the whip flailed his back, leaving it raw and bloody.

The pain was overwhelming. Vomit spewed from his mouth, much to the pleasure of the crowd. "The rope!" cheered someone and others joined in the chant.

Seth was pulled to his feet and forced to stand on the chair. He leaned forward, only to be caught by the noose. With tearless eyes he looked out over the swarm of people. Livid faces sneered back at him. They accused him, spat at him. He tried to speak to them, but there wasn't enough air.

The noose tightened. "Let it be quick," prayed Seth. The chair disappeared from beneath his feet. He gasped one last breath. His neck snapped and his body twitched. The entire world went black.

It was finished.

The crowd cheered as Seth's body twisted and contorted. His face turned blue and seemed to swell. His eyes bulged and his tongue lolled out of the side of his mouth, blue and lifeless. His body gave one last shuddering twitch and then it was still.

The crowd erupted into wild cheers. The mayor watched with a look of satisfaction. A few people took the time to spit on the corpse. Others slapped his dead, bloated face. Most just left. The entertainment was done for the day, and they had work to do.

"What do you want with the body?" the mayor asked Mr. Walters.

The man looked happily at the corpse. "I was commanded to bring it back to Emriville so that our people can be satisfied that the criminal is dealt with."

"It is a long walk," mused the mayor. "The corpse will stink by that time. Why don't I provide you with a wagon? It will make the trip much faster."

"Much appreciated."

Even with the wagon, the trip took Walters three days of steady travel. He brought the corpse into town like a hero, but some noticeable faces were missing. He looked around for the king and queen, but they were not there. Neither were any of the men-at-arms. Walters scowled. What type of king did not believe in justice?

Knocking at the inn, as he had been told by the king to do when he arrived back, he waited for a response. To his surprise, it was the king himself who opened the door. Walters bowed deeply. "Your Highness, I've come to inform you that the criminal has been properly dealt with. I have his body now in the wagon if you want to see for yourself."

"Very well," replied the king. He motioned to some men in the inn. Walking out, they reverently picked the corpse up from the cart and carried it toward the inn. The doorway filled with men as soon as the bearers had passed by.

"Attend to his burial needs," demanded the king before they were out of hearing range. "But, do not nail the coffin. The Queen will want to say her goodbyes." Turning to Walters, he scowled. "You may leave now. Your job is done."

"But... but..." stuttered Walters. "The town needs to see. I should show them..."

The king stared at him with cold eyes. "He's dead. Aren't you satisfied?"

"Sir?" Walters asked.

"Aren't you satisfied? That man... he asked for forgiveness, and the best you could offer was vengeance. Well, *vengeance is mine* declares the Lord. Let his blood be on your hands if you are proud of it, but I will not rejoice in the death of my brother."

"Brother!" sputtered Walters. "That man is a murderer—a rapist, and you still call him your brother. What kind of king are you?"

King Henry glared at him, and Walters shrank away ever so slightly. "That man was washed in the blood of Jesus Christ. If Jesus, the perfect sacrifice, covered his sins, then I have no choice but to forgive him. Now, are you done here, or do you want another chance to insult your king?"

The subtle hint was lost on the infuriated man. Ignoring the crowd of soldiers that was gathering, Walters blathered on. "King? You call yourself a king? You can't even handle a criminal properly. No wonder the country is going to ruins."

The slick swish of swords being drawn filled the air. Walters gulped when he saw the menacing looks on the soldiers' faces.

"Mr. Walters," stated Henry crisply, "you have on more than one occasion committed a crime that is punishable by death. I have given you mercy before, but just now you have overstepped your bounds. By insulting me in front of my men, you have forced my hand."

Henry turned to the crowd of men, looking for one in particular. "Shoals."

The soldier stepped forward, sword drawn.

"To make this easier on yourself, Walters," said Henry, "I would suggest you kneel." The man dropped to his knees in panic.

"Please," he begged, "I didn't mean anything by it. I swear it."

"Arnold Walters, you are guilty of insulting your king and your country, a crime which is punishable by death," stated Henry. Shoals placed his blade at the man's neck. "Before this crowd of witnesses I therefore sentence you." Shoals pressed his blade lightly against Walters' neck. A drop of blood squeezed out and drooled down his throat.

"Enough," Henry said. Shoals pulled away his sword. "I think we have seen enough death for today."

"Yes sir," replied Shoals. "But, if I may be so bold, Your Highness, Mr. Walters seems set on justice. I was just wondering how you plan on carrying that out."

Henry sighed and rubbed his jaw. "You are right, of course. We will have to think of something suitable... do the stocks still stand in town?"

"What!" squeaked Walters. "The stocks haven't been used in over ten years." Henry's glare cut him short.

"It is a pity that so many towns have given up the practice. It really is a practical punishment—within moderation of course," sighed Shoals.

Henry nodded his agreement. "Bring Walters to the stocks. He will remain in them for the foreseeable future with a sign about his neck. The sign shall read, 'an example for those who slander the name of the crown,' or something like it. I think that should do."

Walters started screaming as Shoals dragged him away. A couple of soldiers followed Shoals' progress, laughing at the pitiful man being dragged to the stocks.

Back at the inn, Henry turned to find Rose staring at him. Tears welled in her eyes. "It's over, isn't it?"

Henry pulled her into his arms and together they wept for their brother. "I want to bury him," whispered Rose, "in the meadow, next to Mark. He would have wanted that. I'm sure of it."

The small crowd of mourners huddled around the freshly dug grave. The funeral had been simple. There was no minister to say extensive prayers or preach a sermon of hope. There were only witnesses. Witnesses who had loved the man who now lay beneath the earth.

Elizabeth clung to John's hand and wept into his shoulder. Henry took the freshly made cross and planted it firmly into the ground at the head of the grave, right next to Mark's. Katy wrapped her arms around her husband, allowing the tears to fall freely down her face. Rose knelt on the ground, scattering flower petals in a bed across the freshly turned grave.

"I love you, Seth," Rose whispered. "You are my brother, and I know that you are with our Father in heaven." Tears dripped from her eyes, and a sob caught in her throat. "I'll miss you, though. Don't forget that."

"Do you really mean that?" The small group turned and watched as Bill stepped toward the queen. "Did you really mean it when you said he was your brother?"

Rose wiped her eyes and stood. "Seth has been my brother since the day I met him two years ago. I loved him then even though I only knew him as Caleb Taylor. When I found out who he really was, I only loved him more."

Bill nodded. "I guess I'm the only Hepton left now," he muttered. Picking up a clump of dirt, he rubbed it through his fingers. When it had all fallen back to the ground, he stared blankly at his hands.

Henry reached out and placed an arm around his shoulders. "Come on Bill. We have a lot to talk about."

Slowly, the small gathering turned from the grave. Just before they left the meadow, Elizabeth ran back and knelt by the cross.

"One more thing, Seth," she cried. "You have it now, don't you? I don't just mean the forgiveness part. I mean the *it* that Mark had. You have it all now." She wiped at her eyes, but the tears kept coming. "I can't help but say I am a little bit jealous about that. But, I also want to thank you. If you weren't here, I don't think I would have found any of it at all. So, thank you."

Leaning over, Elizabeth touched her lips to where she thought his cheek might be. "I love you," she whispered. Standing up, she turned and ran to her father. He took her hand and squeezed it gently.

Together they took a step forward. She didn't look back. He wasn't there anymore. *It* wasn't there anymore. It was with her.

She sighed and wiped the remaining tears away. She would see him again, she reminded herself. He was waiting with their heavenly Father, and when her time came, she would find him at the gates as she entered. He would smile and take her hand, and together they would walk forward.

CPSIA information can be obtained
at www.ICGtesting.com
Printed in the USA
BVHW062145030720
582935BV00007B/105

9 781770 692220